meet me on love lane

a novel

Nina Bocci

USA Today bestselling author

CE

Praise for Nina Bocci

ON THE CORNER OF LOVE AND HATE

"Romance at its finest with a colorful cast of characters and a couple to root for."

—*New York Times* and *USA Today*
bestselling author Sylvain Reynard

"Emma's everywoman appeal lends charm to the story, and her self-deprecating humor is a plus. This is a fun bit of fluffy entertainment."

—*Publishers Weekly*

"I flew through *On the Corner of Love and Hate*. Written with wit, quick banter, and heartfelt moments, I wished and rooted for Emma and Cooper's happily-ever-after, for that opposites-attract heat to smolder and catch fire. And Nina Bocci delivered!"

—Tif Marcelo, author of *The Key to Happily Ever After*

"Fans of Hallmark Channel rom-coms will flip over this sassy love story. . . . What follows is a rediscovered spark, steamy banter, and the art of finding love in unlikely places."

—*Woman's World*

"Impossible to read without smiling. *On the Corner of Love and Hate* is romantic fiction at its finest."

—Lauren Layne, *USA Today*
bestselling author of *Passion on Park Avenue*

"Bocci's warm, romantic novel deals with love, friendship, and family ties. This page-turner is filled with quick, witty banter from likable characters living in a realistic small town. The character-driven novel will have readers rooting for the confused friends. Fans of Jill Shalvis will thoroughly enjoy this swoon-worthy story."

—*Booklist*

"Fans of enemies-to-lovers rom-coms (such as Sally Thorne's *The Hating Game*) will enjoy, as will political junkies."

—*Library Journal*

"A delightful slow-burning romance that I adored!"

—Mia Sheridan, *New York Times* bestselling author of *Archer's Voice*

"Charming. . . . Bocci puts her characters through an emotional wringer, but balances the pining and misunderstandings with humor and an overall uplifting message about community involvement, family and hope. Readers looking for a feel-good romance set in a diverse, quirky small town will be entranced by *On the Corner of Love and Hate*."

—*Shelf Awareness*

"Plenty of wit and feisty characters. . . . If you're looking for one last summer read, something comfortable and warm to help you settle in and get ready for even cozier reading this fall, you most definitely don't want to miss *On the Corner of Love and Hate*, because it's everything you're looking for . . . and probably a little bit more."

—*Hypable* (4 stars)

"With its picturesque cover and super cute (and clueless) hero and heroine, *On the Corner of Love and Hate* was an absolute joy to read. I can't wait to see what entertaining story Nina Bocci has for her readers next."

—*Harlequin Junkie* (4 stars)

"Nina Bocci is a wonderful storyteller. I love her characters. . . . *On the Corner of Love and Hate* is a delight with a cast of characters that you will adore. Brava, Nina Bocci."

—*Fresh Fiction*

"Slow-burn romance with great banter and plenty of laughs!"

—*Daily Waffle*

ROMAN CRAZY

WITH ALICE CLAYTON

"A comedic and deliciously whimsical romp only this pair could deliver. Alice Clayton and Nina Bocci have struck gold."

—*New York Times* bestselling author Christina Lauren

"I went CRAZY over *Roman Crazy*—this is simply a perfect romance!"

—*New York Times* bestselling author Jennifer Probst

"Remarkable, refreshing . . . Clayton and Bocci have written a tender love story . . . all nestled within a love letter to the beauty of Rome."

—*RT Book Reviews* (four stars)

"There are books that make you laugh out loud, make you teary, make you hot and bothered, make you smile. And then there are books that make you want to crawl inside them and live within their pages. That's what *Roman Crazy* is."

—*New York Times* bestselling author Emma Chase

"*Roman Crazy* is a laugh-out-loud romantic comedy about second chances, friendship, and the beauty of Rome. You won't simply read this novel, you'll devour it as Alice Clayton and Nina Bocci transport you to Italy and guide you on an unforgettable adventure."

—*New York Times* and *USA Today* bestselling author Sylvain Reynard

"*Roman Crazy* is a sexy, steamy slow burn. A visceral reading experience that takes you from the cobbled streets of Rome to the bedroom and everywhere in between. Get your fans out! Five stars of smolder."

—*New York Times* bestselling author Helena Hunting

ALSO BY NINA BOCCI

On the Corner of Love and Hate
(The Hopeless Romantics Series)

Roman Crazy (with Alice Clayton)

MEET ME ON
LOVE
LANE

NINA BOCCI

G

GALLERY BOOKS

NEW YORK   LONDON   TORONTO   SYDNEY   NEW DELHI

Gallery Books
An Imprint of Simon & Schuster, Inc.
1230 Avenue of the Americas
New York, NY 10020

First Gallery Books trade paperback edition December 2019

GALLERY BOOKS and colophon are registered trademarks of Simon & Schuster, Inc.

For information about special discounts for bulk purchases, please contact Simon & Schuster Special Sales at 1-866-506-1949 or business@simonandschuster.com.

The Simon & Schuster Speakers Bureau can bring authors to your live event. For more information or to book an event, contact the Simon & Schuster Speakers Bureau at 1-866-248-3049 or visit our website at www.simonspeakers.com.

Manufactured in the United States of America

10 9 8 7 6 5 4 3 2

Library of Congress Control Number: 2019950521

ISBN 978-1-9821-0204-3
ISBN 978-1-9821-0206-7 (ebook)

To the real Nana.
I think I miss your laugh the most.
I hope you're having a beer with Pop Pop.
Love, 6-pack

PROLOGUE

We ran across town, holding hands and laughing as we darted through yards. The warm summer night was sticky, the humidity heavy on our skin. Neighbors shouted over the crickets and the owls, yelling for us to get home. It was well past dinnertime, but we'd made each other a promise that we wouldn't stop until it was safe. What exactly safe meant was another story.

We didn't *exactly* have a plan. Who does when you're ten and running away from home? The idea had formed after we'd read *From the Mixed-up Files of Mrs. Basil E. Frankweiler* together at the library. We had packed the essentials, just like Claudia and Jamie from the book: clean underwear, our life savings of eighteen dollars and forty-seven cents, a change of clothes, and pajamas.

"I brought some LEGOs in case we get bored," I told him, holding up a plastic bag filled with a few dozen random pieces.

The tips of his ears turned bright pink. "I brought, uh, some books. You know, in case of boredom." He opened his backpack to reveal a small library inside.

"Some?" I teased, zipping it back up for him. "Come on, we've got to get moving."

The streetlights flickered on one by one, almost as if they were following us, lighting the way for our families, who were by now surely trying to find us.

"Do you think Emma is mad we ducked out on her party? She

hadn't gotten to the presents yet, and you know how much she loves opening them with an audience," he asked, rubbing the back of his neck nervously.

We'd skipped out on our friend Emma's birthday party just after the cake had been served. It was the height of excitement, and no one except the birthday girl herself knew that we had scooted out the back door. But that was at least thirty minutes ago, and our dads would be at Emma's to pick us up by now.

"I told her what we were doing. She was going to try to keep them distracted to give us more of a head start," I explained.

"Was she mad?" he asked, wondering if our mutual best friend was upset that we were running away.

"Worried, I think. You know Emma."

He nodded in agreement. Our friend was always looking out for us.

"I promised that we'd write to let her know once we arrived safely at your aunt's house. Are you sure your aunt won't tell your mom where we're going?"

He nodded. "She hasn't talked to my mom in years. They're mad at each other for something."

Adults!

Dogs barked, nipping at our heels as we climbed the fence that spilled into the small backyard behind my grandmother's office.

She wouldn't come out and yell. Not at us.

Glancing behind me to the large brick building that sat in the fading darkness, I saw her cheering me on from the back window. I couldn't hear what she was saying, but I had a feeling what it was.

Run. Or maybe: *I love you.* At the moment, they both meant the same thing.

If this had been any other day, she might have stopped me, talked some sense into me, as all grandmothers enjoyed doing. Maybe she—Dr. Bishop to everyone else, but Gigi to me and my friends—would have suggested that I stay with her as an alternative, either tucked away safely in her big sprawling house or even hidden away inside the doctor's office where my dad was staying during the divorce. Anything instead of leaving me to listen to my parents' constant fighting.

But not today. I think she hoped we would get away with our plan, given the circumstances. Not many people urged two ten-year-olds to run away, but Gigi suggested it without actually saying it. Better than anyone, she understood why I was desperate to leave.

I needed to leave, so that I could stay.

We scaled the last fence, leaving the majority of the small town behind. All that was beyond that was the railroad tracks and the woods.

Freedom.

But as I jumped down from the fence, a strangled cry spilled from my lips. With a thud, he hit the ground beside me, but just far enough away from the prickly branches that grew behind the fence.

The ones that I had landed right on top of.

"That looks really bad, Charlotte," he said worriedly, glancing down at the two long gashes that had appeared on my leg. Bits of spiky branches poked out from the wound in my pale skin.

"It's okay. I'll be fine," I bit out, wincing when I tried to stand. "We have to keep going." I wiped a muddy hand through the blood that slid down my leg.

"Maybe Gigi should look at it? Clean it up?" he asked, glancing down at the blood squeamishly. "She's right there. I just saw her looking through the window when we cut through the yard behind her office." He looked from my leg to the direction of the building over the fence behind us.

"No, they'll look for us there," I explained, trying to blink back the tears that welled up.

We both turned to look behind us. We'd heard the loud voices at the same time.

"If you're sure."

"I am. Promise."

He nodded. "I can tie a tourniquet," he offered, looking surprisingly steady as he examined my leg. "It's how I got my first-aid merit badge," he said proudly.

"Always a Boy Scout." I smiled, but it faded quickly when we saw the telltale sign of a flashlight beam signaling above the fence.

Waving him off, I felt guilty not letting him show me his skills, but we didn't have time. I rolled back my shoulders, wincing again through the shooting pain. "I'll take care of it once we get to the river," I said, limping away.

The sound of voices was getting louder. Shouts from our parents, concerned neighbors, and the—

We both looked back at the fence worriedly at the sound of the police siren.

"How did they get Birdy here already?" I asked, hearing the static from the walkie-talkie.

"Your dad probably called him as soon as he found the note you left. Between him and my parents, there's no way that they wouldn't get Birdy, if not all the police, involved."

I felt defeated, wishing I hadn't left the note stuck with a magnet on my dad's refrigerator. "I hoped we would have had more of a head start," I explained, trying to keep the weight off my injured leg.

Seeing my struggle, he frowned. "Here, hop on," he offered quickly, turning so his back was to me.

I looked at him, then down at me. I had a couple of inches and at least ten pounds on him. "I'm so much bigger than you! You can't carry me!" I said, just as another shooting pain radiated through my leg.

"I can do it. Trust me, Charlotte," he insisted. "We have to hurry."

His sky-blue eyes shone with kindness and compassion, the sentiment that I knew in my heart was honest and real. That's what best friends did—they helped when you needed it. And this might be our only chance of getting out of Hope Lake.

I hopped on, wrapping my arms around him. "Are you okay?"

In response, he gently squeezed my legs and took off as fast as he could toward the river, the chorus of voices fading behind us.

When we finally made it to the train tracks, he helped me slide down to sit on one of the large rocks that lay between the tracks and the river.

Our tracks. Our parents and the others searching for us wouldn't know to look for us here. It was our secret spot. Sure, it was an odd place for a couple of kids to run away to, but in a small town you're limited to where you can disappear.

That was the first lesson I remembered clearly from my decade in Hope Lake: you can't keep many secrets; everyone knows everyone's business.

We would escape here when my parents fought. Or if he was getting picked on at school. Anytime we needed a friend, we knew to head here. Because that's what best friends did.

"Are you okay?" I asked, swiping the hem of my shirt across his sweaty forehead. He was breathing heavily and collapsed beside the rock I was sitting on.

He nodded, his dark hair slicked with sweat. "I can't believe how hot it is," he said, still panting.

It was unseasonably warm for the end of September. "It feels more like the middle of summer," I groaned, wiping the sweat from my forehead.

School had barely started, which brought up another sad realization. "I won't be here this winter." I felt the tears well up. "No snow tubing or sledding through the woods. I won't even get to be in the Christmas pageant this year."

"That sucks. It's our year to be Charlie Brown and Lucy," he said, reminding me of the parts that we should be performing in this year's play, A Charlie Brown Christmas.

"Your mom can't just let you stay until June when school's done?" he asked hopefully.

I shook my head. "She said her new job in New York starts next week. We have to get settled, so that's why we're leaving tomorrow."

He hung his head, keeping his eyes down. "And she won't let you stay with your dad?"

"He won't be here. He's going on a mission trip to Ghana for the next four months." I couldn't keep the tears from plopping onto my hands. "And before you ask, there's no way she'll let me stay with Gigi. I already asked. So did Gigi. It's hopeless."

"What about Emma? The Peronis would let you stay with them. They'd love it. Or, me. You can come stay with us!"

The hopefulness in his tone was heartbreaking. We had been best friends for as long as either of us could remember, walking into kindergarten holding hands and being virtually inseparable ever since.

He sighed, long and hard. "We should have brought food and water." He rubbed his stomach. I heard it growl when he leaned over to check on my leg.

Blowing out a shaky breath, he looked up, worried. "You've got to clean this, Charlotte. It's going to get infected. I knew we should have stopped at Gigi's," he mumbled.

I dug around in my pack for napkins or tissues but came up empty. Sliding off the rock, I hobbled over to the river to splash water on my leg. "It burns." I watched the diluted blood slide down and color my white socks pink. "I don't know if it's supposed to sting like this."

When I looked up, he was beside me, handing me a shirt from his backpack. "Use this." His face was pulled tight, expressionless.

"No way," I said, pushing the Transformers shirt back to him. "That's your favorite."

He shrugged, tipping his head back toward the rock I was on.

"It's what best friends do." With the shirt balled up in his hand, he bent down and soaked it in the river. Then, with careful hands, he blotted the white shirt against the cuts on my leg, careful not to rub too hard.

"I'm sorry," he said with a sympathetic voice when I winced from the sting. I couldn't imagine how sad he was using that shirt. He'd saved his own money to buy it from the mall in Barreton.

Now it was streaked with blood and dirt because of me.

It's what best friends do. There was a sticker on the pole beside my makeshift seat that read BEST FRIENDS. We had put it there last year when we had coincidentally taken off from another birthday party. That time, it was mine. "I remember that," I said, pointing up to it. Seeing the sticker brought back the drama my mother had caused at my tenth birthday party.

My father and Gigi had planned all of it: the invites, the food, securing the location and getting a copy of the movie *The Goonies* for all of us to enjoy. My mother's only job was to get me a cake. It should have been simple, but she arrived late and forgot to pick it up. When she ran to the bakery to get it, she insisted someone else had bought it—with my name on it—which was *unlikely.*

My father drove me to Gigi's with my presents, but the embarrassment was thick and heavy around me and I couldn't enjoy anything. When we pulled up to her house, my friend was already there waiting. As if he knew that I would be upset and need to escape. We took off for our spot until the sounds of crickets told us it was time to go home.

This time, we were ignoring the crickets. We didn't have a home for me to go back to.

I smiled up at the sticker, trying to shake off the overbearing sadness creeping in. The sticker looked as though it was brand-new. "I wonder if that sticker will look that good when I come back to visit."

We both knew that running away wouldn't work and that we would have to face the inevitable. But it was still worth a shot.

"Of course it will. You'll be here next weekend," he said, with his usual hopeful tone. "Your mom promised."

"Of course," I lied, hoping to spare him the pain that I was feeling. I didn't know when I'd be back, but I was determined that it would be soon. I took out the Polaroid camera that was a gift from last year's doomed party and snapped two pictures. One for each of us.

"What's this for?"

"To help us remember the good times." Even though I was leaving, I'd have people back here as an anchor.

We looked at each other as best we could under the darkening sky. "This place won't be the same without you, Charlotte," he said, taking my hand in his.

My belly erupted in flutters. My usual defense mechanism was humor, so I went that route, tamping down the nervous energy that I started to get when he looked at me. "Quite literally." I laughed, pointing over his shoulder.

"They will be building houses over there soon," he said, nodding his head toward a sign that was stuck in the wet ground. It read FUTURE SITE OF THE LOVE LANE COMMUNITY. The sign sat on the edge of a steep embankment that would be the location of a new housing development. All the houses would look over the rest of the town below, and a massive yellow dump truck was already parked there for when construction started.

"It's a silly name, isn't it?" I scoffed. "*Love* Lane."

He shrugged. "I don't know. I guess it's nice, you know, if you like someone."

My eyes swung to him, wide and curious. "What are you saying?"

"Nothing, *nothing*. I'm just saying it's not that bad," he mumbled, kicking the dirt. "It's sad that people are going to be so close to this spot, though. It won't be a secret anymore." He looked up, and my heart plummeted when I saw the tears in his eyes. "This was supposed to be just for us."

I nodded, holding back my own tears. "My dad said they're not building up this far, but it's only a matter of time before someone does," I said, patting him on the knee.

"I'm going to miss this place." I stared up at the chipped white railroad-crossing sign, my hand resting on the BEST FRIENDS sticker.

"Aren't you going to miss anything else?" he asked, sitting beside me and stretching his legs out. Side by side the size difference between us was comical. His legs were bony, pale, and shorter than mine. My father said I'd had a growth spurt and that eventually he would have one, too, but there was also the chance that he was going to be slight in stature like his mom and not built broadly like his father, who was practically a giant.

It wasn't just our height, though, that made us appear so different in age. He still looked like a little boy, whereas I—much to my dad's dismay—was moving solidly toward preteenville. Doctor or not, my dad was jarred by the fact that his baby girl needed a training bra. My hair was growing faster, becoming more wayward with its curls, and my skin was starting to get the telltale signs that acne was going to be starting soon. Hormones were awful.

The only real similarity between us was the road map of scars, scabs, and black-and-blue marks that marred both of our limbs. It was thanks to hours of horseplay outside with friends. Friends I wouldn't see every day anymore.

"Charlotte?" he said, bumping my leg with his.

"Oh, sorry, I was thinking. What did you ask?"

He sighed. "I asked if you were going to miss anything else."

I smiled sadly. "I'll miss my dad most of all. Three hours is a long way away to visit me, and he's already so busy."

"Are you going to miss anybody else? Teachers, classmates . . ." He paused, shrugging his shoulder. "Friends?" In hindsight, I should have realized what he was referring to.

Friends.

Him.

"I'm afraid."

"Of leaving? New York is so cool! And you're going to be so close to the city. Just a train ride away! We went with Cooper and his parents. There are shows on Broadway that you'll love and the park has a zoo!"

I smiled weakly. "I know that. Dad mentioned it when he was trying to cheer me up."

I sniffed, wiping my tears away with my shirt. "I'm worried everyone's going to forget about me."

A lump in my throat prevented me from continuing.

Taking my hand, he held it gently between his. "I'll remember you, Charlotte."

"I think I see them!" someone shouted from behind us.

He looked at me; the look of sadness and heartbreak that must have mirrored my own was written over his face. We lunged at each other at the same time, and I held him in the tightest hug I could muster up.

My tears plopped onto his shoulder, and I felt a wall, brick by brick, form around my heart. Protecting it from the hurt that I was feeling. This wasn't a pain I ever wanted to feel again. I wouldn't allow it.

What I didn't realize was that by shutting out the pain of leaving him, I pushed him away completely. And I wouldn't know what I was missing until I returned to Hope Lake.

1

The bus rolled to a stop. A blinking yellow light hung over a pair of rickety train tracks. They looked defunct with the chipped white safety bars remaining at attention on the rusted metal poles. Squinting through the darkness, I spied a large green sign next to it. It swung back and forth in the May breeze.

HOPE LAKE

25 MILES

It was barely legible in the dense fog. It's what happened in valleys like this—the fog would blanket the town until the sun burned it away. *Everything settles in Hope Lake. The weather, the people.* My mother's voice echoed in my head. *Remember that, Charlotte. Don't go back, it sucks people in.*

I remembered her words wearily, rolling out my neck. Every inch of me was stiff, cramped from the fabric seat and the stale bus air. It didn't help that I was wedged against the window thanks to the mountain-size guy in my neighboring seat. His long legs were outstretched into the darkened aisle, perfect for tripping an unsuspecting person on his or her way to the onboard restroom. He was snoring away, oblivious to the fact that he kept half the bus awake with the sound. It only added to my sour mood.

The ride should have been a couple of bumpy hours by bus to my destination, a sleepy Pennsylvania town in the middle of nowhere. But with weekend traffic, roadwork, and a dozen drop-off stops that I didn't realize were a part of the route when I bought the one-way ticket, it had taken almost five and a half hours, and it still wasn't over.

"I'll never complain about the subway again," I groaned, shifting side to side, hoping to jar the lumbering snorer, and my rear end, awake.

The bus rumbled along in the darkness, eating up the last five miles slowly. The snorer jolted awake when the driver sounded the booming horn as we finally pulled into the tiny bus station in a town called Mount Hazel. I wasn't back yet, but this was as close as I could swing relying on public transportation this late at night.

I descended the bus stairs, my purse and carry-on bag slung over my shoulder, and looked around. Everything seemed nice enough, at least in the transition between night and the wee morning hours. A small, clean bus shelter sat near the street, free of graffiti. The rental car place behind it looked freshly painted and well-kept. The only noticeable problem was that it was closed. Wasn't everything open twenty-four hours like it was in New York? As the last passenger disembarked from the bus and got into an awaiting car, I realized I didn't have many options to get those last couple of miles to Hope Lake.

"Ma'am, are you expecting a ride?" the kindly bus driver asked, scratching his well-past-five-o'clock shadow with his meaty hand. "I can wait a bit so you're not alone with, uh, everything."

He peered around me to the semi-pitiful stack of suitcases that I had begged and borrowed from people with the promise of returning them as soon as I could. The ragtag bunch contained most of my worldly possessions. He had removed them from the built-in bus storage and neatly propped them against the side of the small, darkened depot.

It may not have seemed like a lot when my roommate, Parker, and I were packing up the necessities, but now seeing it in two piles with no way of getting it to where I was going, it appeared mountainous.

I smiled. "I did have a rental car, but clearly that's not happening." I waved back to the closed Enterprise booth. "I didn't realize they weren't open twenty-four hours like they are at home."

"No, ma'am, not here. Most stuff closes about five or six in the evening."

"It wouldn't have mattered. Sign said they closed hours ago," I admitted sheepishly, checking my watch. It was just after four in the morning.

He looked at me disbelievingly. "So no one is coming? Are you from Mount Hazel?"

I shook my head wearily. "I'm headed to Hope Lake."

Realization dawned on him. "Is there someone I can call for you? I don't want to leave you here by yourself."

He yawned, and a nugget of guilt wedged itself in my stomach. This guy didn't have it any easier than I did with the traffic and delays. He was just as tired, or more. "I'll figure it out. Thanks, though."

The driver looked uncertain. I didn't know if there was some unwritten code that would prevent him from leaving a passenger alone. "If you're sure," he said finally, looking around the empty lot. The side with the rental cars was filled. I wondered which would have been mine.

"I'm just going to sit tight until the Enterprise people come," I said, glancing at the hours on the glass door. "They should open at eight o'clock, so it's not too bad."

The only things surrounding me were the sound of crickets, a couple of hooting owls, and a suspicious-looking three-legged cat with a Mohawk that was wandering around the parking lot.

"Maybe you could call someone for a ride?" he suggested, seemingly unconvinced with my willingness to just sit under the street-light. "Those fancy-app drivers are just starting to come around here."

"Really, I'm okay," I insisted, not wanting to add anything else to my nearly maxed-out credit card. The rental car was prepaid without a refund. "I have a book right here . . ." I paused, pulling out a tattered print copy of *The Alchemist* that I'd borrowed from the Brooklyn Public Library. A hefty charge would be waiting for me by the time I got to return it. "I'll be fine. Promise."

Nodding, he reluctantly walked to the far end of the lot. His black pickup truck sat under a flickering lamppost that was teeming with some sort of large moth.

I tried giving him the most reassuring smile I could when he tooted the horn and pulled onto the quiet, deserted road. I didn't falter in my decision to sit it out until I heard the damn owl hooting again.

The outdoors and I were not copacetic. It was warm and sticky, and it wasn't even summer yet. My skin tingled thinking about the insects. I wasn't a Girl Scout. I needed AC and a glass of wine. *Can I make it back to New York before the end of August?*

Clearly, I didn't think this plan through.

I swallowed thickly. *Do I even have a plan?*

Sort of!

I pulled out my phone and dialed Parker. She'd be up now readying for work.

"Shouldn't you be asleep?" she mumbled through a yawn.

"Are you working?" I sunk down onto one of the suitcases.

"Yep, just slid two cakes into the oven. On track for a banner day."

Parker owned a boutique bakery called Delicious and Vicious. Her cakes were traditionally flavored with not-so-traditional messages and theming to go along with them. Her business had boomed a couple of months back after being featured on the Food Network.

"I need you to keep me company for the next few hours," I explained, curling my legs under me. "A plan would have been smart."

"No shit."

"Shut up, I just meant that the car rental place is closed."

She sighed into the phone. "Get an Uber, Charlotte. Or better, call your dad." She punctuated each word with a short pause. It was an argument we'd had for the past few days. I didn't want to let him, or anyone in Hope Lake, know that I was coming.

"Obviously, you're going to have to see him, and explain things, eventually. You know, like when you show up on his doorstep and say, 'Oh, hey, Dad, I'm home—'"

I interrupted. "Here."

"What?"

"I'm *here*, not home. Home is where you are. *Here* is not home. This is a bump in the road. A sad little pit stop in my life. Nothing more, and certainly *not* home."

She huffed. "One thing is for certain."

"What?"

"You're not going to be writing the Hope Lake tourist advertisements," she barked, laughing as she repeated, "'Sad little pit stop.'"

"I'm serious. I can't let this, *whatever*, distract me and make me lose focus of the end goal. Getting back to New York." I paused, feeling a sense of unease wash over me. "To civilization," I finished.

"Whatever it is, a pit stop, a roadblock, or the start of something new, you can't just sit on the side of a highway alone in the middle of the night. It's like a Stephen King novel. Or better yet, an M. Night Shyamalan movie. He's from Pennsylvania, right? I'd be worried sick."

"You're enjoying my imminent demise a little too much, thanks," I lamented. "Wait a minute, the 'start of something new'? You're either living in a Hallmark Channel movie or *High School Musical*, Parks."

She sighed, no doubt dreaming about Zac Efron. "Whatever, send me your exact location so if you go missing, I can have a lead to give to the hot country detective who'll want to question me about your disappearance."

"This isn't the country *exactly*," I corrected. "It's just not the city." I put the phone on speaker so I could share my location with her via text.

"Brilliant explanation, Sherlock. You know that anything outside of New York is the country to me. Okay, I'm sending you an Uber now. You're limited out there in the sticks on what type of vehicle will come pick you up, so hopefully whatever comes fits all your crap."

I sighed. "You don't have to do that, Parker. That's not why I called you."

There was a long pause. I could hear pots and pans clinking and clanking in her kitchen.

"I know it's not." I hated the thought of my recently not-so-broke friend sending her super-broke friend a charity Uber.

Then, something howled. It was coming from the thick wooded area next to me. *Are those eyes in the darkness?*

Okay, maybe I didn't hate the charity Uber that much. I wasn't going to last five minutes out here. This didn't exactly bode well for my being stuck in Hope Lake for the foreseeable future.

"I'll pay you back," I insisted, knowing that it would be a bit before I could. Things were *tight*. It helped that I was saving on not having to rent a place when I got to Hope Lake.

Parker grumbled. "Unnecessary. This is me helping you after you helped me manage everything after the coverage from the Food Network. Now, if you just took the job I offered you, you would still be here with me, in New York, instead of leaving me here all alone." She sighed longingly. "Now I have to let my idiot brother's idiot friend move in."

Even with all the press, she had thankfully stayed the same witty, generous best friend I had for the past twenty years. Even if it meant offering her untalented-in-the-kitchen best friend a job.

"I'm sorry about that, but we both know my working as your assistant would have been disastrous. I burned water and destroyed your favorite caramel pot. With my luck, my first day on the job would involve my burning down the entire place instead of a small stove fire. No, thanks."

Parker laughed just as a car drove past. *Not the Uber.*

"I didn't think it was possible to be that bad at boiling, but, surprise, it was. I'm sure the fire department is still telling that story."

I pinched up my face, not that she could see me. "In my defense, I forgot about the stove because my phone rang and I got tied up."

"Fair enough, I know that was the last phone call you were hoping to get," she said kindly, having been there to witness my pathetic mood after I got the bad news.

The caller was the head of HR at the Brooklyn Botanic Garden, After almost three months of trying to find something new, I officially gave up the search in New York after my last job prospect didn't work out. Sure, I could have gotten a job almost anywhere else, but I wanted a job in *my* field. Wasn't that why I was still paying off my student loans? The position at the BBG wasn't exactly what I had hoped for, but it was close enough and I would have been happy. Plus, there was the idea that the change of scenery would have been a good move for me. Getting out of the flower shop and into more of a business role with greater responsibilities and a chance to move up would have been worth it.

It was just after they courtesy-called to say they went with another candidate with more community-engagement experience that I decided to head back to Hope Lake with my tail between my legs. There were options, of course.

Sure, I could have found a way to stay—cater-waitering, something soul sucking in Times Square, tour guide on the Gray Line tourist buses—but how long would that have lasted before the boredom crept in? I was in debt, desperate, and after a come-to-Jesus conversation with Parker about my options, Hope Lake seemed like the best, well, *hope* to get my life back on track.

Plus, I figured that if I ducked out of the city for a couple of months, the gossip that my former boss Gabrielle had started about me would die down and I wouldn't be shunned in the floral world any longer.

"Hey, not to beat a dead horse, but has there been any more Gabby gossip floating around?"

Parker sucked in a breath. "Do you want me to be honest?"

My stomach dropped. I thought it would get better if I left. "No, but yes," I responded, nibbling away at my thumbnail.

"She said you were trying to steal clients from her and that some of the accounting was *off*. Which we know is a lie, but it's added to people not wanting to hire you because they think you're shady. I'm really sorry, Charlotte. It's my fault that she's going after you."

The worry latched onto my heart and squeezed. If this kept up, August wouldn't be enough time for the damage to fade away.

"No, it's not. She was always looking for a reason to give me the boot. The cupcake incident just added to it."

"Still, I'm sorry. I should have done my due diligence with that order. I knew they were for her, but it was just so busy that day—I let the assistants handle that one and never checked what the message was."

Parker's bakery, known for its brutally worded messages, had delivered a dozen cupcakes to Gabby. They were ordered by her philandering husband.

"It's not your fault that her husband was cheating," I told her.

"With her sister."

"Still, where he dips his nib isn't your fault. Or mine for that matter."

"No, it's not, but if it wasn't for *his* message on *my* signature Bananas Foster cupcakes, she wouldn't have taken it out on you."

I snorted. "Maybe not, but it is what it is. I can't keep losing sleep over it. Besides, I'm here now, and maybe she'll find someone new to torture."

"You're so positive! This trip is working already."

I tried to focus on that sentiment. "It'll be good for me to help my dad with Gigi. She's getting older, and although he won't admit it, I know he could use the help. And let's be honest, I've been a pretty lousy granddaughter when it comes to visiting her."

As in not coming back to visit in—checked watch—twenty-one years . . .

"Yeah, but they loved coming to visit you in between all of your dad's incredible service trips. It's not like you haven't seen them often," she insisted, knowing how much I loved having both my dad and Gigi come to visit me in New York. "Remember how much fun Gigi has here?"

I nodded into the darkness. The rumble of an engine drew my attention. "I think the Uber is here."

Sure enough, a large diesel-engine truck pulled into the lot, headlights streaming across the cracked pavement. The driver was shrouded in the darkness of the vehicle. He didn't look like he was going to come out and help me with my bags. *What a gentleman.*

"Don't hang up. Keep me in your pocket until you're delivered to your dad's doorstep!" Parker insisted.

"It's like I'm a pizza." I laughed. I stood, slipping the phone into my shorts pocket.

Pulling up the first suitcase, I tipped my chin up toward the truck bed. "Can I put everything back there?" I shouted through the partially open window.

As I asked, he picked up his cell phone. The brightness of the screen highlighted his face. Thankfully, he didn't look like a serial killer.

Neither did Ted Bundy.

Waving me back, he started yelling into his cell.

"Great, this will be a fine addition to the trip from hell," I mumbled. Then the first raindrop plopped onto my forehead.

I hurried as best I could with flip-flops on, running back and forth to lug the suitcases. I did a pretty good job, considering some didn't have working wheels. The truck bed was thankfully empty, and had one of those covers over the top in case of rain.

Just my luck, by the time I slid the last suitcase inside, the skies opened up in a light summer rain. At least my things didn't get soaked.

*

THE RIDE WAS painfully quiet. The driver didn't mutter a single word to me except for "Sit on the plastic bag in the back," when he saw that I was wet. Parker was still listening quietly in my pocket. This was the perfect setup for a murderous tale. After all, I was in the middle of nowheresville, in a truck that barely functioned, with a man I didn't know. I pulled out my phone and was texting Parker from the small back seat he'd wedged me into, the plastic sheet crinkling under my butt.

> **ME:** If I die, I'm going to be so pissed.

PARKS AND REC: You won't be anything but dead. I, on the other hand, will be super pissed. Don't haunt me either. That'll just piss me off more.

> **ME:** This is absurd.

Thankfully, a WELCOME TO HOPE LAKE sign welcomed us about a half hour later. It was slightly faded and weather-chipped around the edges. It hung crookedly on a tall wooden pillar at the edge of town. Like the town it would soon welcome me to, it had seen better days.

Stop being so negative, Charlotte.

I tamped down the snarky response but only for a second. A streetlamp above the sign flickered to life, highlighting something I'd missed on the first pass. What was more depressing than the beat-up sign was the small oval plaque attached to its bottom.

POP: 9,723

Nine thousand seven hundred and twenty-three. *Total.*

My street in Brooklyn had more people than that.

As we drove into town, the sun was trying to color the sky pink after the rainfall. Even though I was exhausted, miserable, and soaking wet, I could admit that it was a stunning landscape: something I wasn't used to seeing over the concrete jungle around my apartment. The tree-lined horizon was a sight to behold as we took the last hill over another pair of unused tracks that led into the Carey Mountains.

The beautiful scenery wasn't the only thing that I was examining. Google Maps was providing me with a clear path to follow . . .

1. To make sure he was actually taking me back to Hope Lake.
   He is.
2. To see if anything at all looked familiar. *It doesn't.*

How could that be? How much could change in a place in two decades? *Probably not much,* I wagered.

> **ME:** I have to admit something weird.

> **PARKS AND REC:** Oh boy. Do I need wine? It's a little early—even for me.

> **ME:** No, ass. I was just going to say that this place doesn't look familiar. Like, at all.

> **PARKS AND REC:** Nothing? Not even your dad's place?

> **ME:** Just got into town. Haven't gotten there yet.

"Are you sure this is Hope Lake?" I looked skeptically out the dirty window. "I mean, there isn't another one, right?" We had just ventured into what appeared to be a newer residential area, with rows of beautifully maintained townhomes. Another sign appeared just after that development that said we were heading toward the historical section of town. *When did that happen?*

The driver snorted. "This is it. The one and only Hope Lake. Listen, the request just said to bring you here, there wasn't a real address plugged in. Unless One-Two-Three Anywhere Street, Hope Lake, actually exists."

Oh, Parker. "It's Dr. Bishop's place on Main Street," I explained. "One-Forty-Five, please."

Nodding, he made a sharp U-turn next to an entrance to the school campus. It looked like that hadn't changed much. At least not from what I remembered. I was at the elementary school for only a couple of years before we moved.

As the sun cut through the trees, I found myself leaning against the window, amazed at the town's welcoming appearance. "Are you sure this is Hope Lake?" I asked again, disbelievingly.

"Lady, are you high?"

I scoffed. "No, I'm just trying to figure out why nothing looks familiar. Or dilapidated."

"When was the last time you were here?"

"A long time ago," I said flatly. My eyes were seeing the well-kept buildings, the newly planted flowers, and the maintained yards. New sidewalks lined the streets, and businesses looked ready to open instead of being shuttered. No matter how much I stared, my brain wasn't processing it. Whether it was from lack of sleep or just disbelief, I wasn't sure, but I'd be finding out soon enough.

"A lot has changed. Especially in the past year and a half with the new mayor," the driver said.

He turned onto Main Street. Just like every other part of town we'd driven through, nothing looked familiar.

> **ME:** Just pulling up now.
> **ME:** Parks, I lived here for the first ten years of my life.

ME: Nothing looks the same.
ME: Not even the house.

The two-story, brick-front home looked like it had just been cleaned up. The black shutters appeared newly painted. The landscaping boasted beautiful hydrangea bushes, a pair of holly shrubs, and a rhododendron. At each of the lower windows hung sturdy black flower boxes that exploded with gorgeous chartreuse potato vines, blue lobelia, red dracaena, and yellow million bells.

It made me wonder if there was a florist in town who needed some help from a disgraced and blacklisted flower junkie and event planner. *Not that they need to know that I am disgraced.* I could be anything that I wanted to be here. My lousy history didn't have to follow me back. I could be successful, revered, impressive. An admired astronaut or lauded lawyer or even a talented teacher.

I laughed to myself. Or someone who loved alliteration way too much.

As I stared up at the house, Parker's words from earlier played in my head on repeat before I hung up. *Start of something new . . .*

Whatever this trip to Hope Lake turned out to be, one thing stayed the same: I had to make the most of it.

Entering the house was a good place to start. And yet . . .

My grandmother, whom I had always called Gigi, loved her bright-red office door. She felt that it welcomed everyone into the practice. It did have an addition to it, though: a large bicycle wheel covered in white anemones, hanging from the front door like a wreath. It definitely wasn't something I would ever think Gigi would pick out, but there it was. It seemed that my dad left the door the same when he took over.

As my eyes scanned the building, the sun winked against the familiar brass plaque just to the left of the front door. My chest warmed seeing that it still read THE DOCTORS BISHOP: DR. IMOGEN BISHOP & DR. ANDREW BISHOP. I wondered why they didn't take the sign down to reflect Gigi's retirement.

As I contemplated my next move, my phone buzzed with a response text from Parker.

PARKS AND REC: It's been years, C.
I'm sure a lot has changed.
P.S. Glad you're not dead.

> **ME:** Yet
> we don't know how my dad
> will react.

PARKS AND REC: Oh, please.
PARKS AND REC: I'll probably hear his joyful crying from here.
PARKS AND REC: Call me after a nap.
PARKS AND REC: Love you.

> **ME:** You too.

"Lady."

Startled, I jumped. "Sorry, what?" I'd been so zoned out I had forgotten all about him.

"Are you going to get out or just sit here staring at the building?" the driver asked, turning around with an annoyed expression. "I got another call back in Mount Hazel."

I shook my head to clear it. "Sorry about that. I feel like I'm lost. I mean I *was* lost in thought." I stopped myself. This guy couldn't care less about my life story.

Stuffing my phone into my purse, I slid out of the truck, the plastic bag I was sitting on stuck to my butt. I sighed, mentally measuring the distance between the sidewalk and the porch with ten steep steps leading up to the front door.

Just like before, the driver didn't offer any help with my luggage, instead choosing to play Candy Crush on his phone. By the time I got to the last suitcase, I'd added his rudeness to the list of why I already hated it here.

After he'd pulled away, I sat on the top step, leaning against the pile of what made up my life. The town hadn't quite opened up yet. There was a startling difference between the little shops of Hope Lake and those on my street in Brooklyn. There were no pull-down cages to cover the front doors. From my vantage point, it didn't look like the doors were deadbolted or hardwired with a security system.

Across the street there was a grouping of small businesses, not a chain store in sight, which was refreshing. A tiny bookstore, a small café that looked like it sold coffee and ice cream. I made a mental note to visit that one later.

As I glanced around the office's small porch, I noted that all the store signage was bright, cheerful, and free of cracks or chips, at least from where I was standing. Maybe it was an odd thing to focus on, but when you expect the place to resemble something out of a dystopian novel, you tend to pick up the small and odd details.

The one thing that was similar to New York was that the birds were loud, chirping away on the tree-lined streets surrounding the office/house where I'd be living for the next however many months.

Months.

I had a lot of unanswered questions. The living arrangement had been on the top of the list. Something about the unusual burst of flowers outside the office made me think, *Maybe Dad has a girl-friend.* It wasn't something that we ever brought up. My parents' personal lives after their contentious divorce was a no-fly zone that all of us respected. Right up until my mother's death, I had no idea if she was seeing someone. It was something that neither parent ever brought up with me around.

If my father did have someone staying here with him, I wasn't about to cramp their style by staying in the house.

Where am I going to go?

Know what would help?

A plan.

I ignored my darkening thoughts and stood up to stretch. There was a police car circling the roundabout that surrounded the town square. As the sun brightened the sky, burning off any remnants of the rain and fog, I found myself unable to focus on anything but one word.

Sleep.

That was the goal, at least. Except the policeman slowed his cruiser in front of the building, quickly flashing his lights for a moment, almost as if it was accidental. Or as if he thought I was a hardened criminal who had just robbed the place and decided to take in the sunrise with my stolen goods.

"Can I help you, miss? The doc doesn't open until eight," he said through the opened passenger window. He shifted, glancing around me to see the suitcases. "Ma'am?"

I didn't want to shout, given that one of the ground-floor office windows was open. Descending the front stairs, I smiled at him, remembering him, sort of. He looked the same as he'd been back when I was ten, still pudgy around the middle, but his once-black hair was heavily salted at the temples now.

"Do you remember me, Officer Birdy?" I asked, smiling. I tried remembering the last time I had seen him. At school? Maybe at the house during one of my parents' riotous fights? That wasn't it. There was a memory scratching at the surface that I couldn't quite put my finger on.

He tapped the badge on his chest. "It's Chief Birdy now," he said proudly, his whiskery mustache still curled up at the edges when he smiled. "And you?" He paused to take a good look at me.

Twenty-one years later and I still had the same curly reddish-brown hair that never seemed to do what I wanted. At least with it shoulder-length, the waywardness didn't appear so unintentional. Though I *did* still look a lot like Little Orphan Annie.

I smirked as my identity dawned on him. "My goodness, I dare say you're Doc Bishop's little Charlotte. I'd recognize you anywhere."

His little Charlotte.

I guess that's how people here remembered me. The only child of the prominent small-town doctor and his always-wandering ex-wife. I would forever be "little Charlotte," regardless of my age.

Birdy slapped the steering wheel excitedly. "What brings you home?"

This is not my home. I swallowed the first answer that popped up, instead blurting out, "Just visiting!" I hoped it sounded genuine, but judging by the look on his face, I'd failed.

Word traveled fast in a town like this, and soon, people would be waking up to the breaking news of the day.

Charlotte Bishop has returned to Hope Lake.

It sounded like the opening line of a mystery novel.

Would my reappearance make the front page of the small-town paper? From what Gigi and my dad have told me, Birdy had a tendency of treating town gossip like it was a campy eighties television drama. The more salacious, the better.

Would people park themselves outside my father's office trying to sneak a peek at the girl who had never returned? So much for blending in and not drawing attention to myself.

Birdy widened his eyes. "How did you get here? Do you have a car? Does your pop know you're here?"

Was he interrogating me?

Why did my first official conversation with someone in town have to be with a cop who noticed everything?

Because you have no plan.

"Whoa, okay. Slow down," I said. "I haven't slept in a while. Bus to Mount Hazel. No. Uber to here. Not yet."

He was on a roll. "Why didn't your dad let us know you're coming?"

"*Us?*" I asked, wondering exactly whom he was referring to.

He laughed, jolly, like a small-town Santa. "Us is everyone! The town. Why didn't he let the town know you were coming? We could have done something special."

Like what? A parade? I thought, trying to keep myself from laughing at the notion. I would have to practice my wave. Elbow, elbow, wrist, wrist.

"How long are you staying? Those are a lot of suitcases."

What's with all these questions?

I held up a hand. "Honestly, I can't keep up. I'm storing some stuff here since there's no room in New York. Where I live. Home is New York, but, you know, New York apartments are shoeboxes and all. No, I'm not staying. He doesn't know I'm here. Surprise." I laughed awkwardly, realizing I'd said New York three times in twelve seconds.

Am I trying to convince him or myself that I'm not living here more than the next couple of months?

I turned to wave my arm toward the suitcases behind me to reiterate that I was just storing things temporarily, but my arm, and purse, swung out . . . and made contact with someone.

Turning, I saw that I had hit a well-built man around my age, give or take a year. He was lying on the ground, with one of his hands cupping his nose. Thank God, no blood was spouting out, but judging by how tightly his eyes were squeezed closed, I must have really done a number on him.

"Oh my God!" I shouted, kneeling beside him on the damp side-walk. "I'm so sorry! I didn't see you. You're so quiet for being so big!" My hand throbbed from where it had connected with the man's face, but it was nothing compared to what he must be feeling. I supposed that I knocked the wind out of him because he wasn't answering. He just kept squeezing his nose and moaning. He was lying on his back, looking a bit dazed when he finally opened his eyes. They were a beautiful shade of blue, like the clear sky that appeared right after a summer storm. There was something so comforting about them.

When I stepped forward to help him up, he was just about to roll over.

I stumbled, my foot connecting with his lower half. He howled in pain this time, a sound far worse than when I hit his nose. He rolled away from me, with his legs curled up to his chest, maybe to help him breathe through the pain.

The man now lay in a small puddle, but it didn't seem to bother him. He wasn't crying, but there was a shallow, whimpering noise coming out of his mouth that made it quite clear how badly I hurt him. He was breathing deeply—deep breath in and then a cleansing breath out. I found myself mirroring it in the hope of calming down.

"Birdy, help!"

Birdy was out of the cruiser in a moment and kneeling beside the injured party, whispering to him.

"Oh my God. I'm so sorry!" I apologized again frantically.

I bent down to help him and gently touched his sweaty shoulder. His once-light-gray shirt was soaked through from either the earlier rain, sweat, or both. He was facing away from me, angled toward the office stairs that I so desperately wanted to run up so I could disappear behind the door and hide.

"I'm so sorry," I said. He whimpered again, sounding a bit like the animals I had encountered at the bus stop. "I'm here less than an hour and I'm wreaking havoc. Do you need ice? A warm towel? Flowers? I don't know what to do for this type of ailment!"

Great! My bright idea is to offer him a bouquet for the pain.

The exhaustion was getting to me. I felt a sense of delirium mixed with embarrassment and a nice heaping spoonful of guilt. The perfect blend of *why I didn't want to come back here in the first place.*

"Should I get my dad?" I asked Birdy, not knowing how to care for a stranger who had been both knocked down and unintentionally kicked in the balls. "I mean he's a doctor and can, I don't know, help with manly business problems?"

Oh my God. Stop talking!

"Henry, son. Is everything okay?" Birdy asked, gripping the man's shoulder. "You know, down there?"

I snorted.

Glancing up at me, Birdy scowled lightly. "It's not funny. You've hit a man in the worst possible place."

I grimaced. "I think I broke his nose, too."

Birdy looked scandalized, but also a touch eager. "Well, you're certainly bringing the excitement on your first day!"

My hand flew to my chest. "Oh, no, no, no!" I rambled, knowing that gossip-loving Birdy was probably salivating over sharing this news. "No one needs to know about this." The last thing I needed, or wanted, was a slew of attention on day number one.

Nodding faintly, he still had a glint of mischief in his eye, and I had a feeling the town would know about this by lunchtime. Birdy turned back to the man he'd called Henry. "Are you okay, son? Need Doc Bishop?"

Henry shook his head slightly, whispering something that I couldn't hear. I hoped it wasn't "Arrest her for assault"—that would have been the icing on this already lousy cake.

"Charlotte," Birdy said, and I felt the man's body stiffen under my hand. I hadn't even realized I'd kept it there. "He said he's fine. Son, are you sure? The doc is right there."

He nodded again but made no motion to sit up. I pulled my hand away briefly, and he exhaled loudly as if he was relieved that I'd moved it.

"I'm so sorry, Henry," I apologized again, his name feeling strange in my mouth. "Do we know each other?" I asked, his chest seizing up again.

"Charlotte, maybe you should go ahead inside, give ol' Henry here a little bit of room to pull himself together a bit," Birdy said, patting ol' Henry on the shoulder.

I shifted away from them and stood. Staring down at him, I could see that he was very well-built, clearly a runner, but I knew he must do more than that. Football? Was there a sport where you needed to be even beefier than that? Something where you tore trees from their roots and tossed them?

Even with Henry semi curled up I could tell that he was very tall. He probably had at least a foot on me, if not more. The gray shirt he wore was tightly wrapped around his biceps, just as it had been stretched across his chest. His shorts hit a spot on his legs that highlighted calves that looked like he had sewn a softball into each. I admired him for a beat.

On a scale of one to ten, what are the chances of hooking up with a guy after you hit him in the business?

Probably slim to none, with slim out of town.

"Okay, well," I began, and part of me was talking to myself but I was also talking to Birdy, and Henry on the ground, too. "Like I said, I'm sorry. If you want to come in and see the doctor, I can, you know, put in a good word." I laughed. It was lame and I knew it, but this whole situation was awkward as hell.

"Thanks, Offi— Sorry, Chief Birdy."

He nodded to me before bending down to help Henry up. When Henry finally stood, he turned away from me with his shoulders hunched. I guess I really did do a number on him.

Chief Birdy opened the car door for him, and he collapsed inside, his head against the seat. He never glanced my way, and part of me was glad. The other part was disappointed that this was another lousy first impression. I watched them drive off.

I was at the top of the stairs about to ring the doorbell when it swung open, my father looking surprised, elated, confused, and concerned all at once.

"Charlotte!" he shouted, pulling me into a crippling hug. "I was having coffee with Reese, and I swore I heard your voice. What's all this?"

Reese. So, there was a girlfriend. *Now what?*

"Surprise! I'm here for a . . . *bit?*"

2

"What a surprise," my father said, keeping his arm wrapped tightly around my shoulders as if I would disappear. The act made my heart twist up. I hadn't stepped over that threshold in more than two decades.

"Shouldn't we bring my stuff in?" I asked worriedly. There weren't any people around, but I didn't want to leave everything out there sitting in the open.

"Oh boy, that's a lot! But we'll get it later." He paused, seeing my worried expression. "It's Hope Lake, Charlotte. The last bit of excitement Birdy got was Mrs. Mancini parking her car on the sidewalk illegally to run in to get ice cream at Viola's. No one will steal your stuff."

"Well, I just gave him some excitement this morning," I said, gesturing toward the front door.

My father raised his eyebrows in shock.

"Not that kind of excitement. Jeez, Dad. I accidentally hit some poor guy in the face and then in the manly business and sent him to the pavement in tears."

His eyebrows raised even higher toward his hairline.

"Okay, there were no tears, but I did a number on him."

"Charlotte. You can say that you injured a man's penis and testicles, you know. I'm a doctor; I won't blush."

"Penis and testicles, ladies and gentlemen. And it's not even eight in the morning!"

"Oh boy. You're here for, what, ten minutes and you're causing a ruckus. I should probably warn you, once word gets out that you're here, it'll only get more ruckusy."

I laughed, following his lead into the office portion of the building. "Is that even a word?"

He smiled. "Damn it, Charlotte. I'm a doctor, not a grammarian."

I rolled my eyes. "Still pulling out the *Star Trek* references, huh?"

It was his schtick. Need a pick-me-up after being diagnosed with a cold? He would "Live long and prosper" you daily when he called to check on you. Want to argue about a flu shot? You'd get a "Resistance is futile."

"You're still pulling those lines with patients? I hope they're at least laughing."

"Always. The kids love it, even though most of them only know the new *Star Trek* films and not the classic show," he explained. I made a mental note to get back to "the kids" later.

To my knowledge, there weren't many people my age here. It was part of why my mother insisted that I never come back when I was still a kid. Well, that, and the fact that there wasn't much here for me to do. The place was stagnant—"like a hamster on a wheel," as my mother used to say. Even if I did want to return, she made sure there was a reason why I couldn't.

My dad led me into a small room off the foyer. While the rest of the town may not have jogged any memories, this house felt like it held a lot of them.

The foyer emptied into what served as the administrative office for my father's practice. A wall of glass partitions welcomed me, and filing cabinets lined the space behind the two currently unoccupied desks.

A massive stone fireplace sat against the far wall, surrounded by patient seating. The mantel was filled with photos of my dad on volunteer trips. Ethiopia, Haiti, Syria—anywhere he could travel to lend a hand, he did. Not as often as he did when I was a kid, but at least one trip a year now, when his time allowed. On the opposite end of the waiting area was a small section reserved as a kid zone.

"That's new," he said proudly, motioning to the child area. "We have a pediatrician coming in. She's using the offices until she can find her own place. Or until I convince her to join the practice. I'm getting old, you know."

"You're not. You haven't aged a day," I said, smiling when his cheeks turned pink. He looked exactly the same as he did when I saw him last, when he stopped in Brooklyn on his way to the UK for a seminar last year. Our weekly FaceTime chats didn't count. You couldn't *see* a person that well on video calls.

He was sporting a few more grays mixed through the reddish brown at his temples. At least he didn't look tired like he did the last time I had seen him in person. Running between two towns could be exhausting. Overall, he still looked like Dad. Too tall, too lanky from all the cycling he did before he saw patients, and too harried from all the hours spent at the practice. *A hazard of living where you worked*, I wagered.

"Is a full-time pediatrician really needed here?" I asked, curious to know how many patients she could possibly see in a town with fewer than ten thousand residents. I supposed it could be a handful.

He looked at me curiously. "Of course. She's swamped, actually. She started coming once a week, then twice. Now it's four days a week, and she's splitting time between us and Mount Hazel, trying to decide where she's going to settle. I'm hoping she chooses to stay here."

My father sounded so hopeful, and I wondered if he would be repeating the same phrase to me by the end of the summer. Or, by the time I got my shit in order—whichever came first.

"Did you get a couple of days off with Memorial Day last weekend?" I asked, noticing that the purple shadows under his eyes looked lighter than when we'd FaceTimed last week.

Our weekly calls were scheduled for Tuesday nights during dinner. It was after his last patient of the day, and it gave me time to get home and make something other than ramen or canned soup. Anything to give him the appearance that all was well. *Even when it isn't.*

He frowned, rubbing the back of his neck. "I meant to, but there was an emergency in Mount Hazel. Fireworks displays never seem to go off properly there."

I winced. "What happened? Anyone lose a finger this year?"

"Thankfully no," he explained, looking relieved. That had happened on more than one occasion. "Someone did get a Roman candle to the forehead, though. I went up to help with a couple of burns and stitches."

"Never a dull moment with you, Dad," I teased, bumping his shoulder. "You can't just sit with a cigar, whiskey, and slippers, and relax. You've got to start taking care of yourself."

"Never a cigar, you know that," he said in his doctor voice. "Whiskey—hell, I'd probably take a sip and fall asleep. But the slippers? I should get a pair of those this winter."

Mentally, I added them to his Christmas list.

We wandered through the exam rooms, which had been converted from the formal dining and family rooms into four smaller patient spaces.

Everything looked pretty much the same as it had when I visited the office as a child. If you didn't know it was a house prior to the office, you'd think it was built this way. My dad's living quarters on the floor above us mirrored the ground-floor plan—but without the clinical feel.

"What's so funny?" he asked, cocking his head.

I smiled again. "It's funny what memories resurface and when."

He frowned, pulling his doctor's coat from the hook in the hallway. It must have been closer to opening time than I'd realized. "What do you mean?"

"I'm just thinking out loud, that's all. I remember running down this hall when I—well, before we left."

His expression darkened. My leaving was still a sore spot that we avoided. "Gigi loved it when you visited the office growing up. So did I."

I smiled, hooking my arm through his as we walked down the hall. This was good. Comforting, too. We passed an air freshener, and I had a sense of déjà vu so strong that he held on to my arm when I swayed.

"Sweetie, are you all right?" he asked, his hand flying to my forehead as if to check for a fever.

Oh, Dr. Dad, always worried.

"I mean, the walk down memory lane, the luggage out front . . ."

"We'll get to that in a minute, Dad." I laughed and walked ahead toward the back of the building. I stopped at a collage of photos of my father and Gigi spanning from his med school graduation to what looked like a recent one of her in her fancy new wheelchair.

"New paint?" I said, trying to change the subject from my staying to something benign. The walls remained the sunny, pale yellow I remembered from childhood, but they looked freshly done.

He nodded. "Reese had a friend in Barreton that needed work, so we got him to come up a month or so ago. He fixed up the moldings, too. Great craftsman."

"Who's Reese?" I asked, racking my brain for a reminder. Did he tell me about this person, and I spaced out? It wouldn't be surprising given that my brain wasn't firing on all cylinders lately. "Another general practitioner?"

Hiring another doctor would make sense, since he was inching toward retirement age, but two general practitioners *and* a pediatrician? That seemed like lofty aspirations for a tiny practice in a small town.

"Speak of the devil," he said, turning toward the swinging doors that opened up to the mudroom and back parking lot.

If he was the devil, sign me up for hell. In walked a tall man with dark, closely-cropped hair and a knee-buckling smile. Hello, Idris Elba's look-alike. He appeared to be in his midthirties but dressed like he was in college, with a faded AC/DC T-shirt and a pair of ripped, worn denim jeans. There was something classically handsome about him with his sharp, stubbled jawline and piercing brown eyes. Judging by his gait, he was very confident. He strode in with purpose. And his smile was blinding. Good Lord, who knew Hope Lake was hiding all the hotties.

Here I thought Reese would be Dad's girlfriend.

"Dr. Reese, this is my daughter, Charlotte. Charlotte, this is Dr. Maxwell Reese. He officially joined the practice as of last week," Dad explained happily.

"Dr. Reese." I smiled and extended my hand but pulled it back quickly as I realized something obvious. "Oh!" I shouted.

"Please call me Max," he encouraged, clapping my father quickly on the back.

I extended my hand again, and he held it for a beat longer than customary.

My father looked at us curiously, his eyes darting before sliding a keen eye over at our clasped hands.

"Well, it's nice to meet you, Max," I said, enjoying his soft hands on mine. I kept my eyes down, feeling the heat creeping up my neck.

"It's so wonderful to finally meet you, too. I've heard so much about you. We plan to venture to Brooklyn next month to take you to dinner. There's a conference we're attending in Manhattan."

Still reddening, I looked up, hoping that no one noticed. "Surprise! I beat you guys to the visit. I'll be here in Hope Lake." Max looked pleased, but not nearly as happy as my father, who was positively beaming.

"For a little while at least," I said nervously, hearing the back door open again. Soft voices carried down the hallway. I realized that their office would be opening, and I still had yet to explain my situation to my father. Though Max seemed nice, and was certainly attractive, I didn't exactly want to air my baskets of laundry in front of a stranger.

"I know you're swamped, so I'll just crash upstairs for a little while. I haven't slept in twenty-four hours, and I'm beat. Oh, but all my stuff is still outside. I have to get that first. My God, I'm so tired, though. No one will steal it, right? I can sleep for a couple and then grab it all and unpack the nightmare."

I was rambling and didn't notice my father trying to get a word in edgewise.

"Oh, honey. I wish you'd told me of your plans," my father finally said when I paused to take a breath.

Yeah, I don't exactly have a plan, Dad.

"This was sort of spur-of-the-moment," I said, leaving out that I had zero plans and was just winging it. Something that my super-organized father never did.

Dad's mouth was a perfect O, his brows were furrowed, and his normally pale skin was flushed pink. "We have a slight conundrum, you see. Max hasn't closed on his house yet."

"Nearly there," he said, clapping his hands together and pointing them to the ceiling. "Soon, I hope."

"And the B and B is filled with the crews who're trying to finish up all the renovations and expansions before the summer tourist season starts. I didn't think you'd be here, so I invited him to stay with me at the house instead of doing a short-term lease somewhere else."

"Oh." My voice sounded flat. "Congrats on the future house." He wasn't much older than me. Six years give or take, and he was moving into a practice and buying a house. Meanwhile, my life was piled up on my dad's front porch and I couldn't remember if I brushed my teeth last night.

"Okay, no worries," I replied, thinking of the layout of the second floor of the building. During the divorce, Dad moved out of the house we'd lived in together and into the doctor's office. Over the years, he transformed the second level into his living quarters. It was the perfect bachelor pad. Besides the kitchen, two bathrooms, and living room, it had a bedroom and office, the latter of which I was hoping would have doubled as my guest room. Now it seemed that Dr. Max was there.

"Maybe the couch in the living room?" I asked. Having two roommates would be like college, but with less . . . *questionable dating practices*, since, you know, my dad lived here.

Dad frowned. "Honey, I wish."

"So do I," Max mumbled.

Well, well, maybe my chances are a bit better.

"I SHOULD HAVE made a plan," I complained, stuffing the last suitcase into the back of my dad's SUV. Of course, because the suitcase was older than I was, the zipper split open, spilling underwear and bras over the rest of the stack. "Awesome."

My father had pulled his Mercedes SUV to the front of the house, jumping the curb to make it easier for me and Max to load up the car while he tended to his first patients.

After the awkward exchange in the office, we decided that it was best if I stayed with my grandmother Gigi, until Max moved out, whenever that would be.

"I'm really sorry about this, Charlotte. I do wish we were meeting under different circumstances," Max apologized, carefully avoiding the ladywear as he restacked what I'd just shoved into the back to make it easier for me to remove everything later. Before he came outside to help, he had changed out of the random AC/DC shirt into a respectable polo from the Hope Lake Country Club, since he was expecting patients soon.

"It's fine." But it wasn't. *I wasn't.*

"I feel like you're angry with me," he said, partially sitting in the trunk. I wasn't mad at him, per se. The stranger in my house. *It hasn't been your house in, well, ever.*

I shook my head, smiling genuinely.

"I'm not mad at you. I don't even know you," I said honestly. "I'm frustrated with the outcome of the day, and I'm exhausted. And that usually means I'm a verbally stunted nightmare. I'm pretty sure that I smell *not great*, and I have a wicked headache, which is making everything feel a hundred percent worse."

He laughed lightly and reached out to touch my shoulder. "Your dad didn't prepare me for you," he said with a gentle smile. "I knew you'd be beautiful; I've seen that in photos that he has around his house, but funny I didn't expect, since he's so dry and straitlaced. Amazing, well, I knew you would be the way your father described you." He stood, raising his arm to close the trunk.

"Oh yeah? How did he describe me?" I asked, wondering how much this Max knew about me, especially when I knew nothing about him.

"He said you were feisty, wildly intelligent, stubborn, and while a bit harried at times, incredible. All of which are rolled into a fire-cracker of a daughter. Just from the few moments we've had, I'd say that I fully agree with his summation."

My face warmed under his gaze.

A horn beeped behind us; a pale arm extended out the passenger window. "Looking good, Dr. Reese!" a woman yelled.

He ducked his head, smiling until the car was gone.

"Seems like there's a Dr. Reese fan club in Hope Lake," I teased.

He smiled shyly.

"I don't know if it's a fan club so much as one persistent fan *pair* of women who like to rib me incessantly," he explained. "Your father thinks it's hysterical."

"So do I! How long have you been here to have accrued a fan club—sorry, fan pair?"

His lip quirked up on one side as he took a step forward. Just then, another woman passed by on the sidewalk and gave Max a delicate wave.

He flushed pink. "Not that long. I can tell you that I didn't draw nearly as much attention when I got into Hope Lake as you did."

I find that hard to believe.

"I'm thinking you have plenty of attention tossed your way, seeing as that woman nearly walked into the stop sign because she was staring at you."

Max laughed, briefly glancing her way. When he brought his focus back to me, any embarrassment was erased.

"How about this? You get settled, relax this afternoon, and tonight maybe we can have a walk around town and get to know each other a little bit? I'm not an expert on this town, but we can explore Hope Lake together if you'd like."

Dr. Max's confidence was palpable. While I wasn't always attracted to alpha-type guys, it was sort of working for him. Or I was just that tired and, frankly, a bit more gullible than usual.

"Like a date?" I blurted out. Immediately I wanted to swallow the words. Sleep was so needed right now. "See what I mean? Verbally stunted."

He barked a laugh. "Not exactly what I meant. I was just thinking that you must have a reason for being here, and maybe a friendly face would make things easier. Of course, if you'd like to call it a date, I'm certainly not opposed to it."

Is dating something I'm going to entertain while I'm here? I wondered. Then I looked at him again with his deep, dark eyes and perfect face and decided. *Why not?*

"Uh, sure. Gigi doesn't live far. I'll text you. What's your number?"

Taking my phone, he dialed his. "Done," he said, handing it back.

"Thanks." I clicked on his number and listed him as Dr. Max in my contacts.

He looked over my shoulder. "I like that. Dr. Max."

He winked, and my mouth went dry. I swear my flirting game was in desperate need of a life preserver because it was drowning.

If I wasn't so tired, I'd have had a sexy quip in response.

Instead, I snorted, depositing the phone back into my pocket.

"I'm sorry, I'm a mess," I said, staring up at the house. "Not even a hot mess at this point. A tepid mess who needs so much sleep and a long, screaming-hot shower."

"How long have you been up for?" he asked.

I scratched my head, trying to think. "At least twenty-four hours. I figured I would sleep on the bus and get here on time last night to crash at a normal hour. Clearly that didn't happen."

Max looked concerned, glancing at his watch and then at the car that had just pulled up to the curb. It was likely a patient. "Are you okay to drive? I can take you if you'd like."

I smiled gratefully and took the keys from him. "Thanks, I'm okay. It's just, I focused on this place the whole trip here."

Dr. Max, as I was now calling him in my head, leaned against the car, crossing his arms. I couldn't clear my head, my emotions were all over the place, and I was so tired that I was becoming delirious.

I was about to tell my inside voice to shut the hell up when Dr. Max spoke up. "Judging by the fact that I'm pretty sure you just fell asleep while standing up, why don't we push our walk to tomorrow, since I suspect once you fall asleep, you're not rousing until morning. And if it'll make you more comfortable, come here for dinner after. It'll be my night to cook, and I'll make my specialty as a welcome-home gesture. I know your father wants to get to the bottom of this unexpected journey you've embarked on, and admittedly, I'd like to spend some time getting to know you when you're coherent."

A woman got out of the car that had just parked at the curb, drawing Max's attention away from me. He waved before turning his attention back to me.

Dr. Max walked me to the driver's-side door and waited while I got situated. "Until we meet again," he said, tapping the roof once before walking away.

I watched him until he disappeared into the house, welcoming the patient as she walked in the front door. She leaned up to give him a kiss on the cheek. She, like the other women, looked smitten.

Small-town doctors, man. No wonder he had a fan club. My smile faded as the door closed. *What the hell are you doing, Charlotte?*

THE DRIVE TO Gigi's wasn't exactly easy. It should have been, considering it was only a couple of miles outside of town, but I kept having to stop to check the directions on my phone.

Where was the miserable, depressed town that my mother always talked about? I expected abandoned buildings. Run-down homes and pothole-riddled streets. At least that's what my ten-year-old brain remembers combined with my mother's descriptions. Instead, it was nearly the polar opposite of anything she'd ever told me about it.

Just one street behind my father's practice, I rolled to a stop sign outside a development that lined the perimeter of the forest leading toward the river. THE LOVE LANE COMMUNITY, the stone sign read. *That's familiar*, I thought, impressed by the breadth of hostas, zinnias, and hydrangeas at the sign's base.

My phone chirped with a message just as I was about to accelerate through the stop sign. I glanced at it quickly when I heard the quick *bloop* of a siren. Panic struck. Shit, did I run the sign? No, I stopped and looked, I didn't even move yet. Then what was the reason for being pulled over?

There in the rearview mirror, I saw the red and blue lights flash quickly before shutting off. I pulled over beside the stone wall and waited. Then I waited some more before the policeman rapped at the window with his nightstick. Beside him was another officer, significantly younger than the one with the stick.

I half expected to be greeted by Chief Birdy again but instead, there were two new faces.

Officer Stick's shiny brass name badge read DUNCAN, and I couldn't read the apprentice's from where I was sitting.

I lowered the window and smiled, as innocent and calmly as I could. "Hi, there. Beautiful day we're having, huh?"

I could imagine what my face looked like. Deer in headlights came to mind. I had never been pulled over before. Hell, I didn't even have an updated lic— *Oh, shit!*

"License, registration, and proof of insurance," Duncan said gruffly, placing the nightstick back in its holder on his belt.

"Funny story about that," I began, leaning over the console to reach into the glove box. I riffled around for the insurance papers, finding them in a neat, organized little leather folder labeled NECES-SITIES.

Jesus, Dad, does everything need to be so orderly?

"Ma'am?" he said. I could hear the officers whispering between themselves.

"Yes, sorry, uh, so funny story," I said, smiling as broadly as I could. "I have the insurance and the registration, but, well, you see, my ID, well, I don't really hav—"

"Step out of the vehicle, ma'am." *Well, damn, this has escalated quickly.*

Think, what happened on Law & Order? *No one got pulled over on that, it was crime-scene stuff.* I set the little folder on the passenger seat and stepped out into the unseasonably warm day. It was only around nine, but the weather was already muggy and humid. I pulled the hair tie from around my wrist and pulled my curly hair up so it was at least off my neck.

"Ma'am, whose car is this?" the seasoned officer asked, casually resting his hands on his belt.

The younger man stood behind him, watching his every move, mirroring his position and trying to look as authoritative.

"It's my father's car. Dr. Bishop . . . ? Do you know him? I'm sure if you just call—" I began, but Duncan held up his pasty hand.

"Yes, I know him well, which means that I know his daughter doesn't live here. Are you claiming to be her? Yet you have no ID to prove it."

I swallowed, feeling the perspiration beading up on my forehead. "I *am* Charlotte Bishop. I just came back this morning for a visit, of sorts. I'm going to Gigi—sorry, my grandmother's—now. Imogen Bishop . . . ? Out on—"

He cut me off again. "Yes, we're aware of where Imogen lives. Do you know why we pulled you over?" There was no trace of kindness in his tone. All business with this one.

"Is a taillight out? I don't know. I mean, I live in Brooklyn, so I'm not too familiar with—" I stopped talking when I realized I was essentially digging my own grave.

"I don't drive in New York," I finished, twisting my fingers together anxiously.

"When was the last time you held a current driver's license?" Duncan said, and I felt the color drain from my face.

"Um," I began, thinking back to when I had taken the test. Almost thirty-one minus sixteen equals *I am so screwed.*

"A while ago?" *Brilliant, Charlotte, how the hell did you plan on renting a car without a license?*

"I know how to drive, though. I mean, I passed the test with flying colors. It's just there's not really a huge need to drive in the city with all the public transportation, you know? Ubers are for birthdays." I laughed, and it was so damn awkward.

His face didn't crack. He was stonewalled like the actual stone wall behind me.

"Ma'am," he began.

"I'm only thirty-one; I'm not really a ma'am."

It slipped, and I slapped my hand over my mouth quickly, but the damage was done. It appeared that I was already on his short list of people to hate today.

"Teddy, you're going to have to drive Dr. Bishop's car to the station," Officer Duncan explained, ignoring the fact that my mouth hung open.

"The station? Sir, with all due respect, is that necessary? I'm being arrested? This is a joke, right?"

If I wasn't at the top of his list before, I sure as hell was now. His face reddened so quickly, I thought his head would pop off. "I'll have you know, ma'am, that you can't roll in here driving illegally and texting your fancy New York friends and get away with it. You can sit at the station until we can run your background and see just how long you've gone without a valid license."

My eyes burned from flattening my lips together so hard. I was already in a heap of trouble, and I had been in this godforsaken town for only a couple of hours.

Officer Duncan ushered me into the cruiser, opening the back door with a smug grin on his face. I stared at him.

"In the back? With the cage thingy? I'm not a criminal, for pity's sake!"

He didn't answer except for raising one bushy eyebrow to his graying hairline. I huffed, swallowing every snarky retort swirling in my sleep-addled brain before sinking into the pleather seat. He was kind enough to keep the door open while he radioed into the station.

When he was off the phone, I put my hands together and tried to look like someone you wanted to help. "Can you at least call my grandmother or my dad and let them know I'm here so they're not worried?" I begged.

He snorted. "This isn't *Who Wants to Be a Millionaire*. You don't get a phone-a-friend until you get to the station."

Suddenly, he straightened up, smoothing back his wayward hair. I turned around to see a shiny white Jetta pulling up behind the cruiser.

"Oh, I see what's up," I mumbled, but he'd lost interest in me thanks to the visitor.

The car stopped, and a woman got out. Her long hair was pulled up in a loose bun, wide tortoiseshell sunglasses were perched on her nose, and she was dressed as if she were headed into fashion court, with a red pencil skirt and a black-and-white polka-dotted blouse. Wrapped around her was a thick, knotted black belt that accentuated every inch of her slight frame.

"Hello there, how's my favorite policeman today?" she asked, click-clacking across the road in her impossibly high heels.

Officer Duncan was trying, and failing, to act cool by leaning against the hood of the car.

"Oh, you have a criminal! Exciting!" the woman said, clapping her hands. "When was the last time we had one of those? Probably when that tourist from Philly lost his pants, but that wasn't really criminal as much as hilarious."

I laughed. Finally, she turned and looked at me slumped against the pleather seat with my forehead pressed against the window.

Her perfectly shaped eyebrows raised from shock. Turning to Duncan, she shouted, "Wait, you're arresting Charlotte?"

3

———

"Well, I'll be damned. What the hell are you doing here? And by here, I mean both in the back of Duncan's cruiser and in Hope Lake," she said with a laugh. "And how did I not know you were coming?" Her voice sounded hurt.

"You don't know how happy I am to see you. The rest will take a bit to explain. It would go faster if Officer Duncan here cut me loose," I teased. I had never been so grateful in my life to see a friendly face. "*You* should have been my phone-a-friend."

She looked at me, then to Duncan, utterly confused.

"Figures you'd know her," Duncan chimed in, rolling his eyes. He pushed off from the car and walked toward us.

Emma hushed him with a playful swat to his arm. "Be nice. Charlotte is one of my oldest and dearest friends. Though she was terrible for not letting me know she was coming. We could have planned something!"

What exactly did this place plan for people who came to visit? Gift baskets and special tours? Though, if it was a gift basket, sign me up.

Turning to me, she smiled broadly and winked. "Duncan," she said in a cloyingly sweet voice, "can we let her out? I don't think she's a danger. In fact, I'm not even sure if she's awake."

Duncan harrumphed.

She glanced over at him with the same sweet smile. "I haven't seen her in ages, and I'd love to chat. I promise I'll bring her to the station if she breaks any laws."

He rolled his eyes. "She's unlicensed. You can't let her drive."

"Never. I'll chauffeur her around."

"And she should pay a fine," he said sternly, hiking his pants above his round belly.

My stomach dropped. This, too, would be on my nearly maxed-out card.

"Emma, I'm serious," Duncan said. "I'm not going to let this fly just because she's friends with you or because she's the doc's daughter."

"I know you're serious, Duncan. That's why you're my favorite policeman and why I brought you this package of cookies from my mom."

"Your mother made me cookies?" Duncan said, his voice suddenly soft and sweet.

Emma nodded and pulled a small white box from her massive tote. "I was coming to bring these to the station when I saw you pulled over here."

She handed him the box, and watching him open it was like seeing a child on Christmas morning.

"You're like magic," I whispered through the still-open door. "And honestly, what does your mother put into these cookies that they've reduced a grown man to this?"

"Shhh, you're not out of the woods yet, lady. He's got to agree to release you to me. And you owe me an explanation," she whispered back as we intently watched Duncan shove an entire beautifully decorated cookie into his mouth.

"Why I'm here . . . ," I began, snickering when Duncan dived into the box for another cookie. "That's sort of a long story."

"I figured as much, since I didn't even get a text that you were coming." A tinge of hurt peeked through her voice again.

Emma Peroni was the only person I reconnected with as an adult, more because she was so persistent that I couldn't say no. Besides my dad and Gigi, I should have told her I was coming.

With all the love I had for her, I wasn't sure *now* was the best time for a reunion or an explanation. Emma knew everyone in town and was engaged to the mayor. Running into someone like her when you're literally a hot mess isn't exactly an ego boost.

"How about the condensed version? I have fifteen minutes to spare," she said, checking her watch.

"Fifteen minutes. Okay, condensed version. I'm in Hope Lake for the summer—" I stopped when Duncan choked on the cookie he'd just shoved into his mouth. "Or I can leave earlier, depending on how things go."

Emma nodded slowly, as if she was deciding how to react. "But why? And what are your plans while you're here?"

I laughed, slapping my thigh. "That, my friend, is the million-dollar question. As an aside, if you have an answer that pays a million, please let me know."

"We need more time to get to the bottom of this. I'm clearing my morning for you," she exclaimed, sliding her phone from the tote.

"How do you find anything in there? It's like Mary Poppins's carpet bag."

Emma sucked in a breath, offended. "Carpet bag? This is Gucci! Cooper bought it for me for our anniversary. I'll have you know, everything is organized within an inch of its life."

"That doesn't surprise me."

She mock frowned. "I'll let that slide since you look like you just spent the weekend partying in Vegas. I'm assuming you're feeling like it, too. For now, I'd like to know why you're in the back of Duncan's car."

I winced. "Partying in Vegas? That bad, huh?" There wasn't a mirror nearby, but that might have been a good thing.

"Charlotte, your bags have bags."

"If someone would have just let me go, I'd be at my grandmother's by now and snoozing the horrible day away but, noooo," I said, stretching the word out dramatically. "I had to go and get pulled over without a license."

"And driving with your phone in your hand," Duncan chimed in around a mouthful of cookie. "Let's not forget all the fun stuff."

"What does that mean?" Emma asked suspiciously.

Duncan smiled. "It means that if she steps a toe out of line, you're in trouble. Keep her in line, Peroni."

"That's it?"

"Did I forget to mention the hefty fine?"

The urge to give him the finger was strong, but I was sure there would be an added charge for that.

"And we're taking the car back to the station. Your dad will have to come for it later." He whistled, and the other cop pulled away in my father's car, tooting the horn as he sped down the road.

Emma smiled at Duncan, blinking her eyelashes softly at him. "Duncan, if I bring you some of Sophia's pasta fagioli tomorrow, will you let my friend go with a little old warning?"

Duncan turned, considering what she had just offered, wiping the crumbs from his uniform as he grinned at her. "I suppose, since it *is* her first offense, but you'd have to sign for her."

"Emma, it's fine, you don't have to," I protested. "I can wait for my dad to be done with his patients before he gets me at the station."

She glanced at her watch again. "You don't look like you're going to make it that long, Charlotte. You're going to sit there, half asleep and looking like hell—no offense—for a couple more hours? I don't think so. What kind of friend would I be?"

Duncan shrugged and mumbled something like "Your funeral," but Emma appeared unfazed.

"Do I have to sign something, or is my word good enough for today?"

He rolled his eyes. "I know where to find you."

She reached up and planted a quick kiss on his cheek. "I'll bring the soup in time for your lunch tomorrow."

Duncan blushed and thanked her, not sparing me a second glance. Fine by me.

"My morning is cleared now. What are your plans after I spring you? Can I buy you brunch, or do you want to head to Gigi's to sleep?" She slipped the phone back into her pocket. "Not that I would blame you."

"Brunch sounds like the best thing in the world right now. Food, then sleep," I said as my stomach unleashed a cacophony of hangry sounds.

"Emma," Duncan grunted, pointing a meaty finger in my direction as he sank back into his cruiser. He handed me my purse and nearly-dead phone before pulling away and shouting, "Don't forget, stay outta trouble."

"Aye, aye, Captain!" she said, with an awkward salute.

"Can we call my dad to let him know you're—what did you call it? Springing me? Make sure we use those words," I insisted, knowing that he would find it hilarious.

"Already done. Once Duncan agreed to let you go, I shot your father a text. He said to stay out of trouble."

I had a feeling that was easier said than done.

WE ARRIVED AT the 81 Café after Emma rummaged around in her purse to find me a phone charger.

The deli was a quaint little hole-in-the-wall not far from where I'd been pulled over. It was a random weekday, around mid-morning, and yet it was filled to the gills. Cars streamed in and out of the lot, some parked sideways in the empty grassy space next to the door.

"What are they giving away?" I asked with a laugh. She pulled into a spot labeled RESERVED FOR MR. MAYOR, which was just to the right of the blue-painted disabled spots.

"Oh, look at you, fancy pants. Getting hitched to Mr. Mayor has loads of benefits."

"That it does!" She preened, flashing the giant diamond on her left finger for me to see.

"Is that a mayoral perk for everyone? When your dad was mayor, did he have a prime spot, too?" I teased, but a sense of unease still rushed through me. I was trying to keep a low profile. Having lunch with the former mayor's daughter at a busy deli in town after nearly getting arrested wasn't exactly flying under the radar.

"Maybe we should try somewhere else?" I asked nervously, seeing a crowd through the large windows. "Or just get takeout?"

"Nah, it'll be fine. They have the best sandwiches in town. We can pull up a stool at the counter if need be," she insisted, sliding out of the shiny white Jetta. "I'm actually surprised the guys aren't here."

"What guys?"

"You know, the guys. Cooper, Nick, Henry." Her eyes searched my face as if I should have known who they were. I knew Cooper was the mayor and her fiancé, but I didn't have a clue who Nick and Henry were. "They're here a couple of days a week. If not all three guys, at least one is usually planted on a stool at the counter."

"All this for a sandwich?" I asked, wringing my hands as I walked through the front door.

The counter was filled with about a dozen people crammed together on a row of tall stools. Mismatched tables filled with diners dotted the black-and-white-checkered floor. There was enough room to get through the maze of tables, but barely. Each plate was piled high with a sandwich that covered its entire surface. What space wasn't sandwich was filled with a pickle spear and chips.

"This is nuts!"

Emma nodded excitedly, scanning the room for an empty table.

A stout waitress with a smoker's rasp called out from behind the packed counter. "Emma, honey, take the booth in the corner. I'll be over in a second to clean it off."

"It's been wild here since JOE opened," Emma exclaimed, sinking onto the light blue vinyl seat. "Tourism is up almost forty percent from this time last year, and it's not even the busy season yet."

Somewhere deep in my brain, a needle scratched.

"Who's Joe, and really? Tourists? Here?"

I had vague memories of weekends away from Hope Lake. Anywhere my mother could take me to for a couple of days *just to escape*.

"Oh yeah, and it's only going to get worse, but better, if you know what I mean. Crazier and busier. Insanity! I love it!"

"And who's Joe?" I said, holding up the menu so the waitress could clean off the table.

"Oh, it's not a *who* but a *what*. It's this kick-ass outdoorsy spot out on the river: Jackson Outdoor Extreme—JOE. White-water rafting, paddle boats, canoeing, kayaking—you name it, they do it. They're even building a zip line through the mountainside that ends at the lake on the other side of town. You should check it out while you're here!"

"Sounds like a lot, but sure," I agreed, having no intention of doing so. I wasn't planning on dying here because of a zip line.

She carried on for a few minutes. "Rail biking, fishing, hiking."

My head was spinning. With her schedule being as crazy as it was lately, I only ever saw Emma's life via her Instagram, and that was an innocuous look into her, not the town. We'd kept in touch, but it had been sporadic since the engagement.

"Help me understand something," I began sincerely, shifting in my seat to lean a bit closer to her. I didn't want to attract attention to us, let alone the conversation. "What happened to this place? How did you get tourists? Big companies? And what the hell is rail biking?"

Emma furrowed her brows, looking confused. "I'm not sure I follow, but to be fair, I have wedding brain on top of a bunch of projects that I'm working on, so talk slowly and I'll do my best."

Ah, another distraction to keep the heavy topics away from me. "How's the wedding planning going?" I asked, remembering her story from last week that showed her, and her family, outside a bridal shop.

"Oh my God. Don't even ask. They're all driving me insane. At this point I want to *E-L-O-P-E*," she whispered the letters, ticking off each one on her fingers.

I smiled.

"Don't change the subject to bridezillaland," she said. "Now, what do you mean, 'What happened to this place?' The deli? Hope Lake? Pennsylvania? The States? I can wax poetic about each one of them, so buckle up. Oh, and why are you here again?"

I chuckled, not doubting for a second that she could go on forever. Emma was always a force to be reckoned with. I took a sip of the water that the waitress left after she cleaned off the table and thought about how to broach the subject.

"I'll preface this by saying that I'm tired, hungry, probably smelly, and mentally exhausted, so don't expect any sort of rational thoughts here. But, to sum it up, I just got fired from my job and blacklisted in my field in basically the whole of New York City."

"Oh my God, that sounds awful. Do you want to talk about it?" she asked, sympathy and empathy oozing out of her.

"We'll come back to that, over beer preferably."

"I know the perfect place! We'll go as soon as you've recovered. Now, stop stalling! What do you want to know about Hope Lake?"

I exhaled, feeling some of the weariness seep from my body. "I mean, I obviously haven't been here in a while, but I always thought it was *different*." I wasn't sure exactly what I wanted to say *I thought it was a hellhole? A depressing one-horse town? Somewhere to avoid at all costs?*

"I just grew up thinking it wasn't somewhere I ever wanted to come back to. So what happened to it? Mind you, I hardly remember a thing from when I lived here as a kid. It's like I blacked it all out."

Emma's mouth flattened into a thin line, a crease forming on her forehead. "There's a lot to unfold in that ramble, but for starters, why did you never want to come back here? I just always thought your mom wouldn't let you."

I took a deep breath. My brain was growing wearier by the second, and I couldn't come up with something nicer to say. "It started out that way when I just left, but as I got older my mother always made living in this town out to be her greatest regret. So as the memories faded for me, I just started believing her."

I held up my hand when she drew in a deep, scathing breath. "I know, I know. Trust me, it wasn't great hearing that she hated everything about this place—which included my dad, grandmother, and essentially me, since I was a product of her time in Hope Lake. I think she hated it so much that that was why she never let me visit. In hindsight, that's pretty shitty to do to your kid. But I'm sure you know, she wasn't exactly a Mother of the Year candidate. I feel like it says something that I waited to return until years after she died."

Emma reached out over the table to take my hand. "When you first left, I used to hear our dads talk about it sometimes. It was always vague, since I was only a kid, but it still made me feel so badly for you." She squeezed my hand.

"She wasn't always . . . I mean, the problems with depression and anxiety sort of came and went," I said, taking another sip of my water. Then the tears welled up. "They flared up whenever my dad would try to get custody of me. He knew what was going on but couldn't prove it. She hated taking the meds the doctors gave her to try to manage the symptoms. She said they made her feel awful. But I don't think she realized how bad it was when she was off them. Whenever he brought her to court, she would take the meds and be hands-on, and present. When it was over, and the family court denied him custody, she'd toss the prescription and I'd lose her again."

Emma sighed. "I never understood why the judge kept siding with her. My mom tried explaining it to me, but I don't know that she knew the whole story with the meds and the visits. Your dad kept a lot of that to himself."

"Once, a few months after I left, I tried getting her to let me visit but my dad was in Mozambique. She wouldn't let me stay with anyone but him. Somehow it was part of the custody agreement. Even Gigi was excluded."

"Which sucked," we said in unison.

"I think she knew that's what the judge was looking at. All his travel kept him from gaining any sort of meaningful custody."

"Not to sound cold, but why didn't your dad just not go?" she asked, and it was a question that I struggled with for ages.

"He tried to explain the circumstances, but the trip to Africa was planned for a year. He was part of a research team and was going to be gone for six months. He tried finding someone to go in his stead, but it was too little notice for anyone in his field of study.

"It still hurt and I know he was crushed by it, but it really solidified the judge's decision to keep things as is.

"By the time I was old enough to realize how important his mission work was to him, I couldn't ask him to give it up to bring me here. Besides, by that time I was so hell-bent against this place, it was a nonissue. There weren't many people who knew about the struggles I had with my mother or what led us to uproot ourselves from this place, so that was isolating. Coming here just felt like it would exacerbate that feeling. I had enough going on; I didn't need more to deal with."

I smiled ruefully to myself. How long did I wait to tell someone all of this? First day here and I dump a quarter of my life on someone I hadn't seen in ages. Looking up at her, I saw her eyes swimming with tears.

"Maybe we should look at the menu," she suggested, and I was grateful for the reprieve. "We've got all summer to talk about it. About everything we missed out on."

Opening the menu up, I had to bite back a moan as I examined the choices. It was just as she said—a sandwich lover's dream. Perfect for a carb-loving gal like me. "What do you suggest? If you don't tell me what's the best, I'm going to order the whole menu, and I can't afford that."

She slapped her menu down. "First of all, it's your first day back, so lunch is on me. Second, get the Classic. It's the best thing you'll ever put into your mouth, I'm not exaggerating. Don't tell Cooper." She added the last bit with a quick laugh.

I crossed my heart. Reading the description, I frowned. "Seems pretty simple compared to the rest." Fresh mozzarella, fresh spinach, sliced tomatoes, and a basil pesto mayo on a soft bun. "It's just that, compared to the city—"

"I'm going to stop you right there," she said, a bit snippy.

"Sorry, sorry. I'm just so used to, never mind. I'm keeping an open mind."

"About the sandwiches, or Hope Lake?" she asked, waving the circling waitress over.

"Sandwiches for now. The latter is going to need some convincing."

"Challenge accepted," she said happily.

"Oh boy."

"YOU WERE RIGHT. That was the best thing I've had in my mouth in ages," I said, slapping my hand over my mouth when an older woman walked by and laughed.

"I told you. Don't ever doubt me. I am all wise and ever powerful."

I rolled my eyes. "Okay, Oz."

I dug my phone out of my purse. "Oh, my dad texted saying that Dr. Max is driving him to get his car and then is going to help him deliver my stuff to Gigi's."

She smiled. "I can help you unload later, if you want. Or I can just nonchalantly be there when Max shows up."

"Oh no, not you, too?"

"Me too, what?" she asked innocently.

"You're a part of the Dr. Max fan club," I accused, throwing a sugar packet at her.

She tossed it back, laughing. "I don't know what you're talking about. I plead the Fifth!"

My eyebrow raised silently in questions. "Do tell, nearly married lady."

"Please. Cooper knows I love him dearly, but Max is really unfairly attractive. Sometimes, I catch myself just staring at him," she said with a dreamy sigh. "And before you say anything, Cooper does the same thing. The first time he met him he said, and I quote, 'He's absurdly handsome, right? It's not just me?'"

"You're not wrong," I said, lowering my voice. "And he seems possibly interested. But he also seems like he's got the interest of every woman in town."

"You're not wrong," she repeated my words back, smiling broad and bright. "You said yes, right? I'll live vicariously through you."

"He didn't actually ask me anything."

"If and when he does, just say yes."

I smiled. "I've got enough on my plate right now. Dating while I'm here seems like it should be the very last thing on my to-do list."

Emma laughed. "Dr. Max should be at the very top of your to-do list."

"This conversation has gotten way off track," I said.

"Not surprising, I have a way of derailing conversations. It's a gift." She gave me a cursory glance. I could tell she was cooking something up in that head of hers. "I'm canceling everything I have for tomorrow."

"Okay . . . ?"

"What do you have planned?"

"Let me check my calendar." I pretended to open and close a calendar. "Nothing. I was just going to hang with Gigi."

She clapped her hands happily.

"Excellent. I'll drop you at Gigi's now. Get some rest, because tomorrow I'm going to give you the insider's nickel tour of Hope Lake. We'll see the old stomping grounds, all your old friends, and if by the end you're not hopelessly in love with this place, I'll drive you back to New York City myself."

This was too good to be true.

"Deal."

4

"When was the last time you saw her?" Emma asked as we pulled into the long, winding gravel driveway up to Gigi's house.

The words caught in my throat. "Almost two years ago. Once she needed the wheelchair full-time, it was too hard to bring her to visit me in the city."

Emma frowned. "Why didn't you, you know, just come here? I get why you didn't as a kid, but as an adult—"

"Another million-dollar question, Peroni," I said, trying to bring in some levity. "My mom never liked my career choice. Dare I say, she hated it. After she died, things were hard for months. I couldn't focus on work, but I had to, because, hello, expensive-as-hell city to pay for." I paused.

"Surely your dad would have . . ."

I nodded vigorously. "He offered for ages. Flights to visit him on his trips, cars to pick me up, bus tickets. But my pride got wounded every time I had to ask him for something."

She touched my hand. "What do you mean?"

"I was a wreck after my mom died. Literally a wreck. Hell, even before she passed, I wasn't exactly in the best frame of mind. Afterward, I didn't have time to take off from work because it wouldn't have been paid. I'd go to work, be in a fog all day, and come home. My best friend, Parker, tried helping, but it wasn't working. She reached my dad through the organization he volunteers with, and they got through to him. He cut his work in Malawi short because I needed help with the funeral arrangements and taking care of all the legal stuff. Her family—well, that's another story—but they weren't any help. I had to lean on him so much. I carried a lot of guilt from that. My mom was so imperfect, but she was still my mom, and he swallowed all his anger toward her to make sure that she had a nice service."

Emma's eyes were watery, much like mine.

"We don't have to do this now, Charlotte," she suggested.

"It's okay. It's like therapy, except you're a lot cheaper."

"This is very true."

Rolling my shoulders back, I looked up at Gigi's big house. "I tried, desperately at times, to prove that I could make it without any support. You don't think of event planning or floral design as particularly cutthroat professions, but let me tell you, they are."

"It's that tough?" she interjected, slack-jawed at my revelation.

I shook my head. "If Bravo wanted to, they could have a successful spin-off for *Real Housewives* by focusing on all the small businesses they use and underpay, and the staff that works to the bone to make their parties television-worthy."

"That sounds awful, and also something that I'd hate-binge."

I laughed ruefully. "If you don't know the behind-the-scenes, it *is* entertaining. But so many people don't see the other side of things. I guess they don't want to. The shows focus on the lives of the rich and gorgeous, and the incredible designers and caterers who create the lavish parties are ignored."

"You're right, I never even thought about that." Emma looked stricken at the realization. "So work was keeping you there?"

"It's part of the reason. It's not an excuse by any means, but my dad understood how important it was for me to prove myself. I was working sixty hours a week or more, and the pay was hysterically bad. I was doing everything I could to get somewhere within the company I worked for, and then— Poof. One incident that wasn't even my doing gets me fired, blacklisted, and crawling back here trying to figure out what step two is."

Emma folded her hands on her lap. "Whatever happened, it's in the past. You're here now, and we're going to make the most of it!"

"Thanks, Emma. I sure have missed you."

"I've missed you more. Now, cheer up and don't focus on anything other than how happy Gigi's going to be to see you. And that you'll be staying here with her!"

We sat silently for a few minutes, staring up at her sprawling white Victorian. It was an absurdly large house for an elderly person who was basically confined to the first floor. But I loved it, and I knew Gigi did, too. My father had begged her to consider moving to an assisted-living facility, but she patently refused, citing her staunch independence. It was for that reason that she wouldn't let him move in.

While Gigi had agreed to let me stay at her house, I didn't know what type of reception I was going to get from her. I had to just rip off the Band-Aid.

"Okay, I'm heading in," I said, taking a deep breath.

"She'll be happy, Charlotte. I promise," Emma reassured me. "I'll call you in the morning."

I waited in the drive until she pulled away, tooting her horn as she waved.

Climbing up the house's wide, weathered stairs, I smiled at the overflowing flower boxes hanging from the slightly chipped white banisters. On both sides of the stairs, two enormous barrel planters were filled to the brim with vibrant lipstick-pink zinnias, pale yellow petunias, and bright green ivy. Bright blue lobelia blooms poured out of hanging baskets that were placed evenly around the wraparound porch. It wasn't even June yet and her yard and floral decor were enviable.

It made me wonder who in town was responsible for all the work. *And did they want to hire me?*

"Of course, it's not locked," I muttered, knowing some things never change. I turned the ornate brass doorknob.

"Gigi, I'm here!" I shouted from the doorway before pushing the doorbell a few times.

I heard the telltale sounds of her motorized chair coming from what I remembered being the kitchen. Sure enough, Gigi zipped through the swinging door on her trusty, ruby-red mechanical steed.

"There's my girl. Your father told me you were coming," she said, checking her Apple Watch. *What was a ninety-year-old doing with an Apple Watch?*

"Although, that was a while ago. Anything to confess, young lady?"

"Give me a hug first and I'll share all my secrets." Dropping to my knees, I took her hand and kissed her delicate cheek.

When I pulled away, a tear slipped out, but I brushed it away before she could see it.

"Let me look at you," she said, holding my arms out at my sides. "You're tired. Why?"

I frowned but schooled my features before she noticed. "I'm okay, Gigi. Long night of travel. Long day of nonsense."

She pulled me down to her, and I sat on the floor beside her chair. She smoothed her hand down my cheek. I leaned into it and smiled.

"How I've missed you," I said.

"You're here now, that's what counts."

I smiled, remembering how much I missed her sweet face and gentle touch. "Did Dad let you in on the news?" I asked, looking up at her kind eyes.

"That you got arrested, yes."

Welp, so much for that moment.

"No, not that, and it wasn't arrested, Gigi. My God, you're a nudge."

She laughed. "You love me."

I nodded. It was true. "Did he tell you anything else?"

"That you're going out with Dr. Reese?"

"What?" Between getting detained and seeing Gigi, I had forgotten all about it. "It's nothing, just a walk. Dr. Max told him?"

"Apparently so. Then your father told me. By the way, I heard dinner was involved, too." She waggled her eyebrows.

"This day has been the worst," I lamented.

Gigi patted me on the head like I was her favorite pooch. "Oh, don't forget that you knocked poor Henry to the ground. Yes, he mentioned that, too. Poor Henry, right in the balls, huh?"

"Gigi! You don't say balls!"

"I don't? I'll have to remember that. Nads? Nuggets? Meatballs? What's the term these days. I'm not in the know."

"This isn't happening."

"Oh, but it is. You nailing poor Henry in the testicles was the highlight of the morning. I think they lit a candle for him at the daily mass."

"God, the whole town must know."

"You're not wrong, unfortunately. Gossip burns through this place like a wildfire through dry brush."

"That's concerning. Dad didn't tell you anything else about me?"

Gigi smiled, her gray eyes twinkling. "My darling, he always talks about you, so you'll need to be more specific. But first, what good news do you bring for me?" She pulled me closer, forcing me to look in her eyes.

"You've got a new roommate!" I feigned excitement.

"Oh, he did mention that. I couldn't be happier. I need someone to dust the ceiling fans for me." She squeezed her thin fingers through mine. "Oh, and how are you with laundry?"

"You're a regular comedian, Gigi."

She beamed, though her eyes were a bit watery. "I try."

Holding hands on her front porch, we sat silently watching a hummingbird land on a bright red feeder. Suddenly, with the wind blowing through the front door, Gigi's demeanor shifted. With her eyes glued to the fluttering bird, she whispered, "This is your house, Charlotte. You stay, you leave; you're welcome here as long as you need to be. Get your feet back underneath you."

Embarrassment bubbled up in my stomach. I didn't want to admit all my failures. Disappointing my father was hard. Disappointing Gigi, who only ever championed me and my frivolous dreams, was devastating.

"Gigi, I—" I began, but she held her hand up to stop me.

"Not now. We've got time. All summer to mend fences."

I smiled, giving her another kiss on the cheek. Summer. I could handle that length of time. A finite amount of time.

She always understood me. "You're the best."

"You say that now. I'm being literal. You'll have to mend the fence out back. The deer keep coming in and eating all my apples."

I laughed. "Never change, Gigi."

She patted my hand. "Okay, enough of the sappiness. I'm too old for all this sentimentality. My heart can give out at any moment, and I'm not going out like this." She paused, waggling her eyebrows. "Anything interesting to report? I have to live vicariously through all you young people."

"'All you young people'? What does that mean? Male suitors?"

She smiled, her eyes twinkling. "Some. I'm irresistible, what can I say. It works for the old guys with money, why not me? Now tell me, what sort of excitement rained down on the town upon your arrival? Suzanne hasn't stopped talking about it, but she embellishes. I want to hear your side."

"Suzanne? Suzanne. Why do I know that name?" I asked, scratching my chin.

"My neighbor, Suzanne Mancini. You remember her, right? Loud, great cook, busybody, and my best friend." I vaguely remembered her name, but I couldn't place her. Confusion must've been evident on my face.

"You must remember Mrs. Mancini!" Gigi insisted, inching her chair up to the still-open doorway.

I shrugged. "The name rings a bell, but I'm drawing a blank."

She sighed and continued to rattle off relatively ridiculous descriptors. "A couple sandwiches short of a picnic, often inappropriate, runs the senior social circuit around Hope Lake. She taught you how to play gin rummy."

A memory surged up like a wave.

A flash of an oval table in a bright yellow kitchen with pennies and playing cards splayed across the table. Gigi sitting at the counter teaching two other kids how to play chess, boys about my age. The house smelled like fresh-baked cookies, and a burst of happiness exploded in my chest.

"Lots of curly hair, sort of stout and sturdy, with long pink nails, and a laugh that made you giggle right along with her."

"Yes! That's her. I'm so glad you remember!"

"Not really, she's just walking across the yard right now."

"Suzanne. I thought we said tomorrow?" Gigi called, but the woman ignored her.

"Look at you," she said, wheezing a bit as she slowly climbed the stairs. She was decked out in a lime-green tracksuit with white stripes down the legs and rocking an old-school pair of Stan Smith Adidas. I balked at how fashionable this woman was when I looked like I hadn't combed my hair in days.

"I'm so happy to see you again. I heard you were here and baked cookies for you! Just like I used to do when you were little," she explained. I looked down at her empty hands, confused.

"Oh, I ate them. And then my dog, Whiskey, well, he got the rest. I'll make more tomorrow. I just wanted to say hello and welcome you back to Hope Lake. It's wonderful to have you home."

I couldn't get a word in edgewise. Thankfully she turned to Gigi. "We have our meeting tomorrow. I'll see you guys then."

Mrs. Mancini pulled me into a crippling hug before descending the stairs with care. "That was . . ."

"She's a lot to take in. I'm ticked about the cookies, though."

"What meeting do you have tomorrow?" I asked, watching Mrs. Mancini's dog, a Saint Bernard, greet her at her side door. He was wagging his tail, his large body shaking with delight.

"Senior citizens meet twice a month to discuss old-people things. She's hosting tomorrow, so I'll need some help over the gravel," she explained, as if it was just a normal day out and about.

I supposed that it was. She could zip herself down the road if she wanted to. No one said she had to be stuck in this big old house all day. Maybe people picked her up in a fancy van, or something. There was so much that I didn't know.

The guilt continued to bubble, reminding me that I had missed out on a lot of time with her. I was going to apologize again, when she zipped her chair closer to me.

"So you really got arrested?" Gigi asked in a maniacal whisper, rubbing her hands together expectantly. "Was it because of Henry? Or did you assault another poor handsome man in the short time that you've been here?"

"You're ridiculous. It was a misunderstanding regarding the lack of a license . . . and some other things," I added quickly.

"If you're already riling up the town, this summer is going to be fun!"

I sighed. "I've made quite the name for myself with the policemen in town. I wasn't arrested. I mean, there were no cuffs. I promised to stay out of trouble."

"Too bad. Cuffs could have been fun. *Trouble* is fun."

"Gigi!" I said, feeling my cheeks burning.

"What?" she said, shrugging. "Prude."

With a practiced flair, she pushed the steering stick on her wheelchair and hit the gas. She made a perfect circle turn and headed back toward the kitchen.

"I hope you ate already, because I burned lunch!" Gigi wasn't much of a cook, something I assume I inherited from her. Luckily for her, my grandpa Stanley did all the cooking. At least until he passed away nearly twenty-five years ago. After that, my father took over either cooking and bringing it over, much to my mother's annoyance, or they grabbed takeout together.

"I can make you something. I ate with Emma," I called from behind her. She left me in her dust.

"I was just teasing. No need to put yourself out, cookie. I ordered Chinese. It should be here soon. Besides, you cook as bad as I do."

I shrugged and followed her into the kitchen. "You're not wrong."

*

AFTER CLEANING UP her lunch, Gigi said it was time for her programs.
I assumed that meant daytime television talk shows or soap operas.
I couldn't have been more wrong. Gigi was addicted to the *Queer
Eye* reboot and Netflix crime dramas.

And if it wasn't murder shows, it was murder books.

"This one is good. It's based off of a podcast that NPR did. Fas-
cinating stuff. This is about Jack the Ripper. Oh, and this is about
the Golden State Killer," she prattled on, handing me each book and
insisting I read them. From the top of a stack on her nightstand, she
took her newest favorite.

"*This* is your bedtime reading?" I asked, holding up a book about
Belle Gunness, who was apparently a rare female psychopath. "How
do you sleep at night?"

"Like a log. I'm ninety. Not much keeps me awake."

"Yeah, but you live alone. In a massive old house with one elderly
neighbor for company, Gigi," I said, laughing when she rolled her eyes.

"Charlotte, you realize that Pop Pop was a mystery writer, right?
He wrote all sorts of crazy stuff—especially for his time. These are
no different."

"I beg to differ, ma'am. Mysteries about stolen French paintings
and jewelry heists are one thing. This one faked her own death!"

Gigi snickered. "I'm glad you've read Pop Pop's books. Admittedly,
I haven't read any in ages. I should start again when I'm done with
this one." She held up a book about Sally Horner, aka the real Lolita.

"I'm going to check on you at night."

"Oh, petal. You're adorable when you're nervous. Grab that one
and take it upstairs with you."

I followed her finger, which was pointing to the stack of books,
and plucked the next one from the pile.

"You can come to the bookstore on Sunday with me to discuss it
with my book club. If you finish it, of course. It'll give you a chance
to apologize for ruining Henry's likelihood of having children."

"Henry runs the bookstore?" I asked.

She shook her head.

"He doesn't run it but helps out a lot when they need it. Especially in the summer, when he's not teaching."

I looked at the book in my hands. "Lizzie Borden? This is your book-club pick?"

She nodded. "I'm in four book clubs. We meet once a week, a different day each week. True crime is the most popular one, though. The young-adult group is probably second busiest, and no, I'm not the oldest person in it. Most of the people are interested in the books, but with tourist season approaching, a lot come to listen to Henry."

"Why? I can't imagine spending my summer vacay at book club."

"Come to one and you'll see why. They listen but mostly look." She winked before bringing her hand up to her mouth to cover her yawn.

"You're a marvel, Gigi."

I helped her from her chair to her recliner, a fancy leather number that pushed her up to an almost standing position to make it easier for her to get herself back into the chair. We were in what once was her massive living room but now was serving as her bedroom.

"When did you move in here?" I asked, looking around. It was cozy. She had a small basket in the corner with skeins of yarn piled high inside it. A half-finished blanket lay on the small wooden table next to it. The room was a pale gray, but it didn't feel cold or clinical. It was inviting and comfy.

"Eighteen months ago," she said sourly. "Your father insisted that I needed to either be in a home or on the first floor. He didn't trust me going up and down the stairs, even with one of those goofy electric climber things. Not that I would allow any of that to ruin my woodwork," she scoffed.

"Why didn't you just let him move in with you?" I asked, picking up the crocheted blanket to examine her perfect loops.

"Your father is still in his prime. I did not need him giving up his life for me. Besides, I'm fine." She sighed, picking up a frame of her and my grandfather. "This house has everything I need. A nice bathroom with an old-person tub. Books, the television, my MacBook, and my knitting. It's like my own studio in a big house."

"You sound more like a hipster than a grandma," I teased, brushing some of her icy-white hair from her forehead.

"I'm not a fan of the almond milk, so they took my hipster badge away," she said quickly. I was glad that her wit and wits were still sharp as a tack.

She looked so tiny, so frail, it made my heart break a little more at all that I'd missed. Her hair was whiter than I'd ever seen it. She looked healthy . . . but tired. I could see why my father worried.

"Can I ask you something?" I sat on the edge of her bed.

She nodded, leaning her head in her hand. "The house looks like you've been doing a lot of remodeling. This room aside, the kitchen has a fresh coat of paint, and your stove is brand-new." While I hadn't traveled around the whole house, I wagered that I would find similar updates in every room.

"I'm ninety, you keep forgetting. Truth is, honey, the more I get done now, the less your dad, or I suppose you, have to worry about when I finally join Stanley. That's what all the visitors are for. The boys help me with projects when they can. They make sure that I'm not being taken advantage of from contractors or the real estate agents who sniff around. This place, and Suzanne's, are on the historical registry, so they've always drawn interest. I've had offers, but, well, it's not time yet. I feel like I have something holding me here. At least for a little while longer."

Another quiet yawn escaped, though she tried covering it up with a laugh. "Look at me being all morose when you've finally come home. There's food in the fridge if you're hungry."

My lower lip quivered, but with her eyes fighting sleep, I didn't think she noticed. "Gigi, I'm going to go unpack," I started, swallowing the lump in my throat. Maybe getting fired and having zero options except to come back here was exactly what was supposed to happen, so I had time with her.

"You'll be good with Netflix?" I asked, watching her eyes droop.

"I'm happy you're home," she said as she drifted off. I didn't have the heart to correct her, to tell her that my home was in New York, not Hope Lake.

TEARS SPILLED OVER as I climbed the wide oak stairs. My hand slid up the polished banister to steady myself as I fell apart. It wasn't just what Gigi had said, or how easily she embraced me back into her life and home. It was just being with someone who loved you no matter what. The truth of how much I'd missed that feeling was squeezing my heart in a vise. And the house—the presence it held and the significance I felt standing inside it again after so long—only made the feeling stronger.

The memories flew by like a film as I climbed higher up the stairs. Breaking my arm when I decided to slide down the stairs to see if I could make it out the front door without crashing—I couldn't. Playing hide-and-seek with foggy figures whom I couldn't place. Gigi getting a rent-a-pony for my sixth birthday and my getting lost with it in the woods behind her house because we busted through the fence. The fence that she'd still never fixed.

The last real memory I had of Hope Lake was the worst one, barreling at me like a freight train. My begging Gigi to keep me with her instead of letting my mother take me away to New York. Screaming as my mother dragged me from Gigi's house. My mother backing out of the driveway with me practically clawing at the back window to get out. I cried watching a crumpled Gigi on the front porch, my father sitting on the steps with his head in his hands, defeated. I, too, felt defeated now. And angry at my mother all over again for pulling me away from them. And frustrated with myself for allowing myself to stay away.

I paused halfway up the stairs; my eyes traveled up the richly decorated wall. It was a personal museum highlighting everything Gigi loved. Not surprising, it made me feel a bit better. Seeing her with her family and friends, and shots of this town over the years. A place that she and my father loved so much. Dotted among everything were more than a dozen photos of me at every age. I touched the frame that held one of me, Gigi, and my dad at my Temple graduation. I had a similar one with Emma and her parents from her graduation at UPenn.

A less familiar photo that I needed to ask Gigi about was a close-up of me as a little girl with a slight boy about my age, maybe younger, judging by his size. A thick head of dark brown hair, a smattering of freckles on his nose, and incredible blue eyes framed with long black lashes. We had our arms around each other and two beaming toothless smiles. I plucked the frame off the wall and carried it down the hall, into the bedroom where I'd be staying while I was here.

True to his word, my father and Dr. Max had brought all my boxes to Gigi's house before I arrived.

The top box had a note taped to it.

Gigi insisted you have the master.

Love, Dad

I opened the dresser drawers, which were completely empty of Gigi's belongings. Unpacking was quick, because I didn't have all that much here—just some clothes, shoes, and a box of toiletries. In no time flat I was done, but I was bone-tired and ragged and wishing I took that nap.

Another note was propped on the small nightstand, folded like a card.

I look forward to seeing you again soon.

"Huh," I said, holding the card. I knew it wasn't my father's handwriting, so the only person it could be was Dr. Max. Odd he didn't sign the note, but I guess he figured I'd know it was him. It was a sweet gesture, one that I'd be thinking about later, when my brain wasn't so full of mush.

I placed the card from Max and the framed photo of me and the young boy on the nightstand next to my bed.

It took everything left in me to muster up the strength to step into the shower and head back downstairs for dinner. After I checked on Gigi, who was fast asleep, I popped into the kitchen to see that she'd left me a plate. On top of the foil was an explanatory Post-it in her doctor scrawl.

It's safe to eat.
Suzanne made it and brought it over.
I'll see you in the morning.
Take your time and get used to the house again.

XOXO, G

Underneath the foil was a too-large piece of lasagna and a slice of garlic toast. I popped it in the microwave, and my mouth watered while it spun. The lasagna was delicious, and I hadn't realized how hungry I was until I looked down and it was gone.

Once I was done, I was tired again. By the time I made it back upstairs, I felt like my limbs were Jell-O.

The bed called to me with its pile of cushy cream-colored pillows that leaned against the antique iron headboard. I reasoned with myself and sighed as I sank onto the lush bed.

"I'll just rest my eyes for five minutes." *Said no one ever.*

5

"The basement is flooding."

"The house is on fire."

I swam up from sleep to the strangest conversation. Maybe I was still dreaming, but why would Keanu Reeves be telling me the house is on fire instead of John Wick–ing us the hell out of there?

"The police are here . . ."

I sprang up, clutching the sheet to my chest.

"I didn't do anything!"

I looked around nervously but only saw Emma, looking perfect and put together with linen capris and a robin's-egg-blue cardigan. She was sitting on the edge of my bed giggling at me.

"It's about time," she said, poking my arm with her well-manicured fingernail.

I groaned, flopping back onto the sea of pillows. "It can't be morning. I only took a nap." Rolling over, I fluffed up one of the pillows under my head, hoping to fall back to sleep, but by the way the sunlight was streaming through the three windows, it looked like morning. I realized that I must have crashed hard last night.

She laughed. "You're right, sunshine. It's not morning. It's almost one in the afternoon."

My eyes flew open, landing on the antique silver alarm clock on the nightstand. "Holy shit!"

"I'll say." Emma patted my head the way someone would a toddler's and stood, the bed springing back. "Gigi was worried, since you'd been asleep for so long and hadn't eaten. She wasn't sure what time you went to bed last night."

I sat up, my head swimming from still being half asleep but also from being scared awake. "I'll be honest, I have no idea what time it was. I remember eating and thinking I'd take a nap and that's it. Poor Gigi, she must have been so worried. I suck."

"She *was* worried, but it's not like she's mad. Relax. You were exhausted and clearly needed the rest. That being said, get up and do something with that," she said, motioning to my hair. "We've got plans."

Sliding from bed, I glanced in the mirror and groaned at my appearance. "I fell asleep with it wet, so it dried like this."

"Oh, please, you look great."

"Lies! Unless you have time for me to take another shower, you're getting ball cap Charlotte today."

"I'll take whatever Charlotte I can get!"

I disappeared into the bathroom and came out with my toothbrush in my mouth. "What's the plan?" I mumbled, smiling when I found Emma walking around the hall, peeking at all the photos. "I have to check to make sure Gigi will be good without me here for a bit."

Emma leveled me with a look. "Honey, she's been living alone for decades. I think an afternoon without you is okay. Besides, I saw Mrs. Mancini walking her dog when I was coming in and she said she'll be over around two for their weekly chess match before the senior meeting."

That made me feel marginally better. "I'm glad she'll have company. I am fighting with some guilt and I don't know how to squash that."

Emma nodded. "I get it. You've got this chance now to get some of the lost time back. Instead of focusing on the guilt, focus on moving forward, what you're going to do while you're here. There are plenty of people who want to catch up with you now that you're back."

I laughed. "We can check off the Hope Lake PD from that. They'll be happy to see me leave, I think."

Popping back into the bathroom, I washed my face and moisturized. When I came out, she was picking up candlesticks from the fireplace and trying to pull sconces off the wall.

"Uh, Emma? What are you doing?"

She smiled, looking guilty. "Looking for hidden secrets. Do you remember as kids trying to find this house's secret passageways?"

My mouth hung open. "Wait, are you being serious? I don't remember that."

And I practically lived here as a kid.

"Memories are interesting. I think you'll remember soon. Maybe you'll even remember where the secret passageways are!"

I laughed, watching her lift and poke her way around the room. "We can just ask Gigi about the supposed hidden passageways."

Emma raised her eyebrows. "That's just it. *I have.* I know others have, too."

"And?" *I can't believe I don't remember this.*

"She always says it's fiction, that the hidden passageways were something that your grandfather made up in one of his novels. But imagine if it's true? He based so many of his books on Hope Lake and this house. It's like the Goonies or Indiana Jones. Treasure or secrets. They might know who shot JFK or what's in Area 51!"

I threw my head back and laughed. "You're insane. If there are hidden passageways or answers to the great mysteries of the world, we would have found them already."

"You say that now. I know Nick and Henry have looked for years. They haven't found a thing," Emma said before reaching up to try the shelf in the walk-in closet.

Henry. The guy I almost maimed yesterday in front of my father's house. *Why does my brain trip on that name?* I shook off the feeling.

"Okay, Sherlock. Keep searching if you want, but I've got to get dressed." I dug through a drawer, trying to find something to stroll through town in. "Stay in there unless you want a free show."

I changed into a pair of old jean shorts and a Temple T-shirt that had seen better days while she searched behind my clothes and knocked on the walls. "There's a square in the ceiling," she called out. Using an empty hanger, she stabbed at the small block. "This doesn't count as a passageway. It's in plain sight," she explained, stepping down from the ladder.

Joining her in the closet, I looked up. "Where did you find the ladder?"

"Behind the door. It was convenient to have it there to aid in my snooping."

"You're nuts. I think it's the attic. Before they put in those pull-down ladders that hide in the ceiling, they used these old ones that you leaned against the cutout and hoped you didn't fall off. I saw it on HGTV."

"Well, aren't you a fountain of useless knowledge."

"I've been on my couch for almost a month, lamenting life and trying to figure out what the hell to do with my future. HGTV filled a lot of time."

Emma smiled sadly, taking my hand. "What happened anyway? I don't want to push, so if you don't want to talk about it, that's okay."

Do I want to talk about it? Not really, but I would have to eventually.

I nodded, slipping a Giants cap on my head and pulling a chunk of curly red hair out the back. "Yes. But first, coffee."

AFTER COFFEE IN the kitchen with a very cheery Gigi, we headed out in Emma's car with a promise to bring her back scones from the grocery store, wine from the liquor store, and her special order from the bookstore.

"You know, she's really quite with it for her age," Emma remarked, pulling out of the driveway as Gigi sat on the porch in her chariot.

"Don't do anything I wouldn't do!" she howled, waving at us.

"What exactly would that be?" Emma shouted back.

"It's a short list, trust me!"

"Gigi!" I mock scolded.

"If you get into trouble, record it! I have an AMEX, so don't worry about bail!"

She sang the last bit before zipping herself back into the front door.

"She's a trip, that's for sure. I'll be honest, I don't know how I'm going to keep up with her," I admitted, trying to put into words what I was feeling. "I kept thinking she was going to be this helpless creature because of the motorized chair, but she's not. She's a maniac in the best possible way. Seeing her so chipper has helped me realize that this is a great opportunity. It's like you said, the guilt is there, but I have a chance to fix it."

"You know," Emma began, her voice barely above a whisper. Which was hilarious, as we were the only two in the car. "She really helped us with Cooper's campaign. She and Mancini were invaluable. They busted their asses working at the poll stations for him. That may not seem like a lot, but it is."

I was astonished. "I had no idea."

Emma nodded. She pulled out onto the main stretch of road that led back into town. "The two of them were always helping my dad out when he was running, so we weren't sure if they'd be able to for Cooper, since they're a lot older now. I couldn't have been more wrong. Gigi played hostess for a couple of meetings and organized a postcard campaign to maximize our efforts. She even helped register voters at the high school. The kids loved that because she was their doctor growing up. I think it made her day to have so many remember her as a positive influence on their lives."

I smiled, glancing outside at the town passing by. "I don't know anyone who doesn't love her."

As the town rolled by, I thought about Gigi's face when I got to the house. There wasn't a shred of sadness there. She radiated happiness. But why did I feel so lousy all of a sudden?

"Why so glum, chum?" Emma asked, perhaps sensing the shift.

I shook my head slowly. "I can't believe how much I don't know about her or, hell, even my dad. Their lives here are so full, and I've never asked. It's like the subject was off-limits and we only stuck to happy things like reality television and our favorite sports teams."

Emma patted my hand. "You said it yourself: you've been busy. They understand that you were trying to advance your career in the city. Working that much couldn't have been easy."

"It wasn't, but it's not like I was that busy that I couldn't have visited at least once in the past couple of years. I'm surprised they've been so welcoming after how shitty I've been."

The gnarly twist took hold again in my stomach when I glanced at Emma's expression. She knew I was right. And shitty.

"I know that I'm their daughter and granddaughter, but if it were me, I'd be mad if my kid didn't have the decency to visit."

"Really? After knowing everything that went on between you and your mom, you'd risk alienating your kid? While I won't discount your feelings, I think you're being hard on yourself. You staying away from here was what you thought was right. Maybe you weren't supposed to come back until now."

I nodded. "Fate, man. I believe in it."

"Now," she said, lowering her voice to a stern, mom-like tone. "I do think you do need to have a come-to-Jesus with Gigi and your dad about some of the guilt you've been feeling. No use keeping it bottled up if you're going to be here a while."

Emma lowered her window, letting in a sweet-smelling breeze as we passed the apiary.

"Keep in mind, I'm here if and when you need me. To vent, commiserate, swoon, whatever. Don't forget that."

I smiled, looking down at the remarkably clean floor in her car. "I won't forget. Wait, swoon?"

"Hey, who knows," she said with a laugh. "Keep your eyes open, you never know what this place will present as an option to you. Ahem, Dr. Max."

"You act as if this place is magic, and my God, you're as subtle as a peacock."

With a wink, she continued. "We're doing a bit of a scenic tour. Nothing too boring. I won't inundate you with historical facts and figures. I'll instead stick to the hot spots," she explained, beeping and waving to almost every person we saw outside on the quick ride into town. "Unless you want the facts and historical mumbo jumbo, because I will totally deliver."

I laughed. "Maybe another time. Let's ease into the riveting fun facts of Hope Lake."

Emma turned, wide-eyed. "Oh, hell, that's a great idea!"

"What is?"

She looked at me as if to say *Duh*. "Fun Facts of Hope Lake! I can have little signs made up and put by different landmarks. The river, the lake, the brewing company—which we're stopping by soon."

My mouth fell open. "There's a brewing company here?"

Emma furrowed her brows but kept her eyes on the road. "I should rethink the crash course in Hope Lake history. HLBC— I'm sure you can guess that it stands for Hope Lake Brewing Company—was started a couple of years ago, but in the past two years it's really taken off. The owners, Drew and Luke Griffin, got some help from the Community Developmental Office—where I work—and opened this amazing place down by the lake. It's right on the water, it's got indoor and outdoor seating, firepits on the lake's edge. Fun get-togethers every weekend, and theme nights starting in June. Lots of great, unique beer flavors, and it's all made in-house. Brought in a bunch of jobs, too. It's a big hit with the tourists."

I continued to gape. "Wow, kudos to you and your department. So this is in the past couple of years? That's awesome. By the way, you should totally be doing their advertising. I haven't heard anyone talk about beer so swooningly in ages."

"Swooningly?" Emma laughed, turning onto a road canopied by dense trees on either side. She slowed as we reached a bank of houses. It was a peaceful lane, with large front yards and literal white picket fences.

"Now, does any of this seem familiar?" she asked.

"It really doesn't," I admitted, trying to put myself in ten-year-old Charlotte's shoes. "Maybe I blocked it all out for being traumatic. I mean, I didn't talk to my mother for almost a month after we left."

"Really? How did you manage that?" she asked, turning onto the next street and pulling over.

I picked at a fuzz on my shirt. "I'd leave her notes, and she'd either answer them on the paper or ignore me. Eventually she would just talk to me, and if I didn't respond, I'd get punished. I learned pretty quickly that if I didn't play along, I'd lose the small connection I still had with my dad and Gigi."

"Charlotte, I'm so sorry."

I shrugged. "It's in the past. A lot of therapy got me to the point where I could talk about leaving, or my mother, and not totally break down."

"Well, I certainly don't want to bring up any old wounds, but if it's any consolation, I'm glad you're here now, and I know Gigi and your dad are, too." Emma smiled. "That is what friends are for."

"Speaking of friendships, I'm glad that we've got this do-over, too. I know I wasn't exactly the best person at keeping in touch," I admitted.

"Hey, Facebook is my method of communication, too, a lot of times. We've established that you're busy, and Lord knows I am, too. Just seeing you pop up in a text box or with a notification every now and then is enough sometimes. But now that you're here, we're tossing the digital friendship aside for an old-fashioned one."

"I could do with a little old-fashioned in my life. It's been missing. Maybe this place will help me slow down a bit and realize what's, I don't know, important? Does that sound cliché?"

"Yes, but I don't care. I like it, and we're running with it! If we had two beers, we'd toast to clichés!"

"And we'd also get pulled over by Duncan. I've got a sinking feeling he's waiting in the wings for me to step out of line."

"You're not wrong," she said, laughing and pointing to the cruiser that was on the side of the road, shrouded in a grouping of trees.

We beeped as we drove past. Duncan gave a half-hearted wave.

Emma pointed toward a street with a DEAD END sign next to the street sign. "We're getting into your old stomping grounds and— oh my God, I just sounded like my mother. When you see her, don't tell her."

I crossed my fingers over my heart. "Promise."

Smiling, I focused on the impression that Emma's mother left on me. Sophia Peroni was the kind of mom I always admired. Kind but firm. Endlessly loving but also took zero shit. If I ever decided to have kids, I wanted to be like her.

"How is she? Still as fabulous as ever?" I asked.

"You're not wrong there. Don't let her know I said that, either; she'll be insufferable. It's bad enough Cooper gets her riled up all the time."

"Speaking of, where is he today while you're playing hooky?"

"Cooper, Nick, and Henry have a standing man-date on the last day of every month. Weekday, weekend, doesn't matter," she explained, rolling her eyes when I gave her a smirk.

"So they're all besties, and they do what? Go golfing, hit the movies, braid their hair, get their backs waxed?"

She turned, glaring. "That's a very specific comment. Experience with the back waxing?"

I shuddered. "A guy I used to date would get his whole body waxed once a month."

I laughed when she shuddered. "Enough about waxing and weirdos."

"Agreed. I have a very uncomfortable visual of what Cooper would look like being totally waxed. We'll be catching up with them soon, by the way."

"Where are we going?" I asked as she readied to make a U-turn to head back onto the main road. "You said stomping grounds. I know the house my mom and I lived in is gone. Right? She said it burned down just after we left."

Emma slid me a glance. "What?"

I looked at her expectantly.

"Seriously? Burned down?" she parroted.

I nodded. "Yeah, she told me a couple of months later that it was some sort of freak fire, that's why we couldn't— Oh my God, I am an idiot," I groaned, slapping myself on the forehead.

She barked a laugh. "I'm sorry. I don't mean to laugh," she insisted. "You're not an idiot, Charlotte. You were a kid whose mother lied to her to ensure her story remained what you believed. The house didn't burn down. It's not a house anymore, but it's still standing."

"I can't believe that I believed her." I held up my hand when she started to disagree. "Worse, I can't believe she went as far as lying to me about it so I wouldn't ask questions. Who does that?"

Your mother, that's who.

Emma opened her mouth and closed it a few times, unsure of what to say.

"I know what you want to say, I was a kid, yes, but still. I'm an adult now, for pity's sake, and I still thought it was true. I never even bothered to ask my dad about it."

"You've got a look," Emma interrupted my thoughts. "Is something ringing a bell here?"

"Sort of? But I mean, nothing is jumping out at me. Let's follow your plan for now. I'm not sure if I'm ready to see the house anyway," I admitted.

Once we turned off the main road, going toward the school complex, the memories started again. Bright yellow buses climbing the hill toward the school. Kids playing on the sidewalks and the concrete alongside the building. The front entrance to the property was flanked with large brick signs labeled HOPE LAKE EDUCA-TIONAL COMPLEX. We drove up a long, wide driveway that led to the three schools.

"Elementary school," I said happily, pointing to the first building we drove past.

"Yes! And this is the middle school," she explained, waving toward a similarly designed building just up from the first.

"And let me guess—Hope Lake High School is that big one on the hill?"

"Yep. Henry is an English teacher there. Not that his line of work was a surprise. He never went anywhere without a book in his hand growing up."

"I meant to ask earlier, but you keep talking about this Henry as if I am supposed to know who he is." I felt foolish asking, but it was driving me nuts why I couldn't place the name. "Who exactly is Henry to me? I mean, I know I hit a Henry yesterday, but you talk like I should know him—"

Emma slammed on the brakes, jolting me forward sharply. Thank God we were on a closed drive and not the main road or we would have surely been rear-ended.

"Ems, what the fu—"

"Did you just ask who Henry is?"

6

"Yes?"

"Henry," she repeated, looking exasperated. Her hands were gripping the steering wheel, but she was fidgeting.

"Yes, Henry. You make it sound like I'm purposely trying not to remember. It was a long time ago, and don't forget, I didn't exactly leave under the best circumstances. I probably blocked it out. That's what one of the therapists I used to visit said."

Emma gasped. "Wait, your dad and Gigi never mentioned Henry? Or any of us?"

I realized that this revelation was going to sting. "Well . . . I think they caught on pretty early that talking about Hope Lake was not great for me. So eventually it just never came up except for random town gossip." I shrugged.

"Wow. I don't know what to say." Emma just stared at me, and we sat in silence for a bit until she said, "Rewind. You're the one who hit Henry in the nuts?"

I rolled my eyes. "You're like Gigi with the gossip. Good Lord. Keep in mind, I was exhausted and trying to get into the office when Birdy pulled up in the cruiser.

"It was a total accident," I added quickly. "Honestly, I can't believe you, the heartbeat of this town, didn't hear about it."

"Oh, I heard about it, but I didn't know it was you. I was on a call, and people were asking Cooper if Henry was still able to father children."

"Oh, come on! It was a tap. Nothing a little ice or whatever couldn't fix," I said, feeling ridiculous that this was still a topic of discussion.

I hadn't actually considered that this town would operate exactly how my mother said it would if I came back. "It's not even been two days and it's like Page Six in here."

"It's not that bad."

"Ugh, I should just shut the hell up already."

Emma nodded. "I have an idea. Let's go somewhere we can sit for a bit to calm down."

After agreeing, I remained quiet, staring out the window as we drove up a long, twisty hill that opened up to a beautiful park.

The spot Emma chose overlooked the town below. I could almost see Hope Lake in its entirety.

"This is quite the view."

Emma smiled smugly. "You keep doubting the power of Hope Lake. I can't wait to prove you wrong."

BY THE TIME Emma pulled back into Gigi's driveway, I had learned three things: (1) It felt as though no time had passed since Emma and I saw each other at our college graduations, and (2) I was exhausted. Not just physically but mentally. Emma was a lot to take back then, and things hadn't changed at all. When she was excited about something, she talked *endlessly*. I barely got any questions in. And (3) Dr. Max was definitely interested. He'd sent a text on our ride back asking if I was settled and might want to take the promised walk through town tonight.

"What are you going to say?" Emma asked, as we situated ourselves on Gigi's front porch.

"I don't know. I'm still thinking."

We sat, listening to the crickets. Again, something as simple as an insect noise was giving me a sense of calm that I hadn't experienced in a great while. I was beginning to appreciate being able to sit in silence with Emma. It was comforting.

"Listen," I said finally, rocking back and forth, enjoying the creaks of the porch and the chair. "I might take Dr. Max up on his offer and I might not. I'm still trying to figure out if dating is something I want to do while I'm here."

Emma grinned. "You do whoever is going to make you happy. Sorry, *whatever*."

"My God, with you and Gigi, I'm sandwiched between two screwballs."

Her phone buzzed, breaking the contemplative silence. She glanced at it, smiled, but left it unanswered.

It made me think about who was texting her. Cooper was the obvious answer, but she had so many people who loved her, it could have been anyone.

"Can I ask you something?"

"Always," she answered immediately.

"Why'd you come back here once we graduated? I mean, you could have gone anywhere, done anything, been anyone, and yet . . ."

"I came back to the one place where everyone knew me?" She laughed. "I thought about leaving briefly when everything hit the fan with Cooper in college. Even when he was running for mayor, and things looked like it was all going to go south, I considered it, but when I weighed all the pros and cons, I realized there wasn't anywhere else I'd rather be than here. I love it. There are good, honest people who love Hope Lake as much as I do. I like being in that mix. Helping give back to a place that gave me so much. It was part of the reason I wanted to make sure Cooper won when he ran for mayor . . . even though we had our differences."

I laughed. "Seems like you got over those differences."

She smiled. "Oh, we did. A lot." She stood and stretched her arms over her head. "This was a good day."

"It was," I agreed, stifling a yawn.

"I know we were supposed to have dinner, but I think you need to catch up on sleep first."

I groaned. "I think I'll spend tonight vegging out with Gigi and starting to formulate some kind of plan."

"Do you really want to say no to Max's offer on a stroll through town?"

My lips pursed as I thought about it. Spending time with an attractive guy certainly had its benefits. "I'm not saying no indefinitely," I reasoned, as much for me as it was for Emma.

"Okay, I'm just saying—be open to the possibility. I have to run, but I'll see you soon." Emma bounced down the steps and got in her car.

"And don't even think about leaving!" she shouted, tooting the horn before pulling away down the quiet street.

I TRIED TO relax, but I couldn't. Emma had left a few hours before, and I'd been trying to do things to pass the time. Reading wasn't keeping my interest, and neither was the thousand-piece puzzle of the Great Wall of China that Gigi had started on her dining room table.

Instead, I sat on the porch and pondered. Not about anything in particular, but just pondered. At least, until a very sleek car pulled into the driveway next door.

Max stepped out, wide smile and a bag around his arm. He was poised to climb the steps to Mrs. Mancini's when he saw me sitting on the porch.

Long strides carried him across the yard, and I straightened. I wished I had my phone to sneak a peek at how I looked, but alas, it had been a long day, and I was sure it showed.

"Fancy meeting you here, Dr. Max," I said, sliding over on the porch swing to make room for him.

He sat and pushed us off so that the swing moved in the warm breeze. "I was stopping by to check on Suzanne, and, I admit, hoping to run into you."

"Really, now. How convenient that I'm sitting out here," I said, bumping his shoulder with mine.

"Convenient indeed. What brings you out here? Just enjoying the beautiful night?" he asked, waving to the setting sun lighting the sky in orange and purple.

"Yes, actually. I was antsy and couldn't seem to shake off the day. This, well—this wasn't something that I could do in New York. Just sit in the fresh air and *be*. It's exhilarating."

"There's nothing like this place at sunset. If you're ever back behind Gigi's house at this time of night, trust me. Magic."

"Maybe I'll do that later," I said, bumping his shoulder again.

"Maybe, you'll have some company," he said, bumping mine back.

Just then, Mrs. Mancini walked onto her porch and waved her arm over. "Yoo-hoo, Max!"

"I'm being summoned," he said teasingly. "If I don't bring her this, she'll stomp over and take it."

"What is it? Never mind. I'm not sure I want to know."

"Contraband of the highest order. Diabetic shakes," he said, showing me what was in the bag. "We order them for her at the office, since it's cheaper for her. I deliver them, because, well, she gives me cookies."

I laughed. "Her cookies are a thing of legend."

"Maybe I'll see you later, then?"

I smiled. "Maybe."

Later was twenty minutes, and when I heard his steps crunching across the grass, I turned. "You're right, this is magic."

With the bright moon above us, we wandered around Gigi's property, skating past the woods and not dipping inside because who knew what sort of beasts hid among the trees. By the time midnight rolled around, I was exhausted and a bit chilly and Max was extending an invite for another magical midnight stroll.

7

After a couple of days of much-needed rest and relaxation, I was up before the sun, which was typical of my old life and schedule. The commute to Manhattan was pretty easy, even if the hours were hellish.

"Gigi, I'm running into town, do you need anything?" I asked, sliding into the kitchen with socked feet.

"My goodness, what made you do that?" she asked, smiling at my feet.

I shrugged. "I don't know, why?"

She laughed, pushing the motorized scooter's joystick to make her roll slowly toward me. "Because you used to do that all the time as a little girl. Slide into the kitchen or dining room. Anywhere there was a hardwood floor."

I thought about it for a moment, but nothing came to mind. I was finding that the more I wanted memories to reveal themselves to me, the less likely they would.

"I don't remember that but as long as it makes you laugh, I'll keep doing it," I said, bending down to kiss the top of her head. "I'm not going to be long. I thought I'd grab some wine or dessert to have with dinner since Dad and Dr. Max are bringing dinner here."

"Thank God," she said, followed by a barking laugh. "I was worried that we would have to fend for ourselves and cook. Lovebug," she added quickly. She reached into her pocket and then held her hand out to me. "Take this." She deposited some cash into my palm. Before I could protest, she cut me off. "Grab wine and get a cake from the store. There isn't an actual bakery anymore, but the grocery store ones aren't awful."

"A ringing endorsement!" I shouted, earning another laugh from Gigi. "Anything else you need from town?"

She shook her head, yawning as she did it. She couldn't have been up for more than a couple of hours, but she was already eager for a nap. "Why don't you lie down while I'm gone? That way you won't get into any trouble with Mancini next door."

"No, I'm fine. Henry is popping over to help me with something, so I have to stay awake."

"Oh, Henry's coming?" I asked, trying not to linger. I was curious about this guy whom I apparently had a whole childhood of memories with. I had already said I was leaving; how would it look if I happened to stay until he arrived?

"Yeah, soon, I think. He's probably bringing lunch, if you want to hurry back."

I shook my head. "No, I'll let you spend time with your friends. I was just going to apologize again for—"

"Almost leaving him sterile?"

"Gigi!" I shouted, much like a mom would at her misbehaving child. "Between you and Dad and the medical terminology, it's enough to make my hair curl."

"Oh, hush. You go, and I'll say you're sorry. By the way, Suzanne will be over later. She fancies Dr. Max, too."

"Wait, what do you mean by *too*?"

She gave me a pointed look, her gray eyes alight with mischief. "I saw your face when you were texting him. There were also a couple of nice-looking young people walking around the property in the moonlight. . . . He's very attractive and single. You're single and very attractive. It's simple math."

"Gigi, are you advocating a dalliance with Dr. Max?"

"I'm saying you're only single and young once. And the field is green here in Hope Lake. Explore, my darling. But if you tell your father I said that I'll hit you with a frying pan."

I inched away. "I'll be back. Love you."

"Love you more. Oh, wait!" she called out just as she pushed the saloon door forward with the motorized scooter. "How are you getting into town? Sure, I can't drive anymore, but I'm not keen on my car being impounded because you're a criminal."

"God almighty, I'll never live this down. And wait, do you even have an impound here?"

"Of course! If you get into trouble, Birdy keeps your car in his driveway. No one dares steal it from there."

"Well, thankfully I won't be having anything impounded. As far as my ride, Emma texted this morning to let me know that she was sending someone to pick me up, since, you know, I'm not a legal driver."

She yawned again, but this time, it was fake. "Good luck with that. Let's hope she doesn't send her father! I love Enrico, but that man can talk paint off a wall. He's one of those Ubie drivers now that he's retired."

"It's Uber, and no, I don't think it's her dad."

I kissed the top of her head again just as a horn beeped outside. "My mystery date is here. I'll see you later!"

"Have fun!" she shouted, as the front door closed.

I half expected her to follow me out to see who it was. Sure enough, she wheeled herself to the side windows and peered outside. She gave me a thumbs-up as soon as she saw the car.

In the driveway was a sleek, navy-blue BMW sedan. The driver slid out, and I recognized him immediately—it was hard not to, living in this town. "Mr. Mayor," I said, walking toward him with an extended hand.

He shook it, but kept it held tight. "It's good to see you again, Charlotte. Long time."

Cooper was dressed casually for an on-duty mayor on a Wednesday afternoon. He had on a light green polo shirt and khaki pants.

He smiled, releasing the full-blown Cooper charm, and I saw exactly why Emma had fallen hard for him.

"How did I win getting chauffeured by the mayor? Or did Emma bribe you to come way out here for me?"

Cooper's eyes twinkled. "I'll have you know, I offered to pick you up, *and* I had to nearly fight our previous mayor for the honor of taking you into town."

"Oh, really? Why is that?"

"I'm here to welcome our newest resident. Welcome back to Hope Lake." He held out his hand and unleashed another grin.

"Visitor," I corrected him before the pleasantries went any further. "I'm not sure that I'm staying."

He mocked surprise by placing his hand on his chest. "Oh, really? Emma didn't mention that."

"Uh-huh, I'm sure. In all seriousness, though, thanks. It's rough not having easy access to cheap public transportation."

Cooper laughed. "This isn't public, but it is cheap."

"I think we have very different definitions of cheap, Mr. Mayor. Nice ride. This new gig must pay you well." I was teasing, and we both knew it. Cooper was old money.

"What's the plan, Mr. Mayor?"

"You realize you can just call me Cooper, right?"

"This is more fun."

Cooper sighed. "I've got strict orders to deliver you to Emma."

"Deliver? What am I, a sofa?"

Cooper barked a laugh as he opened the passenger door for me. "Can I give you a warning?"

I rolled my eyes before sinking into the plush leather interior. "Something tells me that you're going to give it whether I agree or not," I mumbled once he shut the door.

Cooper walked quickly around the front of the car. He glanced up at Mancini's house and waved knowingly. The curtains quickly shut.

Once we were inside the car, Cooper drove down the empty street, beeping quickly to a Jeep that had its turn signal on.

"Slow down a second. Is that Henry?" I asked, turning to see the Jeep pulling into Gigi's driveway. She was back on the porch, waving to the large man lumbering up the steps. He bent down, kneeling on one knee and taking her hands in his. My heart skipped a beat at the tenderness, and I wished that Cooper would have just stopped so I could watch what happened next.

"Yep. Whenever Gigi has a book question, Henry is her number one guy," he explained, tapping a rhythm out on the steering wheel. "Come to think of it, he's her number-one guy for everything. Maybe except gardening. That's when she calls Nick."

"Jealous?" I teased, smiling when Cooper nodded.

"Everyone in town vies for Gigi's love and affection."

That didn't surprise me one single bit.

"Can you swing back around? I wanted to tell him something."

"Do you mean apologize?"

"I swear, news in this place spreads like a flash fire."

He laughed. "That's an accurate assessment. I'll give you five minutes. I'm not going to be on the receiving end of angry Emma."

"Deal," I promised.

Making a quick U-turn, he pulled back into Gigi's drive. I took the steps two at a time and slid to a stop at the front door.

I walked in, trying to be quiet so I didn't interrupt Henry and Gigi's conversation.

Just as I reached the pocket doors, they began to emerge, and panic struck. Why, I will never know. Maybe it was the shocking blue of his eyes or the genuine beaming smile that he gave me.

Whatever it was, I spun too quickly without saying anything and ran into the standing coatrack. Which then fell into Henry.

"Oh my God, I am incapable of normal function!" I howled, but it was covered by Gigi's cackling in between asking poor Henry if he was all right.

"Just go, girl, before you kill the man!" Gigi shouted, continuing to laugh.

Henry looked fine, red-faced, but fine.

I descended the porch stairs as fast as my legs could carry me. Back in the passenger seat, Cooper was laughing.

"How did you know?"

He shook his head. "I saw the whole thing through the window."

"I am hopeless," I insisted, my head falling into my hands.

Cooper remained silent while he pulled back out of the drive and zipped down the road. "You're not hopeless. I do think you're overwhelmed, though. This place is a lot to take in. Especially for someone like you."

I turned. "What does that mean?"

At the stop sign, he put up his hands in defense. "Not in a bad way. Just in a *you were already here* way, and people have all these expectations that you have to live up to. Or deal with. To complete strangers, this place is a lot. To someone like you, with a history, it's got to be even more confusing."

"Well, you're not wrong there. It's definitely an adjustment. One that I didn't quite anticipate. This whole place feels like it should come with a warning. Speaking of, what's your warning, Mr. Mayor?"

Cooper looked around as if Emma were listening and going to surprise him. His expression turned from playful to concerned.

"Emma has plans. Somehow . . . ," he started, blowing out a deep exhale. "Somehow she's convinced you fit into those plans."

"What are these plans?" I asked, wondering what exactly I was walking into.

"Oh, no. I'm not going there. That's your conversation to have. Just do us both a favor."

"What?"

He turned the car in to a small parking lot behind an old stone building. Workers milled around outside, some taking a smoke break, others chatting over a copy of what looked like building plans.

"If there is no hope for you to stay here, don't encourage her. It'll only make things harder when you leave." He slipped out the door and came around the front of the car, shaking hands with a couple of the workers before stepping over and opening my door. "I understand that you don't remember your childhood here, but Emma does, and when you left the first time, it really hurt her. All of us, really, but mostly her and Henry."

"About that—" I began, but he was already continuing.

"I'm glad you're here, Charlotte, but I have to look out for Emma first. I really don't want to see her hurt because she thinks you're here to stay."

I opened and closed my mouth a few times before simply nodding. I knew what he meant, even if it did paint me in a less-than-flattering light. That was a hard pill to swallow, and I didn't want to admit it, but it hurt knowing that she was hoping I was going to stay but preparing herself if I decided to go.

BEFORE COOPER LEFT, he blew a kiss to Emma, who was looking out at us from a window that overlooked an alley. She knocked on the window and waved excitedly for me to join her at the front of the building. At least, I think that's what she was motioning with her hands. It was either that, or she was doing some sort of aerobics.

I walked through the alley where a building opened out onto Main Street. Cooper had driven in from behind the building, and I hadn't realized we were in the center of the town square.

"The town looks great, doesn't it?" Emma asked, standing beside me. We stayed there for a moment, side by side, staring at the hustle and bustle of the town. "It's not even busy yet. Give it a month. This place will be packed."

"Wow. I can't imagine it. I look forward to seeing that."

She nodded and rubbed her hands together. "Oh yeah, the B and B's are already booked through mid-September, that's a few hundred people right there. We have some local families using Airbnb and VRBO to rent out their places for a couple of weeks at a time while they're traveling. The Jackson family, which operates the JOE facility here, are even talking about venturing into the boutique hotel market and are taking over an old textile plant near the lake opposite the brewery."

"I'm just . . . ," I started, unable to find the words. "Impressed."

"Why, thank you," Emma said, the happy and excited expression evident on her face.

"It's something to be proud of. It's a destination, Em," I said honestly.

There were customers milling about in front of the antiques store that had wares out on the sidewalk. Across the pedestrian walkway there was a bookstore with signs in the window that I couldn't read from this distance. Nice to see the independent stores were alive and well.

After a while of talking about the town, Emma turned around to face the building we were standing in front of. The building, whatever it had been or was becoming, had a killer storefront location. Its four large, rectangular front windows looked out over the busy section of Hope Lake.

To the left of the massive stone building was an ice-cream shop called Viola's Sweet Shop. It didn't look open yet, which was too bad, because I had a sudden hankering for some sweets. It wasn't just because I was itching for ice cream but because a certain handsome gentleman was helping move tables from inside the building to the small, fenced-in area outside.

"How did he get here so fast?" I asked, pointing toward the man.

Emma looked over quickly, then whipped back around smiling. "Where was he, and why are you paying attention to his schedule?"

Henry had changed the white shirt he had on when I saw him at Gigi's to a navy-blue T-shirt that was pulled tight over his back. *Does this guy have any shirts that fit him?* I watched him carry a round, wrought iron table with ease. He placed it down, then marched back inside to carry out two chairs without missing a beat. He made it look like he was carrying pillows.

The more I stared, the more I could see Emma out of the corner of my eye watching me, watching him. "Interesting," she said, and her hands twisted together in what I was realizing was her way of keeping her excitement in check.

"I wasn't sure you'd recognize him," she said with a laugh. "Wait, let me yell to him to lie on the ground and whimper." She laughed even after I slapped her arm.

"It was an accident, Jesus!"

Upright, and not cringing in pain, he was more attractive than I'd realized—even at this distance. I couldn't see his face when he was on the porch, or when I knocked the coatrack into him, and certainly not when he was bowled over in pain.

"I still can't believe you don't remember him from way back," Emma said, scrunching her face in confusion. "I mean, you guys—"

"I know, I know. Inseparable."

She nodded. "You're a baffling mystery, Charlotte. Before you get distracted by the muscles, I've got something to show you."

"Emma, listen—" I began, but she cut me off.

"I'm sure Cooper talked to you. I know he means well and is just trying to protect me, but I'm a big girl. I'm not hanging the moon and the stars on thinking that you're going to stay. This idea that I'm about to share with you is just something for you to do while you're here. Honestly, it would be helping me out just until you leave."

"Nothing like being super vague, Peroni."

"I'll explain, but I need you to have the full effect when I do. All the bells and whistles."

Some unknown emotion was niggling at me. Something between elation at the what-if and trepidation.

Whatever it was, I pushed it down and followed her through the doors of the great stone building.

Inside was a wide, cavernous hallway that had sectioned-off quarters with large windowed walls lining the main walkway.

"This whole lower floor was a bank—upstairs were offices and storage—up until about ten years ago, when the bank pulled the branch out and left it abandoned. The town recently got to buy the building when the market was good, and we were hoping that we could rent it out or even sell it once it was renovated. So now we have businesses that want to lease the space to open stores and even a restaurant out of the lower level. We found a company to design and manage loft-style apartments upstairs that will all be for rent."

Emma really did have vision.

I looked around, marveling at the building's interior. The ceilings were copper tiled, and while they weren't shiny any longer, they still had a gorgeous patina that drew your eye upward. A massive crystal chandelier hung in the center of the space almost like a disco ball over a dance floor. The sunlight reflected off the crystals, sending a rainbow across the floor.

"It reminds me of the shopping areas in Grand Central. Have you been?" I asked, walking up to the first newly remodeled storefront on the right. It, like its mirror on the other side of the building, looked out onto the square. The one I'd entered was still empty, but you could see that with only a little bit of work, it would be ready for whatever they had planned for the space.

The other empty space across the short hall had a sign on it that read COMING SOON in big red letters on the white plastic board.

"What's going in here?" I said, crossing over the threshold and setting off the jingly doorbell.

"This is what I wanted to talk to you about."

Here it comes.

"Hit me."

She smiled, giving me a playful tap on the arm. "So you're here for the summer and need a job, right? Well, what if I told you that this"—she motioned around the empty shop—"could be your job?"

I looked at her skeptically. "What exactly is *this*?"

"It was supposed to be a flower shop, but our resident florist is having second thoughts about starting over again in a new space, especially one this big."

My brain stopped processing when she said *florist*. "You have a florist?"

She nodded. "Lucille. She used to work at the grocery store doing the floristry work there. It's nothing fancy, a bouquet when you're in the doghouse. Something to congratulate your kid at a job well done at school. You know, small things. Nothing on a grand scale. Anything like that we might need, we have to go to Mount Hazel, Barreton, or online."

"And she, what, retired? You're trying to get her back in the saddle?" I asked, attempting to keep the excitement out of my voice. It was difficult, because I was already thinking about what this space could be.

"She was never *really* working in the first place. It was a side gig that she did to keep herself busy once her husband died. This came up as an opportunity, and she jumped on it because the grocery store decided to do away with the small flower department they had. She had money, and this was supposed to be her project. Now, honestly, I think the minutiae of running a business is more than she wants to handle at her age. She realized coming in, arranging, and doing the business side was just too much for her," Emma explained, walking deeper into the shop.

The setup of the room was making sense now. The blue tape would be where the coolers would sit. The marble top was a quick workstation or for taking orders. As I wandered, pieces fell into place where things should, or could, go.

"What are you thinking?" she asked, following behind me as I perused the space.

"The setup is not totally functional as is. I can see what she was originally thinking, but it's all so compact, probably because she based it on the small location she's used to."

"That's likely a yes. By the end of the meeting with the contractor, she was zoned out. At this point, she's thinking about ponying up the money and only being a silent partner. I won't be shocked if in a couple of months she tries to just sell it outright."

"Must be nice," I mumbled.

"How would *you* want to see it set up?" she asked, tapping her pen on her small notebook.

I narrowed my eyes at her. "Is this a test?"

She laughed. "I'm genuinely curious to know what you'd do here."

"I'm imagining coolers along this wall. The counter here is for orders?"

She nodded. "A Square or whatever financial system here," she added, placing her hand on the edge of the table.

And with that I went off, explaining how I would organize the entire space to maximize storage. I was rambling, but Emma didn't seem to care or notice. She was feverishly typing away on her phone. Looking over her shoulder, I saw that she was taking notes.

"What else?" she asked.

"See who her wholesalers are. I'm not sure if we can get the same ones out of Jersey like we did in New York. But it's not that much farther."

"Noted."

"Wait, wait. You can't just go with what I'm suggesting. You need to talk to this woman or whoever's going to run this for her, get their opinion. You've got to see what her vision is for the place. I could be way off here."

"I know her, she won't care. Trust me, she's only interested in managing the business side and hopefully turning a profit. She doesn't care about details," Emma insisted, pulling out a notepad from her purse. "I'm leaving notes for the guys. They'll be here tomorrow to start putting things together. What else are you thinking?"

"Emma, slow down. What exactly is it that you think I'm doing here?"

"Running the flower shop, of course."

Six little words that made my head spin while my heart skipped a beat. "What?"

"You heard me. We need someone to run this, and fast. She hasn't even named it, and it's supposed to open in two weeks. This train is on the track and pulling into the station whether there's someone professional at the helm or not. I'm a firm believer that without someone professional, it'll go to hell. You're here for the summer, and once you go back to New York we can find someone to take over. You'll get paid—well—and with you living with Gigi, it'll all go to whatever you plan on spending it on or saving it. I feel like this is a no-brainer."

"Of course you do, because you've had longer than three point eight seconds to think about it!"

I was shouting, but in reality, I knew she was right. This was an easy answer, but my brain wouldn't let my mouth respond. A simple yes, and I would be set for the next couple of months.

"I get that, I do, and I know I'm hella pushy, but I sort of need an answer right now, because if it's not you, I've got to find someone else," she said honestly, looking nervous as she paced. "You came at *the* perfect time. I know Hope Lake isn't your long-term goal, but this would be great short-term, right?"

I nodded.

"I believe in providence and people being in the right place at the right time. I believe you came here now for a reason. Why after twenty years you choose now to show up?"

"Because I got fired and needed to regroup?" I answered, not intending it to come out as snarky as it sounded.

"Yes, but you've never felt the need to come back here before when things got sticky."

"Okay, so let's say there's some type of cosmic intervention that sent me here now. You think it's because you suddenly need a florist? Why?"

She smiled. "Ask me when I found out about this falling through?"

The answer popped into my head before I even asked, "When?"

"I got the message as I was driving to the police station to drop off the goodies to Duncan. The day I saw you pulled over. Charlotte, you can't deny the timing is crazy, right? I believe you're here—"

"For this reason," I finished for her.

"Among others. I think Gigi has a lot to do with it. And your dad. All the reasons stack up to be pretty convincing, at least in my book."

"This is nuts, you know that, right? I mean, things like this don't just happen."

"Maybe they do. Who really knows?" She shrugged. "Maybe your coming here was part of some grand design."

I paced, contemplating whether this was a smart move. "What if you're wrong?" A hundred scenarios—all ending badly—popped into my head.

"Then I'm wrong and you work in a job doing what you love for a couple of months, earn some cash, and go back with a solid reference to help you find something else in New York. All this without a psycho boss riding you all the time."

"Be my own boss?" I liked the sound of that. I scratched at the nagging itch on my chest. Something still wasn't sitting right. I couldn't place it. "Could it be that simple?"

Emma shrugged again. "Don't overthink it. What's your gut instinct?"

I didn't have to even think about it.

"To do it."

Emma fought back a smile. It was tough, I saw the struggle, but I think she was trying not to gloat, and I appreciated that.

"I should totally not just say yes. I should want to talk it over with Gigi and my dad."

"And yet . . ."

I smiled.

She clapped excitedly. "YES!" she shouted, and this time, the beaming smile broke through.

"Emma, this is for the *summer*. Don't get your hopes up."

Using her finger, she crossed her heart. "I promise."

And yet, somehow, I didn't believe her.

8

Emma left about a half hour later, leaving me in the shop to collect my thoughts and gather up any other ideas I had for what to do with the space. *You know, if you decide to take the leap,* she said as she was leaving. Not to mention I had to list, in detail, everything I'd need for the shop, prices included, so we could float it past Lucille. We tried calling her, but it went straight to voice mail. She did text a minute later saying what my budget was, though—much more than I expected, by the way—and that she just wanted a list with costs. She was grateful that I was possibly willing to help her out. She just had two rules.

1. I was in charge of the labor and the creative side of the shop.
2. She would handle the finances and the business side of things, leaving me to be creative and build the business as best as I possibly could.

All this for the same salary I was making in New York.

Every cynical part of my body was making sure I was *not* letting myself get excited, but this honestly seemed like a sweet deal that only a lunatic would pass up. Either way, I ticked off the negatives while I toured the shop for the tenth time in a half hour.

- What happens *when* you fail? *That sounds an awful lot like my mother's voice.*
- *When* you fail, you've ruined someone's business. *Again, my mother.*
- What if this makes you want to stay in Hope Lake? *Guess who?*

Even with those thoughts running through my head, I imagined myself there. Taking orders, creating beautiful arrangements, planning parties with Emma . . . even if it was only for a little while.

This was what I had wanted for so long, and here it was on a silver platter for me.

Granted, it wasn't *where* I wanted but it was *what* I wanted. Couldn't I just focus on the positives? For once? A shop of my own that put me in charge and not having to deal with irate bosses who had a ton of money but had zero design talent.

In my head, the aesthetics of the shop were already coming together. That would be the fun part. I sent Lucille all my thoughts and ideas via text and she confirmed, insisting that she trusted Emma and then, by default, me. She started forwarding emails, bills of lading, receipts, and business contacts she already had set up. It really wouldn't take more than two weeks or so to get the majority of it lined up, considering she had given me one hell of a head start. With Emma's help and Lucille's checkbook, this could be the sweetest summertime gig I had in, well, ever.

I made sure the door had closed behind me before turning back toward the ice-cream shop, Viola's. It was charming in that small-town adorable sort of way. White clapboard across the front, with a large window highlighting a couple of the wrought-iron bistro tables inside that matched the ones that Henry had been moving earlier.

I looked around for him, but he was nowhere to be found. "Too bad," I said to myself, walking down the center pathway that joined the north and south sections of the town square. It looked like how a movie would envision a small town. I imagined this place in all four seasons. In the fall it would be bursting with colors stretching throughout the woods. In the winter, it must look like a snow globe, with swirling snow that danced through town.

Spring would bring new beginnings, with flowers billowing over colorful, widemouthed planters that dotted every corner. And I could tell already this place must be pure satisfaction in the summer.

In a bit of a la-la-land scenario, I found myself daydreaming, and I ended up at the bookstore that was directly across from where my shop—*the* shop—would be.

Evan's Books was another delightfully quaint building with just the right amount of old meets new. It had a brick-front facade and two massive rectangular windows highlighting the dark wood shelving that stood like sentries in the shop. The large, ornate brass door had a glass center with stunning intricate leaded trim work that drew your eye to its artistry. An iron bench sat out front just beneath the left window with two wine-barrel planters spilling over with potato vines and spike plants.

It was when I bent over to scoop some wayward soil back into the planter that I noticed who was inside.

There, in the center of a crop of little kids, was Henry. At least, I assumed it was him. From the neck down, he was dressed the same. Distressed jeans hugging him in all the right places and the super-fitted navy T-shirt. But now he wore a large red dog head.

You could hear the children laughing even from outside. Hearty giggles every time he stomped over to the colorful carpet they were sitting on and "barked."

A horn sounded from behind me, and I turned. Someone was waving at the older man next door at the dry cleaner. I hadn't noticed him before. By the time I turned back, things had gone belly-up. Henry, large and decidedly *not* in charge, had been tackled to the ground by the kids. I chose that moment to push the surprisingly heavy door open. A chime sounded through the store. In unison, the children called out, "Welcome to Evan's Books!"

"Thank you," I responded, and if I wasn't watching Henry being tackled and jumped on, I would have missed his body tensing up at the sound of my voice.

An elderly man appeared seemingly from thin air. I was so focused on Henry with the children, I hadn't seen him enter from the back of the store. He moved slowly with a cane in one hand and a notebook in the other. In a weary British accent, he called, "Come on, little friends, it's time for pickup, your parents are all in the parking lot out back. Let's stop treating poor Mr. Henry like a trampoline. You'll see him next week."

There was a resounding chorus of boos, but like little soldiers, they stood and lined up. Each one gave Henry either a fist bump, a high five, or a hug around his long legs before they marched off after the older man. At the mouth of the other room, they called out, "Bye, Mr. Henry!"

With the children in the back, the store was blissfully empty and quiet. Henry didn't move for a few seconds, instead choosing to sit with his back to me. After a few moments, he began stacking the books that were strewn across the carpet. The oddest part was, he kept the big red dog head on.

"Hi there," I said, entering farther into the store. I descended the step to join him in the sunken lounge area. "We've seen each other around a couple of times . . ." *I kicked you in the balls* was implied along with an *I'm sorry,* I hoped. "Anyway, I saw you through the window and thought I'd see how you're doing."

His shoulders shook slightly—I hoped with light laughter. Maybe he found this as ridiculous and awkward as I did. When did I become incapable of conversation with a man? There was something about him, though. We hadn't yet had a conversation, but I felt a familiarity with him. Maybe it was what Emma had said, that we had a history. *But why can't I remember it?*

With a gracefulness I didn't expect from someone so large, he rocked back on his feet and sprung up with ease. The movement caught me off guard, and I stumbled back.

With a whip-fast movement, Henry reached out and grabbed me, keeping me from falling backward onto the hardwood. His arm wrapped around my back, his large hand resting against my rib cage. I was leaning back dramatically, my hands gripped around his shoulders while he was holding me steady. It would have been a wonderfully romantic gesture had it not been for the enormous red dog head.

"Thanks," I said breathlessly. I wanted to slap myself for being woozy over a simple gesture of kindness. It was such a rare commodity of late that I was grasping at any morsel offered.

"Henry, it's good to see you. You know, upright," I said awkwardly as he straightened up, helping me to become steady on my feet.

He nodded, but then tapped the red dog head. "Currently, I'm Clifford." His voice was deep, muffled through the costumed head.

Without warning, he popped the dog head from his own, setting it aside on one of the tables. His hair was matted, sweaty from being encased in the ridiculous thing, but it didn't matter in the least. He was knee-buckling handsome in a classical patrician sense, with a strong, angular face. His hair was rich chestnut brown that curled a bit around his ears.

I hadn't noticed the first time, but small, clear wires disappeared into his ears. He had some sort of hearing device, and I realized that I didn't know how much he heard that first day. Was he reading my lips? Or were they simply to amplify sound so he could hear me?

"Henry," I said slowly. Something was scratching away at my memories. I couldn't place it, but a strange sense of familiarity was washing over me.

"Yep, still me," he said with a joking lilt.

"This was always a bookstore, right?" I remarked, having the strangest sense of déjà vu.

He nodded, waving toward the top level that had a coffee bar. "Coffee?" he offered, climbing the three stairs and disappearing behind the bar. There was a deep recess that served as a lounge area with squishy chairs and mismatched tables dotted throughout.

There was a shelf to the side that housed a complicated-looking silver coffee machine with many bells and whistles. Lining the walls next to the coffee were cups in varying shapes and sizes. A couple cookie jars were set up, and the stools looked inviting. This place was cozy, like the one on my street back in Brooklyn.

I told Henry as much. "So that's where you're living now? Brooklyn?" he asked, and I slapped my forehead realizing I hadn't introduced myself.

"Yes. And I'm Charlotte, by the way. I'm sure you figured that out already, you know, with all the obvious clues and my sparkling conversational skills."

"Wow, you really have no memory of this place, do you?" he said disbelievingly with a frown, setting down a steaming cup of cappuccino.

I figured that Emma had mentioned something. After all, they were best friends. "Emma told you, huh?"

He nodded, making himself a cup and setting it down beside mine. Like much of the shop, things were delightfully and artistically mismatched. My cup had a small green symbol on it, and his emblazoned with Penn State's logo.

"I know it seems odd, but I really don't. I get these brief flashes, but it's like my brain won't let the memory train fully back into the station," I said honestly before taking a sip of the coffee.

"That's quite the metaphor." He smiled, and it lit up his face. His skin had just started to pick up a summer glow, making his light blue eyes sparkle and stand out against the tan.

"What are you doing here? Emma said you're up at the high school? English, right?"

He nodded again. "Yeah, I help out here a lot during the summer. I come to read to the kids every week. Run some of the book clubs." He looked down into the cup. The slight lines around his eyes deepened. "I just can't believe you're here. I'm sorry if I'm being rude."

"I think you're allowed, after what I did to you. Actually, I'm surprised you're being as kind as you are, all things considered."

He threw his head back and laughed. "Noted. Seriously, though, it's just hard to be the only one with these memories. We were best friends. It's like I've imagined my childhood because no one else is there to remember it."

"What do you mean?"

He looked contemplative, a line deepening on his forehead as he scratched at the five-o'clock shadow on his chin. "Emma said you don't remember much, but I don't know if I should fill you in. Or if you want me to. I'd rather see if you could remember our friendship, and this place, yourself. I'd hate to give you my version and have it cloud what memories you might recover."

"That's just it, though, I have none and no clue if I'll get them back," I answered, growing perturbed at myself. "I remember bits and pieces, but so far, you're not one of them. Emma is, but barely. I think being near her in college helped with that. I wish I could remember you. Emma said we were inseparable."

"She's not wrong. We did everything together. Me, you, her, our friends Nick and Cooper. Mostly it was you and me, though." He blanched at the last statement as if it bothered him.

"Does that hurt your feelings?" I blurted out, wishing I could pull the question back in. "I mean, it would bother me, so I'm just wondering."

"It bothers me a great deal, but what can I do but help you—hopefully—remember what you can?"

That was an offer that I not only appreciated but, for some reason, was also looking forward to. There was something in his eyes, a promise, a memory of a lost time, something that made me want to spend time with him. Maybe it was the former friendship manifesting itself into something other than a clear memory. Whatever it was, I found myself wanting to get to know Henry.

Again.

"I have a feeling the longer you're here, the more will come back to you. I mean, look at it this way. You knew this was a bookstore. Do you remember anything about it? The layout hasn't changed since you were last here."

I tried desperately to think back to ten-year-old Charlotte. Sliding off the stool, I spent a few quiet minutes taking my time to look around. I stopped at the large, round oak columns, sliding my hand over the smooth wood, and turned to Henry to see him watching me curiously.

I nodded. Swallowing my nerves and confusion, I said quietly, "I remember story time here. I don't know what, when, or why I do, but I have a feeling I was here for stories. Could that be?"

Henry smiled and nodded, following behind me but letting me explore the area without disruption. After doing a full lap around the perimeter of the store, I took a seat on the tufted armchair in the sitting area. Henry looked as if he was not sure where to sit, choosing instead to lean against the wood column, crossing his arms over his chest and waiting.

The cuckoo clock ticked by as we continued to stare at each other in a quiet bubble. The phone didn't ring. Customers didn't come in, and I was hell-bent on being charming and in control.

"Remembering story time was one thing, why don't I remember *you*?" I said. I hated the way the light dimmed in his eyes.

Finally, he shrugged. But it wasn't just a shrug. His face displayed every emotion. "I guess I'm not very memorable."

My initial reaction was *Yeah, right. Look at you.* But I chose a simpler, less insane approach instead. "It's not you, it's me. I think I spent so many years blocking out Hope Lake and its presence in my life that it's hard to find my way back."

He nodded, pushing his large body from the pillar to join me. "I hope that your time here is helpful in remembering what you loved about this place the first time you were here."

I straightened. "I hope so, too. I don't know how long it'll be, but it's at least the summer," I rambled, wondering why this guy made me so uneasy. Not in a creepy kind of way, but a rug-being-pulled-out-from-my-feet kind of way. Maybe it was the supposed history, or just that I felt an attraction crackling in the air. Whatever it was, I didn't know how to process it.

Henry turned, walking back toward the counter.

"Is everything okay?" I asked, following him to the coffee bar with my still-full mug.

He shook his head, looking at anything but me.

"I know I don't remember—"

He looked up, right at me but straight through me. As if I weren't even there. "Like I said, I guess I was pretty forgettable. I wish you all the luck while you're here. I'm sure I'll see you around."

And with that, he turned on his heel, descended the stairs, and went out the door that the children had used. I caught a glimpse of him before the door closed. He reached out to greet some parents, a handshake, a man hug, and a kiss on the cheek of one of the women. His attitude turned sunny again the moment he got away from me.

What had he said earlier? *Noted.*

9

When Dr. Max arrived at Gigi's later that night, he brought with him more food than I'd seen in ages. When you're single and living with someone like Parker—gone all hours of the night, sleeping in spurts throughout the day—you tended to grab small bites here and there. I hadn't prepared a meal of that size in, well, ever.

"Max, thanks for coming," I welcomed, leaning into his offered one-armed hug. "Is Dad running late?"

"He got tied up in Barreton. Next town over. There was a couple-car pileup and they called him to lend a hand. I couldn't go because I still had two patients to see. I'm not sure when he'll get here."

"That's disappointing. I'm glad you still made it, though." He set the bags with dinner on the side table, and pulled something from one of them.

"What's this?" I asked, taking the small wrapped package from him.

"Just a little something to make Hope Lake feel a bit more like home."

Tearing open the paper, I smiled. "It's beautiful, thank you," I said, carefully holding a thin square painting.

"Your father said that the Brooklyn Botanic Garden was one of your favorite places to visit as a kid." He stepped behind me, looking over my shoulder at the hand-painted piece. "It's linen paper, so it's fragile. I couldn't find a frame for it at the antiques store."

I shook my head. "I have the perfect place to put it." I set it gently on the table in the foyer. "I'll run it upstairs after dinner, which I see you brought a lot of."

He shrugged. "I tend to get carried away."

We walked into the dining room.

Gigi joined us, scooting over to Max, who enveloped her in a hug. "Thanks, my dear. You're too good to this old gal."

"Gigi, you're not old!" Max said, smiling down at her.

"I was talking about Charlotte. You're kind to bring her dinner."

I rolled my eyes, and Max threw his head back with a bellowing laugh. "Gigi, you're a gem," he insisted.

"So tell me about your day," Gigi asked, again. She'd questioned me as soon as I got back home.

"I told you, I'd tell you when Dad gets here." I had already played the conversation in my head at least a hundred times over. The more I thought about the possibility of the flower shop, the more excited I became.

Only for the summer, Charlotte. As if I could forget.

"Yes, yes, well, I was hoping to get the scoop. I could just call Emma," Gigi offered, taking out her brand-new iPhone.

"Where'd you get that? Good Lord, woman, that's like three versions better than mine!"

Dr. Max laughed. "She had to teach your father how to use his Apple Watch. She's a pro."

"Come live with me in New York and you can work at the Apple store on Fifth," I teased.

"I would actually love that. I've been looking at the new Mac mini." *This woman.*

My and Dr. Max's phones buzzed at the same time as Gigi's watch face lit up. I checked the message. "Dad will be here in five."

"That means you share your news in six minutes," Gigi announced, her tone leaving no room for argument.

In my heart, I knew this decision was mine alone, but I still wanted them to be in on the details.

The doorbell rang, jolting me from my thoughts. "Dad doesn't ring the bell, right?"

Gigi shook her head. "What time is it? Oh, crap. I forgot about Nick coming over. Do me a favor, sweetheart, grab my checkbook from my room. It's on the dresser. I need to get him out of here before your father gets here."

"Why is he coming here?" I asked, but there was a flurry of activity.

Without giving me a response, Gigi took off in her chair toward the front door. I looked to Dr. Max, who was just shaking his head, laughing. Apparently, this was another story that I needed to get later.

I took off for Gigi's room, not glancing at the front door. I heard his voice, though—deep, rich, and yet still somehow playful.

"Gigi, I'm here for our date. Where are your dancing shoes?" Nick teased, and I couldn't help but smile at the silly giggle that escaped my ninety-year-old grandmother.

Her checkbook was tossed open haphazardly on her dresser. The checks were unexpected. They were splattered with polka dots and read *I'm not adulting today*.

"Gigi, you're full of surprises," I murmured.

Joining them in the foyer, I came to an abrupt stop when I saw the man in the doorway. Just where were they hiding these guys in Hope Lake? And what were they feeding them?

This man was sitting on the floor, legs outstretched before him and smiling at my grandmother like she was the only light in the sky. It was the second-most-endearing thing I had seen all day, and both involved handsome men and my grandmother. He looked tall, maybe not as tall as Henry, but definitely over six feet. A rich, tan complexion made him look surprisingly boyish. On his shirt was a logo with the script ARTHUR LANDSCAPE ARCHITECTURE beneath it. Ah, that explained the tan and the forearms. Then I remembered Emma saying he was responsible for the beautiful flowers across town and at Gigi's.

"Hello there," I said, walking up to place my hand on the back of Gigi's chair.

When he looked up, I was greeted with warm, inviting brown eyes. He stood, patting Gigi's hand gently as he rose.

He pulled me into a bone-crushing hug and murmured, "Good to see you again, Charlotte."

"Nick Arthur, right?" I said, still smooshed against his shoulder. "We used to ride bikes together?"

"Yes! Among other things. Mud biking, river fishing, anything outdoors. You used to be my reading partner, too. Drove Henry crazy," he said, laughing at what was I'm sure a shocked expression.

Unlike the blank slate that I had with Henry, something about Nick brought back a flood of memories.

I closed my eyes briefly to catch a flash of a little boy with dark brown hair and big brown eyes with lashes that touched his cheeks when he closed them. He was sitting at a table laughing, with a glass of milk in one hand and a large cookie in the other. A chessboard sat before him in the crowded kitchen.

"We used to play chess, too, right?" I asked, surprising myself and both he and Gigi, judging by the expressions they wore. "Maybe I'm wrong; these memories don't seem to make much sense."

His smile was all the answer I needed. It lit up his face in a way that made me want to smile back. "Yes! You remember, I can't believe it. Henry said you didn't remember him at all, and I figured if you didn't remember him of all people, I didn't stand a chance."

"Charlotte, you really don't remember this town? You didn't tell me that."

I saw Nick look over my shoulder to where Dr. Max's voice came from, and for a brief moment his expression faltered.

"Sorry, Gigi, I didn't realize you guys had company," Nick said, tipping his chin toward the dining room.

"Oh, I'm not really company, right, Gigi?" Max said confidently, strolling over toward Nick. "I consider the Bishops family; I'm sure that Nick feels the same way, right?" Max clapped his hand on Nick's shoulder the way that guys tended to do. "Hey, golf next week?"

Nick shrugged. "Sure, I guess my ego can stand another blistering defeat. I'll see if Henry and Cooper want in. Though Henry hates golf."

Gigi groaned as my father's car pulled into the driveway. "Oh, here we go."

Nick turned to glance outside, then quickly turned back to me. "While this has been a fun, short trip down memory lane, I have to run. Gigi, I'm popping out the back door. Charlotte, don't be a stranger. Gigi will tell you how to find me," he said, dropping to his knees and kissing her cheek again. "I think you owe me a rematch at chess!"

Nick, clearly familiar with the house, jogged through the swinging kitchen door.

"Gigi, why does Nick avoid my dad?" I asked, just as a car door slammed outside.

"That, my dear, will require some wine," she responded just as my dad appeared in the doorway.

"Why was he here?" he asked no one in particular. "Did he come to talk to you, too?"

I shrugged. "No, Gigi was going to give him a check," I answered, hoping Gigi would back me up. "And this isn't *The Bachelorette*, Dad. I'm not looking for Mr. Right among the available guys in town."

Dr. Max stayed silent, leaning against the wall that led into the parlor. He just smirked at my dad, who continued to ramble.

"So why'd he stop by?"

Gigi slapped him on the arm. "He cleaned out my gutters for me and did all the work on the flower beds and baskets. He wouldn't take the money the other day, but I convinced him to take a check as a donation to that Little League team that he and Henry coach."

Dad huffed, but it didn't seem like he was really annoyed.

"Do you not like him or something, Dad?" I asked.

He frowned. "I wouldn't say that I don't like him. He's just a pain in the ass and likes to push my buttons. Well, everyone's buttons. He's a bit of a nuisance, you could say."

I waited for him to explain further. "The boys—and Emma, too; she's not excused from this—used to always dare each other to do the most idiotic things, most of which Nick talked them into. Some of which had lasting complications."

"Poor Henry," Gigi said, touching her ear absently. "For how smart all of them are, they really got into some sticky situations."

"What do you mean?" I asked, turning to Gigi.

"When they turned sixteen, Nick managed to break Henry's arm and Cooper fell out of a tree, breaking his leg. We still don't know how that happened." Gigi shook her head.

"Whatever they all did, it sounds like I missed a hell of an exciting childhood by not living here. The most exciting thing to happen to me in New York was when Mom left me on the subway and I ended up in Long Island at midnight."

Gigi gasped, her hand flying up to her heart. The color drained from my father's face, and again, I wished that I had a working filter.

"What?" he said, in a quiet, even tone. I almost wished he screamed it, because at least I would know he was mad. This was a terrifying reaction, because it meant he was beyond pissed and entering into irate territory, which only ever happened when he was discussing my mother and her many flaws.

"I mean, I was okay. No one bothered me. She found me eventually at the police station— You know, I'm going to stop talking."

My father's face was shockingly pale. More so than usual.

"Good idea," Gigi said, trying to take my dad's hand. He looked grief-stricken, his light blue eyes awash with unspilled tears. As if something *had* happened to me. I couldn't imagine what he was thinking. It was one thing for him to assume that my mother wasn't the best parent, but to have proof? After everything he had done to try to gain custody only to be told his travel made him unfit? Good thing she wasn't around to be on the receiving end of what was sure to be a riotous argument.

Dr. Max took that opportunity to save the night. "Dinner is ready! Charlotte, I hope you've brought your appetite. I may have gotten carried away. I set you a place next to me."

AFTER WE CLEANED up dinner, Dad thankfully had calmed down. The four of us sat in the parlor, Dr. Max and I on opposite ends of the couch. He had engaged Dad and Gigi in a discussion about some sort of medical mumbo jumbo and I pretended that I understood a third of what they were discussing. *I didn't.*

"You know, I did my residency in New York," he offered, popping a mint into his mouth. "I thought about staying, but I like it here. It's slower and not as chaotic. I love the city, don't get me wrong, but this seems like a great place to have a life and family." He winked, offering me a mint. "Someday, of course."

"I can see the appeal," I admitted, wary of the fact that my dad and Gigi were not-so-secretly eavesdropping on the conversation. I wasn't going to lie, though—even with them listening. I could see the attraction to this place. It had a lot to offer a family. Good schools, activities, nice people. What more could you want?

"It seems like more and more younger families are moving in. At least that's what Emma said," I stated.

"She'd know. She has her finger on the pulse of Hope Lake."

That she did. "I suppose since news travels at lightning speed in this town that you're all aware of an offer that Emma made to me today?"

"Kiddo, I've waited all night for you to bring it up. Spill," Gigi said, taking a sip of her decaf coffee. "Emma mentioned to me that there was a job offer, but she wouldn't tell me what. I have an idea, but that's only because I was at the last town-planning meeting with Cooper."

She added quickly, "Not because Emma told me what she was thinking. Or that Lucille told everyone she hated how much work the shop was becoming."

"This place can't keep a secret." I chuckled.

"Don't be mad at Emma, honey," Dad said gently. "She was excited and wanted to tell . . . well, everyone."

"And?" I asked.

"And, I may have said that I thought it was a top-notch idea and that you'd be silly not to take it."

"Yeah, but what if they—"

"What if they what, dear? Honestly, I love you more than anything, but stop living in what-ifs." Gigi turned to Dr. Max. "Emma asked Charlotte to help open and run the new floral shop Lucille bought!"

Gigi was not pulling any punches. If she was able, I imagined she would have stood, grabbed a chair, and placed it directly in front of me to drive her point home.

"Charlotte, this is a no-brainer," Dad said, brushing his hair back from his face. "It's a great opportunity. Besides, you never know—"

"I'm going to stop you right there," I said, holding up my hand. "Yes, this is a great opportunity to help Emma, and this Lucille, and also earn some money this summer. But I'm not going to walk around pie-eyed thinking that this is going to be smooth sailing and that it has an extended future. It could all blow up in my face. So let's not start assuming I'm going to stay here."

It came out harsher than I anticipated or intended. Everyone's eyes were trained in their laps, and I felt like crawling under the table. "I'm sorry, that was mean. I just meant that—" I began, but Gigi cut me off.

"Sweetheart, we're all just so happy you're here. You can't fault us for hoping that this would be a permanent change if you found that you were really, truly capable of being happy here. We'll take you for as long as we can."

Dad nodded. "Whatever your decision ends up being, we'll support it. I know Emma will, too. She's just as glad as we are that you're home. Sorry, *back*."

"I know I sound awful, I just don't want anyone to count on me in the long term and then be disappointed or, worse, mad, because I want to leave." Cooper's words had taken a firm hold in my thoughts since he asked me not to give Emma hope that I was staying.

Gigi smiled. "Just promise me one thing."

"Anything," I said quickly, meaning it. I would give her anything I possibly could.

"Keep an open mind. I know you've got a lot of preconceived notions about this place, but someone or something might have you totally surprised. I'd hate for you to miss out on something great because you've got your head in the sand."

I smiled reassuringly, even though I was feeling anything but reassured. "I promise. I will go into this with an open mind."

"That's all any of us can ask for," Dad said, checking his watch.

"Have somewhere to be?" I asked, hoping that we'd be able to have a couple of minutes to chat.

"Early appointments tomorrow, and I promised Barreton's ER staff that I'd pop back up there beforehand to make sure everything was okay after the accident."

"Then we've got to pack for Manhattan," Max said, standing and stretching his arms over his head. "I'm not sure if you remember what we talked about the first day you arrived. You were a bit worse for the wear."

I thought back. "A conference or something, right?"

He nodded, and while Gigi pulled him into a conversation about more medical mumbo jumbo, I checked him out. He wasn't quite as big as Henry, but he was tall, well-built, and I could see why so many women were drawn to joining his fan club.

"How long is the trip again?" I asked, standing and walking over to my dad for a hug.

"Soup to nuts, we'll be gone five days." Dad pulled me into a hug.

"I'm sorry that we're leaving. Had I known you'd be here, and not there as we planned, I would have tried to reschedule or cancel."

I squeezed him back. "Dad, I can survive five days without you here. I promise not to get into any more trouble," I said, laughing when he whispered, "How'd you know I was going to suggest that?"

As Gigi retired to her room and Dad took off, I walked Dr. Max out.

We stood side by side on the porch, looking out at the miles of field before us. "I heard what you told your dad about not looking for Mr. Right while you're in town."

I blushed. "I partially said that because he would be a worrywart if I said I *was* looking for someone. Which I'm not, but I'm not *not* looking."

He turned, facing me. One thing about Max that I liked was that he gave me space. I didn't feel confused when he was around. It was easy. No pressure. "How about this—when I come back from New York, you think about us having dinner. Or maybe drinks."

"You're okay with that? Keeping this casual?" I asked.

"That's perfect." Max took my hand and laid a gentle kiss across my knuckles.

"Good," I responded, feeling the tingle his lips made against my skin fade away.

10

"Are you sure all of these people are necessary?" I asked, tugging on the hem of my shirt. I'm glad I listened to Gigi and ironed it, though there were still a few errant wrinkles in the blue peplum top.

A few days after I accepted Emma's proposal, I went to meet her at her office in the Borough Building, a beautifully restored, multi-story building toward the center of town. Besides helping Lucille get the shop ready to open, I had been given my first big job: the annual Fourth of July festivities in the park. I needed to attend the town council meeting where the festival would be discussed. She wanted to "blow the doors off the town," and, apparently, I was the person for the job. From what I was told, I just had to be there in case they had questions.

I really didn't want to draw attention to myself, but I definitely felt like I was under the microscope when I walked in to see a group of curious-looking people in a large, dimly lit room. At least I had come prepared in case anyone wanted specifics.

Rows of chairs lined the main expanse of the room. At the head of the space was a long, thin table filled with what I assumed were the important people in town.

Cooper was off to the side chatting with Emma's dad, Enrico. They had their heads buried in what looked like blueprints. "Hey,"

I said, motioning to Emma's fiancé and father. "I thought you said your dad wasn't in an elected position anymore?"

She huffed. "He's not officially on anything. He keeps offering to create these subcommittees and chair them. I wish he'd enjoy retirement!"

Suddenly a thin, weary-looking man in an ill-fitting suit cleared his throat before pounding a gavel on the long wooden table where he sat at the front of the room. "Attention. Attention."

"Oh, grab a seat. I have to be up front, but you'll be fine. They just want to make sure that you can handle the event."

My eyes grew wide. "Emma!" I whispered, tugging on her shirt-sleeve to keep her near me. "You said this was to talk about budgets and designs with a couple of people. You never mentioned that I needed to speak in front of a crowd."

She looked guilty. "I didn't? I thought I did. I'm sorry, my brain is mush with wedding, work, and my mother trying to figure out a way to be the mother of the bride *and* the flower girl because she saw it on *BuzzFeed*."

"Wait, what? You know, never mind. I'll figure it out," I said, realizing that Emma had way too much on her mind.

I hope.

The man in the center of the table clutched the gavel as if he were afraid someone would take it away from him. Cooper sat at one end of the table with Enrico on the other. The smile never left Enrico's face.

The gavel wielder seemed annoyed that he wasn't the only person on the dais, judging by the side-eye he was giving everyone.

"Attention. Welcome to the June town council planning meeting. Tonight's agenda is long. I plan on being here for the foreseeable future, examining each and every single detail thoroughly, so settle in for a long night." His remarks were met with a chorus of groans and people shifting uncomfortably in their seats.

Just as he turned the first page on an impressively thick stack of papers, my phone's shrill text tone rang out in the otherwise silent room.

Gavel man's eyes whipped up, as well as the eyes of every other person in the room. Emma snorted but covered it quickly with a fake cough behind her hand.

I dived into my purse, scrambling to find the phone to silence it. Whoever was texting was firing off multiple messages, so it continued to ding incessantly. Finally, at the very bottom of the bag, I found it and switched it to silent.

When I looked up, everyone was still staring, but to add insult to injury, they were now whispering behind their hands. Gavel man gave a quick rap on the table, which drew everyone's attention back to him.

He cleared his throat. "Excuse me, but did you not see the sign?"

I kept my head down and focused on the phone. In my effort to silence it, I managed to make a call to Gigi, who was now answering. "My God, this night can't get any worse," I whispered, hanging up and sending her a quick text apologizing but that I'd explain what happened later.

"*Excuse* me?" the voice shouted, louder and more persistent this time.

"Charlotte," Emma whispered, and I glanced up.

Mr. Gavel was staring down at me as if willing my chair to be sucked into the floor. "I said, did you not see the sign?"

I shook my head. "I'm sorry, are you talking to me?"

He huffed, looking indignantly to the rest of the panel, all of whom glanced away.

"The sign upon entering," he barked, pointing toward the wall where a sign clearly read

SILENCE YOUR CELL PHONES

My attention slid back to him. "I'm sorry, I didn't see it. My grandmother was just checking in on me," I lied, because in reality I had no idea who had sent the barrage of texts. I'd check once the focus wasn't on me any longer.

He adjusted his seat. I noticed his chair was larger than the others at the table. *Compensating much?*

"Carrying on," he said, turning another page on the impressive stack. If he planned on going over every page there, we wouldn't be leaving until sometime next week.

Curling the hem of my shirt over the phone on my lap, I scrolled through the messages, smiling when I saw they were all from Max.

MAX: Hey
MAX: Sorry
MAX: To
MAX: Text
MAX: During your
MAX: meeting
MAX: But
MAX: Was just thinking about
MAX: You
MAX: And thought
MAX: I'd
MAX: Say
MAX: hi

I smiled down at the phone but schooled my features when I heard a throat clear. He had been sending a message here and there, just to say hi.

The gesture was thoughtful, and it let me know that I was on his mind. It earned another smile despite the earlier embarrassment, but I wondered if he had ever sent flirty messages, hell, any message, to another human being before. He wasn't much older than me and yet, he was sending texts in the same fashion that my father did.

As I was replying, another popped up.

I hid the phone under the fabric of my peplum top, trying to discreetly read and reply.

MAX: Sorry, I was on the treadmill in the hotel and I was trying to send it from my watch.
MAX: My bad.

> **ME:** No worries. Focus on running.
> **ME:** Thanks for the "hi."

Something about the texts was weighing on me. He was the one who initiated the contact, not me. Did I find him attractive? Of course, I'm human. But that feeling, those butterflies in the stomach, weren't there. Maybe it was a sign that a summer fling really wasn't what I was looking for. Or maybe I needed to spend more time with him that wasn't a stroll at midnight.

Paying attention to the meeting was harder than I thought. I tried to relax, but nothing was working. I felt sweaty, cold, and on fire all at once, and everything was from the prospect of having to talk to this crowd, especially after what just transpired with the phone and gavel man's rebuke. Being thrown under the bus wasn't my cup of tea. I was trying to give Emma slack, but this wasn't how I wanted to have to meet the town.

Ten minutes into the meeting, I found myself fighting to stay awake. The seat was plastic, and hard under my butt, and I was starting to doze off even though I was woefully uncomfortable. The speaker's voice was flat, with zero inflection. Like the teacher in *Ferris Bueller* who repeated Ferris's name. *Bueller. Bueller.*

If someone spoke out of turn, he banged the gavel against the table, furiously trying to get the attention back onto him and the conversation on track. If someone sneezed or, heaven forbid, coughed, he would pointedly stare and wait until they were done before continuing. I caught Cooper chuckling a few times. Enrico continually rolled his eyes, and Emma—well, Emma looked like she wanted to vault over the desk and strangle him.

After about thirty of the longest minutes of my life, the door creaked open and Henry appeared apologetically in the doorway. He gave a small wave to Cooper, then proceeded to glance around the room, I assumed to find somewhere to sit. I had two seats near me, and an unexplained eagerness to sit next to him.

With a deep breath, I tried to school my features. There was excitement building to talk to him that I couldn't quite squash. He was attractive, smart, employed; he didn't appear to be married. There was an innocence about his look, though. Max was sure of himself, poised, and *very* alpha. Henry took more of a subtle *I don't know that I'm the hottest dude alive* approach that I found endlessly attractive.

I gave him a small wave, trying to get his attention. Just after Henry closed the door quietly, Nick came bursting through with zero regard for the fact that a meeting was in session.

Gavel man was so irritated at Nick's intrusion that he slammed the gavel repeatedly on the table until Nick finally looked over to him. He just waved him off and kept shaking hands with people he walked by as if he wasn't aware that he was disrupting.

Smothering a laugh, I waved to them both. Nick slapped Henry's arm and motioned to come toward me. They couldn't have been more opposite.

Henry walked quietly toward me, while Nick lumbered over with heavy boots thunking against the carpeting.

"Hey," Nick whispered, taking a seat to my right.

Smiling at Henry, who was trying to stay out of the way of the people behind us, I tugged on his hand and slid over, so he could sit between Nick and me. Like Nick, he appeared to come straight from work: in his case, the school. I wondered when school was over. His polo shirt was untucked, but he didn't look sloppy, anything but. His khaki pants were well tailored to fit him.

"Hi, guys. What are you doing here?"

Nick scoffed. "We were summoned."

"Emma," Henry and Nick said together.

I smiled. "I can certainly appreciate that. I'm here thanks to her, too. I can't believe this turnout. Is it always this busy at town meetings?"

Henry shook his head but kept his eyes forward as he spoke quietly. "No, it's the Fourth of July festival. It always draws the crowd. People come to sign up and help. You just happened to pick the busiest meeting to sit in on. After the festival, it'll just be Kirby, and the rest of the council, and that'll be it."

"Kirby?" I whispered toward them.

"The dope with the gavel," Nick offered, hooking his thumb up toward Mr. Gavel, who was now seething because someone's cell phone rang. "He's the head of the town council and houses the biggest stick up his ass."

"What's his problem?" I asked, shushed almost immediately by an angry-looking woman sitting in the row in front of us.

"Hi, Mrs. Rogers. Nice to see you," Nick said sourly.

She leveled him with her heavily made-up gaze before turning around and beaming at the man up front.

Wife? I mouthed, and they both nodded. I pretended to swing a gavel. *Kirby?* I mouthed again, and they nodded with an added matching eye roll that made me snort-laugh.

Henry tipped his chin up at Cooper, who was pretending to nod off himself. Every time we whispered between one another, Kirby's wife would shush us.

After a few minutes, Nick waved to me for my phone, which was still sitting on my lap. I unlocked it and handed it over. He pulled up my text app and typed in some numbers before handing it back.

Looking down, I saw two numbers with the Hope Lake area code.

ME: New phone, who dis?

UNKNOWN NUMBER: This is Nick.

I assumed the other was Henry, but he didn't have his phone out. Quickly entering their contact info, I shot off another message.

ME: This is Charlotte.

Brilliant conversationalist, Charlotte.

NICK: This is easier than getting
shushed.
NICK: Plus, now you've got our numbers.
NICK: If you need anything.
NICK: We're your guys.

Nodding gratefully, I set my phone back onto my lap and tried paying attention to the meeting.

The majority of the comments and discussion were certifiably boring. No one was paying any attention until Kirby said, "And now on to the annual Fourth of July festivities. You should know that this year the mayor's office is taking on a greater role.

"Emma Peroni will be explaining the breakdown."

Emma stood, straightening out her blouse. I still wasn't exactly sure what her job was, but it seemed like if something happened in Hope Lake, she and her department were in charge of it.

"Hello, everyone. This year's festivities will be a bit more structured than in years past." You couldn't miss the way her eyes slid slightly toward Kirby. "We'll be breaking out into subcommittees and having separate meetings before coming to the collective meeting and sharing our thoughts and progress." She smiled before continuing. I couldn't help but notice how engaging she was.

Emma, though not on a mic and amplified, still completely captivated the room. All eyes and ears were on her with the exception of Kirby, who had a death grip on his gavel, and his wife, who actually pulled out a nail file.

Emma continued, unperturbed by the rudeness. She read off her iPad, where, I assumed, she had a list.

"The floral arrangements will be done by Charlotte Bishop. I know you guys were thinking someone from Barreton, but Charlotte has agreed to help Lucille get the florist shop in the former bank building open for us."

"Excuse me," someone from the front of the audience said. "Did you say Charlotte Bishop? As in Rose's daughter?"

My face grew hot. Apparently, word hadn't traveled to every single person in town. It wasn't just that more than a couple of eyes swung toward me, seeking out a way to place the new face. It was that the woman specifically used my mother's name. Not the easier, and more fitting, Dr. Bishop's daughter or Gigi Bishop's granddaughter. No, they had to bring her and all the bad memories into it.

"Is that her?" someone whispered from behind me. Then the rest started murmuring.

"I didn't know she returned."

"Wow, takes a lot of nerve showing back up here after so long."

"She looks just like her mother," another said.

At the last comment, Henry placed his hand atop mine. He didn't try to hold it or pat it consolingly. It was just resting there as a comfort and weight. I didn't feel so alone in that moment.

Trying to shut out the whispers and the stares, I closed my eyes. The photo on Gigi's wall with me and the little boy with our toothless smiles flashed in my mind. "Henry," I whispered, and my eyes shot open.

He leaned over, and I took a deep, steadying breath. "Is everything okay?" he whispered, this time taking my hand and sandwiching it between both of his.

An image of a little boy laughing at a birthday party danced in my memory.

"Just thought of something," I said, smiling. "Thank you."

"Ms. Bishop," Kirby sneered.

I had two choices. Deliver what I had come for or bolt from the room.

"Yes, that's me," I said, standing up.

Kirby slammed the gavel down on the table so hard, the wooden disc it hit jumped. I geared up for a confrontation. I didn't like bullies, and this guy was obviously one. "Hi, Charlotte Bishop here, newly returned—at least for the moment—Hope Lake resident. I'll be designing the floristry work for the event; I have many ideas for how to really amplify the look of the festival. Nothing too mundane or traditional but eye-catching and bold. Something that really knocks the socks off the tourists who come in from the larger towns and cities. I'll put together something to show the planning committee to see. You'll have them rebooking their stays in Hope Lake if I have anything to do with it. I just wanted to say thanks again for the opportunity. I'm really looking forward to it. Stop in the shop in a couple of weeks after our grand opening. I'd be happy to help you."

As I moved to sit back down, my heart fluttering wildly in my chest, I was peppered with question after question.

"What made you come back?"

"Where are you staying?"

"Are you qualified to handle this?"

The last question was one that couldn't be ignored. I stood back up, rolling my shoulders confidently. "I'd say I'm more than qualified, actually. The last event I designed in New York was a society wedding at the Plaza. It featured more than one thousand authentic Dutch tulips that were flown in two nights before the event that needed to be incorporated into the design last-minute. Besides the decade of high-society design work and planning on my résumé, I graduated from Temple with a degree in business. I studied advanced floral design and ornamental horticulture in both traditional European and Asian designs under the best event planners and florists in the country. Any other questions?"

When I finished, I stood waiting for something, anything, to be said, feeling winded and drained. I was tired of trying to defend my capabilities and experience. I did enough of it in New York.

Henry took my clenched fist in his hand and gently pulled me down into the seat. Once I was seated, he took my hand between his again and just pressed. It was the calmest I'd felt in ages, and something that I couldn't explain away.

Emma walked over to Kirby, grabbed the gavel from his hand, and slammed it down onto the table. "Don't worry, I've got this under control. Ladies and gentlemen, while I understand that Charlotte being here is amazing and exciting news, let's just welcome her to Hope Lake and show her all the incredible things this community has to offer. Now, carrying on."

Emma floated into more about the festival. The urge to run out of the room screaming was palpable, but thankfully the whispering stopped. The group was instead hanging on Emma's every word as she discussed the food trucks that would be there, and the local bands from neighboring towns that would perform.

By the end of the meeting, Emma looked as exhausted as I felt. She and Cooper made their way over to me, Henry, and Nick.

"When you told me to come and introduce myself, you couldn't have prepared me for what I would face?" I asked, trying to sound lighthearted, but inside, I was a nervous wreck.

"You did great. But you need a break, and frankly, so do I," she explained. "Get some rest. I have a feeling we're all going to need it."

Giving me a quick hug, she took Cooper's outstretched hand to leave. Before they reached the door, she turned back. "And, Charlotte, I'm sorry if you felt like I set you up in front of a firing squad. I didn't think it through."

I gave her a small smile, not feeling like much more. Cooper bro-hugged his friends, and they walked out of the meeting room with a flurry of people following behind them.

"So," Nick said, turning to me. "Hungry? We're headed to Casey's to get some wings. Unless you're a vegetarian. Then we can . . . I don't know—eat grass?"

"Nick," Henry groaned. "You're endlessly tactless."

"I'm what?" Nick asked, scratching the back of his neck. "I'm going to assume that's an insult."

I laughed. "I'm not a vegetarian. I'd love to go for wings. Is that all right with you?" I looked at Henry. Nick glanced between the two of us curiously, then smiled.

Henry shrugged. It wasn't a yes or a no. It was an indifferent *whatever* if I ever saw one.

"Okay, great. Can I, uh, catch a ride with one of you? I am un-licensed, in case you hadn't heard."

It was Henry's turn to laugh. "Oh, we heard. Birdy was on a roll about it. Apparently, Duncan is considering you a more impressive collar than when he busted this one driving his tractor naked in O'Shea's field."

I raised an eyebrow at Nick. "Well, I'm sorry to have beaten you out of such an illustrious honor."

Nick wasn't blushing like I expected. If anything, he looked proud. "I wasn't naked, I'll have you know. I had something on."

"Something?" Henry barked, rolling his eyes. "Ask him what."

"Not sure I want to know!"

We were drawing attention to our conversation. "Let's get those wings," Nick suggested, ushering us out of the emptying room.

"How far away is this place? Maybe I can just walk?" I said as we exited the front doors of the town hall. It was a grand old building with a great big weeping willow out front.

"It's just down the street on the left. I drove, but my truck doesn't have room for three. Henry, I'll throw your bike in the back. You guys can walk so you can make sure she doesn't get lost. I'll meet you there." Nick took off toward the parking lot before we could answer.

"Well, I guess that's settled," I said, looking up at Henry. His head skimmed one of the low branches from the willow tree. The drooping leafy branches framed his head like a wig.

"What?" he asked when he saw me staring and smiling.

"I'm not sure," I said honestly. There was a flash of the same young face from the photo, but this time, those big blue eyes held an expression of pure sadness. "I can't explain it. Sometimes I get these weird, I don't know, I guess visions? Memories?"

"What was this one?" he asked, stepping forward to lead the way toward what I assumed was Casey's.

I stayed silent a beat too long.

"Of course you don't have to share," he said, sounding self-conscious.

"No, no, it's not that I don't want to. I'm still trying to get a handle on them. I never experienced something like this before, so it's an odd sensation when they hit me out of nowhere."

"Do certain things trigger them? The memories?" he asked, slowing his stride so I didn't have to struggle so much to catch up.

It was a sweet gesture.

"The first day I was here, I remembered a nurse from my dad's office, but only when I walked down the hallway. I mean, I have a hard time remembering college, and that was only nine years ago. I haven't lived here in twenty-one."

"And you were young. That doesn't help."

I nodded, leaving off the parts where my mother insisted for years that anything from Hope Lake was poison that would try to ruin my life as it had hers.

"Just inside, at the meeting, you pressed your hand on mine like a weight, and I think I remembered you doing that before. There's this crazy sense of familiarity, and yet I can't put the pieces together."

Henry smiled. "When we were kids, I used to take your hand like that when you were worried or anxious. You used to say that Gigi told you that it was like a hug—just feeling the weight would help. I'm not sure what made me do it tonight. I'm not even sure *if* I thought before I did it. It was like muscle memory, I suppose."

I smiled, putting my hand out. He sandwiched his over mine. "Whatever the reason, I'm glad you did."

He nodded. "I'm happy to help however I can, Charlotte."

Shivering a bit when the wind picked up, I tried tamping down the nervous feeling so that I could just enjoy the walk. It was a beautiful summer night, with a clear sky smattered with thousands of stars.

"I couldn't tell you the last time I saw a sky like this," I said dreamily. I imagined lying down on a blanket in the middle of Gigi's yard. Falling asleep under the stars.

"Yeah, New York isn't exactly the best place for stargazing."

I hazarded a sideways glance at him. "Visit the city often?" I asked curiously.

A beat passed, and then he shook his head.

It felt like there was a story there, but I didn't think he'd tell me tonight.

"While I'm thinking of it, we have a pretty good telescope at the school, if you're ever interested," he said, looking down at his feet. I couldn't miss the hopeful tone in his voice. "I'm no astronomer, but I could get a book for help."

"I'd like that, Henry." I liked saying his name. Simple, classic, and earnest. For as little as I knew about him, it seemed perfect.

"We're here, by the way," Henry said, pointing toward a building with a bright neon sign that read CASEY'S. "Nick's not here yet."

"How do you know?"

"He has his own parking space," he said, pointing toward a sign labeled:

PARKING FOR THE WING-EATING CHAMP ONLY

"You're kidding."

"I am not."

"This is a thing?"

"At Casey's it is. They host it every year. Nick has won every year. Between this and the Peep-eating contest on Easter, he's quite the food-consuming champion."

"Amazing. This place never ceases to amaze me," I said, thinking of the Nathan's Hot Dog Eating Contest every year. "You know, this is the first year that Parker—that's my roommate—and I won't be at Coney Island on the Fourth. That's so weird."

"You should invite her here. The wing-eating competition is on the Fourth."

I bumped my shoulder into his as we walked the last couple of feet into Casey's. "Maybe I will."

"I mean, we're no Coney Island, but we do have a couple of bounce houses and a dunk tank that yours truly volunteers for every year."

Henry wet and shirtless? Sold.

"Oh," he said, scrolling through the messages on his phone. "Nick just bailed. He has a *thing*."

I laughed. "That could mean a myriad of reasons."

We stood on the sidewalk, under the neon sign that illuminated the ground around us. We looked everywhere but at each other.

"So," we said together.

"You first," we said in unison followed by a laugh.

He held up his hand, waving it toward me. "Ladies first."

I mock curtsied and smiled. "I'd still like to have dinner, if you're up for it."

11

_____

held my breath waiting for him to answer. Maybe he was just interested when Nick was there as a buffer. The two of us alone may
not have been something that he was willing to sign up for.

His answer—a smile—made my heart skip two beats.

"I'm hungry," he replied simply. It wasn't exactly the glowing
acceptance that I was hoping for, but it worked.

Plus, I, too, was hungry.

I followed him into Casey's, a dimly lit space with an elbow bar
and a dozen or so tables of varying sizes. It was surprisingly crowded.

"Every night of the week, there's a special, so it's always crowded
at dinnertime. Even though the bar is up front, they allow families
at the tables," he explained, pointing over to where a couple sat with
their two kids.

He held up two fingers to a young waitress, who glanced in
our direction. She then proceeded to stroll up to us, beaming at
Henry.

"Henry, I've been wondering when you'd show up again. It's
been ages! I needed to thank you for everything you did for me and
Bridget with the Hemingway paper. It really pulled up our grades."

Oh, that wasn't what I thought she was going to say. I assumed
she would be flirting with him. That's what I would have done. I
rocked back on my heels and watched Henry's reaction.

He smiled; the tips of his ears pinked in the dim bar light. "No problem. I'm glad the extra help paid off. Never hesitate to ask. I'm always here to help former students."

She grinned. "Appetizer for you two is on me."

"Thanks, that's kind of you," I said, glancing around at the tables. "Anything open for two?"

"For you and my friend here, always."

But it was so crowded; our choices were limited. Instead of something cozy, she ended up leading us to a quiet table for four in the corner close to the long oak bar.

"Thanks," Henry said, smiling briefly.

She deposited two menus and flicked the beer menu that was already on the table with her long red nail. Henry walked around me and slid the chair out for me.

"Thanks," I said, sinking down onto the slightly wobbly seat.

There were three other seats, and I wondered which he'd choose. Where did I want him to sit? Either next to me or across from me. Next to me would be closer, but then I'd have to turn every time I wanted to look at him. If he was across from me, he'd be farther, but I'd be able to glance up at him over the flickering candlelight.

Okay, Charlotte. That's a bit much. It's a bar and dinner, not moony eyed romance.

He took the seat on my right, which meant I had to turn to talk to him, but if I wanted to, I could accidentally-on-purpose brush up against his hand. Or grab fries from his plate.

But I was jittery. Pulling the paper napkin into my lap, I tore at it systematically. It helped keep the nerves at bay.

Through the silence, I kept tearing small bits of napkin, piling them up in my lap. Glancing down, it looked like I was practicing making confetti.

"So, English, huh? Do you like teaching?" I asked out of the blue.

The reason for the nerves eluded me, but I thought they stemmed from having a history with Henry and not remembering it. Maybe it was the vestiges of a crush that I harbored at ten, or just the safety and innocence of reacquainting with a childhood friend again. Either way, there was a feeling simmering that made me fluttery.

"Yep, English." He smiled, pausing when a little girl wobbled between the tables. Henry cooed down at her, earning a toothless smile. It reminded me of the gentle expression he had when he kneeled down to speak to Gigi.

"I knew from a pretty young age that I wanted to teach. Reading was always a favorite pastime for me, so I put two and two together. The bookstore is an added bonus. I teach at Barreton U in the summer as an adjunct," he rambled, and I wondered if he was as nervous as I was.

A different waitress came over asking if we were ready to order. "I'm sorry, I didn't even look at the menu." I remembered a chalk sign with specials near the door. "Just two slices of pizza and an iced tea, please."

Henry looked surprised. "We can wait if you want to check the menu out. They have a ton of options."

I waved him off. "This is good. I like judging places on their pizza."

The waitress grinned and turned to Henry.

"I'll have the same as the lady," he said, smiling over at me.

After the waitress left, he said, "So, florist, huh?"

"Yep, I love it. And while I'm a nervous wreck about starting this place with Lucille, I'm excited, too."

"I think it's a great idea. Emma seems to think so, too. A vote of confidence from her is going to go a long way. She has a lot of clout in Hope Lake. How's Lucille to work with?"

I smothered a laugh. "Honestly? I have no idea. We've never met."

"Say what now?"

The waitress brought out the drinks and pizza, and I knew the pizza would be good. It was thin, cheesy, and looked like it had just the right amount of crunch to the crust.

"Yep, haven't met," I said, pausing to take a sip of tea. "We've talked and texted, but she said she's too busy running between here and Barreton, where her grandkids live, to actually meet in person."

"I have to admit, that sounds pretty awesome," he said, taking a large bite of the pizza. "Nerve-racking but awesome. What does she do, give you a budget?"

"Yep, exactly, and then I follow it and ask her for some direction if I need more money or need to change something."

I folded my slice together and bit down, moaning around the slice. "Delish. And, yes, it is totally nerve-racking, but she keeps insisting that I just do my thing. It's sort of crazy, but I think Emma worked her magic on her, so she trusts me. Plus, I promised I'm not out to screw her. That wouldn't have flown in New York, but here, you guys are unfailingly honest. It's refreshing."

"Thanks?" he said, laughing. "It's true, though. Most of the people here are kind and honest. Don't get me wrong, there's always a few weeds in the field, but for the most part, it's wildflowers."

I glanced up at him wide-eyed. "What did you say?" I asked, the words taking hold and settling. "I feel like I've heard that before."

Henry remained silent, instead, sipping innocently on his tea.

"Henry?"

"It's something Gigi used to say when we were kids," he said, and he seemed to feel guilty about admitting it.

My mouth fell open. "Why would she say that?" I asked, remembering the phrase but not the context.

"There were some . . . kids in fourth grade who were a bit on the cruel side. Gigi wasn't having it and would say things like that to make it a little better."

"Wow, really? I don't remember anyone making fun of me," I said, scratching my head. "Not that I remember much, but I figured that would have stood out."

He shifted in his seat, the wood creaking beneath his large body. "It was to make *me* feel better."

I blinked. Once again in sheer disbelief. "Kids were making fun of *you*?"

He nodded. "It's in the past. Gigi and, uh, some others were great for helping me through it. Once I had a growth spurt, the teasing faded away. It was tough being the smallest ten-year-old."

It was a growth explosion, not spurt, I thought, but judging by the way the waitress who'd just reappeared laughed, I said it out loud.

"Check?" she asked, still smiling at me.

It felt like we had just sat down, but after glancing at my phone I realized we'd been sitting there for nearly three hours chatting about work, his love for teaching, and my irritatingly inconvenient lack of memories. The time flew by in an instant.

Henry, to his credit, didn't laugh, but it looked like he wanted to. "Check is great, thanks."

After he settled the tab, we walked back into the town square area. Crowds milled about, tossing coins into the fountain in the center.

There were empty benches scattered throughout the walkway.

"Want to sit a bit?" I asked.

He nodded, waving his hand for me to have a seat. The bench wasn't exactly big, in fact I think I stopped in front of the smallest one. The one that put us nearly on top of each other. He shifted; I felt his thigh brush mine.

I placed my hand on my lap, and my pinky touched his knee. My face warmed, and I thought about how silly I was being over a slight pinky brush.

"What a gorgeous night," I finally said, leaning my head back. I was trying to focus on anything but the stretch of warmth that was building between our touching legs.

Henry mirrored my position, outstretching his long legs well past where mine ended but keeping them close to mine.

"I keep thinking about when you said that you were the smallest ten-year-old. I think I remember being really tall for ten. Now look at us."

Henry's long left shoe bumped into mine. "You were tall. You dwarfed me when we stood side by side."

I tapped his shoe back with mine. "Oh, how the roles are reversed," I whispered, feeling the rogue pinky brush his.

His hand fell to his side, putting it in the perfect place to touch mine. Intentional or not, it was the only thing I could focus on.

A peal of laughter filled the night, and I sat up quickly. I stood, stretched, and turned in a circle to take stock of our surroundings. Couples were kissing good night beneath the large trees that lined the pathways that surrounded us. This town pulled every bit of magic out of each night. It was convincing me in the best of ways.

He, too, stood and bent to touch his toes briefly before walking toward the road. He looked both ways and scratched his head. Henry didn't have a car or his bike, since Nick never dropped it off, and I had no clear way to get home, but I didn't worry about any of that. There was something peaceful about spending time with him, just us, and I wanted to do it again and soon.

"Henry," I said softly, feeling the flutter when he turned to me. The size difference was very noticeable here in the open. Without the walls of the bar closing in, he seemed like he was larger than life.

"Charlotte?"

I swallowed, swayed, and tried to find a focal point. That point just happened to be his lips. I leaned as he leaned, but his eyes cleared of the fog that had settled over both of us.

With my heart thundering, I took a shot. "Would you want to have dinner again sometime? One that's planned with just us in mind," I asked, hopeful. It was the first thing that came to mind and I didn't feel a stitch of regret. *Say yes. Say yes.*

He looked up to the sky. "Have you changed your mind?"

"My mind?"

"About staying? Here in Hope Lake?" he asked, and that hopeful tone nearly made me fall to my knees. "You said at the bookstore that this was temporary."

"No. I mean, I'll be here for the summer. That's sort of temporary, I guess. That's three months for us to get to know each other.

Again," I said honestly, thinking, *What guy wouldn't want something casual for the summer?* As soon as that thought entered my mind, so did Dr. Max. We'd been texting and it was nice, but for some reason I didn't feel guilty. Probably because we hadn't even been out on a date yet.

He exhaled, remaining quiet for a beat. "I'm sorry, Charlotte. But the answer would be no."

"Can I ask why?" I asked, more irked than hurt. I couldn't decide why I was annoyed, but I was. "I see you looking at me. I know you're attracted to me. I'm pretty sure you can tell that I'm attracted to you; if I'm wrong, that's on me."

Henry rubbed his large hands over his face, frustrated. His handsome face looked conflicted but steadfast. "You're not wrong, but Hope Lake is my home. Not New York or San Francisco—here. I'm still hopeful I'll have a life with someone who wants the same thing. *Here* is a part of that. You're right on all those other points, but I'm not a short-term or casual type of guy. I can't be, especially with you. You leaving again would really . . . well, let's just say something temporary wouldn't be good. It's not how I'm wired. Maybe it's old-fashioned dorky, but that's me, and I'm not going to—"

I held up my hand. "I get it."

Henry looked taken aback. "I'm sorry, that was rude of me."

I shook my head. "It wasn't. It was straightforward, but that's good. I know where you stand."

"I didn't mean to offend you." He began to reach out for my hand before he caught himself. "If I were a different man, I'd have asked you on a date the first day you arrived."

"Even though I'd just kicked you in the no-fly zone?" I teased, hoping to lighten the mood.

"Your efforts to get me an ice pack from your father would have sealed the deal."

"I'll remember that for next time," I sputtered, when I saw his wide eyes. "I don't mean when I kick you— Oh, never mind. We can still be friends, right?"

A sadness flickered in his eyes.

"Well, friends again."

Henry smiled, and for what was possibly the first time in my life, I had a grown-up discussion, semi-disagreement, and resolution with a man.

Like an adult.

And while the outcome may not have been exactly what I had wanted, I felt good about having another friend in Hope Lake.

"Friends, again," he parroted, and this time, he did take my hand. It wasn't a handshake or a fist bump. He just held my hand sandwiched with his for the briefest of moments, and I missed their warmth once he pulled his hands away.

Looking up at him, I felt the pull again. An invisible thread seemed to float between us. The Charlotte and Henry history may have been a mystery to my memories, but my feelings knew the whole story, and it seemed that they weren't going to make ignoring our history easy.

12

About a week after the council meeting, I was full steam ahead on the festival plans, and the work on the shop. It felt good to be making strides toward something that I was excited about.

"Can you guys see this okay?" I asked the four heads that appeared on my iPhone.

Screen: Emma, Dad, Gigi, and Parker. None of them could be here at the shop with me because of their hectic schedules, and in Parker's case, distance, but I wanted their input. The flower shop might be temporary, but there was no reason I couldn't make it as awesome as I could while I was here. Emma had surprised me with a conference call where everyone could see the progress unfolding.

"All good," Emma said.

"Yep," Parker replied, a smudge of flour dusted across her cheek.

"Looks great, Charlotte!" Dad said proudly.

"Put the camera back by that guy in the tool belt," Gigi shouted, earning a chorus of laughs from the workmen.

"Mom!" Dad shouted, gaining another round of shouts.

"Oh, live a little, Andrew," she cackled. "You're always ruining my fun."

"Dear God, control yourself, Gigi," I teased. "Just let me hook this up to the selfie stick Emma left."

Once my phone was on the stick, I toured the entirety of the shop for my family and friends. "The color green on the accent walls is perfect. Emma, good call. It looks beautiful against the other two cream-colored walls."

"Glad you like!"

"Charlotte, turn ninety degrees," Parker shouted over the sounds of the band saw the workers were using.

"What's going in the two large windows?" she asked. "Shelving or shirtless models?"

"I like the way she thinks," Gigi chimed in.

"Are those really my only two options?" I asked, smirking when I caught the workers listening in on the conversation. Not that it was hard—the phone was on speaker.

"Yes!" Gigi and Parker said in unison.

"I'm doomed with you two." I laughed. "Sorry to disappoint, but it'll be shelving." I aimed the camera toward the stacked wood planks on the floor.

"Listen, I'd love to stay on here and check these workmen—I mean your progress—out, but I have eleventy billion cakes to bake, frost, and deliver today. I love you, C."

With that, Parker was gone.

"What are those?" Gigi asked, pointing to something behind me.

Not something. *Something*.

"Oh, uh, just a test bouquet," I lied, turning the camera so they didn't see the vase full of flowers that were front and center on my worktable. The ones that were just delivered by FedEx and that didn't include a name—just a card with a single violet flower drawn on it. The bouquet was bursting with zinnias, foxgloves, irises, and sweet peas. It was beautiful but not exactly my taste.

"You don't have those types of vases," Emma chimed in.

Damn it. She knows the inventory that well?

"You're right, I don't," I said flatly, hoping the topic would drop.

I watched realization dawn on Gigi that they were *flowers*. Not of my own design, but from *someone*, and she had the most Gigi-like response.

"Oh, speaking of cakes to bake or something," Gigi said before clearing her throat loudly. "Andrew, we have that thing to do. Bye, Charlotte."

"What thing, Mom?" Dad said confusedly, looking at his mom, who had already hung up her phone and suddenly appeared in Dad's screen view, zipping over to him with her chair. "Hang up!" she howled, shaking her fist at her only child.

"Ow, uh, bye!" Dad said just as Gigi's hand connected with his arm.

"I'm going to pretend that all of this isn't hugely suspect and just go with the flow because I'm damn busy. Are you staying or also going in a weirdly suspicious fashion?"

Emma laughed. "I'm staying on for a bit longer. I'd like to know about the mystery flowers. So unless you want me to keep asking . . . spill."

Truth was, they were as much a mystery to me, too. "They showed up a couple of hours ago. Just the box and vase."

"No card, huh. I mean, they have to be from Max, right? Who else would send flowers?"

I shrugged, walking the phone over so she could see them clearly. "They're pretty. Not exactly what I'd pick for myself, but I can appreciate the design."

"They are a bit ostentatious," she agreed.

"This company isn't cheap, either. They're the kind that sell a design and then upcharge to get fuller bouquets. This has to be the top of the line," I explained, admiring the fullness of the arrangement.

"Are you going to ask Max?"

I nodded. "I texted him after they arrived. He hasn't responded yet, but he usually doesn't when they have patients all day."

"Are you still thinking of dinner? Drinks?"

"I know I've been on the fence with Dr. Max, but if I'm being honest, it'd be nice to socialize and get out to have some fun. At least he doesn't care that I'm not staying in Hope Lake.

"Yeah, I mean besides the stroll behind Gigi's house that night, there hasn't been a lot of time for us to get to know each other. Since he got back from New York he's been busy, and I haven't had a free minute to breathe, let alone date. I've been here twelve hours a day! Once the shop opens and I'll have normal hours again, I'll take him up on the offer."

I looked around the shop. Things were coming together, but there was still a bit of work to be done. I made a mental note to send a message to Lucille, telling her that we were in good shape but that we might not have all the product by opening day. The delivery schedule was a bit of a mess, but she said she'd handle it. A couple of more brutally long days on my end and things would be ready to roll. With any luck, I'd have a normal eight-to-four day—something I had been dreaming about for years.

"I can't believe this place opens so soon, Emma. Are you sure you don't want to wait until July for a big grand opening?"

"I'd love to," Emma said, her head moving in and out of the phone screen. "But with the festival, the timeline is too tight. At least this way we can get some excitement built for this place. PS, if I haven't mentioned it, Late Bloomers is a great name for the shop. Catchy."

I smiled. "I always said it's what I'd name my own shop if I ever got one. It's because you're never too late to find your *thing*. I think that's what sold Lucille on it, too. When we spoke before she left to visit her daughter, she said that she still hadn't come up with a name for the place. When I suggested it, she was sold."

"I love that she went with your idea. It's perfect. And I told you she wanted to be super hands-off."

"She is. It's a little crazy when you think about it. I keep thinking it's too good to be true, but she has agreed to everything I suggested so far."

Emma looked like the cat that got the canary. "Told you."

"Yeah, yeah. You were right. This has been great so far."

Emma smiled and pretended to brush off her shoulder.

"Oh! Have you seen the final logo? It's absolutely perfect. Tell your friend at the print shop thanks again for the design work. I adore it. I love that it's not super traditional but quirky with the stem being an actual stem to spell out the word. I just hope people like it. Like this place."

"Me too! And are you kidding? They're thrilled to help. Don't forget, this is business for them, too."

"True, true. I'm glad you keep as much as possible in town. Let's hope other people feel the same and want to order flowers from the new girl in town," I said nervously, wondering if they would pay it forward.

"They will! A couple people I spoke to are raring to go for the grand opening."

"Oh, that's good. A couple is good."

"Charlotte, I know that you're nervous, but you really don't have to be. I have a feeling that it's going to be great."

"How great?" I asked.

Emma laughed, not missing a beat. "More than great."

"Like, *superhero* great."

I closed my eyes, ignoring the looks from the workers, and from Emma, who was still staring at me expectantly from FaceTime. When I closed them, I saw two small girls, and I knew immediately it was me and Emma. We were at school and playing tag against a few boys, but we were dressed like characters from *The Justice League,* the DC comic that Emma and I were obsessed with. I was Batman and Emma was Superman.

Seeing all of us clicked something together piece by piece. I was seeing Cooper, Henry, Nick, me, and Emma.

"Huh," I said dreamily, opening my eyes again to the bright shop lights.

"Huh? That's all you got is *huh*?" Emma said exasperatedly. "You hardly remember anything, and you only give me a huh?"

I laughed, not out of humor but disbelief. "Okay, calm down, Dr. Phil. It's not like this was some magnificent discovery. It was a flash, barely a blip. Not even on the radar."

Yet, it didn't feel insignificant. It wasn't monumental by any measurable standard, but it wasn't anything to sneeze at, either. Locations, people, the smell of the town—the strangest things were bringing back the memories. The longer I stayed here, the more I'd remember. But the question that kept nagging me was *Do I want to remember?*

"Keep me posted about the flowers. I've got to run. Cooper has a couple of meetings that I want to sit in on."

I laughed. "You're a control freak."

"You're not wrong. Kisses!"

THE WORKMEN LEFT the shop just around dinnertime and around the same time that Max texted back.

MAX: If the flowers are from a secret admirer, the card is never signed . . . 😌

Okay, so does that mean he sent them? Or what?

ME: Well, whoever sent them, they're gorgeous.

Which they were. It wasn't a lie. They just weren't my taste. About twenty minutes later another text came through.

MAX: I was thinking.

ME: Sounds dangerous.

MAX: What?

My fear with text messaging/flirting/discussions was always that the sarcasm wouldn't come through. Clearly, Dr. Max wasn't as nuanced in the text game as I had hoped.

ME: Never mind. Bad joke. What's up? 😊

MAX: Notte's has an opening next Friday

ME: The restaurant?

MAX: Yep, with a new section that
overlooks the water.
Table for two . . .
Delicious pasta . . .
Wine . . .
MAX: Sound good?

It did. My stomach growled at the thought of a delicious Italian meal, but a romantic meal for two overlooking the water . . .

ME: What about wings and
pizza at Casey's?

It was a quick counter, but I wasn't sure why I rejected romantic and private for the casual and cozy.

It took Max more than a half hour to respond. I chalked it up to being busy instead of what it might have been—a bruised ego.

MAX: Pick you up after work? 😊

ME: Looking forward to it.

As the sun faded behind the mountains in the distance, the town square lit up in a magnificent color palette of oranges and yellows. The beams danced across the light gray stone of the water fountain that sat in the center of the square, creating an effect that looked similar to a crystal chandelier with the sprinkling water winking in the sunlight.

The stool for the workstation and the desk chair that I'd ordered for the office in the back hadn't come in yet, so I planted myself on the floor, my legs outstretched before me, staring out at the town. The floor was cool under my bare legs. My bones felt weary. Days of harder work than I'd done in ages were catching up to me. I kicked off my sneakers, wiggling out my sore toes. I'd need to get something with more support or in a week I'd be unable to stand, let alone work all day. My old once-supportive work shoes back in Brooklyn were a mess. Certainly not worth the money to have Parker ship them.

The last of the sun streamed into the stained glass window that was above the door, sending colors dancing around my bare legs. I closed my eyes and daydreamed, but the longer I sat there, the sleepier I got. It was getting so warm, even on the cool tile. The warmth wasn't helping the sense of exhaustion I was feeling. My father had texted earlier that he was on duty, which meant he was stuck picking me up after his last appointment to deposit me at Gigi's. But that wasn't for another half hour.

I started running through my list of everything that I needed to do:

1. Finish the shop, easy enough. *Not.*
2. Finish planning the grand opening.
3. Get some sort of plan together for the Fourth of July extravaganza.
4. Get a license? Maybe a scooter was easier than a car.

The list kept going on and on in my brain, exhausting me even more. How was I going to get all of this done? Was I insane? Yes, but I had to keep focused on the fact that this was a great opportunity. If I could pull this off, it would look outstanding on my résumé for when I started applying back home again.

Which would hopefully be soon.

I lay back fully, staring up at the copper-tiled ceiling. *One thing at a time*, I thought, counting the rows of old tile. A nap wouldn't hurt, right? It helped when I was feeling overwhelmed, and I was certainly up to my eyeballs with that.

Just as I was about to shut my eyes again, a shadow appeared in the window.

There were few people who could fill a space like Henry. The antireflective film on the window prevented him from seeing me wave. By the time I got up from the floor, shoes back on and out the front door, he was already jogging up the street.

"Henry!" I called out, but it was no use. The traffic, the birds chirping good night, and his hearing issues probably made it impossible for him to realize I was calling to him.

What were you going to say if he turned around? I thought, watching his fading form disappear around the corner and into the alley that ran behind the buildings on my side of the street.

My phone beeped just as I stepped back into the darkened store. Pulling up the Notes app, I added a reminder to get some nightlights so when I was here late, I wasn't wandering around in the total darkness until I could get to the light switches.

I checked the message.

NICK: Hey, goin' to Casey's with the
crew. Hungry?

> **ME:** Starving! Meet you there!
> **ME:** Oh! But I need a ride to
> Gigi's after.

NICK: I got you, no worries.

I called my father on the way out the door to let him off the hook for driving me around town. He was disappointed, but he also sounded relieved, and very tired. If he brought me to Gigi's, he would have to stay for a bit, and he sounded as exhausted as I felt.

"One of these days, I'd like to spend some time with my daughter. I feel like I'm seeing you less than when you lived three hours away. Why is that?"

"What can I say, I've been exceptionally popular since I've been back? This place knows how to keep a girl busy, Dad."

"Well, take it easy. I don't want to see you running yourself ragged like you did in New York. Limits are good, and you need to take care of yourself."

"Yes, Dr. Dad."

"Funny, but I'm being serious. Make good decisions."

"Are we still talking about my health?"

"Charlotte," he chided. "I'll see you later."

The walk to Casey's was quick. Even though the entirety of Hope Lake was about the population of my street back in Brooklyn, it didn't feel like I was missing much by not being in New York. It had so much within walking distance from work. It was kind of perfect.

The smells of Casey's hit me the moment the front door swung open. I popped inside, making my way toward the center of the place. I held my breath while I was looking around for Nick.

Just as I was about to give up, the door swung open again, and in walked Henry, not Nick. I felt a flare-up of nerves. *Friends, Charlotte.*

"Hey there!" I said, a bit too cheerily. I startled the couple at the next table. "Fancy meeting you here."

He looked confused. "Wasn't this planned? Nick called me and said we were all coming for dinner."

I covered my embarrassment quickly. "Oh yeah, yeah. I just expected Nick to be here first."

"He's never on time. We can sit and order, and he'll probably arrive just in time to eat. Let's grab a table," he suggested.

He guided us to an open table, his hand hovering near but never touching my back. I felt that same sense of familiarity—that burst of calm you felt when a friend was with you—but this was mixed with something else that I wasn't willing to address yet.

We chatted amiably about the shop; he was impressed with how much work was accomplished in such a short amount of time. We discussed the bookshop and how his being done with school gave him more availability there to run his book clubs. His explanation of genres and upcoming events made me realize how behind I was on popular fiction.

"When I'm done at the shop one afternoon, I'll stop in for a recommendation," I said, and he smirked. I got the feeling Henry could chat about books all day, every day.

"You guys ready to order?" the waitress said, sliding up to our table. I was so busy eyeballing the dimple in Henry's cheek that I didn't hear her approach.

"How about you order your favorites, and I'll help you enjoy them."

"Sounds good." He looked to the waitress. "We'll have two dozen garlic-Parmesan wings, that meatball appetizer with the mozzarella inside, and a couple of the HLBC grapefruit on draft. Oh, and Nana's special pizza. Anything else?" he asked me, folding up the paper menu and putting it back behind the napkin container.

"Is that enough for Nick, too?"

"Yeah, but he'll order more food when he gets here, I'm sure."

"Oh!" I shouted, waving to the waitress to come back. "Extra crispy on the wings, please. You mind?" I looked to Henry.

"Huh, that's how Henry always gets them," the waitress responded before walking away to put our order in.

Henry blushed.

Our phones buzzed at the same time. "Nick's not coming."

"Again?"

He shrugged. "He got tied up."

"Does he mean literally?"

"It's certainly possible. If he doesn't come home by morning, I'll send up the red flag." Henry chuckled. "You know, tonight is my only night off from everything. No tutoring, bookstore, or running around for Emma. I'm glad that I cut my run short to meet you here."

I glanced at his tattered shirt. It seemed to be a favorite of his to work out in. Flustered, I choked out, "You love to work out, huh?"

Again, Charlotte. You are a master conversationalist.

"Yeah I do. It helps clear my head after a busy day. It's solitary, though."

The waitress had brought over our beers, frosted mugs filled to the top with sweet-smelling grapefruit beer. Henry raised a mug. I mirrored him and waited for him to make a toast.

"To Late Bloomers," he said, clicking his glass lightly to mine. I smiled down at my lap.

The server brought out the food. It was way too much for just the two of us.

"This is a lot."

Henry smiled. "I figure—what you don't finish you can bring to Gigi. She loves these wings. We bring them over for her all the time."

"Another thing I didn't know about her," I said, finishing off my beer.

"The good news is that you have a lot of time with her now," he said, pulling a slice of pizza from the tray.

Henry waved the waitress over to get me another beer.

"None for you?" I asked.

"Nope. I'm a one-and-done kind of guy."

"Who's the Nana the pizza is named after?" I asked as the waitress brought me another frosted glass. I took a sip, loving the feeling of the chilled glass on my lips.

Henry looked up curiously. "Really? You don't know? I'm sorry, that was insensitive of me."

I shook my head, keeping the *How would I know?* snarky retort to myself. "Who?"

"Gigi, of course."

My hand held the mug in midair. "My Gigi?"

"The one and only. She's sort of like the town Nana, so Casey, who owns the place, named her favorite pizza after her as a bit of an homage."

Sipping the beer, I tried pulling my heart from the pit of my stomach. "I had no idea."

Henry took my hand over the table, rubbing the skin lightly. "Gigi means a lot to a lot of people here. You'd be hard-pressed to find someone that doesn't love her."

As I finished the second slice of Nana's pizza, I wondered if unbuttoning my pants would have been an acceptable move. "This is a lot of food, and I am done, after this one." I was uncomfortable, and so full of cheese and garlic, but I didn't care. I was happy, and a bit buzzed after the grapefruit beers.

My phone began ringing from my purse. "Oh, it's my dad. Give me a second."

I excused myself, standing up to wander between the tables. "Hey, Dad, what's up?"

"I'm just making sure you don't need that ride. I'm stopping into Casey's to grab dinner for Max and me, and I was going to run you to Gigi's while my order was getting done."

The joys of living in a town the size of a shoebox.

"Oh, I'm at Casey's now. I met Henry for some wings."

"Henry Mercer? Excellent. Glad to hear it. I'll be there soon if you want me to drive you to Gigi's. Or you can just stay with Henry. That works for me."

"Yeah, give me ten minutes to finish up."

I rejoined Henry at the table to find that he had already packaged up the leftovers. "You said you were done, and I figured you might be in a hurry, so I packed it," he explained, looking sheepish.

"Thanks, I'm in a bit of a hurry. My dad is coming, and I'm going to catch a ride with him."

"Oh, I would have driven you home," he said, sounding disappointed.

"Another night. I know Gigi has been asking where you've been. She mentioned needing to talk to you."

"I see. Um, tell Gigi I've been busy trying to square the summer up. I'll be sure to stop over soon."

He handed me the take-out bag, his hand brushing mine. I flashed back to the pinky brushing the other night on the park bench, and my stomach filled with butterflies again.

"I'm sure Gigi will call and thank you for saving her from eating my cooking."

The waitress dropped the check on the table, but Henry snatched it before I could grab it. "My treat. No arguments. I know you're going to try, and just know that you're going to lose."

I opened my mouth to argue but thought otherwise. "I'll just simply say thank you, then."

"You're more than welcome."

"This was fun. We'll have to do it again sometime."

Henry's eyebrows raised expectantly.

"As *friends*, Henry. We could make sure everyone comes next time."

Henry and I walked toward the front of the restaurant, just as my dad walked in.

"Henry," Dad cheered, clapping him on his broad shoulder.

"Dr. Bishop," Henry responded, holding out his hand to shake my father's.

"Good to see you. How're your parents? Haven't seen them in a bit. Tell your father we'll have to go golfing," Dad rambled. I dare say he might like Henry more than I did.

Henry turned to me. "This was fun. I hope we can do it again. Maybe after the grand opening, when your life has calmed down a bit. We'll get the whole gang back together."

I hazarded a glance at my dad, who was trying to look anywhere but at us. Which meant he was trying and failing to avoid listening to the conversation. "I'd like that. Sounds like fun."

Henry slid forward, gently gripped my bent elbow, and kissed me lightly on the cheek. My eyes closed, and I leaned in as he was backing up, making it an awkward transition.

Middle name, thy name is awkward.

After he left us, Dad rolled his eyes, earning a playful slap to his arm.

"Stop it. He's nice, and we're adults."

"He *is* nice, and you are adults, but—"

"Father, don't."

"Don't make me give you the talk again. I've got plastic anatomical models to really bring the point home," he offered, and I had the worst flashback of my father and Gigi trying to explain the birds and the bees to me in a Manhattan hotel room when they had visited sometime around my twelfth birthday.

"No, please and thank you. No need for the talk again. I'm still scarred from it the first time around."

"Suit yourself. My anatomical dummies have been improved.

Someone drew happy faces on the ovaries," he said, hiding his smile as best he could.

"I sincerely hope you're still using them *with* the happy faces."

"Of course I am. It's hysterical and helps to put kids at ease when they have questions. Anyway, enough about smiling ovaries. How did this whole dinner arrangement happen? Just curious. Are you remembering your connection?"

"Not exactly. I get blips on the radar. I'm hoping the more I'm around everyone the more I remember. Nick, Emma, and Cooper jarred some stuff loose. Henry, well, he seems to be my sticking point."

"From a medical standpoint, it's amazing to know that you're gaining some memories. From a fatherly perspective—well, for me, it seems like no time passed with all of you. You're still the same little kids you were all those years ago. Henry still looks at you like . . . you know what." He paused, glancing at his watch. "Oh, look at the time. I have to go."

I touched his arm. "Looks at me like what?"

"I shouldn't have said anything," he apologized, looking mad at himself for the slip. "I don't want to mess with whatever's going on. I have a feeling you'll remember everything in time."

Once we were in the car and on the way to Gigi's, I texted her to see if she was awake. If she was, my dad would come in. If not, he'd just drop me off. Her response was pure Gigi.

GIGI: Tell your father he doesn't have to check up on me. I'm not dead yet.

> ME: I love you, I'll see you in a couple minutes.

GIGI: Go out, have fun. Make bad decisions.

> ME: Dad literally told me I needed to make good decisions only a couple hours ago!

GIGI: God, he's a buzzkill.

I barked a laugh, making my father jump in the driver's seat. "What is she saying?"

I slid him a glance. "You don't want to know."

"She's a spitfire, but, Charlotte . . ." His tone got serious all of a sudden. "I'd like you to try to convince her to let a nurse come in. Just once in a while."

I knew it was coming. I could see how tired and how stressed over her well-being he was. It was another point reminding me how unavailable I'd been. How little I knew.

I sighed. "I know that would be best for her, but I doubt she'll go for it. She's so independent. She won't let me help her with anything." Part of me wanted to say, *I'll be here. I can help*, but there was no point in offering. We both knew there was no guarantee on that.

"You say independent, I say stubborn. She had a pretty bad fall earlier in the year that she hasn't fully recovered from," he explained sadly.

"I didn't know that," I said, trying to keep the hurt from my voice. "You didn't mention it."

He shook his head. "You were stressed and so busy with your job. I didn't want to give you something else to worry about."

I nodded. He was right, but it didn't make it okay, and it certainly didn't feel good. I should have been here.

"I should have come sooner," I whispered. "Spent time with her before all this happened."

Dad took my hand. "Put that thought out of your head. You're here now. The best thing you can do is have quality time with her."

I nodded weakly. "I'll see what I can do to convince her. Maybe if it's a male nurse she'll go for it."

"If she would, I'd find one tomorrow. I'm worried all day long when she's alone."

He pulled into the gravel drive, the stones crunching beneath the tires. "I'll try to see what I can do," I said again.

My dad squeezed my hand. I got out slowly, carrying the pizza that Henry had packed up. My father waved, waiting in the car for me to get onto the porch before pulling away.

With the bag at my feet, I sat on one of the rockers, enjoying the warm breeze. The clear sky reminded me of a week ago, when Henry and I had walked to Casey's the first time.

I tipped my head back against the chair and closed my eyes, hoping to let the ache and worry ease out of my body. I tried to enjoy the sounds around me—the crickets that were being noisy on the edge of the porch; an owl that hooted from the massive oak tree that grew beside the master bedroom window.

Checking my watch, I weighed my options. Head to bed a bit on the early side, or stay up watching television awhile and risk getting my second wind.

I yawned just as something howled in the distance. "Bed it is," I said, standing and stretching my arms over my head. Grabbing the bag, I opened the screen door and stopped short.

Lying by the front door was a small, hand-tied bouquet of wild-flowers: a few black-eyed Susans, coreopsis, and lupines. They were common in this area, some even growing near Gigi's fence. *These are far more my speed*, I thought, wondering if Max had realized that his original, overly designed bouquet wasn't exactly my taste. A pang of guilt hit me. Here I was getting upset that Henry didn't want to date me, when there was a wonderful, handsome doctor who sent me flowers.

A small cream-colored envelope sat beside it, wedged by the door. Carefully, I pulled it out, admiring the artistic penmanship.

> *Not sure if a florist gets flowers.*
> *Thought they might brighten your day.*

I floated into the house with a smile on my face.

13

"Hey," I said, looking up to see Max standing beside my booth at 81 Café.

"Hey, yourself." Max smiled, tapping the menu in his hand against the corner of the table.

"Fancy meeting you here," I said, surprised that he managed to escape the office for lunch. I looked around, for what I didn't know. "Want to join me?"

I shifted in my seat awkwardly as he took his. Do I ask him about the flowers? It's not that I was nervous, but I had an overwhelming feeling of being in a bit over my head. Thank him? Buy him lunch?

I kept my eyes on the menu trying in vain not to smile, but he made it hard. He was just staring at me and smiling. No sexy quips, or cute jokes. Just his presence left me unsettled—in a good way. He was almost hard to look at, if that made sense. He was that attractive that I think a nun would take a second—or third—glance in his direction.

"So what are you getting?" I finally asked. "I mean, do you have time to eat, or are you just grabbing takeout?"

Max folded his hands on the table. "I'm free for about an hour. A patient canceled, so I thought, why not. Nice day to get some fresh air. Running into you was a bonus."

The heat crept up, warming my cheeks. "I agree. How've you been?" I asked, wondering if he would bring up the flowers.

He took a sip of the water that Clara set down. "Busy. I'm sure
you can say the same," he said, glancing at the long to-do list that
was beside my phone.

I slapped the list with my hand. Maybe if it was out of sight, it
would be out of mind, too. Unlikely, considering that it was almost
noon and I hadn't even started it yet.

"Can I help?" he offered, pulling one finger at a time off the
paper. He glanced at it, reading down the extensive list. In truth, it
wasn't *that* bad, considering all of it was to be done at Gigi's. It was
just a matter of gearing up to get it done.

"I appreciate the offer, but it's not really anything that anyone
can help me with," I said, the guilt spilling over. "Truth is, I've been
so swamped with the shop that I feel like I've been neglecting Gigi,"
I said honestly.

He shook his head. "You're busy. Anyone can see that, but I'm
sure she doesn't feel that way. In fact, I know she doesn't. She's so
proud of you and happy that you're opening the shop."

I smiled. "Still, I feel guilty. I'll just keep it in mind that you
insist she's okay."

"Well, if you change your mind, you know where to find me."

As I was about to invite him over to help, his phone dinged
loudly. He sighed, looking utterly disappointed. "Apologies. It
appears I have to go after all."

"Well, it was a nice run-in—even though it's been cut short," I
said, genuinely sad that he had to leave. "Another time."

"I'm going to hold you to that. I'll be in touch," he promised,
offering a wink before departing.

"GIGI, I NEED to know why on earth you have so many Tom Hanks
movies? Doubles and triples of each one?" I yelled, but I was met
with silence. Four copies of the *You've Got Mail* DVD in hand, I
came out into the hallway, only to stop short.

She yelled up, "Because he's an American treasure."

"Agree, but that's no reason to have four copies of one movie."

In the past few days, I had become quite the expert at dancing and pivoting around boxes, shimmying between large plastic tubs full of unopened wares and obscene stacks of boxes filled to the brim with DVDs. Gigi was a DVD hoarder of the most ridiculous order. She had full seasons of *Baywatch*, *The Carol Burnett Show*, *The Dean Martin Celebrity Roast*, and every season of *The Muppet Show*. Plus, every single Tom Hanks movie ever made. My dear Gigi had turned one of her spare bedrooms into a Blockbuster.

When I finally reached the end of the hallway, I spied her at the bottom of the steps, exactly where I'd left her. A small wooden table sat next to her with the house phone—yes, she still had one of those—and a bottle of beer.

She wasn't answering me because she was too busy laughing while sitting in her wheelchair. "I love you, but don't poke fun at my stash. No one messes with that room."

"What the hell does that mean? Is it like something from Stephen King? Is it haunted? If I turn around and there are creepy twins at the end of the hall, I'm burning this place down. Am I going to go insane now?"

"Short trip," she mumbled with an added snort. "That room is full of essentials," she howled. She pointed her wiry arthritic finger at me. "None of that is to be thrown away or sold until the perfect time."

I rolled my eyes. "Oh yeah? When is that perfect time?"

"You'll know it when it gets here."

"Gigi, you're being obtuse."

"Oh, look, someone got a thesaurus. Or maybe it's because you're hanging around Henry Mercer lately and he's rubbing up on you."

I barked a laugh. "It's rubbing *off* on you, and you know that. Stop changing the subject. The first spare room I cleaned out for you was a breeze. The rest of this seems excessive and, frankly, wasteful." Which I thought would be the opposite of Gigi.

"Well, it's over now, anyway," she said, looking genuinely sad.

"What is? The shopping spree?"

She nodded, then scooted herself closer to the stairs. For a moment, I thought she was going to climb them. I stood, ready to head down the stairs to help.

Instead, she just touched one of the low frames, this one of her holding a very young Andrew Bishop. "Your dad stopped in one day when UPS was delivering, and he had a bit of a hissy fit. The driver usually brings it all upstairs for me since, you know . . ." She motioned to her chair. "If he's unable, Nick or Henry usually does it."

"So what happened when Dad saw the guy?" I asked, but I knew the answer before she said it. Knowing how my father worried about her, this must have made him crazy.

"He wasn't mad at the driver. He's the usual guy who's all around town. Everyone knows him. I'm pretty sure he went to school with the boys," she said, referring to Cooper, Nick, and Henry. I had come to find out she called them that often.

"It was the situation, right? You had a stranger walking around your house. A thousand what-ifs probably worried Dad sick, Gigi."

She nodded. "What-ifs put an end to my fun." As she said it, her eyes skirted away.

"Gigi . . . ," I said suspiciously.

"What?" she replied innocently.

"You haven't stopped, have you?"

Her pale skin flushed the slightest pink. "Technically yes."

"Imogen Genevieve Bishop, are you still shopping online in mass quantities?"

She pursed her lips. "I've cut way back."

"Gigi . . ."

"And they're not delivered here anymore. Henry lets me send them to his house."

"Gigi! You've made him an accomplice!"

She laughed. "Oh, calm down, your little sweetie is safe. Andrew loves him."

I wanted to explain, *He's not my sweetie*, but this wasn't the time nor the place.

"Is this why the door was locked with two deadbolts and a skeleton key?"

She shrugged as if it was perfectly normal. None of this was ordinary, but really, when was Gigi ever a typical grandmother?

"Gigi, why are you really keeping all this stuff?"

"A rainy day?"

I walked down the steps, only to see her wiping away a tear. Sitting on the bottom step, I took her hand. "Gigi."

"When your mom—" She paused, biting her lip as if to not say something negative about her. "When you left Hope Lake, all of us took it really hard. Some more than others, but all of us had to find a way to deal with the emptiness however we could. Mine was this," she whispered, squeezing my hand. "An Easy-Bake Oven, Barbies, LEGOs—you know, whatever you liked. I would buy them and store them away for when you visited. I know it's not great to spoil a kid in a divorce, but I didn't care. I just wanted you to come back and be happy for a while."

"But then I didn't come back," I said, feeling the tears well up. "And you just kept buying things and hoping that I would."

She nodded. "I know it's ridiculous, but it made me feel better. I went through and donated a ton of it to charity when you outgrew it."

"Too bad, I would have still built the LEGOs."

"They're in the closet stacked along the wall. They were always your favorite. I didn't have the heart to get rid of those."

Leaning over, I gave her a gentle hug. "Thank you, Gigi. I'm sorry I didn't make it back until now."

I felt the tears on my shoulder. "You never have to apologize for that," she whispered. "You have nothing to be sorry for."

"I do. Maybe it was my mother's fault when I was younger. But after she died, there is no excuse." A tear dropped down my face. "On a serious note, how are we going to hide all this stuff from my dad?"

Gigi took my hand. "Oh, cookie, I'd never make you lie to your father. I'll come clean one of these days. I just . . . ," she began, but her soft smile faded. Her watery gray eyes looked resigned, sad.

"Sometimes, I get lonely and I still like getting the deliveries. The visits and the friends stop after a while. When you're my age, time passes slowly while you're waiting for what's to come. When I'm alone, I think a great deal about my legacy. What people will remember me for. Was I a good mother? A good doctor? A good wife? My Stanley will long be remembered for leaving his mark on the world with his imagination and words, but what about me? It's a bit selfish, but I'd like to be remembered, even if it's just for a small fraction of my very long life."

She looked so small in that moment and I hated myself more than when I arrived. Not that I was the answer to all of her problems with loneliness, but if I had been here, I could have helped quell some of it. Stave off the sadness she felt by spending time with her more often. Knowing this, I needed to remember to make time for Gigi, no matter where I ended up living permanently.

"Gigi, I think people are going to remember you in a way that will have them talking about you for decades," I said, a tear slipping down my cheek.

Wiping it away, I smiled, hoping that any trace of sadness was gone. "As a hoarder."

"Oh, you're a smart-ass," she laughed, punching my shoulder weakly.

"Seriously, though, I was thinking you can sell it. Most of this stuff was for you anyway, so why couldn't you have a big old yard sale and pocket the cash," she said.

"Gigi," I said sternly. "That's not funny. This is your stuff."

She harrumphed. "What did I say the first day you showed up on my doorstep looking like a couple of miles of bad road? This is *your* house. Not your dad's, yours, which means all the crazy shit inside is yours. Sell it, burn it, give it away to charity. It's your choice."

The possibility of a yard sale had merit. And it's not like it was a secret that I needed the money. "I'll make a deal. We'll go through it all together and save a couple of the truly classic Gigi purchases. We'll put the rest up at a yard sale, and we'll celebrate with a fancy dinner and some of that wine you sneak when you think I'm not looking."

"Deal."

With a weak squeeze of my hand, she gave a small yawn. "All this excitement has me in need of some shut-eye. And maybe another beer," she said, tapping her empty bottle on the table. "This was the last one I had." She looked at me expectantly.

"How, pray tell, do you expect me to get to the brewery or the store without a car or a license? Fly? Do you have a magic carpet somewhere, Aladdin?"

Gigi looked at me sagely but also like Jafar with the lamp. "I have a special guest stopping in to help you with the last room down the hall from yours. Upstairs, the last room on the right."

"That sounds like a horror movie," I teased.

"Hush now, that room is a favorite and I miss it. It was my Stanley's, and I haven't been in there in forever. After you peruse that room, our special guest will take you to HLBC afterward for a beer, and don't forget to get me a case. I prefer the blood orange, please, and thank you."

"Is that all I'm going to get? I just sit here and wait for someone to appear?"

Gigi laughed. "No, my sweet and silly girl. You're going to go back upstairs, put all that shit back into the room neatly, shower, do something with your hair, and he'll be here in an hour."

Vague much?

With that, she wheeled herself down the hall and into her room, where she promptly closed the sliding doors, leaving me on the step confused.

I WASN'T PACING, per se, but I wasn't *not* pacing, either. The shiny hardwood floor creaked beneath my feet as I wandered back and forth in front of the front door. I kept it open, hoping to be able to see the car when they pulled in.

I had a sneaking suspicion it was going to be Henry. I couldn't place why he was my guess, but he was. Gigi seemed to favor him. Maybe it was wishful thinking.

I was so deep in thought that I hadn't noticed that the double doors to Pop Pop's office were propped open. Normally, they were always closed. Even as a kid, I hardly ever went in there because it always made Gigi sad. This year would mark twenty-five years since he had passed.

Tonight, I didn't know if it was accidental that they were open or if Gigi had been in there and didn't close them all the way. I tiptoed over and peered inside. Like every other room, save for the As Seen on TV room, it was meticulously maintained. Gigi had a pair of cleaning professionals come in weekly, but this was more than that.

The shelves were all perfectly aligned with rows and rows of books. Peppered in between were photos, much like the ones that dotted the walls throughout the house: Pop Pop stationed at various locations in World War II. His and Gigi's wedding, Dad's first birthday, and more highlights of their amazing life together.

Pop Pop's desk appeared as if it was in the same condition as it had been just before he passed away. The wheeled leather chair was even pivoted as if he were going to walk in at any moment and sit at his typewriter. There was even a sheet of paper popping out of the top of the typewriter waiting for his words. "Do you remember him?" Gigi said from behind me.

My hand flew to my chest, and I turned. "Gigi, you scared me."

"Apologies. I was just wondering. I'm at the age where I'm forgetting the little things, and that bothers me. It never felt like we had enough time together."

"Quality not quantity, right?" I said, taking her hand.

She smiled in agreement, squeezing my hand. With a quick sputter, she pushed the joystick to guide us around the room, pausing every few steps to explain a detail.

"Nearly everything in here is older than you; isn't that incredible? These books have lived such a life. There's so many stories in here."

"I bet there's a lot that aren't even in the books," I said, taking a book down from the first shelf in the corner.

"Is this Pop Pop's first?" I asked, reading the dark green spine. It had ornate gold letters on the fabric cover.

No dust jacket like the newer books had. Just old craftsmanship.

THE CATACOMB MYSTERY

Gigi took it carefully, cradling it in her delicate hands. "Yes, I was so proud when this came home with him. It was the first copy ever printed, too. He got to watch it being made. I don't know if that's even allowed anymore."

"Maybe Henry will know. We can ask him when he gets here," I said, hoping she'd nod or give me some indication it was Henry we were waiting for.

"Good try. Be patient. That goes for everything, too. Don't be in such a rush. Time moves fast enough the way it is. Don't go chasing it with a stick to get it going quicker."

"Okay, okay, wise one."

Gigi slapped me on the rear end before scooting forward with the original book on her lap. Each one she picked up had a story. I knew Pop Pop was prolific, but I hadn't realized how many books he'd actually penned. "Gigi, have you read all of these?"

"Most, not all. Once he got sick, I had a hard time keeping up with them. He had so many written and they were publishing them slowly, I think to stretch it out after he died. After he passed away, dozens more came out in the years that followed. They sent them, of course, but I just had Mancini, or your father, put them away in here. I never opened many of them."

"Can I? I won't have time for all, but I'd love to read some of them."

Gigi smiled. "Darling, these are as much yours as they are mine. Read whatever you like."

There was a quiet knock on the door. "Coming!" I called, looking to Gigi for some indication of what was going on. Of course, I got nothing.

"Have fun. But not too much fun." Gigi winked.

"Scandalous!" I joked, kissing her cheek before stepping out of the room.

I braced myself, still hoping it was Henry.

But Henry made it clear . . .

I know, I know.

I took the final step to be directly in front of the door and looked up expectantly, only to have my heart speed up double-time.

"Hi, Charlotte," he said, standing on the porch, looking shy and awkward. I couldn't understand why, but whenever I saw him, he appeared unsure of himself.

"Henry." I gave him a small wave.

"Oh, for pity's sake, invite him in, girl!" Gigi howled, zipping behind me to wave to Henry.

"Blood orange, don't forget it!" she shouted before disappearing down the hall and into her room.

"Oh, this was on the door," he said, holding up a small white envelope.

My eyes grew wide.

"Oh, shit. Thanks, I'll be right back."

The envelope felt like a grenade in my hand the way Henry eyed it suspiciously. In the small first-floor bathroom, I tucked it into the closet between two fluffy ivory towels and joined Henry back in the foyer.

"Everything okay?" he asked, glancing at my empty hands.

I nodded, adding a forced smile. Truth was, I didn't have an honest answer for him.

14

If anyone in town didn't know we were preparing for the grand opening of Late Bloomers, they weren't paying attention. We papered signs all over the place. All over every. Single. Business. I was pretty sure my dad had informed everyone he knew in Barreton and Mount Hazel as well. Between his and Dr. Max's coverage in the surrounding towns, we had almost the whole county covered and excited.

Between them, Henry, Nick, and Cooper, it was teamwork at its finest. Of course, Mancini and Gigi threw in their support by emailing the senior groups. Apparently, they were well versed in social media, because they offered to run a Facebook page for me.

I was starting to see why these people, my friends, loved Hope Lake so much. Everyone pulled together. There wasn't a one-upmanship where one business tried to get ahead of another.

"Are you ready?" Emma asked, when I opened the door after she picked me up at Gigi's to take me to the shop. The sun was barely up, just rising over the mountainside in a brilliant orangey-red like the petals of a lily.

"As I'll ever be," I said honestly, the butterflies erupting in my belly. "I can't believe today is the grand opening."

We pulled down the road, heading toward the diner. "Plan the same?" I asked.

The plan was to hit the diner sometime around ass-crack-thirty, then go to the shop by seven for one more walk-through/panic session. Gigi suggested I try a bit of yoga to calm down somewhere in there, but that wasn't going to happen. I was way too anxious for that.

"Yep, breakfast and then your big day."

"I'm not sure I can eat. I'm not nervous. Just sort of, I don't know, overwhelmed."

"Overwhelmed I can work with," she insisted as we pulled into the lot of the 81 Café again. No surprise, even at 5:30 a.m. it was packed to the gills with cars.

"Again, I say to you, are they giving something away?"

She laughed. "Charlotte, you only had lunch here one time, and unless someone else brought you, you haven't been back since."

"Well, I did see Dr. Max here during lunch last week . . ." I raised an eyebrow, waiting for her reaction.

"Oh, really." She pulled up her sunglasses to give me a look. "And?"

"Dr. Max has been great. He's giving me space to figure out what the hell I'm doing with the shop, and with Gigi and the house. My free time has been at a premium, but he doesn't seem to mind. I'm sure after the opening today, we'll find time to get together again."

"That's a good sign. A guy who isn't trying to wedge himself into your life in every free second."

She zipped into the reserved spot for the mayor. "We don't have a lot of time. What do you want?"

"It's breakfast, Em. Get whatever you want. I trust you," I insisted, really meaning it. Next to Parker, I knew that Emma was creeping into best-friend territory and that I could count on her for anything.

After she returned with our breakfast, we were on our way to Late Bloomers.

"SO ARE YOU still overwhelmed?" Emma asked as she moved some papers off the counter.

"Don't take this the wrong way, but I'm just worried about your prospective numbers for the business."

Emma had submitted projected reports to both me and Lucille of how the business would do. It was how she rallied support behind it. While I didn't necessarily need to worry, I still did. If I failed, the business failed, and then I ruined a chance I had to really build something.

Emma looked mildly offended with thin lips and her brows furrowed, but it passed quickly, and her dark eyes twinkled. "I'll have you know I'm like Santa. I always make my list and check it twice."

"Ho, ho, ho. I get it. It's just a lot of pressure. What if this is a categorical failure?"

She shrugged. "You have numbers to support it. If we didn't, no one would have gone through with this in the first place. Charlotte, why the sudden onset of doubt?"

I sighed. "I really didn't want this to turn into a friggin' therapy session."

"If I promise not to charge you for the advice, will you let it all out?" she said, grabbing my hand.

"Maybe not all of it—that still needs those beers you promised."

"Deal."

"I just keep hearing my mother in my head telling me that this place ruins people . . ." I took a deep breath.

"Why now, though? Or has she been in your ear since you arrived?"

I swallowed, thinking of a way to explain this without sounding like someone who needed to be committed. "It feels like whenever I think I'm happy, or could be happy here, it starts up."

"I suppose that's possible, but I also think you're afraid to let yourself *be* happy."

I parroted the words back to her. "I suppose that's possible. My focus has been on the grand opening since you told me about this harebrained idea. To make it wildly successful, to drive excitement, but think about it, would people be interested in a flower shop?

Especially one run by a has-been florist? Could this town even sustain it after being so used to whatever was included in the Shop n' Save?"

Emma cleared her throat. "First of all, it's a little late to be asking that now, Charlotte." She tried sounding aloof, but worry betrayed her smooth voice. "Charts and numbers seem to think so, but who knows for sure. Death and taxes, my friend. Those are the only two guarantees."

I shrugged. "What's the second of all?"

Her answer was quick this time. "Honestly? What do you care if it fails? You won't be here."

I reared back. "Ouch."

"Honesty, my friend. I'm not a fan of lying. Especially not to friends who are doing me a serious solid. If this goes belly-up, it's my head on the line, but—and this is a very big but—I don't believe it will. I've seen what you can do and what you've created in a short amount of time. I think people are going to fall in love with your creativity and your infectious spirit and keep finding ways to come back to Late Bloomers. So, chin up. I have faith in you. You need to have it in yourself."

"You're right. Okay, let's get to work," I said, putting all my fears aside to open my first shop.

WE WERE HIDING out in the back room. We'd done the walk-through, artfully arranged the vases what felt like a hundred times, re-arranged my desk by stacking and restacking the order forms that would hopefully be filled. Emma even went so far as to vacuum the floor because it would *pass the time*. With just a half hour to go before showtime, we holed up in the back near the coolers so we couldn't obsessively stare out the front window looking for potential customers.

"Maybe we should just take a peek?" she sputtered, and it was a relief to see a nervous Emma.

"Aren't you nervous? Why aren't you nervous? Why am *I* nervous? You look calm. What the hell, man? This isn't my venture, it's yours," Emma rambled, biting at her smartly manicured nail.

I spun around, pointing a finger accusingly at her. "You ass. I wasn't nervous, but now I am. Why are you talking? Stop talking."

"What if no one shows? What if the flyers blew off the poles? What if it's just your dad, Dr. Max Hotness, Gigi, and Mancini here?"

"Dr. Max Hotness?" I laughed, grateful for the bread crumb to focus on instead of the doom and gloom what-ifs.

She looked at me with a confounded expression. "Don't tell anyone that I call him that!"

"Sure, sure. I'll keep your squirrelly nicknames to myself."

Emma turned, advancing on me so quickly I stumbled back. "While I'm thinking of it. Did you ever figure out if he sent the obnoxious bouquet?"

I nodded, popping a Tic Tac into my mouth. "He basically said it was him without actually confirming it was him."

"What the hell does that mean?"

"I asked him, and he said something like 'Secret admirers never sign their cards.'"

"Oh, good. At least you know it was from him and not some rando trying to fix you up."

"There have been a couple others, though. He hasn't mentioned them, and I haven't brought them up, either."

"Other what? Flowers?"

"No, no. Envelopes with nice messages. Heartfelt quotes from famous poets or lines from love stories. I've been researching them because I'm not familiar with any of it."

"That's wickedly romantic, and I hate you just a little for it. Cooper isn't a love-letter kind of guy. More like a sexy look followed by . . . TMI. Sorry. Anyway, the secret-romance stuff must be nice. Max doesn't strike me as the romantic type, but I've been known to be wrong."

"Anyway, you can keep swooning over Dr. Max, and I'll keep it from your beloved fiancé."

"Oh, please. He knows. I get a bit tongue-tied."

I waggled my eyebrows. "Oh, really?"

"About a month ago, I stopped by Henry's parents' house to say hello, and Henry's father was still on the treadmill. Sweaty gray T-shirt, Harrison's normally perfectly coiffed hair was drooping in his eyes. Needless to say, I took one look at him, sputtered something incoherent, and promptly walked into the doorframe, knocking my sunglasses off my face."

"Hopeless," I added playfully.

Emma looked at her watch. "I can't take it anymore. I need to look." With that we both went up front and saw a group of people waiting out front.

"Still worried about my numbers?" Emma said with a laugh.

"THE LINE IS down the block," I said, shaking yet another hand of a person whose name I couldn't remember. Dozens of people poured through the front door when we opened and hadn't stopped since. It was so busy that we had Nick working the door to welcome people in and chat while they waited outside.

"The good news is, the other businesses down this end of the square are loving the foot traffic!" Emma said excitedly, waving to someone she knew.

"Thank you! See you next week for the birthday flowers," I said, smiling as the elderly woman teetered out of the shop holding a small bouquet of daisies.

Turning to Emma, I whispered, "We need someone else to take orders. We can't keep up with me designing and taking payments and you schmoozing and barking orders."

"I'm type A! I like to organize. Besides, forget the walk-ins for a minute, you need to hire someone to help with these orders. There are enough special orders here to keep you here day and night for the next six months!" Emma beamed, ripping another order slip off and filing it into the M–F binder she designed. It was going to help me stay organized and not overwhelmed. Until I looked inside and saw how many orders I had to complete, that was. "I'm going to be here all night just getting the wholesalers' orders placed." I called for Gigi to take over as I started going through all the order slips. "Wait, some of these are months from now?"

She shrugged. "I'll cross that bridge with whoever takes over after you leave."

"Listen, Em . . . ," I began, but another wave of people had just been let in by Nick, who was helping manage traffic since the shop couldn't hold more than about a dozen or so people at a time. I still hadn't been able to thank him for the help or the snack from Casey's he brought as a congrats gift.

"This is going to be a long day," Emma said, eyeing the crowd.

Around lunchtime, it began to slow, but I had a feeling once it rolled around to one o'clock, we'd see an uptick again. Hopefully, not as many at once.

"Where's Henry today?" I asked. I was disappointed that he hadn't been able to make it yet.

Emma slid me a glance. "Barreton U? He started his summer-school teaching a few days ago."

"Oh, I was hoping he was going to be able to stop in."

"I'm sure he'll make it. I know he wouldn't want to miss it," she said, handing me a small knife to open another pack of order forms. Emma had made it clear that she thought I was walking a very tight rope without any safety net beneath me when it came to Henry.

The other night, I had explained to Emma what I was feeling toward Henry. She wasn't surprised by it, but warned in the kindest way possible that while he might look big and imposing, he was soft and squishy on the inside.

"Emma, I know you're looking out for him, but—"

She turned, smiling. "Henry is a grown man. I just don't want to see his heart go through the blender again."

"What's that supposed to mean? Why would his heart be pulverized?"

"First of all, do I have to remind you about Dr. Max? You've been texting him since you got here. And while I'm a big advocate of that, I can't sit by while you pine for Henry, too. And secondly, there is something about Henry's past that explains why he doesn't want to get involved with you. Henry should be the one to tell you this, but I know he won't. Please, for the sake of our friendship, don't repeat this." She waited for me to nod before continuing.

"Henry had a girlfriend, Sarah, who we were all convinced he would marry because we never really saw him with anyone seriously. They weren't together long, but he seemed happy and invested. Then she tells us one day that she got a job offer in San Francisco and that she was going to take it. She never even mentioned it to him. He had no idea she was looking for a job elsewhere, and certainly not that she was planning to up and move cross-country in two weeks.

"He was crushed. He's had dates here and there since, but nothing serious. Then you come back and all of a sudden that light is back in his eyes. He seems like the Henry we used to know and love, but when you leave, he'll be back to square one, and we'll be left to pick up the pieces."

"Oh," I replied, finally beginning to understand where Henry was coming from. *He's looking for long-term,* I reminded myself just as the knife I was using to open the order forms slipped, nicking my already battered fingers. "Shit."

"You okay?" Emma asked, concerned at the amount of blood pouring from my finger.

I rolled my eyes at my stupidity while grabbing a napkin to contain the bleeding. "Yeah, can you hold down the fort while I bandage this up?"

She nodded, smiling at the crowd that looked on. "Okay, folks, I'm creating your arrangements! Who's excited!?"

I headed toward the small office space to find the first aid kit I'd purchased. Rummaging around the storage shelves, I finally spied it on the very top shelf. "Of course."

There wasn't a step stool in the back—I had to add that to my list. But for now, I had two options: try to scale the shelving, or bleed to death.

Always so dramatic, my mother's voice said in my head.

With my foot on the first shelf, I was about to pull myself up when the back door popped open.

"Allow me," a deep voice said from behind me. I startled, but not from being frightened. I knew exactly who it was.

"Henry," I breathed, waiting for him to walk into the room before I turned around.

"Emma told me you were back here."

He walked over quietly, moving behind me to reach up to the top shelf without any aid.

"Here you go," he whispered, his lips against the shell of my ear.

It took a moment for him to back away. It wasn't like I was in a rush, either. He inhaled deeply, and I swore I felt his chest rumble against my back. How long had it been since I had a reaction like this to someone? My face felt burning hot; my chest was heaving. I leaned back just enough for my head to fall to his shoulder. That snapped him out of it.

With his hands steadying me by holding on to my hips, he backed away. I turned quickly, but I got a rush. Leaning against the shelving, I glanced up at him. He, too, was flushed, cheeks pink and eyes wild.

"L-Let me help," he stuttered, reaching for the first aid kit.

As he reached out to grip it, I pulled it back.

It fell to the floor with a clatter. The lid popped open with the contents spilling out.

"Shit," I groaned, bending to retrieve everything. My finger was bleeding through the napkin I had around it.

"Charlotte, please, let me help," he insisted, holding my hands still.

His were warm and soft compared to what a mess mine were with the years of nicks and bruises marking them.

"It's okay, really. Maybe you should help Emma? Is she still alive out there?"

He laughed. "She's holding her own. She's already recruited Mrs. Mancini and Gigi."

"Oh, good," I said, nervously fumbling with the Band-Aids. "I'll worry about cleaning it and adding ointment later."

"Charlotte, relax. Taking two minutes to clean this is better than having your finger fall off. How will you make beautiful arrangements with only nine fingers?"

His voice was teasing, but it held a touch of real concern.

Gently, Henry took my hand and squeezed. Closing my eyes, I tried not to focus on the slight tremor in his hand or how delicately he cleaned and bandaged me up. I just settled in for a quiet moment, enjoying his mending my hand as best he could. Once he was finished, he held my hand for a moment longer than he probably should have. It wasn't awkward, but unexpected, considering how adamant he had been about not getting close due to my transient status.

"Impressive. Maybe you should have gone to med school."

"Boy Scouts—taught me everything I know," he said, but the words hit something deep in me.

"Boy Scouts," I said simply. "Why does that seem familiar?"

I closed my eyes, trying to remember. All that popped up was a memory of a crop of spiky plants near a fence.

"Charlotte?" he breathed.

Slowly, I opened my eyes. Looking down, I noticed that he'd taken both my hands in his, his thumbs lightly stroking my palms. When my eyes met his, he was staring intently at me, waiting.

"Yes, Henry?" I asked, leaning forward to close some of the space between us.

Slowly, he inched forward, matching my position. I parried, and as he was about to lean in, the door swung open.

I slid back, knocking over the stool beside my desk. Henry, to his credit, hadn't moved an inch.

"Hey, guys, it's getting crazy out here," Nick said, looking between the two of us. I must have looked tremendously guilty, because he raised a dark eyebrow. When I glanced at Henry, they seemed to be having a silent broversation.

"Sorry, sorry, hurt my finger. You know. Thanks, Henry," I sputtered, and slipped out of the room. To my surprise, I ran right into Max.

"Hey there!" he said cheerfully. "Some crowd you've got in here."

I smiled, stepping to the side to greet a woman who just came up to the counter. "Give me a moment?" I explained, but he side-stepped me.

"Come on, take five. I brought ice cream," he said, holding up a paper cup filled with vanilla.

"Oh, Max, I'd love to, but I can't stop now. I've got people to greet and orders to take. It's a great problem to have, but I can't take a break right now. How about later? I'll shoot you a text."

He looked disappointed, but I couldn't be worried about that right now. Not when there was a line of people waiting to place an order.

Thankfully, he got the hint and recovered nicely. "Sure, no problem." He took the ice cream and left.

"Okay, that was both the sweetest and the most poorly timed gesture I've ever seen." Emma laughed.

"I swear, instead of things being easier between us, they get more awkward."

Henry didn't come back into the main area of the shop after I bolted through the swinging door. He must have slipped out the back door, into the alley. *Or, he's still back there . . .*

But he wasn't. I peeked as soon as there was a slight dip in the crazy. With only about twenty minutes left, the crowd, thankfully, thinned to a handful.

The one person I was anxious to see, Gigi, who was zipping around the store trying to upsell everyone, looked as exhausted as I felt.

"Mrs. Mancini, thanks for coming and bringing Gigi. It meant a lot. Why don't you guys head home? I'll bring you dinner after I clean this place up a bit."

Gigi took my hand, pulling me down to eye level. "Tomorrow is another day. Don't wear yourself out, my darling. I'll see you when you get home." She kissed my cheek and waved goodbye to Nick and Emma, both of whom looked like they were ready to drop at any minute.

What was left of the crowd inside split apart as if Gigi was Moses commanding the Red Sea. A few people bent to kiss her cheek; some gave her a soft hug as she was leaving. It was adorable and humbling to see how many people loved her.

"Almost done," Emma whispered, dropping another slip into the file folder. It was bursting open.

"I'm going to have to bring that home to sort through so I can get the ordering done by tomorrow morning," I said, eyeing the folder skeptically. "If the delivery truck comes by midweek, I can put in two solid days before the weekend and get through a chunk of these."

"What can I do to help?" Emma offered, looking at the whole-sale vendors' price sheet and ordering information.

"Nothing, really, but thanks. One of these days I'll teach you how to order tulips straight from the Netherlands." My heart was beating fast, either from excitement at the prospect of filling the orders or worry, because *how the hell am I going to do this?*

"I need to figure out how to categorize the orders," I continued. "Something easier to follow. This was the way I used to do orders back in New York, but the volume wasn't like this, and there were six of us to spread the work out to. This was far more than I imagined for one person."

Emma raised an eyebrow. "You don't trust my system?" she said in mock offense.

I laughed weakly.

"Of course I do!" I said, mollifying her. "You make Martha Stewart look like a slacker when it comes to planning."

Emma preened. "On a serious note, you're going to be extremely busy, Charlotte. Busier than even I thought. I think you really need to hire someone to help, or a couple part-timers. This is too much for one person to do."

I nodded. "I don't disagree, I just don't know the first thing about hiring. I've only ever done the design work and planning."

Emma paced around, collecting errant papers and straightening the shelves as she did so. She moved in contemplative silence. Was this her process? The way she ferreted out issues and found solutions? *She has her problem-solving CDO hat on*, I realized.

"For the events you've done, you had to get subcontractors, right? Caterers, servers, the whole nine?"

"Yes, of course."

"Did you use a service? I'm sure New York has a ton of ready-to-hire companies staffed with people," she said, stacking a set of decorative boxes into a pyramid on one of the glass shelves.

I sank, exhausted, onto a metal stool.

"We did use a service once, but it wasn't the best fit. After that, we just figured out the calendar for the month and my boss hired based on— Oh." I paused, the light bulb coming on.

"See, you *do* have experience hiring people. It just might not be for subcontractors and parties yet." She smirked when I rolled my eyes.

"Okay, fine. I can hire someone to help, but can we talk about this at another time? I'm beat."

With a nod followed by a long, loud yawn, Emma pulled me in for a hug. "I'll see you soon."

"Thanks for today. For everything."

"Always," she said, moving wearily toward the door.

Once it closed behind her, I rolled out a small piece of carpet that I'd found at Gigi's and settled onto the floor again. I wasn't sure why, but that spot in the very center of the shop was turning out to be my favorite place to just sit and think.

If I knew how to do yoga, I would do it here, but my lack of coordination prevented it when a hard floor was involved. The breathing, though—that I could do. In and out, eyes closed, mind wandering. Bliss.

Slowly, the weariness started melting from my bones. Minutes passed in peace and quiet while I contemplated life's great mysteries.

Was Henry going to kiss me today?

I lay back onto the rug to stretch and dream about it. While it wasn't exactly a great mystery, it gave me something to think about. Until an actual mystery jolted me awake.

"Oh, shit! Emma was my ride. How the hell am I going to get home?" With everyone being exhausted, it must have slipped her mind. I know it did mine.

How hard is it to get a driver's license again?

Unfortunately, life's great questions meant I wasn't relaxed anymore.

Customers. Emma had been sure they would come out in support today, but I assumed that meant come for the coffee and snacks she insisted we provide and maybe a photo op with the *Hope Lake Journal.* I honestly didn't believe it would translate to an abundance of orders.

And a couple of leads on party-planning opportunities.

Through a yawn, I rolled over onto all fours to try to pull myself to my feet. My back was facing the door when I heard someone enter the shop. A customer?

I knew I should have locked it.

"I'm so sorry," I mumbled, struggling to get up with my ultra-stiff back, "but we're closed for today."

The snicker urged my eyes to bolt open. "Henry?" I gasped, turning to see him lingering by the front door. He took up much of the frame with his large body.

He had changed his clothes from earlier, but he was still dressed casually, his arms crossed over his broad chest and covering much of the navy-blue polo shirt he wore. His jeans were worn out in all the right places and fit perfectly.

"You were expecting someone else?" he asked, glancing behind him.

I did my best to stand up gracefully. By the way his eyes followed my movements, I would say I failed. "No, no. I was just having a bit of a postmortem. Alone, in the dark, you know."

Postmortem? Jesus, Charlotte! Can you at least try to have a filter? Why was I incapable of normal conversation with this guy?

He laughed. "Not sure I follow."

I sighed, straightening my shirt that had ridden up. Looking down, I realized how filthy I was. Smudges of dirt streaked across my shirt; green foam bits were under my nails. I was the walking, talking definition of a train wreck.

"Pull up an inch of carpet, I'll explain," I suggested, sitting back down on the rug. Classy Charlotte was a futile wish at this point. I might as well try to get comfortable in this awkward bubble we were in.

Henry gracefully situated himself on a corner of the rug, stretching his legs out to the side. "This was on the front door," he said, handing me another envelope.

"Oh!" I snatched the envelope away from him. Max must have left it prior to the ice-cream incident and no one had noticed. I was hoping more would arrive, but what I wasn't thrilled with was the randomness of how they were left. There was no rhyme or reason to them.

"Thanks. I'll just tuck this away," I said, carefully sliding the letter into the back pocket of my shorts. Henry eyed it curiously but didn't ask about it, thankfully.

"What is it?" he asked.

I examined his face—furrowed brows, thin lips, and a worried look. He genuinely looked like he had no idea what they were. While I suspected they were from Max, there was a small part of me that *hoped* they might have been from Henry.

"Oh, just a little letter," I said, not embellishing to see how he'd react.

We sat silently for a few minutes: me decompressing, and Henry seemingly happy to just sit beside me.

Finally, I felt that I either needed to move or curl up and fall asleep on the rug. "So . . ."

"So," he replied, turning toward me. "Tell me about this post-mortem?"

I laughed awkwardly. "Since I don't have a crew, you'll have to be my postmortem buddy."

He looked around the darkening shop. The only lights now were the security night-lights dotted around the room and the tiny desk lamp that sat next to the computer.

"Should I be worried?" he asked, his smile shining through the darkness. "I'm not going to be autopsied, right?"

I chuckled, scooching closer to the center of the rug. It's not that I was trying to get closer to him, but I wasn't *not* trying, either.

"It's not *that* kind of postmortem," I began, just as he leaned back on his arms. He looked so relaxed and put together. Meanwhile, my heart was about to burst from my chest.

Fidgeting with my hands, I tucked in for story time. "When I was in college, I had a part-time job with an event-planning company. It was as close to a perfect job as I could get at nineteen. Anyway, we used to decompress after every event. All of us together, sharing wine, canapés, and desserts. Whatever might have been left over from the shindig. The whole point was for us to chat about the event. The highs and lows, what went right and what could be improved. The owner used to call it a postmortem and take extensive notes. Nothing was ever perfect for her, though. She always thought we could improve."

"She sounds tough," Henry said, rubbing his bottom lip with his thumb. He smiled after he caught my eyes darting down to watch it slide across his mouth.

I cleared my throat. *Maybe I should walk around? Let some cool air pour out of the coolers? Put an ice cube down my shirt?*

Shaking my head, I looked anywhere but at him. "She was actually really awesome. She wanted the best for us and the business. Now, my last boss? She was an overbearing, egotistical nightmare. Anyway, the point is, I was going to have a postmortem with Emma on the way home about how today went, but she left, and now I'm a bit stranded."

Mentally, I was trying to calculate how long it would take for me to walk home, especially given my already-exhausted condition.

"I noticed she zombie-walked out of here. I had to call her to make sure she got home all right," Henry explained, running his hand through his hair. "Once I realized no one was coming for you, I popped in, thinking you'd need a ride."

My heart warmed. "Thank you. That was amazingly kind of you to not leave me here after the day I had."

"It looked *busy*, to put it mildly. Steady stream of people all day. It worked for the bookstore, too, since your customers came to visit every shop in the square after they visited for the grand opening."

"It was great, but I know we can improve the system we have in place. Hence, the postmortem."

"I can do it with you," he offered simply. But there was nothing simple about his words. My face warmed as if a fireplace were lit right next to me.

I swallowed, looking up at him as the remaining solar street-lights clicked on, leaving balls of startling white light on the side-walk in front of the shop.

He, too, realized what he had just said. "I mean, I can drive you home and you can use me for your postmortem. I wasn't here long, but I heard a lot of feedback while I was at the bookstore today."

His eyes stayed locked with mine while I thought about it. I *did* need a ride, and the company certainly was choice. And a willing ear to bend about the day?

I didn't have to think twice.

"Give me five to grab my stuff."

15

"Ready," I breathed, skidding to a halt in front of him. Henry had a bemused expression as he checked his watch.

"Impressive," he teased, taking the tote from my shoulder and placing it onto his.

"Thanks." In under six minutes, I had grabbed everything I needed and tossed it into my bag.

Henry followed me out the front door of the shop. Close, but not too close. I slipped the key into the lock to secure the dead bolt, and I glanced up at the crystal-etched front door that read LATE BLOOMERS in an artfully designed script. Reaching out, I touched it gently.

"If I haven't mentioned it, I think the name is genius."

I smiled up at him. "I appreciate that."

The night was warmer than I expected, making me wish I'd left the thin sweater I wore back at the shop. Like every night I came into town, the people of Hope Lake, whether residents or visitors, congregated in the square. People milled about visiting shops, eating ice cream, or just sitting and drinking coffee under the stars.

"This place is a bit magical," I admitted, earning a beaming smile from Henry.

"I think so."

He led us across the walkway that separated our shops. Well, not *our* shops per se. The shop he worked at and the one I was whatever-ing at. It was just a stretch of wide sidewalk with the fountain planted in the middle. Trees lined the walkway, and benches and potted plants were dotted throughout. It was a nice little spot to congregate.

"This is very Hollywood, you know."

"How's that?" he asked, his stride slowing as we reached the fountain.

Two young giggling girls were tossing coins in while two young boys I assumed they were with looked on.

Leaning in, I bumped his shoulder playfully. "Hollywood. Rom-com? You know, a meet-cute between two single, attractive shop owners. I can see it now, they gaze at each other longingly across the busy pedestrian walkway that anchors their businesses, waiting for the chance to accidentally-on-purpose run into each other. Maybe it's at the cozy café or the delicious ice-cream shop. Maybe it's just the two of them saying a wish at the fountain in the town square that's been known to make dreams come true if you have a true heart." Without stopping, I plucked a penny from my pocket and flicked it in to make a wish.

Here's to making the right decision.

Henry stopped, standing a few paces back, arms crossed over his broad chest. "I would have never pegged you for a hopeless romantic, Charlotte Bishop."

I laughed, walking to meet him. "If you repeat it to anyone, I'll deny it. I have a rep to protect."

"You're ridiculous." He tucked a piece of hair behind my ear. His finger lingered just a moment before sliding down my jaw. I shivered, and it wasn't from the night air.

The wind picked up, blowing his hair out of the artfully arranged style he wore to cover the wires that led into his ears. I glanced at them, staring just a moment before he shifted strands back to hide them.

"You can ask about them, you know. I'm used to it," Henry said, sweeping his arm before him to direct me to lead the way.

I gave him an embarrassed, sideways glance. "I didn't want to pry," I said honestly. "The other day I saw you running through the center of town. I was trying to get your attention and yelled, but you didn't turn around. You just kept going. I shouted again, but nothing. I really thought you were still mad because of *the incident* until I realized that you probably didn't hear me."

"Sorry about that," he began, pointing the way between the bookshop and the dry cleaner, where the alley was shrouded in darkness. "I probably didn't. When I'm outside, there are so many factors that make hearing more difficult. Traffic, for one thing, is a nightmare. I apologize for ignoring you. I promise, it wasn't my intention," he said, winking when we reached the parking lot that ran behind the row of buildings.

There were more cars than I expected. Henry led us to an older-model Jeep Wrangler. A *much* older model. It wasn't held together with duct tape or anything, but it was definitely a classic. It fit Henry perfectly.

He held the door open for me to slide inside. The interior was immaculate. For as faded and questionably sound as it looked on the outside, he clearly took care of it.

"So, the—" I paused, pointing to my own ears. "I'm not sure what to call them."

"The medical term is *cochlear implant*. They're not hearing aids, per se. Those make sounds louder—think what Gigi has," he explained, tapping his ear. "These send sound signals to my brain because my cochleas got damaged when I was younger." He started the engine and inched onto the main road.

Don't ask. Don't ask. Don't ask.

"How did that happen?"

It's like my mouth and brain aren't connected.

"If you don't mind me asking, I mean," I added, wondering what the chances of survival were if I jumped out of the car.

He rolled to a stop, so jumping wasn't going to be an issue. Henry wasn't mad, though—instead, he looked pensive. As if he was remembering whatever had happened all over again.

"Nick and I always horsed around when we grew up. Cooper and Emma, too, but Nick and I took competition to a new level all the time. When we were eleven and watched *A Christmas Story* for the first time, the triple-dog dare became the fabric of our lives. The shit we would try to make each other do was ridiculous."

I reached over, resting my hand over his on the stick shift. "I'm sorry," I said weakly. I had no idea why, but I was. You could tell that the two of them were the best of friends, so whatever had happened must have been traumatic. I couldn't imagine either of them willfully hurting the other.

"Thanks. You should know, I don't blame him for what happened. I'm as much at fault as he was. I just happened to be the most uncoordinated at the time. I had finally gotten my growth spurt, and everything didn't quite work properly yet. I was gangly and Bambi-on-new-legs uncoordinated with my long legs and big feet. I could barely walk across a room without tripping over myself. Anyway, we had just done a marshmallow challenge to see who could fit the most in their mouths."

I laughed. "That sounds both amazing and difficult," I admitted, wondering what it would have been like if I'd have stayed here. Would we have stayed only friends? Or more?

"Nick had the bright idea to see what else we could do. At one point Cooper had a rock up his nose, and I thought it would be smart to put a pencil in Nick's ear. Emma, who was usually the voice of reason, had left to go home."

I cringed, thinking of a pencil being jammed into an eardrum. "Nick said, 'How about you do it,' and triple-dog dared me. I had three pencils in my ear on each side when Nick's dog ran into the living room. I jumped to get out of the way and fell. The rest is history."

I looked at the implants again. In the darkness of the car, you couldn't see them unless you stared, or knew they were there. The wires were clear and disappeared into his ear, and his shaggy haircut further aided in hiding them.

Before I thought twice, I slowly reached out, touching the thin wire as gently as I could. Smoothing his hair back on one side, I inched my way over the center console that separated us so that I could look more closely.

"They're almost invisible," I whispered, wondering if my voice would be amplified because I was so close.

Judging by the way a slight shiver ran through him, I guessed yes. The strangest urge to lean down to kiss him overtook me. Henry turned slightly, making us that much closer in the already tight space of the car.

He cleared his throat just as I was going to lean in, and I was grateful. I didn't feel safe on this tightrope.

"They bother some people. I've been on blind dates before and they've ended before they even began because of them."

My mouth dropped open as I sunk back onto my own seat. "You're kidding," I blurted out, wondering what kind of shallow twits he dated.

He shrugged, trying to play it off like it didn't bother him, but his face betrayed him. Even with the car mostly covered in shadows, I could see that it hurt his feelings.

"Screw those vapid bitches. Their loss," I insisted, squeezing his hand.

He squeezed it back, not letting go until a group of teens came tumbling out of the mouth of the alley, laughing loudly.

With the tension in the car at a fever pitch, he pulled out onto the main road.

With Gigi's house being on the far end of town, we had some time to kill. We were supposed to be discussing the day at the shop, but as much as I needed and wanted his opinion, I didn't want to waste alone time with Henry with talk of work.

"I'm getting better learning my way around the town," I said when he rolled to the stop sign by the antiques shop. "Which streets lead to Emma's and Cooper's. Which roads to avoid because Duncan and Birdy like to sit there to nail anyone speeding."

Henry laughed. "I doubt they get many speeders. We're not exactly a fast-moving town. It does surprise visitors how big Hope Lake actually is, given the low population number. It spans a lot of territory."

"Yeah, it does. It's part of the reason I really need to get a license while I'm here," I said, thinking about how often I needed to beg people for rides all over town.

"It's not a bad idea. Your dad mentioned it when I saw him yesterday."

"Oh? Where did you see him?" I asked, wondering why Dad didn't mention it.

"He stopped into the shop to grab a copy of the club's upcoming true-crime pick for Gigi. I think she's hoping you'll join us, too."

My lips flattened with worry. "Sorry, I'm a bit of a wuss. True crime is a little much for me. What did he have to say?" I asked.

"He asked me to keep an eye out for you. You know, in case you get into trouble. You caught him by surprise showing up here."

Dad and Dr. Max had a busy schedule between Hope Lake and the help they provided to Mount Hazel and Barreton. Which sucked, since I was here. But as Parker reminded me during our phone call the other night, they had these things planned long before I decided to show up on his doorstep unexpectedly.

"I know that; I get it. There's nothing that could be done. Next time, I'll give him fair warning to prepare for my visit." I laughed, but Henry didn't seem to think it was funny. It was just another reminder that my time here was up in the air.

It doesn't have to be, a little voice said, swimming up. I reattached the anchor and sent it back down into the depths. *Not going there*.

Henry was quiet as he turned off on a road that looked all too familiar. There, just ahead, was the small stone wall that read THE LOVE LANE COMMUNITY. It was where I got pulled over that first day.

The community, I found out afterward through some accidental research, wasn't actually *on* Love Lane. After consulting a map that hung in my grandfather's office at Gigi's, I realized that there wasn't even a Love Lane in Hope Lake. No avenue, road, trail, street, or lane.

I was beginning to think it was just a friendly term for the area: aka the road that led to the overlook where everyone from teenagers to adults spent time parked in their cars to *admire the unobstructed view of the town.*

It was a surprising path to venture out toward Gigi's. One that I wasn't about to read into, given Henry's adamant reaction to the two of us being a temporary *us.*

"This area of town is so unexpected. I can't explain why, but the first time I came up this way, I thought I'd left Hope Lake," I said as he pulled next to the stone wall, where I knew a dusting of wildflowers grew.

Not pulling into the area of the overlook where the line of cars were parked for *viewing* was probably a smart move.

"I'm not sure I follow?" he said, doing his best to turn toward me. It was difficult with his large body in a small space.

My face flushed at the thought of being up here, in the car, for the exact purpose of enjoying Love Lane . . .

"Uh, you know. The area below—with the big manor homes and the stately trees and the landscaping surrounding them—is such an old-school, hoity-toity place. The center of town is so small-town chic with the old but renovated buildings, and then right at the top of the hill behind the cul-de-sac you've got horndog teenagers—"

"And some adults," he chimed in.

I suddenly wondered how many trips up here Henry made. He was attractive, employed, a genuine *nice guy,* and I was sure that there wasn't a shortage of women in town who had noticed all of it.

"Noted," I replied, and my stomach did a little flip at the sight of his shy smirk. "I just mean, it's an odd place for such a saucy destination. You've got a development with beautifully landscaped yards and expensive SUVs in the driveways, and then just . . . Then a couple feet away you've got rocking cars and fogged-up windows.

Why isn't the kissing spot up by Emma's parents' house deep in the woods? Or, hell, the area by where Gigi and Mrs. Mancini live? That's a dead end with open space for, well, *whatever*, for miles."

"Rewind a second. You say the first time you visited this area. You mean since you've returned, right?"

"Yeah, why? Was this one of my hangouts before?"

He nodded. "Not this place exactly, but the other end of the development. The section that leads out—never mind. It doesn't really matter."

"No, no, it does!" I insisted, folding my hands up as if in prayer and making an *I'm begging* face. "Things are coming back, but it's been so slow. I keep waiting for a deluge of memories, but it hasn't happened so far."

"It might. It will, actually. I'm sure of it. You just need to be patient."

"You sound like Gigi," I said, laughing when he smiled.

"I take that as the highest of compliments."

"Seriously, though. Did we hang out here?"

He nodded, his expression turning sad. "It was a spot just for us. I know that sounds odd, considering we were ten, but that's just how it was. Cooper and Nick hung out together a lot. Emma trailed after Cooper, of course, though she'd never admit that. This place sort of just became a hangout spot when things turned sketchy for one of us."

He said *us*, but I had the sinking feeling he meant *me*.

"None of this is familiar?" he asked, hopeful.

"If I said it's all familiar, would that make any sense to you?"

He shrugged. "I don't know what you're going through, so I can't really attest to how I would or wouldn't feel. I think that if put in the situation where I had no memories of my childhood, I'd be a lot more panicked than you are."

I laughed. "Oh, I'm panicked. I just can't focus on that because I know it'll make me crazy. I need to keep myself moving forward and hope that something will jog those memories free. The more I visit places like this—spots that meant something to me as a kid—the more I think I'll remember. I'll explain on the way to Gigi's."

Henry pulled back onto the road, kicking up plumes of dust with the large tires.

We bypassed a stream of cars all shapes, ages, and styles on the way in. "Does everyone come here as soon as the sun goes down?"

"Pretty much."

I laughed. "I'll never understand."

"Oh, you will. Love Lane wasn't given its name because it was the prime site for *certain activities*," he said, waving his hand back toward the fading taillights. "It was named after Lionel Lovegood."

"You're making that up," I said, playfully slapping his arm. His hand flexed when my skin touched his.

He smiled. "I'm not. Lionel Lovegood was a physician who came here the same time that Cooper's great-, great-, well—times however many times it is—grandfather Campbell founded the town. You know about that, right?"

"You're saying his name was Dr. Lovegood?"

"Yep."

"Like, *Love Good*?" I emphasized, drawing out both words with an added eyebrow wiggle.

"Yes," he said slowly.

I tried not to smile, and the way his lips were pressed together, I would have said he, too, was trying not to laugh.

"Dr. Lionel Lovegood? Seriously? That's the best name."

Henry chuckled. "Yes, it is a cool name."

"Oh, and yes, I know a bit about Cooper's family history. Go on."

"Lovegood was on the same boat as Campbell coming from England in the 1740s. Immediately, they formed a great bond and had what many people thought was a prophetic vision for the town. I don't know that they had a bit of Nostradamus in them, but I like to think that they had the foresight to plan for many futures after them and that it wasn't just dumb luck.

"After years of focusing on the center of town, Lovegood supposedly wanted to branch out into the wooded areas that surrounded Hope Lake. With the river on one side being used for trade and industry, Lovegood wanted the lake side to be seen as a family spot. Somewhere for picnics and church functions. The woods were hopefully to be kept a safe haven for the wildlife to flourish. He wasn't a big fan of razing the area for the sake of buildings. Some things were meant to stay as is."

"Is that why the B and B's and the park are out that way? Nothing is surrounding those except the woods."

He shrugged. "I suppose that was why those particular buildings became what they did. Every Hope Laker knows the stories, so perhaps they tried their best to keep with the tradition and the original town model. You know, this place loves tradition. The B and B's didn't start out as bed-and-breakfasts, of course. At the time, they were single-family homes; Lovegood saw this huge expanse of untouched land, and he knew it was special."

"So Lovegood, what, lived out this way, too?"

Henry shook his head. "He was supposed to. The story is that he had just built his practice and was in the midst of building a home for his family when his wife got sick. While the construction continued, he devoted all his free time to helping her. Campbell got historical credit for most of the work they did together because Lovegood fell out of sight. Campbell tried to change the perception, but you know how hard it is to change public opinion once it's made up."

I nodded. "Do I ever."

"Put a pin in that, I'd like to come back to it."

I smiled. "Deal. Now, please continue. We're almost there, and we still haven't talked about the shop."

I found this common when Henry and I were alone and chatting. Every topic was discussed except the one that we were supposed to. Time went by absurdly fast when we were together, and I wished that it slowed down just a little, giving me more time to enjoy being around him.

"Oh, and what about his wife?"

Henry frowned. "She passed away a few days before the house was finished."

I felt a pang of sadness that was completely unexpected considering I had no tie to the story or the people involved. "That's so sad."

Henry continued with the Lovegood tale, just as he turned onto the long road to Gigi's. "It wasn't until after he himself died that Cooper's however-many-times-great-grandfather, at a very old age, went back and edited what he could, giving Lovegood the credit he deserved. That included having Lovegood's Forest dedicated to him—the full stretch of land and miles of forest surrounding the area. It was only safe from development because Lovegood saw to it."

"But I looked it up after the, you know, nonarrest," I whispered. "Love Lane isn't on any map."

"It's not technically recognized by anyone in the state. It's not like it's a state park or anything. Over the years it just became Love Lane, but most of us know the story."

I cleared my throat. "You know, Emma should put one of those story signs up there to make sure everyone knows it. That's really an awesome bit of history for visitors."

"Like you," he said, shutting off the engine. "A hopelessly romantic visitor."

"Oh, hush," I said, with another playful slap to his arm. Again, the longer my hand lingered, the more his muscle flexed beneath it. I could get used to that.

An idea had taken hold when we were still on the lane. All the talk of romance was getting to me. The sound of gravel under the tires meant the night was almost over, and even though I was beat, I didn't want it to end.

"This whole time I was regaling you with stories, and we didn't even discuss your—what did you call it?"

"Postmortem," I reminded him. "It's okay. Another day, perhaps."

We sat quietly for a beat, staring out the Jeep windshield at the sky.

After a few moments, Henry cleared his throat. "So."

"So," I replied, looking at him in my periphery.

With every glance at him, I noticed he was staring at me. I didn't know if he was aware he was even doing it.

"Henry?" I said, causing him to shake his head as if he was zoned out.

There was always a zing between us, at least on my end. Something that felt like we were tied together by an invisible string that was an old connection that I was realizing may have always linked us.

Henry shifted in his seat. Perhaps still coming out of whatever deep thought he was focused on when he was staring at me. The tips of his ears were red, like always. I popped open the car door before he could come around and do it for me. "Stay put a second," I insisted, having an idea that would either be brilliant or a categorical failure.

I was sincerely hoping for brilliance.

Sliding down from the Jeep, I crunched my way around the front of the car, loving feeling the warm headlights on my bare legs. He watched me through the windshield, and I wished I could have fully seen his expression.

When I joined him on the driver's side, I gripped the bar, stepped onto the rail, and pulled myself up. His window had been down for the drive.

How did I not notice how good he smells before?

My arm was on the doorframe holding myself up. "Tell me you're changing your mind," he breathed, touching my skin lightly. "About staying here?"

I swallowed. I wanted to say yes and reach over and kiss him. Or have him pull me inside and smother my lips with his, but to what end? It would be a lie just to sate this building urge between us.

Looking down, I shook my head. "I don't know what I'm doing. Literally, I have no idea. I have all these balls in the air and no juggling skills. But I want to spend more time with you, Henry." Slowly his hand fell away, and when I looked back up, he was staring out the windshield, up at Gigi's house.

"I respect that you have your reasons for not wanting to stay here. I wish you'd do the same for me. You may leave again, and while I would love to see what could happen, I can't let myself. I'm built for commitment, stability—not a fling. No matter how much I would love to spend time with you in a nonfriendly *friendly* way . . ."

I smiled, trying to not let the words hurt as much as they did. But as he said, he wasn't interested in temporary, and I couldn't offer him more than that at the moment.

"Good night, Charlotte," he said, his voice strained.

Henry's Adam's apple bobbed, and I knew then he was on the edge: the precipice of giving in. If I pushed him just enough, he would break.

But if I broke Henry, could I live with myself?

16

After that night with Henry, I realized I needed to let go of any hope that Henry and I could be more than friends. And Dr. Max was the perfect distraction. Not only did he not expect me to make any promises, but he was eager to spend time with me.

I needed easy. I had enough to deal with.

What do I wear for a first date that says I'm sort of vibing with you because I find you handsome and interesting, but I'm also 90 percent sure I'll be sleep-eating chicken wings because I worked fourteen hours today?

As I stood in the center of my closet staring up at my clothes, I grabbed a pair of worn jeans and a thin navy blouse. *Nope, that's wrinkled, and I'm not ironing.* I held up a powder-blue top, thinking it might be clean, but— *Nope, also wrinkled.* I tossed the jeans on the floor and grabbed white shorts and a denim shirt. There, no ironing required.

Thanks to a last-minute customer, I decided to just meet Max at Casey's by hitching a ride with Mrs. Mancini, who was heading into town to pick up a book.

Twenty minutes later, I was praying to God in the passenger seat of Mancini's Lincoln Navigator, an SUV that she needed extra-high running boards and a lower grab bar to pull herself into. She drove like a demon.

"Thanks again for the ride," I said, clutching the doorframe nervously. She careened around a corner at a speed reserved for the highway.

How did I get pulled over by Duncan when someone like Mancini was free to drive all over town unchecked?

"Oh, dear. My pleasure," she said sweetly, making another turn without any signals or brakes. "I told your father that I was always keen to give you a ride to and from work, but he seemed to want to take you himself or find you other rides."

Probably to keep me alive, I thought, closing my eyes as she narrowly missed driving up onto the curb.

When we arrived at Casey's, I let out a breath and a silent prayer to whatever higher power didn't have us flying off an embankment à la Thelma and Louise. "Thanks, Mrs. Mancini. I'll bring you and Gigi home some pizza when I leave."

"No rush, honey. You and your suitor have fun tonight," she called out, waving affectionately to me with her pillowy hand.

Inside, it was a frantic but fun atmosphere. Friday at Casey's must have been the go-to place for dinner before heading to the brewing company for a couple more drinks.

Max stood, waving from a table smack-dab in the center of the restaurant. From there, we could see the entire place.

And the entire place could see us.

Normally, that wouldn't have bothered me—considering I had been stared at, whispered about, and pointed to since I arrived—but this particular audience wasn't one I wanted spying me having dinner with the handsome and interested Dr. Max.

Off at the end of the bar, situated among a crowd of chatty people, were Cooper, Emma, and Nick. Suspiciously absent was Henry.

"Casey's is busy tonight," Max said congenially, pulling my thoughts away from why Emma hadn't invited me to join them.

Because she knew you're seeing Max tonight.

"Yeah, the food is so good, so it makes sense," I replied, smiling as he held the chair out for me. I was trying not to allow my eyes to dance over toward where I knew they were sitting. A glass remained at an empty stool. It was half-full, so someone else must have been with them.

Tilting my chair a bit pitched me closer to Max, but also didn't allow me to have an unobstructed view of that corner of the bar anymore. The urge to keep looking to see if Henry joined them was strong.

Max and I chatted amiably about everything and nothing at all. It was nice, but also a bit like dry toast when you're not feeling well. You know it's good for you, but it's also so damn bland.

Was Max good for me? On paper, absolutely. There was no reason that I shouldn't be diving into the deep end with him. And yet . . .

"Maybe one of these weekends we can try out JOE? I still haven't been since I've been so busy at the practice," Max said, shaking me out of my thoughts. For the life of me, I didn't know what he'd been talking about for the past five minutes because I kept staring up at my friends at the bar.

The three of them had the bar patrons in stitches, everyone laughing at something that Nick was prattling on about. His hands moved around his head, and he looked like he was dancing. When he spun around, he caught me staring around the couple beside us and clapped Cooper on the back.

"Oh, damn," I mumbled into my beer, hoping that Nick drawing attention to us wouldn't mean that they would all come— Never mind, that's exactly what it meant.

They filed through the cockeyed tables, saying hi to nearly every patron. Cooper said good evening even to the people he didn't know, in all his mayoral splendor.

"Fancy meeting you guys here," Emma said pointedly. "Max, I thought you were going to Notte's?"

While she was focusing on Max, Nick stared at me with accusation in his eyes. I couldn't look at him, no matter how much I wanted to show him that I was free to see whomever I wanted. His best friend wasn't interested, and Max was. Mentally, I was sticking my tongue out at him and daring him to text Henry to tell him that we were there together.

"We were, but then Charlotte suggested here. Thanks for the recommendation, though. We'll definitely try it another night," Max said cheerily to Emma.

"No problem. Always happy to help the locals out," she said, smiling at me.

"It's just you guys here?" I blurted out, looking toward the bar, where I counted the four glasses again.

Emma followed my line of sight. "Oh yeah. Henry was here, too, but he— You know, I don't know where he went off to."

Cooper and Nick shrugged, although Nick looked like he had more to say on the subject.

"He'll probably be right back. Maybe it was something at the bookshop," Emma said casually, but her fingers tightened around her cell phone.

Max shook Cooper's outstretched hand, promising that they'd get together to discuss a bike-safety initiative. Nick reminded him about golf.

"We'll let you get back to your date." With a quick wink, Emma finally turned and glided back to the bar behind the guys.

"Great friends you've got there," Max said, apparently unaware of the magnificent level of awkwardness that was just displayed.

"The best," I said, holding the beer in my sweaty hand.

I willed myself to enjoy the night, and not read into what Henry's disappearing act meant.

MY DATE WITH Max had gotten cut short because he was on call and an emergency popped up. He offered to stop by with coffee soon so we could continue our pleasant conversation.

Pleasant. Not exactly the word a man wants to hear when describing his dating aptitude.

When he showed up with two coffees, as promised, I was grateful.

"Well, you seem to be the talk of the town," Max said brightly.

"Morning!" I said, glancing up at the clock and noticing that it was actually almost lunchtime. Had three hours passed already? No wonder I felt so tired. "I thought my dad said that you both were booked well into this afternoon."

He smiled, depositing my coffee on the counter next to a freshly cut pile of robin's-egg-blue hydrangeas.

"*He* is, but I had a couple schedule changes and I thought I'd see if you were free for lunch. Pick up where we left off. But judging by this stack, I'd say you're not," he said, eyes widening at the pile of orders under a paperweight labeled TODAY.

"It's been . . . busy. To say the least. Good busy, but busy nonetheless. Thanks for the offer, though. I brought myself a sandwich from the house because I'd be working through lunch because of a meeting with Nick."

"Oh yeah? What's he stopping in for?" he asked, pulling up the stool to the counter.

"We're supposed to go over ideas for this project he has down in Barreton. I said I'd like to take a look. It's sort of nice to have someone else in the business to talk to about things. You know, bounce ideas off of, whatever," I replied, continuing to work with the foam and short, square wooden box that was for a birthday arrangement.

He nodded, then sipped his coffee. Max seemed happy to just hang out and chat, but I was pressed for time.

My fingers were stiffening up. They did that whenever I stopped working for a couple of minutes. I tried stretching them and shaking them out, but Max grabbed my right hand and proceeded to try to examine the nicks and scratches that decorated them. It was both weirdly medical and oddly personal all at once.

He brought my hand to his lips, and I waited for the tingles, sparks—hell, even a blip on the meter.

Nothing.

I thought that the reason I didn't feel anything after he took me home and kissed me on the cheek was because I was bone-dead tired. But again, nothing.

Slowly, I pulled my hand away. I didn't want to be mean or insensitive, but I wasn't in the right headspace for him at the moment. "I'm sorry if I'm being rude, but the people who ordered these are coming in for this in about an hour and I still have a bit to go."

He looked apologetic. "My timing is never great." He laughed. "I can leave. I just thought I'd stop in to see if I could steal you away for a few minutes."

"The offer is tempting. I won't lie." I smiled up at him, and seeing his disappointment mirroring my own, I weighed my options.

I could leave for half an hour, enjoy getting to know Max for a bit, maybe will some excitement into our interactions. But then I'd have to stay late again to catch up.

"Are you free tonight? For a coffee over at the bookstore?" I asked.

I shook my head slowly, but Max wasn't looking at me but at his Apple Watch. I was wondering what in the ever-loving hell I was thinking.

The bookstore? *You. Idiot.*

"Yes, that sounds great, actually. I have to stop in anyway to pick up an order. Gigi talked me into joining the book club this month. I don't know when I'll have time to read, but she's a hard woman to say no to."

"Great."

The bell chimed overhead, and all the energy in the room shifted. I didn't need to look up to know who it was walking through the door.

Carrying two coffees.

I couldn't make this up if I tried.

"Max," Henry said coolly. He looked embarrassed, and awkward.

"Henry," Max replied, just as stiffly.

"I see you have coffee already," Henry said pointedly to me.

Max looked between us quickly but then focused his attention on me. It felt like he was specifically watching my reaction to seeing Henry.

"Yeah, uh, Max just stopped in with coffee as a bit of a surprise," I explained, hoping to make it clear that this wasn't a planned event.

But last night was planned, and he probably saw us, which was why he left and didn't return.

Even if it was planned, Charlotte—who cares? Not Henry, he's not interested in short-term, and Max is.

I was going to push the inside voice in front of traffic.

"Oh, you know Charlotte, too?" Max finally asked, taking an imperceptible step closer to me.

Henry didn't miss the move and took a step forward. "We go way back."

"Oh yeah," Max replied, seemingly uninterested in what Henry said. "From when you guys were kids?"

It was a Ping-Pong match, and I was in the crowd watching the ball fly back and forth.

A dig here, a zip there. I'd never seen either of them act this way before.

"Yep, even walked into kindergarten together," Henry shot out smugly. You could tell that he thought that was game point.

Admittedly, the arrogant banter wasn't something I normally enjoyed, but this was giving me insight into Henry, my past, and just how much the thought of Max and me together was annoying him.

Pettiness, thy name is Charlotte.

Max didn't seem to care about the shared and apparently storied history of Charlotte and Henry, judging by his yawn. With a casual lean against the counter, he picked up one of the hydrangeas and spun it around in his fingers. "Oh, that's right. Gigi mentioned that at the welcome-home dinner."

Henry's eyes narrowed. Coffee now, dinner with the family,

then dinner alone. I could see the annoyance growing in his eyes. The blue darkened like a storm was taking over the sky.

"You're the one she can't remember."

Game, set, match. Max won the day.

Henry stiffened, his fingers clutching the recycled paper cups to the point that I thought they would puncture the cups and send coffee all over the shop. If I wasn't watching him closely, I wouldn't have noticed the way his shoulders deflated just a bit, or how his eyes returned to the soft blue they always were.

"Henry, I—" I began, but he wasn't interested. I couldn't blame him, either.

"I see you're busy, Charlotte. I just thought I'd leave this," he began, setting the coffee down for me.

"And this," he said, stepping forward to set another envelope on my desk. Written on the envelope was a simple C with a small flourish at the end in the shape of a wildflower. Max's eyes followed him and proceeded to stare at the envelope incredulously. "It was on your mailbox, but it's windy, and I didn't want to see it blow away."

Max didn't look at the envelope again. Was that a sign that it was from him but he didn't want Henry to know?

"Thanks, Henry," I said, taking the envelope and setting it on the table behind me.

By the time I turned around, Henry was striding purposefully to the door without so much as a glance back.

I watched him through the front windows until I couldn't see him in the crowd anymore.

"So," Max said, pushing the coffee he brought for me closer, effectively in front of Henry's cappuccino.

Oh, Lord. Male posturing was ridiculous. Even when it was a wickedly handsome man doing it.

"Listen, I think meeting later at the bookshop might be a mistake," I said, shoving the hydrangea stem into the foam a bit too hard, causing it to snap in my fingers. "Damn it."

"It's fine. I can stop there to grab my order before I come here."

"Yeah, that works. If you grab what you need and swing by here later, maybe we can go get ice cream at Viola's? Or something else? We can even just walk around town. I'm finding that I enjoy doing that, especially when it's unplanned and I make random turns onto streets I don't remember."

"Perfect. See you about six. Sound good?" He reached out his hand to take mine. Rubbing his thumb over the nicks and cracks in my hands, he squeezed gently. "I'm looking forward to it, Charlotte."

As he left, he turned to wave. Much like Henry did, he disappeared into the mingling crowd. He was charming, there was no doubt. Handsome, too, smart, single, and yet . . . I didn't know. I wanted temporary. Dr. Max was okay with that. Henry was not. I needed to keep reminding myself of that.

I finished up the box arrangement just in time for the customer, who identified herself as a friend of Henry's parents the first time I met her.

"Charlotte, this is gorgeous. So much more than I expected," she said, holding up the arrangement. "I know you said to trust you with the choice of planter, but this was above and beyond. The perfect shabby-chic design."

"Thanks, I appreciate that and the business. I attached a card with my contact information as well as the store's hours. Anything you need, we're here," I said, wrapping the entire design with recycled paper. She paid, and I walked her to the door.

"You know, I just stopped into Evan's Books and mentioned that I was coming here. Henry was the one who originally told me to come in. I usually drive over to Mount Hazel or just buy online and have them delivered. I'm glad I listened."

Waving her goodbye, I stood outside, enjoying the warm sun on my skin. Emma had a bench installed right below my main window. It was the perfect spot to take five minutes to collect my thoughts.

It didn't hurt that I could see straight across the pedestrian pathway and into the bookstore. I couldn't tell if Henry was inside, just that the shop was open.

Just as I was standing up to head back in to work, a troop of lit-tles marched, literally, toward the bookstore led by a very loud Nick.

"Hup, two, three, four. Hup, two, three, four," they chanted, their small legs marching with high knees behind him. They were wearing uniforms, green with numbers on their backs. I couldn't see the logo on the front.

"That must be the Little League team Henry and Nick coach," I said to myself, sinking back down onto the bench. I could spare another couple of minutes.

A familiar face joined me at the bench a moment later, scaring me since I was focused on Henry's shop.

"Jeez! Are you trying to kill me?" I howled, clutching my shirt near my heart. "I almost jumped out of my skin."

Gigi was wheeled up beside me, inching her scooter closer to me. She patted my leg comfortingly and smiled. "My dear, I called your name three times. You were totally zoned out. You used to do that as a child, too. Stare off into space, or at the television, and we'd have to jolt you out of the funk. What, pray tell, has you fixated today?" She followed my line of sight toward Henry's shop. Henry had just appeared in the front door, opening it for the kids to march in.

"Ah, I see. I can't say I blame you there. I'd stare, too, if I were a hundred years younger."

Gigi's wide, friendly eyes twinkled, and I knew she was fighting to hide her smile. "That one is really special. To me, to everyone really. Even your dad has a soft spot for him. If you chose to spend some time with him, I'd personally be thrilled."

The phrase *spend time with* would have made me chuckle if I didn't want to do exactly that.

"It's not like that. You know how things are, Gigi," I murmured, watching as Henry turned toward my shop. The littles marched away, continuing their *hup, two, three, four* chanting. "Henry and I are just friends. Nothing more. He's not interested in anything else while I'm back."

Back, I said. Not visiting . . .

She turned as best she could, shifting so she was almost fully facing me. It felt like she wanted to see my face and judge my reaction. "Is that so?" she asked, narrowing her eyes as if that would help her see the truth through my lie. And it wasn't a lie after all. We were friends, regardless of how I felt about the situation or hoped that it would have a different outcome.

"And Nick?"

What, is she going to run through every single guy in this town?

"What? Oh, we're just friends," I admitted emphatically. "He's awesome, but there are zero sparks. Less than zero."

"Ah, but Max," she said, lingering a bit on his name. "He's a good choice."

She didn't say more, just kept the suggestion there and waited for me to explain. "We're supposed to get together later."

"Hmm," she said simply, turning back around. "I think young people today miss out on the simplicity of dating that we had back in my day."

I looked at her, smirking. "Oh yeah? Enlighten me."

She gave me such a side-eye, I guffawed. "If you fancied a boy or girl, you sent them a letter. Visited their parents' house and asked if you could take them out."

"Sounds about right," I said, wondering the last time anyone sent a letter of intention to another person.

You've got a handful of them right inside waiting for you to open them.

I jumped up, thinking that I hadn't opened the letter that was left at the shop. That one was still sitting inside.

"Are you all right?" she asked, taking my hand.

I sank back onto the bench. "Yeah, sorry. I just remembered something. You were saying?"

She smirked knowingly. It got wider when I saw Henry out of the corner of my eye walking from the shop over to Viola's for an ice cream.

"As I was saying. Now you have to sort through all the matches and the harmonies or whatever. You're connected by a computer. It's sort of impersonal. At least to me."

Gigi wasn't wrong, but statistically dating sites were successful. "I'm not a huge fan of the sites myself, but you have to admit, sometimes letting an algorithm do the dirty work for you is helpful."

"Honey, the dirty work is half the fun."

"Gigi!" I shouted, scandalized. "You're too much."

"I speak the truth. Sometimes going through the mud is the best way to find what's important. Who'll be there with you to pull you out. Does that make sense?"

I nodded. "Yes, but it doesn't help the current situation."

"I'm aware of that. You've got quite the conundrum on your hands. The dashing and handsome Dr. Reese and the one you seem to have set your eyes on."

She nodded up toward where Henry was walking back, carrying a cup of ice cream, presumably for Mr. Evan, who was now waiting outside on his own bench.

This was small-town life. This was something I could get used to.

BACK INSIDE, I sat on the stool and stared at the envelope. Plucking it up, I held it between my hands, just feeling it. The thin, rough linen paper was so light a breeze would take it like petals on the wind.

> You are the finest, loveliest, tenderest,
> and most beautiful person I have ever known and
> even that is an understatement.

"Well, that certainly gets your attention," I said to the blissfully empty work area in the back of the shop.

"What does?" a voice asked, between the dings of the door's bell. "I hear you're looking for another employee," Nick said, walking into the room carrying a cup of steaming hot coffee.

"I must really look like hell if I'm being gifted with a third coffee today."

"What? Oh shit, this is my coffee. I should have brought two. I didn't think. You're okay. I mean, you look okay? Nice? Good? You can have this, if you want it. It's got a stupid amount of sugar in it, though."

"Nick, have you ever complimented a woman before?"

"Does 'Nice boobs' count?" he asked sincerely.

I opened my mouth to respond but thought better of it. "You know what?" I smiled, grabbing the rag from my workstation to wipe my dirty hands. "Are you looking for a part-time job? I've seen your work. You're hired!"

"Ha!" he cheered, giving me a beaming smile. "I'd love to help, but you can't afford me. I just saw Henry leaving the bookstore looking like someone ripped a page from his dictionary. Charlotte, did you hit him again?"

I laughed in spite of myself. When it came to Henry, I would forever be known as the ball-breaker. "No, I'll have you know that I have not touched Henry Mercer."

Unfortunately.

Nick looked at me curiously. Instead of focusing on the what-ifs of Henry, I dug back into my sketches for the Fourth of July event. They were due to the planning committee at the special meeting Monday night and I still hadn't finished.

"These are incredible," Nick said, sliding one of the finished designs over. "I love the use of blue alliums. It's less traditional and really eye-catching, especially for the planters on the band shell."

I preened. "Thanks. It's risky, but I was trying to go outside the box, you know? I saw photos in the town archives from past festivals so I could get a feel for what's already been done. It was a lot of red, white, and sprayed blue roses or carnations. These are for the main thoroughfare around the pavilion," I explained, showing him the art for it. "The flowers will be pouring out of the planters they set up on the sides. Tons of color, mixed heights to really capture the fireworks feel. It's not like fireworks are only red, white, and blue, so this mirrors that. All bursts and pops to draw your eye to the tiny details. I hope people like this take on things. Most will, I think. I'm not sure about the gavel-wielding guy, though."

"Nothing will please him. Don't even try," he explained. "What's that sketch?"

"Emma said the pavilion is where everyone congregates during the day. Those," I said, pointing to the sketch still in his hand, "are the night bloomers. Moonflowers, nicotiana, and jasmine will be scattered throughout where everyone drops their blankets. It'll be a fully sensory experience. I think they'll really shine with the fireworks blasting off overhead. I even added glitter sticks for Emma, so they sparkle along with the festivities."

"That's a fun touch, she'll love it."

"She's been so stressed out making sure this whole thing is a success, I figured I'd give her a little something that will make her giggle," I explained, pulling out a couple of other sheets of rejected ideas.

It was nice to have someone to chat with who knew the field and was interested in the conversation. At least, I think he was.

"The mayoral ball is something else entirely, I'm assuming?" he asked, looking around the scattered papers for a sign he was right.

"Oh, I know, but I had some ideas that I had to jot down! Wait until you see these," I said as I pulled out another sketch. "I'm helping Emma with the menu and table decor, too, which I'm thrilled with. There's an entire flower wall for photos. Someone suggested a booth with those little stick accessories, but I thought we should go pure class all the way even if it is an outdoor festival. It's stunning, if I do say so myself."

"Flower wall?" Nick said, his eyes widening. "What made you go in that direction?"

I shrugged. "Again, risky. People associate them with wedding photos nowadays, but this isn't anything like that. Emma said Hope Lake has traditionally favored a shade of green as its town color. I was falling asleep in here the other night and I bolted awake with a vision of a couple in front of a crawling-ivy-filled wall that was peppered with baby's breath over its entire surface. That will be the base of the flower wall. At the top, there will be billowing waves of champagne hydrangeas, and cream gardenias in staggering lengths. The smell will be incredible."

"Charlotte, this is going to be a ton of work. I know you're looking to hire more people, but do you have the time for this?"

What else do I have going on?

I scratched my head. Looking around at the shop, I knew I needed help. "The flower wall is the most ambitious thing here. That'll be a lot of time in the walk-in, but I think the payoff will be tremendous. Emma said a lot of state press show up for the festival. I think they will for the mayoral ball, too, if the governor shows up. The publicity for the shop alone is worth all the extra time."

Nick looked confused. "That's a bit long-term, isn't it? The ball is in the spring . . ."

I frowned. "I suppose, but it'll be incredible exposure. Whether it's for me professionally or the shop generically—the publicity is amazing for the town."

He smiled, bright and beaming. "Spoken like a true Hope Laker."

Remaining quiet, I let the words ruminate. Weeks ago, I would have shredded the thought. The notion that I was becoming a part of this town. And now?

"Who knows? There are a couple of options that I'm batting around. I could always travel back and forth between New York and Hope Lake. Spend some time in both places if there was a reason for me to stay. I don't know. I can't think about it now; I don't have the mental space." I laughed when he waved his hand at my desk— or what you could see of my desk—to illustrate my point.

"You know, Emma can't come back here. I think she gets hives from the chaos," I said.

Nick laughed, tossing his coffee cup in the trash. "Doesn't surprise me. Anyone who labels their cabinets would go crazy in here. No offense."

I held up a hand. "None taken. And wait, she labels her cabinets?"

"Doesn't everyone?" Emma said, coming through the swing door and into the back room with a hand over her eyes.

"Your eyes are closed," Nick said plainly. "Did you know that?"

Emma turned toward his voice, keeping her eyes covered. "Your awareness of the obvious is truly awe-inspiring, Nicholas. Thank you."

Nick smiled proudly. "You're welcome."

I'm not sure he grasped her sarcasm.

"I stopped in to check on the progress," Emma said, turning toward me. "If you could kindly carry the sketches out to the safety and sanity of the shop floor, while also directing me so I don't trip and impale myself on what are sure to be scattered florist tools, that'd be great."

"You're completely ridiculous. All right, you two, I'm heading out," Nick said, grasping her elbow and leading her out into the shop, the saloon door to my office swinging behind them. "You got that stuff, C?"

"Yep!" I nodded, rolling up the plans and tucking them safely under my arm. Looking around, I saw that it really was a bit of a mess, but time was a prime commodity that I was sorely missing, and cleaning my office was last on my list of to-dos.

In the front of the shop, Emma had cleared a space on the workstation, even managing to organize it all in neat, orderly little piles. "You're an insatiable fiddler."

"I'm sure I don't know what you're talking about," Emma said matter-of-factly.

The envelopes that were left to be stacked were piled on the metal stool. Emma's hand was hovering near them, and it was only a matter of time before she grabbed the one from my secret admirer in her flurry to straighten up.

"Here, let me . . . ," I said, just as Nick waved at us as he walked out the front door.

"Grab these before I could?" Emma sang knowingly, taking the envelopes that had fallen. With a triumphant grin, she held one up as a high-school-aged girl walked into the shop.

"Hi there, have a look around. I'll be with you in a second," I said. I was cheerful on the outside, wilting from embarrassment on the inside.

"Give it here, Peroni," I said, but she'd already begun reading it aloud.

> They slipped briskly into an intimacy from
> which they never recovered.

"You've been holding out on me!" She fanned herself with the letter. "Here I'm worried that you're doom and gloom without any excitement, but it looks like I was wrong. What's this about?" She held up the paper so I could see the typewritten message.

It was the first time I got to read it. Like the others, it was poetic and vaguely familiar, but I couldn't place it. I shrugged. "Not sure. A couple—okay, more than a couple—have showed up. No idea who they're from." I had been receiving letters steadily for the past few weeks. I opened the first couple, but after those, I never opened any of them. I think the reason I let them sit unopened was because I'm pretty sure they're from Dr. Max, and it's easier to not think about them than face my feelings—or lack thereof—for him.

"That quote's from Fitzgerald," the girl said, walking up to the counter. She was pretty in a pixie sort of way. She had small facial features and was petite, with a shock of platinum hair cut into a severely-angled chop.

"Who?" Emma and I said together.

Emma looked affronted. "I don't know any Fitzgeralds in town," she added with a huff. As if someone had the gall to move in without her knowing it.

The girl rolled her eyes. "You're kidding me, right? Fitzgerald as in F. Scott? That's a line from *This Side of Paradise*."

The two of us looked at her curiously.

I'd had a vague recollection of the words, but upon hearing this girl pair them with Fitzgerald, the blocks fell into place. The other unopened notes were spread out on the counter. Unopened, but now I was curious. I plucked one up and slid out the paper.

I read it, keeping in mind Fitzgerald.

```
I used to build dreams about you.
You know, you're a little complicated after all.
"Oh no," she assured him hastily. "No, I'm not really—I'm
just a—I'm just a whole lot of different simple people."
I love her and it is the beginning of everything.
The loneliest moment in someone's life is when they are
watching their whole world fall apart, and all they can do
is stare blankly.
```

"All of these," she said, taking one from me, "are from Fitzgerald. I mean, they're from a bunch of different books and personal quotes and stuff, but it's definitely all from him."

"Who would send you anonymous quotes from Fitzgerald like this?" Emma asked. I was about to tell her I thought they were from Dr. Max when the girl asked, "Are you in the class?"

"What class?"

"Mr. Mercer's course on American fiction writers. It's brilliant."

"What. The. F—"

Emma slapped her hand over my mouth, murmuring, "Juvenile. No cursing."

"I'm eighteen, relax," the girl said, taking the paper from a still-stunned Emma. "Mr. Mercer would love to see that someone is using his class so creatively. Can I take a pic?" the girl asked, pulling out a battered iPhone.

I slapped my hand over them. "No, sorry, I'm still working out what's— Just, no. Okay? Sorry, I'm so confused right now."

And I was. A tableful of notes would have to wait until I was alone and had time to process the crazy ideas that were rolling around in my head.

"No problem. Just wanted to show him how cool it was that someone was listening. Anyway, I came in because he mentioned you. Or is it you who runs this place?" she asked, pointing between me and Emma. "Need to hire someone? I'm a dub mage in art and business and I totally dig flowers and design. I'm great at Quick-Books and can manage the shit out of your, well, everything."

"She's the one you've got to impress," Emma said, pointing over to me. "I didn't really follow the rest of what you said with my old-lady hearing and lack of teen lingo experience, but it sounds super . . . dope? Wicked? Cool? Are any of those still hip?"

The girl shook her head. "Good try, but no."

Suddenly, Emma went quiet. "You guys chat and get to know each other, and I'll leave. I'm swamped." She started gathering her stuff to make a quick exit.

"Where are you going? We had to go over these!" I shouted, holding up the designs as Emma stalked back. She grabbed the rolled-up designs and headed for the door again. "I'll be back tomorrow."

On her way out, she flipped the OPEN sign to CLOSED and went across the square toward the bookstore. After a moment, she disappeared into the shop. She came and went in a flash, and I was left gobsmacked, staring after her.

My visitor cleared her throat. "Do you have an application or something I can fill out while you're having an existential crisis?"

I laughed. "I don't have an application. Have you ever worked in a flower shop before? How about working events? What flexibility do you have in your hours?"

What am I thinking? She's a smart-ass and has no experience and I'm going to hire her?

"No, unless you call YouTube videos experience. You can learn anything on there. I've been knitting, quilting, and canning veggies with my mom for the past year. Between that and Instagram tutorials, I've found I can hold my own in the world of floral design. I love playing with new ideas and sketching thoughts out on paper. I don't have much of a social life, so I'm free whenever, especially in the summer. My parents split, and my mom won't pay for school if I stay an art major, so I need to get something to help with that."

"Your mom cut you off?" I asked, seeing her in a new light.

The jagged hair that looked like she might have cut and dyed it herself. The fingernails bitten down to the quick. A vacant, scared, and unsure look in her eyes that I recognized way too much. She could have been me just a few years ago.

"You're sure this is a job you'll want to do? It's a lot of standing and designing whatever people want, even if it's ridiculous and you know it'll look awful. It's not easy. Plus, I have no idea how to be a boss."

She laughed, her eyes lighting up. "Do you know how *not* to be a boss?"

I thought about it. Specifically, about my last dead-end job.

"Yes, I know how *not* to be a boss," I answered, knowing that if I modeled every decision based on the opposite of what Gabrielle had done, I would be successful.

"Then I'd say that's the best boss you can be. Treating people like humans and not minions or underlings is the first step," she said confidently.

I never thought of it that way. Here I was getting solid advice from someone a decade younger than me.

"You start Monday," I said, holding out my hand for her to shake. "I'll have to download paperwork and stuff, figure out what the going rate for pay is, but we'll worry about that later. I can talk to Lucille—she's the owner—about paying you a bit more after a few weeks. We'll call it training or something. I'm sure Emma has packets or whatever bosses are supposed to hand out."

"I'll be here at eight. I make lousy coffee, but I brew a mean cup of English breakfast," she said, bouncing lightly toward the door.

When her hand was on the doorknob, I realized something important.

"Hey, I should probably ask your name!" I laughed, thinking how terrible I was at this whole boss thing already.

"I'm Nellie. Pleased to meet you, Charlotte."

"I THOUGHT YOU were coming back tomorrow," I asked Emma, pulling my wet hair up into a bun. She was rocking on Gigi's front porch swing, brushing crumbs off her lap from feeding the birds a fortune cookie.

"It took forever for you to come down," she said, taking a drink from a bottle of green tea.

"Sorry, Your Highness. I was in the shower. Why didn't you ring the doorbell?" I asked, leaning on the railing.

"I didn't want to wake Gigi. I know she goes to bed early. By the way, have you eaten yet? I brought takeout. Although I may have eaten your egg roll," she said guiltily, pushing the bag of Chinese with her shoe. She stood, slinging a plastic tube over her shoulder.

"How'd you know I was going to be here? I didn't even know I was going to be here."

"What does that mean?" she asked, looking at my door curiously.

I turned, spying another envelope stuck to the screen. "I was supposed to have ice cream with Max, but I canceled."

"Why'd you do that?" She was speaking to me, but her eyes never left the door. Or I should say, the envelope that was stuck to the door. "Are you going to get that? And open it while I'm standing here? I'm curious." She bounced on her feet, the floorboards creaking beneath her.

"I canceled because I'm exhausted, and yes, I'll take it, and no, I don't know if I'll open it now or later."

"You had a bunch of letters at the shop. How many total? Roughly?"

I thought back. "Maybe about ten?"

Emma whistled. "Wow, someone sure has been busy. Have you asked him about them?"

"Who?"

"The person sending them?" she said, not looking me in the eye. She crinkled her skirt in her hands.

"No, I don't know who it is. I mean, I thought it was Dr. Max, but then I got to thinking that it doesn't make sense."

Emma remained quiet.

"Emma, do *you* know who it is?" I asked. She still wouldn't meet my eyes. "Emma?"

She cleared her throat. "If I did, I wouldn't tell you. I love you, and this is the most absurdly romantic gesture in the most absurdly ridiculous way. I want to see how it plays out."

I straightened. "Even if that means keeping me in the dark?"

"Furthermore," she continued, "I don't think you *want* me to tell you. I see that you're trying to ferret out information yourself. You need to be the one to solve this puzzle on your own. I can't spoon-feed you the answers. Either that, or those responsible will have to be truthful."

"I hate you," I said, giving her arm a solid pinch.

"You don't hate me. You love me, and you know I'm right."

"I hate that, but you are."

"Now what?" she asked, keeping her eyes glued to the envelope. "You going to open that?"

"We eat, that's what. I'm starving. Do you want to eat out here or inside?" I asked, avoiding her question. "Thanks for dinner, by the way. I was going to have to eat frozen pizza."

She frowned. "You realize that you can come over anytime, right? Or head to my folks' house? Or Mancini's? They'd all be more than happy to feed you. And Gigi."

I shrugged. "Don't worry about her. She's still in the single-lady-of-the-house zone so she eats whenever she feels like it. So many people bring her food, it's a bit hysterical. No wonder she doesn't want to go into assisted living. Besides, she's been giving me a wide berth. I don't see her all that much. When I go to work, she's futzing around waiting for someone. When I get back, she's cleaning up after dinner or getting ready for bed."

Emma laughed, bumping my shoulder as I held the door for her. "I think she's probably trying to give you space. Showing you that you two can coexist in a shared space. Similar to what your dad is doing. It's probably why he didn't cancel the meetings and trips he and Max had planned. They're not trying to overwhelm you or hover so you get spooked and bolt. Trust me when I say they want you to stay. We all do."

She turned to look at me head-on. I stopped short but kept my eyes down.

"Hey," she said, tipping my chin up.

"I see I've caused you to get that deer-in-the-headlights look. I'll stop for now and say kung pao chicken or shrimp with garlic sauce?"

Some of the tension melted. "Is both the wrong answer?"

"Never."

17

"Knock, knock," Henry called from the shop's front door.

"Oh!" I said, trying to steady myself. "I'm just finishing something up."

He looked disappointed. "I see you're busy. I can come back later to place an order. It's my mom's birthday, and one of your masterpieces will beat the book on British poetry that I bought her last year."

"You scared me." I was standing on a stool, my arms placing green foam into an elongated vase that a customer had brought in for a garish centerpiece that she *needed* to have in her entryway. I couldn't reach it without some delicate maneuvering. "Also, a book of British poems sounds lovely."

I was covered in foam, again, and a fleck wedged itself danger-ously close to my right eye. The problem was that both my hands were covered in it, leaving me no safe way to remove it until some-one ventured in to help.

"I'll take whatever you're going to give me as soon as you save my eye," I said, moving from around the counter to stand in front of him.

"Your hands are shaking. Don't blind me." I blinked rapidly every time his fingers came near my eye.

"Your eye is possessed. I can't get near it without it fluttering. Hold still," he said, gently cupping my face. He leaned in, close.

Then closer still, until my eye wasn't fluttery anymore because it was too focused on him.

"Did you get it?" I asked, feeling a spark lick up my spine with every soft touch of his fingers on my skin.

"Yes." Henry pulled back, quickly plucking the green foam from my face before stepping away. "I just wanted to bring this back," he said, holding out the envelope from the other night. "It must have fallen out of your pocket when I drove you home."

He looked uneasy, rubbing the back of his neck.

"What about those?" I asked of the envelopes in his other hand, which he had just pulled from his back pocket. There were two more.

I didn't think it was possible, but he looked even guiltier.

"They were stuck to your front door when I got there. At first, I thought they were for me from you or Gigi. So, uh, I opened one. When I realized that it wasn't from you but *for* you"—he paused—"I stopped. Clearly they're from, well, whoever it is that you're seeing. . . ."

"You read one?"

He nodded, showing me the opened flap. He stood straighter, and his voice took on an edge. "I meant to give them to you, but time got away from me. I've been so busy with the Fourth of July festival, plus some course things, and— Never mind, you're clearly uninterested."

He held his hand out. The grip on the envelopes was tight, almost frustrated.

"I can't believe you," I snapped sourly, taking them from his hand.

"Me? You can't believe me? How do you think I feel? I'm fighting against whatever this is between us, while you're seeing Max, making me look like a goddamned moony-eyed fool."

His hands gripped his hair, tugging at the curly locks. "I can't believe—" he muttered, too low for me to hear. "So stupid," was all I could make out.

"What do you mean?" I pointed at the envelopes. "I've only seen Max a couple of times, not that it's any of your business!"

I stormed into the back room with Henry hot on my heels.

"I'm sorry that I read the damn thing. I would have given you the rest back, but you were probably busy with *Max*," he said, spitting out his name again as the door closed behind him.

"Oh, please. Enough with Max. We barely see each other. And eventually, I'll find a minute to spend more time getting to know him."

"While you're here," he added with a finality that sent a rush of anger through me again.

"Yes, Henry. While I'm here. *He* doesn't have a problem with short-term."

He stepped away. In the back room, alone and in the dim light, he looked even more tired than he did out front. The sparkle that usually lit up his eyes was missing.

My remark had its intended effect, but it felt awful.

"For the record," I said, tossing the letters on the workstation, "these letters are as much of a mystery to me as they are to you. Full disclosure, there was a part of me that hoped they were from you."

"Not my style," he said flatly. "I outgrew writing simple letters."

Ouch. If this was simple, what did it make me that I enjoyed them?

I whirled around. "Well, since these are obviously *not* from you, I hope you'll excuse me. I have some Sherlocking to do since Max is the likely poet in all of this."

He harrumphed. "Max? You think your Dr. Max sent these? Fitzgerald, Cummings, Keats? He has no idea who any of those people are!"

I slapped the envelopes on the table, sending more stems scattering about the floor.

"How many of these did you read to know that? How dare you!"

He had enough dignity to look remorseful at being caught.

I couldn't believe him. And if they weren't from Henry and they weren't from Max, I had no idea who the hell they *were* from, and

I wasn't about to figure it out with Henry looking over my shoulder while I tried to.

The intention was to hold my head high and storm past Henry, but he had other plans.

As I made my way to him, he pivoted so that I had to stop short. "Move."

He blew out a long breath. "I'm sorry." He paused, his head sagging dejectedly. "I was rude. Being mad over the *situation* is certainly no excuse for me being rude. Especially not to you. I . . . just give me a second," he whispered.

We were facing in opposite directions, his right shoulder touching my left. Vibrations rolled through his body as he fought whatever it was that was warring inside him.

"Why are you mad?" I asked, wanting to turn to see him but staying facing forward. It was easier. Almost like there was a confessional screen between us that gave him a chance to be honest.

"What aren't I mad at is probably a shorter list," he said quietly.

I stiffened. "You're mad at me?"

He shook his head. "No, not *at* you. At myself, the situation that I've put us in. Max is a constant thorn, and all the letters you're getting. All of it is a constant reminder that I'm not—that we're not . . ."

"Not what?" I asked.

"That we're just *not*. Not is such a finite and negative adverb."

I smiled. "Spoken like a true English teacher."

The warmth was building at the spot where our shoulders were touching. Who would have thought that a shoulder touch would be enough to both calm my anger and build up other emotions.

"We're just *not*. There's nothing positive about it, and it's been eating away at me."

"Well, you're *not* alone in the frustration. So, I guess in a roundabout way that's a positive."

"Yes, but I am alone and we're *not* and that's my doing."

Turning, I finally got to look into his eyes. They were torn. His brow was furrowed, and the blue was stormy and conflicted.

"Henry," I said, leaning toward him. While the annoyance was still there over the letters, another emotion was at the forefront.

He smiled down at me, a small spark shining through the stormy blue. "Even in this light, your hair looks like it has fire woven through it," he whispered, reaching up to tuck a curly strand back behind my ear. His thumb smoothed down my cheek slowly. His other hand met my cheek, and he held my face gently in his hands.

"Henry," I breathed, my eyes fluttering closed.

He was going to lean in. I felt the shift in his body. The stiffening of his fingers on my skin. The shuddery breaths coming from his mouth that was *so* close to mine that I felt the edge of his lips.

With a deep exhale, he took his hand and placed it over mine. It was a strange feeling, but I loved that his hand shook as our fingers intertwined.

"Henry," I sighed. I couldn't keep doing this. It was a carousel that I needed to get off of and far away from. The feelings were twisting around me like ivy and pulling me under.

"I'm sorry," he said, squeezing my hand once. "I feel like I'm a kettle boiling over all the time. It's making me crazy."

I laughed, but we both knew it wasn't with humor. "I know the feeling," I said honestly, squeezing his hand back gently.

"Can I?" he begged, but what was he asking for? At this point, I would agree to anything if it made the pain go away.

Henry raised our joined hands slowly. He turned mine toward the ceiling so my palm was open and facing him. I wanted to look away. I tried looking away, but my eyes kept drawing back to where I knew I shouldn't look: his lips.

Slowly, he raised my palm to his mouth, kissing it once, then twice before moving up a few inches to my wrist. His warm lips pressed there, and he inhaled. "You always smell like lilacs. Even if you're not working with them. If I catch the smell of them on the breeze, I know you're around. It's driving me out of my mind."

"Henry," I mumbled again, incoherent from the sensations pulsing through me.

These were just his lips. *Just* his lips on my skin, peppering their way up my bare arm until he reached my shoulder. The curve between my shoulder and my neck was almost my undoing. My head lobbed to the side when I felt the tiniest bite of his teeth against my flesh followed by the swirl of his tongue.

"Jesus Christ," I moaned, the sound echoing through the darkening chamber of the back room.

Henry's other hand was splayed across my back, inching its way up until he reached my hair that had fallen out of the clip. I could feel his fingers twirling a strand around. My hands were limp at my sides until he gave a slight tug and they snapped to attention.

"Henry." I chanted his name incoherently as I gripped at his shirt, his waist. Anywhere that I could to hold him to me. I was afraid he'd disappear. That this was all a figment of my imagination. Too delirious from working so much, I manifested all of my desires in this one moment.

Up, up, up his lips went until they reached my jawline. My head tipped toward him. Every inch of my skin felt like it was reaching up to his lips, waiting to be touched. I burned. It was the only way to describe it. My body felt alight with a fire that I hadn't felt before.

Out of nowhere, Henry lifted me up with the quickest of movements. Fear of falling, or fear of him letting me go, made me wrap my legs around him, earning a deep growl. We were in the center of the room. There wasn't a wall to push me against, and the table was too far away to set me upon. He just held me against him, breathing heavily into my hair until he lifted me up, only to catch me with his hand resting on my ass. The thin, flimsy shorts I wore did nothing to shield my skin from the heat of his palms.

Silently, I prayed for his hands to reach up and under the fabric to cup me without having the barrier between us that was driving me crazy. As if he could read my mind, he intensified his grip on one side and slipped his right hand beneath the fabric of both my shorts and my panties.

"Holy shit," I breathed, my head falling back as Henry pressed a single kiss to my breastbone.

Tremors ran through my body. I wasn't cold but on fire, and trembling to keep myself as composed as possible. The other option was tearing off every stitch of clothing, knowing that someone could walk in at any minute.

His fingers, ten tiny pinpricks of heat, were pressed firmly into my flesh. I was convinced I would have bruises. All of this—the emotion sizzling through me, the light-headedness from his lips— and I realized that he hadn't even kissed me.

I giggled, thinking this was the equivalent of two adults dry-humping. The giggle was what zapped him out of the trance he was in: a lust-filled ocean that we were both drowning in.

He pulled back, leaving a small wet spot in the center of my tank top where he'd pressed his mouth.

"Charlotte," he said, a panicked beat to his raspy voice. "I—"

"No, no, don't say you're sorry!" I begged, my hands trying to catch any part of him to be able to keep him near me. "Don't shut down, please. This wasn't a mistake."

The door chimed, sounding through the back room. If it was possible, he looked even more stricken, his face paling and his hands shaking as they held me.

"I'll be right out!" I shouted, keeping my arms wrapped around his head.

If anyone walked back right now, they'd think I was either trying to climb Henry like a tree or smother him in my bosom.

And they wouldn't be wrong on either count.

"I'm not letting go," I said, twisting my hands in the back of his shirt and my legs around his waist.

"Charlotte, you have a customer," he said, sounding pained. I knew then, no matter what magic I did with my boobs being right there in his face, I had lost him.

"They can wait. This can't."

Henry was barely holding on anymore, and I couldn't keep

myself up much longer. Reluctantly, I slid down his body. When I brushed up against him, he sucked in a sharp breath.

"I'd say sorry, but I'm not," I said, as I began to pace, clenching and unclenching my fists.

Glancing at him over my shoulder, I grew annoyed that he looked like the picture of restraint.

Looked being the operative word.

A small vein in his neck throbbed. His breathing was shallow and shaky, and his eyes were a stormy swirl. He was terrible at hiding his emotions.

"Charlotte," he began, and I slammed my hand down on the small table.

He startled, his eyes flying up to finally meet mine. "Charlotte, I'm—" he started again, and I slammed my hand down a second time.

"So help me, I will throw this vase at you if you say you're sorry," I warned, clutching my hand around the thin glass vase.

"I won't say it," he retorted, but he may as well have because his head was down and he was staring at his shoes. "Regardless of what you think of me right now, I don't want to hurt you. This wasn't why I came here."

"Why did you come, then? To bring the letters? To flirt and be jealous a little bit more? To show me that you're unaffected by this?" I shouted, waving between us.

The door chime sounded again and either the first person left because they heard us shouting, or another person came in.

He stalked forward, lowering his voice to a harsh whisper. Henry's lips were a hairbreadth away from mine. Against my lips, he whispered, "I'm selfish and weak. Today, the weakness won out. I want you to stay because this time, Charlotte, you have a choice to stay here. To not leave me. But I won't beg someone to stay again. I won't, Charlotte, and I can't let this happen again. I can't put myself through it."

I remembered Emma's story about Henry's last girlfriend.

"Henry, I'm not her," I said, trying to hold him to me. "I'm not Sarah."

He sucked in a breath, surprised that I knew about his past. "You know about her, that's good. And you're right, you're nothing like her. That's why this would be a thousand times worse than before, because it's you."

18

After Henry left, it was like the shop had a black cloud hanging over it. No one came in the last two hours it was open. Which was good, because I wasn't in the mood to be cheery and cordial. It helped me focus on getting work done, finishing up the rest of the customer pieces. With everything finally ready, I flipped the sign to CLOSED and headed out into the darkening streets to walk home.

As I wandered toward Gigi's, I thought about the last thing Henry said. *You're right, you're nothing like her. That's why this would be a thousand times worse than before, because it's you.*

The farther outside of town I got, the worse the weather got and the less I recognized where I was. Driving through town was one thing, but walking in the dark—I had no idea where I went wrong. Somewhere in my fog, and the fog and rain that had rolled in, I turned up the wrong street. "So much for clearing my head," I mumbled and pulled out my phone.

Emma and Nick went straight to voice mail. There was the option to call Max, but I didn't want to have to explain why I hadn't had time to see him. I should just be honest with him and tell him that it wasn't him, it was very much me, but that was a better discussion in person when I wasn't a confused mess.

I called one of the people I knew I could count on no matter what. Of course, the call was picked up on the first ring. "Hey, sweetheart, how was your day?" Dad asked, and I could hear him shuffling around.

"It was okay. Hey, are you busy?" I wiped a tear that was sliding down my cheek.

"For you? Never. What's up?"

I coughed, covering up the whimper that was choking me. "I'm sending you my location. I got myself lost, and the rain is picking up. My umbrella isn't holding up with the wind. Can you pick me up and take me to Gigi's?"

We hung up and I sent him the ping. I wasn't that far, but I had no idea what the expanse of land between where I was and where Gigi lived looked like. It could be the deep woods or a bunch of hills. None of which I wanted to traverse in the rain.

I just wanted to take a bath, curl up, and relax with my head on Gigi's lap. She could rub my head like she did when I was a little girl.

Suddenly a memory came, plain as day, as I tucked myself under the canopy of an elm tree.

My parents were screaming at each other about my leaving with my mother. Gigi took me upstairs to her room. We curled up on the narrow bench that sat at the foot of her bed. She stroked my head and whispered stories about the many places in the house that she could hide me that my mother would never be able to find me. "If she can't find you, she can't take you away from me."

"Gigi, where are the places? Let's go now," my small voice begged. We stood, and she held my hand as we tiptoed down the hall. There was wood paneling all along the bottom half of the wall. They looked like frames, but one of them wasn't like the others.

"This one is for you, Charlotte," she explained, pulling down the small piece of molding to reveal a latch. When she pushed down on the latch, a small door popped open. "You follow this all the way down the hall and up the stairs. You'll be in a separate room in the attic."

"It's so dark," I said, looking down the short hallway.

"I know, it's the only way in or out of that little room. I keep all my secrets in there. You can stay in there whenever you want."

"Will you be here when I'm ready to come back out?"

"Yes, my darling. Gigi won't ever leave you," she promised. With a kiss on the top of my head, she gave me a small nudge forward. Once I was safely in the passageway, she handed me a tiny flashlight. "This will help."

I shone the light down the dark tunnel and my eyes bolted open. It wasn't a flashlight but my dad's headlights coming down the road. The memory was still fresh in my mind, and now I couldn't wait to get home.

Hopping into the car, I hugged my dad with everything I had.

"What was that for?" he asked, kissing the top of my head.

"I'm just glad to see you. It was a bit of a rough day, but I just had one hell of a memory come through."

"Oh yeah? What?" He pulled out onto the road and took a quick turn. This was where I'd gone right instead of left.

"Did you know Gigi's house had a secret passageway?" I asked. I expected him to say "Of course," but instead he chuckled.

"Don't be silly, Charlotte. There aren't any secret tunnels in the house. I lived there for ages and never found one. Trust me, I looked. So have many other people."

Did I imagine the whole thing? Can I not trust the memories now?

I closed my eyes, thinking back again to that day. My mother storming up the stairs, screaming at Gigi to tell her where I was.

"Rose, she ran down the backstairs and outside. Go out there to find her. Or, better yet, leave her alone until you calm down. You're not helping anyone being this worked up."

"Don't tell me how to raise my daughter, Imogen," she howled, slamming something against the wall that I was hiding behind.

I wanted to jump out, to tell her to leave me alone, that I wanted to stay with Dad and Gigi, but my voice wouldn't work. I was terrified as the flashlight flickered and died. Slowly, I turned myself around and crawled in the opposite direction.

The voices faded the farther I got into the wall. At the end there was another panel but this one had no latch. It pushed away quickly, opening up into the attic.

The main part was on the other side of a door. I knew this door. Dad told me that there were pipes hidden behind it. But it wasn't a utility space at all.

Gigi had turned it into a little space to escape to. A tufted pillow sat in the corner of a wide plush carpet. There was a small round window that let in a shaft of light streaming across the floor. It was cozy, not too big but not so small that you felt claustrophobic. There was a LEGO set and a couple of Nancy Drew books.

It was the perfect spot for a kid to hide when the world seemed too big to handle.

"It feels so real," I admitted just as he pulled into the driveway.

Shutting off the car, he turned to me. "Come on, we can talk inside."

Gigi was waiting in the foyer for us. "I made dinner," she announced just as we crossed the threshold.

"Oh God, Mother, why?"

"Dad!" I yelled. "Not nice."

"You'll say the same thing once you eat it."

"For that comment, Andrew, you'll get seconds and like it."

"Shit."

"Gigi, before we feast on what is sure to be a delicious dish, can I ask you a question?"

She stopped her chariot and turned toward me. "Anything."

"There's a secret room upstairs, right?" I waited, watching for a negative reaction. For her to shoot down the memory.

"You remember," she said simply. My father's jaw dropped.

"There is?" he said, stunned when Gigi replied, "Duh."

"Can dinner wait a few minutes?" I asked, primed and ready to haul myself up the stairs.

"It's already burned, what's a little longer?" she said, winking when I spun on my heel and tore up the stairs.

Pulling out my phone, I enabled the flashlight and found the panel. I recalled the memory one more time to remember how Gigi did it. With my eyes closed, I popped the molding and found the latch. A quick click and it opened just as it did in the memory.

"Incredible," my father murmured from beside me. "I grew up here and she never told me."

Gigi called up from downstairs. "You never needed it, Andrew. You had a good childhood." It didn't take a genius to figure out that she meant I needed it because *I* had a shitty childhood.

"How did it get here? Why did you build it into the house?" my dad asked, his voice echoing when he stuck his head into the passage.

"It wasn't meant to be a secret room. It was an accident, really. When I realized what happened, I had them finish off the passage and the room at the end."

"I'm glad you did," I breathed, nudging my father out of the way. "Gigi, I'm going in!"

I heard her say, "Wait!" but I had already disappeared inside.

It was considerably harder to go through it than when I was ten. I had to crawl slower, and I worried my hips were going to get wedged and stuck. Luckily, the deeper in I got, the wider the space became.

At the end, just as I remembered, I found the panel. Pushing it to the side, I slipped into the attic space.

This time, there wasn't any sunlight streaming through the window, but the moonlight was. The weather must have cleared up, because the tiny octagonal window looked dry.

The rug was the same, although dustier than I remembered. A couple of boxes were stacked up along the wall that bordered the rest of the attic. They were all labeled ROSE in black Sharpie.

"Dad, can you hear me?" I called down the passageway.

"Barely," he said. "I'm not sure we'll both fit down there."

Lifting my phone, I dialed his number. It shut off the flashlight but there was enough of the moonlight to keep my eyes on the boxes. As if they were going to disappear.

"What's the matter?" he asked, sounding worried. "Gigi is having a fit downstairs saying she can explain. You'd better come out."

"Mom's stuff is here," I said unceremoniously.

"What?" he responded shakily.

"Yeah, not a lot, but a couple of boxes. I'm going to try to push them out."

With the boxes stacked in a row in the hallway, I propped my phone on top to light the way. Getting in here was hard enough. Getting out with three boxes was even worse.

My father eyed the boxes as he pulled them out for me. Stacking them in the hall, I heard Gigi clearly now. "Bring everything down. I'll explain."

"You'd better," Dad replied, sounding more annoyed than I had ever heard him with his mother.

He carried two, and I carried one. We took care of them as if they held the finest china.

We settled into the dining room, placing all three boxes in the center. Gigi wheeled herself to her usual space, where the chair was missing, and began.

"I'm sure that you both have questions. I will answer as best I can, but I'd like to say something to start. Rose had these sent to me after she died. I don't know why. I put them away because they hurt too much to look at. I've never opened them; therefore, I have no idea what's inside. I don't like to speak ill of the dead—we all know that your mother had a great many problems and flaws, but know this—whether it was right or wrong, I do believe that in her own way she loved you. Keep that in mind when you're looking through these."

I nodded, unable to speak. The boxes weren't sealed with tape, just folded over, making them easy to open. The first box had my mom's childhood stuff: some report cards, a lot of photos that I'd never seen before, and one of her and my father that he had never seen before, judging by his pained reaction. You could see there was once a great love there—at least on his end. He held the photo reverently, touching her face lightly before setting it aside.

"This was when we got married at the Borough Building. She always said she never got a photo." He didn't look sad so much as resigned. Dad had many years to get over the heartbreak he suffered at her hands. I was hoping that this wouldn't open those wounds back up.

The second box was filled with some things that represented my mom's life in Hope Lake with my father. A copy of their marriage license and my birth certificate. A couple of pictures of me as a kid that I'd never seen. It wasn't the same as the rest of my memory lapse, but that I was far too young to have any clear memory of them.

The third I assumed would be more of the same. I couldn't have been more wrong. I opened the top and my hand flew to my mouth. Pulling out the chair beside me, I sat, taking the box onto my lap to dig through easily.

Stacks upon stacks of envelopes were inside. At least a hundred, but they weren't like the ones that were coming now. These were addressed in a young person's unsure script.

Charlotte Bishop c/o Rose Bishop
644 E. 76th St Apt 4
New York, NY 10021

"What. How?" I mumbled, sifting through the envelopes. They were all postmarked from the day we left Hope Lake until about three years later. "They stopped when we moved apartments," I said, holding up the first one.

"Oh dear," Gigi said, wiping a tear from her eye. "I was afraid of that."

"What are these?" My hands shook as I tried opening the first one. "I can't get it, they're still sealed. I need one of those openers."

I jumped from the chair and slid into my grandfather's office. I remembered seeing one that day I was in there with Gigi. Running back into the dining room, I saw the side-eye the two doctors gave me for running with a sharp object.

"Andrew, I need help with a thing. Let's leave her alone for this part," Gigi insisted.

"If it's all the same to you, Mother, I'll stay. I'd like to see what this is."

As she wheeled out, she ran over my father's foot with her wheelchair.

"Ouch!"

"See, *now* you have to come with me. Put some ice on it, you'll be fine."

Dad looked worried but followed after his mother.

When they left, I hurried to open the first envelope as gently as I could. The paper was thin and old—being stuffed away in the attic didn't help much—but there wasn't anything I could do about that now.

I slipped my fingers inside the envelope and pulled out the first note, somehow recognizing the childlike printing immediately.

> *Dear Charlotte,*
> *We had a math test today. It was easy but it wasn't the same without you sitting next to me. I brought Lego for recess, but no one wanted to play with me. Are you coming back soon? I hope so. I miss you.*
>
> > *Love your best friend,*
> > *Henry*

The next few were much of the same. Various silly details that ten-year-olds care about, and all ending with requests hoping for the same outcome. For me to come back to Hope Lake.

My best friend.

The tears started around the fourth letter. By the twentieth, I could barely read them through the waterworks.

Not a single letter was opened, which meant not one was responded to and yet . . . not a single letter lost the hopefulness that I would come back. With the very last letter in my hand, I collapsed onto the dining chair, staring at all the aged envelopes.

I wasn't sure how or when the memories of Henry would come back. I had hoped that I'd remember him. How we were and what he meant to me. Closing my eyes, I took a deep breath and held some of the letters in my hand.

In my mind, I saw two kids as they climbed the front steps of Hope Lake Elementary. The boy was wearing pants that were a smidge too short and the girl carried a LEGO Stormtrooper in her hand.

Immediately, I knew they were us. In the memory, we turned around to wave to our parents, who were standing by their cars: Henry's mom and dad, and my dad and Gigi, my mother nowhere to be found. I remembered that day. The first day of kindergarten when she said she had a headache and for them to take me without her.

Then another memory came. Henry dressed as Indiana Jones and me as a magnificent peacock, a costume that Gigi labored over for a month because it had to be perfect and she wasn't the craftiest person.

The last memory that came was on Valentine's Day, a few months before I left, when Henry brought me in a cupcake that he made all by himself. On it was a shaky C and a lumpy H in syrup.

And it tasted terrible.

But I smiled and ate the whole thing.

Henry.

"There has to be a reason why I couldn't remember you," I whispered, wiping at the tears on my cheeks.

At the very bottom of the stack was a letter in my mother's scrawl. It simply read *Imogen*. Something from my mother to Gigi was unexpected, especially after Gigi explained how they didn't speak. The temptation was to call her in to explain herself, but then I saw that it, too, was unopened.

Slipping my finger under the seal, I opened it and steadied myself.

Imogen,
You never thought I was right for taking her away from that
place, and Andrew. And you. Maybe I shouldn't have, but it was
my choice to give her a chance to grow up outside of that bubble.
To experience things that I didn't. I trust you'll know what to do
with these things. Take care of my girl.

Rose

That was it. No explanation other than my growing up outside of Hope Lake.

I went to find Gigi and my dad.

I didn't have to look very far. They were giving me space by staying in the entryway: my dad sitting on the steps, his head in his hands much like the day we left; Gigi in her chair beside him, her hand resting on his knee.

"Dad, I need to borrow your car."

"The keys are in it."

"Please call Duncan and Birdy and tell them not to pull me over. I'll go to Mount Hazel for the driving test this weekend if that helps ease the sting of my breaking the law. Again."

I kissed them both before heading out the door and into the light drizzle that had started up again.

Eventually, I found what I thought was Nick and Henry's street. Sure enough, I pulled up in front of the double-block that had the ancient Jeep Wrangler in front of it.

"But which side?" I asked the pale-gray-sided house. Lights were on in both front rooms and upstairs in the house on the right.

I took a shot and knocked on that one.

And Nick answered thirty seconds later. "Hey, hey, are you okay? Why all the tears?" he asked, pulling me into the house without a word from me.

Inside, I broke down again. Glancing in the small mirror by
the door, I sighed. "I look like a mess." My freckles were more pro-
nounced with my skin being so blotchy. My gray eyes looked even
paler than usual, and they were puffy and watery.

"Are you looking for Henry?" Nick asked, pointing to the letter I
still had clutched in my hand.

I nodded, holding it against my stomach. It's not that I didn't
want Nick to see it, I just didn't want to explain it to anyone but
Henry just yet.

"He's next door."

"Thanks, Nick," I said, giving him a quick hug.

I left Nick's and walked over to stand in front of Henry's door.
If there was a doorbell, I couldn't see it. I placed my sweaty hand
flat against the shiny red-painted wood of the door. My nerves were
making it shake.

A moment later, the doorknob turned. Henry stood on the other
side looking like he'd just been in the middle of a rigorous workout.

"That's not fair," I mumbled, lowering my eyes to examine the
cracks on the cement landing.

"What's not?" he asked, taking a step forward. Looking up
through my lashes, I saw him glance up and down the street.

Absently, I motioned to his naked, sweaty chest. "Do you have a
shirt? Or I'll give you mine?"

He choked, a mix between a laugh and a cough. "Out of the two
of us, I think it's safer for you to remain clothed."

In your opinion.

I nodded, making sure that the envelope I carried was protected
from the drizzle and his prying eyes. Asking him about it was something that I had to work up to.

"Did you want to come in?" he asked, moving to the side so I
could enter. When I paused, he took a step forward. "Or I can come
out there."

"No, no, I'm coming in. I just had to get up some gumption."

Inside, I stopped to take in the living room. I guess I expected another bachelor pad. Something that mirrored Nick's place next door, what with its framed sports magazines and rickety coffee table filled with cereal bowls.

"This is nice," I said, glancing around at the refinished floors, the crown molding, and the well-maintained woodwork throughout.

"Thanks. Nick and I work on remodeling the house in our spare time. Eventually we'd like to sell and buy our own places."

"Eventually," I repeated, wondering when exactly that would be.

"Do you want a drink? I can make coffee or tea," he said, motioning toward the couch for me to sit.

"Water," I gasped, watching a single bead of sweat slide down between his pecs. "Water would be delicious."

"Okay." When he turned, I was at first grateful for the reprieve from staring at his chest, until I saw his back flexing as he strode away. It was thick, much like his chest, with muscles stacked upon muscles.

I didn't know what the muscles were called, but I knew I'd be googling it the first chance I had.

I hope this wasn't a bad idea, Charlotte.

Whether it was my nerves or just seeing Henry slick with sweat, I was starting to get hot. The house didn't appear to have central air. Just an overhead fan spinning away, and the front windows cracked open. Neither was doing much to stave off the mugginess in the room.

I looked around while he was gone. Much like Gigi's wall of fame, Henry had photos that spanned many years of his life. There were many scattered throughout the living area.

One in particular stood out.

There I stood with Henry, Emma, Nick, and Cooper. The five of us lined up boy, girl, boy, girl, boy. There were a lot of missing teeth and awkward smiles—we must've been seven or eight. Emma looked exactly the same, with her dark hair and eyes, and she was sporting a pointy pastel birthday hat. I could easily sort out Cooper and Nick thanks to their eyes and hair. But it was the last two kids, positioned side by side, arms slung over each other's shoulders, that I couldn't take my eyes from.

My index finger traced the smiling boy. "Henry."

The bright blue eyes were easily recognizable. Other than that, there were very few similarities between this slight, gangly boy and the man who had just come up to stand behind me. A man I'd grown to . . .

Hearing him approach, I held my breath until he was right behind me.

"I remember this," I whispered, closing my eyes to see the image of all of us running around the Peronis' massive yard. "I fell in the mud that day and you didn't want me to be embarrassed or get yelled at, so you threw yourself in after me."

"I did," he said, kissing the top of my head. It was a sweet gesture, not one that could be misconstrued or misinterpreted to be something other than comforting. Which it was.

I laughed, tears spilling over and plopping down onto the frame. "Sorry," I mumbled, wiping at them ineffectively with my T-shirt.

"Charlotte," he began, smoothing his hands down my arms. He turned me slowly and tipped my head up to look into his eyes. "Why did you come here tonight?"

I swallowed, feeling the lump stay wedged in my throat. I held out the envelope with a shaky hand. "To talk," I said, pushing it toward him.

He backed away but kept both eyes locked on the small white envelope. It was facedown, so I flipped it over, revealing his ten-year-old handwriting.

"Where did you get that?" he asked, his voice wistful. I sunk onto the couch. "You never responded." His hurt was evident, and I quickly scrambled to course correct.

"I just found dozens of them in a box that my mother had sent to Gigi's after she died."

"What?" he asked disbelievingly. "You didn't get them?"

I shook my head, feeling the uncertainty choking me. "I had

no idea you were sending letters. She kept them—why, I'll never know—and threw them in a box. She never told me or opened them. She just sent them to Gigi with a note, but even that wasn't an explanation, really. I just found them tonight. My mother had them sent to her. They've been sealed away ever since."

"What did the note to Gigi say?"

"That she wanted me to experience life outside of the bubble."

"Why wouldn't she give them to you?" He looked up, and that's when I saw ten-year-old best friend Henry staring back. While I hoped that a rush of memories would accompany my remembering him, I only got a handful. It was enough to make me launch myself at him. He held me there, stroking my back as I held him close.

"I think she wanted me to believe that everyone had forgotten about me. I begged for weeks to come back, but she always found a reason to keep us away. I'll never know why she hated this place so much. If I felt unconnected to the people here, I'd stop asking. And I did. Her plan worked. I think I remembered everyone else before you because you were the hardest person for me to remember. The memories were too painful for me because of how much I missed you."

"I'm so sorry," he said, burying his face in my neck. "I wish I knew."

"I'm sorry I didn't know you missed me," I mumbled. I felt every bit like that lost and lonely little girl who didn't have a friend in the world.

"I cried for hours after my parents told me you had left. We knew it was coming, but I didn't think it was going to be so soon. We had plans, in case you don't remember. I kept hoping that you'd show up. That your desk would have you sitting in it when I came back to school on Monday."

"I could tell from the letters that you were hurting. I'm so sorry."

He pushed me back slightly, smoothing the hair from my face. "Where did Gigi have them?"

I smiled, holding his face in my hands. "This hidden room. I can't explain it, really, but she must have put them in there to forget about all the hurt that anything of my mother's brought her. I have no idea why she sent them to Gigi, but she did."

He looked thoughtful for a moment. "Were they in the cubbyhole?"

I laughed. "The what?"

"The passageway in the wall," he said simply.

My jaw dropped. "You *knew*? Emma is going to lose her mind. She's been looking for it for years."

He tapped his head. "I never told anyone. Gigi made me promise." He picked up my hand and held it against his bare chest. "It was supposed to be a secret. Only for people who needed it, she said. I think Stanley wrote about it in one of his books. It's like an old-fashioned panic room."

"Why did she tell you, though?" I asked, but I knew the answer. It was written all over his face. I just needed him to say it.

"I think she wanted to help me feel like you were still here. She told me that you used it when your parents fought. After you left, I needed it for a while. Over the years I stopped going there, but she always said it was there if I wanted it. I can't fit in it anymore, but back then I'd hide out in there and read. I guess it made me feel like you were still with me."

"You haven't been in it in years?" I asked, wondering if he had seen the ROSE boxes.

He shook his head and waved at his large body. "I tried the first day I came back to visit her after college. I almost got stuck, so I figured it was the house's way of telling me that I didn't need it anymore."

"I went in tonight. I had a memory of it and stormed up the stairs to see it. I couldn't believe I hadn't made the whole thing up."

"I can't believe all this time they were hidden away," he said, smoothing his hand down my back.

My hand flexed against his chest. When his pectorals moved beneath it, I sighed.

"Sorry, it's a reflex," he answered, but his eyes darted down to my lips.

Slowly, I brushed my hand across his chest again, adding a slight nail scratch that made his head fall onto the back of the sofa.

"Charlotte," he groaned, and the sense of comfort we both were seeking turned to one of need.

"I know what you said about not starting something if I leave," I said, lowering my lips to his chest. I placed one light kiss over his heart. "I understand why you feel that way. I just can't help but think that we're missing out on something special here."

Placing another kiss on his chest, I worked my way up to his neck slowly.

His body was shaking beneath me. "Henry?" I breathed, dragging my cheek against his stubble. The ball was in his court. These were his rules, and I wasn't going to push him.

Henry drew his hands up slowly, sliding them up my back and into my hair. My eyes met his just as he leaned forward to capture my mouth. His lips moved slowly, tasting and teasing, but never rushing.

It was delicious torture, and my mind was reeling. His hands on my hips were on fire as they stroked, pushing at my shorts slightly.

"Wait," I begged, and his hands froze immediately. In a flash they were on either side of his legs, lying flat on the couch.

I looked down at him. There wasn't a shred of disappointment, but his eyes were filled with worry. Slipping off his lap, I stood before him. His chest was heaving, his eyes straight ahead, not looking at me.

I kicked off my flip-flops, and his eyes followed them as they sailed across the room.

I placed my index finger under his chin, forcing his eyes up. My hands gripped the hem of my shirt and in one swift movement, I whipped the top from my body. The thin bra I wore was next. His hands balled into fists but remained on the couch.

"Help," I said, inching closer to him. Standing between his legs, I waited.

Tentatively, his hands came up and rested on the waistband of my shorts. With a quick pop, he undid the button, then the zipper, and let them fall to the floor, where I kicked them off.

"Fuck," he hissed.

I hooked my fingers under the panties, shimmying them down until they were in a pile with the shorts.

Henry was breathing as heavily as he had been when I knocked on the door. He sat up but didn't reach for me as I thought he would. Instead, he left his arms resting on his knees, and his head fell forward to lean against my chest.

I touched him, rubbing his head gently. He placed his hands on my calves, lightly at first. Then he slid his hands up the back of my legs, over my rear, until they settled on my waist, his thumbs stroking my skin.

It was absurdly hot in the room at this point. The breeze was coming through the window and the fan was overhead, but it still felt like we were in the center of a lit kiln.

Slowly, I pushed him until his bare back was against the leather. He was sweating, but there wasn't anything I wanted more than to touch him.

"Stay here," I whispered, turning to face the window, so my back faced him.

I heard Henry whimper, and I felt another surge of need barrel through me. I took a step backward and sat in his lap, straddling my legs over both of his with my bottom pushed against *him*. With my back against his chest, I sought out his hands and placed them over me. Not *on* me but over me, hovering until he took the leap and placed them wherever he wanted.

We were breathing so hard that it was audible in the otherwise quiet room. No cars drove by. The television next door wasn't on, leaving only the two of us and our sounds filling the room. The streetlights streamed in through the thin, gauzy curtains.

I watched his hands flutter before one rested on my rib cage and the other sat slick on my upper thigh. Leaning back, I rested my head on his shoulder.

"Henry," I breathed, and he snapped.

In one swoop, he stood. With a quick spin, he lifted, holding me with his arm a firm band around my back. His breath was hot in my ear as he moved toward the stairs and climbed effortlessly. Once upstairs, he tore down the hall and into the last room at the end of the hall.

"Change your mind?" he asked, kicking the door closed behind him.

"Not a chance," I said, sliding my hands up to his hair.

His lips found my skin again, this time traversing from my ear down my neck, across my shoulder. Turning me in his arms, he held my head gently in his hands and kissed me. Once, twice, and then a third time before walking forward. I matched his steps back until my legs hit the edge of his bed.

I sat, and my hands immediately found the string on his gym shorts. Untying them proved difficult with shaking hands, but I managed. Sliding them down, I bit back a moan. He kicked them off and walked around the bed to the small end table where he pulled out a condom. Slipping it on, he crawled onto the bed to lie beside me.

"Let me," I begged, and his hands fell away as I climbed up and over until he was set inside.

As I moved over him, my mind was racing with hundreds of things to say, but I couldn't formulate them even if I had wanted to. On my lips were his, no words spoken, until we both collapsed on the bed, sated and exhausted.

"We'll figure it out," he whispered into the darkness, stroking my hair as I curled up onto his chest.

Before I fell asleep wrapped in his arms, I smiled thinking that everything I swore wouldn't happen, did. I was happy, I was content, and I was loved.

All of which happened in Hope Lake.

19

A week after my night with Henry, I was desperate to see him again. To talk, among other things. He picked me up every night and we took the *long* way back to Gigi's. It may or may not have included time on Love Lane. But we needed to have a serious discussion. I think we were both purposefully avoiding it, instead staying in this blissful bubble that we existed in with no need to talk about the future.

"Thank you for calling Late Bloomers, can you hold, please?" Nellie rambled into the phone. When it rang again, she dropped the pencil that had previously been clutched in her hand and cursed quietly.

"Give me the phone. You run to the back and get the delivery. I think you need five minutes of fresh air with the cute driver," I said, taking the phone from her. She smiled at me gratefully and ran through the back door before I was able to say hello to the caller. She'd been a great addition to the shop in just the past week.

It had been hectic all day. With the Fourth of July festival tomorrow, I had limited time to get everything that needed to be done, done.

Henry had dropped me off with a searing kiss against the back door that proved to be difficult to walk away from, but knowing the size of my to-do list, I begrudgingly did so with a promise to see him again later if I didn't fall asleep on the way home.

The doorbell dinged, and Max walked in, looking a little worse for the wear. I held up a finger and turned so he'd see the phone wedged between my face and my shoulder. After I was finished with the order, I turned and smiled, albeit awkwardly.

"Hey." I was a dazzling wordsmith.

"Hey." Apparently, he was, too.

I smiled again, but even I could tell it looked forced. It *was* forced. Not that there was anything wrong with him, at all. He just wasn't right for me.

"I should have done this sooner," he said, giving no preamble or indication of what he meant. "I thought maybe we could work things out, but then I dropped into the shop last week and you and Henry were, well, occupied."

My eyes widened. "You were the one who came in and then were gone by the time I came out from the back."

"I didn't want to interrupt, and I certainly wasn't about to stay out here and listen in, since it looked pretty—we'll say heated," he said with a grimace.

My face flamed. I would be embarrassed if anyone saw it, let alone Max. I handled this horribly and felt horrible. "Max, I'm sorry."

"Don't be," he chuckled. "I can literally see how happy you are. Your eyes are still sparkling even though you look like a deer in the headlights right now. Your skin is glowing, and honestly, you look like a woman in love. Just not with me."

I blew out a long breath. One that I felt like I had held in for a month. "I don't know what to say."

"Don't say anything. Really, it's okay. I've known for a while. That's what I meant by 'I should have done this sooner.' It's just been a bit crazy. For the both of us."

I came around the desk, stopping to stand by his side. "Under any other circumstances, I would be crazy to not fall for a guy like you."

He smiled, patting me on the shoulder. "It's really okay."

I bumped into his shoulder. "I certainly didn't know it. It's crazy how it took coming back here to awaken a lot of memories that I thought I'd lost forever."

The door dinged again, Emma flying through it with her phone up to her ear.

Max looked back to me and smiled. "Good luck. I'll see you around."

As he left, he waved to Emma, who looked frazzled. "What was Dr. Max up to?" she asked, watching him stride over to Viola's. That man sure did love his ice cream.

"Nothing. We decided that we're better off as friends," I said honestly.

"Oh, that's nice," she said, distracted by the stack of slips piled on the countertop. "That looks laborious."

I let out another deep sigh. "You're not wrong, but it's good. Really good. Nellie is coming along, and she's got a friend she's going to bring to interview. I think between the three of us, we'll get it all under control in no time."

Emma nodded and wandered around the shop silently. But I could tell that there was a ton that she was dying to say.

"Oh, for pity's sake, just say it!" I shouted, walking to stand near her at the front window.

"I think you should stay," she said, raising her hand to stop me from answering. "Just give me a second to state my case."

"Emma, you don't need to."

She looked dejected, clearly taking my words wrong. "Listen, I know I haven't been convincing enough, but I think you should give me the chance to convince you."

"Really, you don't have to. I mean, it's something I'm thinking about. I've been for a while, actually, but I didn't let myself get too far into really considering it."

She smiled. "And you are now?"

"I came to a realization that maybe New York isn't my home, at least not in the literal way I've been thinking. My mom was what kept me there and made it home. With her gone, Parker sort of inadvertently filled that role. Everything I love about the city is tied back to either one of them. I'm a literal case of home is where the heart is."

"So you're saying . . . ?" Emma lobbed, rubbing her hands together excitedly.

I rolled my eyes. "I'm saying, maybe even though Parker is there, more of my heart is here."

Emma squealed and launched herself at me.

"I have a lot to think about," I squeezed out with difficulty. She gave a good hug. "A lot to figure out, and while it's a simple solution in theory—stay with Gigi, work here until I figure out how to buy it—I need a plan. While flying by the seat of my pants worked out in my last-minute decision to come here, I don't want to just wing it when it comes to staying."

"I promise, I'm not getting too excited."

"And yet, you're vibrating."

"That's my phone."

"You lie like a rug, Peroni."

We parted, but her smile remained. "Reel it in, sister. Put your game face on. No one else is to know about this. I haven't even talked to Henry—I mean my dad—yet."

Her eyes grew wide as dahlias in July. "I won't say a thing, but Jesus, you have a lot to fill me in on. Though, judging by the neck burn and glowing skin, I can work that out myself."

With a wink, and a cackled "Toodles," she breezed out the door, promising to see me bright and early tomorrow for setup.

As Emma left, Nellie came back from taking in the delivery with a smile on her face. "I take it your chat with the driver was a good one?"

Nellie shook her head. "Oh yeah, he's nice. But I'm more inter-ested in the guy who helps out over at Viola's. Know him?"

"No. We can ask Henry, though," I said as the bell chimed again.

The place was like Grand Central today. Thank goodness it wa nearly time to close.

I turned, smiling when I saw who came to visit. "Dad, what brings you here?"

Coming around the table, I let him pull me into a hug. "I was going to run over to the dry cleaner and I thought I'd see if you needed a ride back home," he said hopefully. "Give us some time to chat."

"You read my mind," I said, glancing up at the clock. "Can you give us ten minutes to finish up?"

He waved to Nellie. "Of course. I'll grab my stuff from over there and come back. Take your time."

As he left, he flipped the antique sign to CLOSED and Nellie set the locks. "You can head out now. I'll finish this up. See you tomorrow."

By the time Dad came back, I was waiting in the alley and ever so grateful for the ride.

None of what had happened so far today was on my to-do list, and yet checking it off felt really good.

1. Uncomfortable conversation with Max, *which turned out to be fine.*
2. Have a come-to-Jesus with myself about staying in Hope Lake—*Still working on the outcome.*
3. Dad and Gigi finding out she has a perma-roommate. *I think that'll be fine.*
4. Conversation with Henry. *This one I'm looking forward to.*

None was work-related, and yet all had to be dealt with before I made my final decision.

"So, before I dive in. What did you want to talk about?" I asked, buckling my seat belt.

He stared out of the window, focused on a spot on the cracked stone wall where our deliveries came in. His lips curled in, and I wondered whether he was listening or zoned out.

"Dad?" I said again, touching his shoulder lightly.

He smiled and glanced down for a moment. When he looked over, his eyes were glassy. "I wanted to talk to you for a moment about your mother. If that is all right with you."

Did I want to talk about her? No, but I knew I had to.

He must have taken my pause as a no. "If you're not okay with bringing her up, we can wait. I want to make sure that you're able to get through this. I know we haven't had ample time to discuss . . . everything, but I can wait. I've waited twenty years, I can wait a couple more days."

I touched his arm. "Grateful as I am, I'd rather have the conversation than avoid it any longer." *If my therapist could hear me now.*

Swallowing hard, I was trying to quell the surprise that I was feeling that he even brought her up. After what was revealed the other night, with her hiding Henry's letters from me, I really thought none of us would bring her up for fear of what it would evoke in the other. But by the same token, with her gone, no one would be able to answer all the burning questions that I still had. Maybe he could at least shed some light on a couple of things.

"What exactly are we discussing?" I asked tentatively, not wanting to upset him more than he clearly already was.

Dad pulled out of the alley behind the building and took a slow ride out toward Gigi's. "I need you to know some important details first, before we get into everything else. I had no idea that Henry was writing to you after you and your mom left. I certainly didn't know that Rose sent those boxes to Gigi, either. We never spoke after you left, unless it was through family court, and even then, anything regarding you went through the lawyers. She wouldn't answer my calls, and after you got older, I gave up trying to communicate with her and went directly to you. Gigi tried, too, of course, but your mother refused to have contact with any of us. I honestly believe if it weren't for the judge and lawyers, we wouldn't have had contact with you at all."

I could tell he was getting angry by the way his voice shook when he spoke. Anytime he visited me in New York, he never, ever spoke an unkind word about my mother. Even now, he wasn't, but it was clear that he wasn't going to sugarcoat things, either.

There was still something that no amount of therapy—whether medical or of the Hope Lake variety—would ever answer for me.

"Why did my mother act the way she did my whole life? The hate, the pure and illogical contempt she felt toward everything?" I said, watching as he gripped the steering wheel tightly. "I thought the note she wrote to Gigi would have given me some clue, but it was so generic. Why couldn't there have been more sentences. Something to give me a sense of closure? I could continue to let it eat away at me, ruining my own life like she had hers, or, I could try and accept the fact that I would never know and perhaps move on."

"I can't answer that, Charlotte. She wasn't like that when I met her. She had a light about her and then she didn't. I think about it all the time. What happened? What did I do to make her spark go out? What made her so monumentally unhappy?"

I took his hand, resting them both on the stick shift. "Being a person who lived with her longer than anyone else, I don't think it was you. I don't even think it was me. I think she just needed to speak with someone and never did. Get some help. I have so much guilt that I didn't see that she needed to talk to someone before it was too late, and then she was too far gone in her misery to pull herself back out. Maybe she didn't have the opportunity when she was younger, or she refused treatment. Again, we'll never know. Once she was diagnosed with cancer, she let that eat away at her, too. Refusing treatment, skipping appointments. It was like she welcomed it.

"I'm to the point now where I mostly feel badly for her. I have so many questions that will never be answered. I just wish I knew why she did what she did. Why she gave up on everything instead of reaching for the lifeboat.

"I will say that you seeing a therapist was the best thing that you could have done. I probably should have done that. Maybe I wouldn't feel so much contempt for the years I lost to her. And the guilt. Maybe I would be able to let that go, too."

"Guilt? What do you have to be guilty about?" I asked, stunned at his confession.

"So much. I loved the travel, the mission trips. The adventure. Yes, I was locked into some of the trips contractually, but I could have found a way out. I should have, and it still eats away at me that I didn't end it all just so I could get you to stay here."

"Dad," I admonished gently. "Let's say you did. You gave up everything. All the *good* that you've done around the world. You still might not have been guaranteed custody! We can't look at the past with regret. We can't. It'll just eat away at us." I stopped to take a breath.

"It's not too late to see someone, Dad. I'm not ashamed of the need I have for therapy. Talking to my doctors over the years made me who I am today. A person mostly capable of dealing with her feelings, which is still a work in progress but I'm getting better. I'm someone who is genuinely looking forward to what the future holds."

He turned, smiling. "What does that mean, exactly?"

I sighed. It was a good sigh, though. Not a sad and resigned to a certain fate type of breath but a content and happy exhalation. "I was always worried day to day in New York about what would happen. If one thing got out of sync, it would throw my day off and would take me a little while to come back from. Here, I don't have that sense of urgency or worry. It's more of a *I can handle anything thrown my way* vibe and I'm grateful to Hope Lake for that. Emma told me once that this place held a little bit of magic.

"While I don't necessarily believe in magic, I do believe that this place brings out what's best in each of us."

Dad smiled, his eyes a bit watery. "It may be twenty years in the making, but I couldn't be happier to hear you say that."

20

As the sun was beginning to set, the male voice announced that the celebration would be starting shortly. The food trucks were lined up and ready. The beer tent was filled, people were enjoying themselves, and the fireworks would be starting soon. He announced the businesses that were a part of making the celebration what it was, and my friends clapped and whistled when he got to Late Bloomers and said my name.

There was a captive audience in Hope Lake Park, where everyone had gathered on the large expanse of green fields. Locals and tourists alike crowded the space that we secured, and while many were listening in on announcements, the immediate group surrounding us was eyeing my blanket mate with delight. Nick was giving them a show. He stripped off his shirt, balled it in his hand, and tossed it behind him, where it landed on a disgruntled Emma. It left him with only a white tank top that he usually did his landscaping work in.

"If I get a rash from this, Nicholas, I swear I'll rip your di—" She paused, spying little ears at close range. "Arm off and beat you with it."

Not much better.

Stepping in to stop his fiancée from maiming his best friend, Cooper stood beside her and handed her a beer.

"This is my favorite time of year. Hot, sticky, muggy—" Nick said, oblivious to the mental beatdown that Emma was giving him.

"Bugs, sweat, smell," Emma responded, and I myself was wondering why I agreed to sit out here when I had Cooper's perfectly good SUV to sit in and watch the fireworks from.

"If you hate the outdoors, why aren't you in the car?" Parker asked.

Emma scoffed. "How can I make sure everything is running perfectly from the car, Parker?"

My friend looked terrified of my other friend.

"Noted. Is she always scary?" Parker asked me.

"Yes, you get used to it, though. I'm still in shock that you came. And pulled off a surprise. You're usually awful at them," I said to Parker, who'd arrived on Gigi's doorstep at five in the morning.

Good thing I had to be up with the chickens for setup, or I'd have killed her for knocking at ass-crack-thirty.

The statuesque blonde, who happened to be my best friend, was sitting next to me on our blanket, watching Nick intently.

"What were you saying? Sorry, I wasn't paying attention because of *that*," she said, pointing haphazardly in Nick's general direction.

Nick was applying sunblock to his nose. He lathered it on thick like an eighties lifeguard.

"Hey, I'm not a piece of meat to be gawked at," he said. And, as if to disprove his point entirely, he gripped the hem of his tank and in a completely *not safe for work* move that I had the feeling was just for Parker's enjoyment, tore it off over his head.

"You look ridiculous," I said, pointing at my own nose.

"Says you. I've got a cheering section," he said, hooking a thumb toward Parker.

"As if," she mocked, but her eyes didn't leave his chest.

What do we have here?

"How are you doing that?" Parker asked, squinting up at him from the blanket.

"Doing what?" he asked, confused.

"You're dewy. I look like I ran up the mountain in a garbage bag and you look like someone is delicately spritzing you. It's annoying."

Except Parker's face was anything but annoyed. It was curious and interested.

Interesting . . .

Nick shrugged, finishing up his application. "I'm naturally dewy. Sue me."

"You're naturally obnoxious," she mumbled.

"Parker, I'm glad you were able to join us this weekend. Charlotte has told us nothing about you," Cooper said jokingly.

"Okay, okay, everyone on this blanket is a regular friggin' comedian. In case you hadn't noticed, I've been busy."

Parker, fanning herself with a paper fan that she carried with her everywhere, looked down at Cooper and Emma, who was enjoying her fourth beer. Cooper mentioned earlier that Emma was hoping to get tipsy in celebration of a job well done. She just seemed to be celebrating a bit early.

"I just decided to come last night. Charlotte told me about the festival ages ago, but I wasn't sure I could swing it. But then I said screw it. Why not, right? I closed the bakery after I finished all the preorders and rented a car. Charlotte's been prattling on about this place since she got here. I just had to see it."

"I wish I knew you were coming; I would have warned everyone that Hurricane Parker was making landfall," I said, laughing when she flipped me off.

Nick was rummaging around the picnic basket when Parker slapped his hand away. "No desserts yet."

"You bought dessert?" he said excitedly.

"*Bought?* Add an *r* and you've got your answer. I baked a dessert and *brought* it," she seethed, this time sounding genuinely annoyed. She recovered quickly, though. I would have to explain later. I hadn't really talked about New York or my friend there because it felt like I was cheating on them when I was with my friends from Hope Lake.

"Well, however it got here, can we, uh, eat it now?" Nick said, taking a long whiff of the small slit in the box before he groaned.

"Really, Charlotte? They know nothing about me at all?"

I shrugged. "Been busy."

Parker rolled her eyes. "She likes to keep me a secret. That way she doesn't have to share the cakes I bring her." Turning to me, she scowled. "I'll remember this in a couple of weeks when you're sniffing around for a birthday cake."

Cooper and Nick looked at Parker curiously. When she realized they really had no idea about her, she added, "I'm a baker. I own a shop in New York."

Emma clapped her hands before wobbling enough that Cooper had to put his hands on her waist to steady her. "I watched your appearances on the Food Network. Loved it! Glad you were able to expand the shop because of all the promo from it."

Parker smiled. "Thanks, Emma. I'm glad someone here knows about me." Parker and Emma had met before, of course, and had been on the call together before the shop opened, but this was their first "in-person."

"The bakery's gotten a lot of business, which is both a blessing and a curse. I'm sure Charlotte can appreciate that."

"Are you staying with Charlotte at Gigi's or are you at a B and B?" Cooper asked.

"She's staying with me," I explained, knowing where this was going. "Gigi would kill me if she knew her favorite Parker was here and not staying with her. Parker always makes Gigi treats that she's not supposed to be eating."

Parker looked guilty, briefly. It's not like she wouldn't make the Bananas Foster cupcakes that Gigi always asked for.

"Well, you couldn't have chosen a better weekend to spend with us here in Hope Lake," Cooper said in all his mayoral glory.

Like the perfect one-two punch, Emma piped up, climbing up onto her knees and fixing her flouncy skirt. "I'd love to give you a tour tomorrow," she offered with a hiccup.

Parker laughed. "Maybe the day after, sparky. I don't think you'll be in any shape to tour anything tomorrow. Well, what do we have here?"

Parker's eyes had traveled to a figure stalking toward us. I would recognize that gait anywhere. Parker knew about Henry. The push and pull and the confusion I felt over all of it. What she didn't know was what had happened between us over the past week.

We hadn't even discussed it because there wasn't time.

"Dibs," she said, reaching into her shirt and pulling her boobs up one by one.

"Stay classy, Adams."

Standing, I moved toward Parker and whispered, "That's Henry."

"I figured," she whispered back. I wondered why she'd angle the girls up for him to notice if she knew how I felt about him. "It's a test. Go with me."

Henry shook hands with Cooper and then Nick. Giving Emma a quick hug, he turned to Parker, smiling.

"Hello, I'm Parker Adams. I have a section of blanket here waiting just for you," she purred, lightly touching his shoulder.

Henry took Parker's outstretched hand. "I'm glad you were able to come. I know this isn't Coney Island on the Fourth, but if you stick around, you'll be able to see Nick partake in a stomach-roiling contest of wills."

Parker laughed. "You told him about our trips to Coney for the hot-dog contest?"

"I did. It's a great time and maybe, just maybe, this place will make us laugh and cheer as much as that one does."

Henry looked back over to me, and the full wattage of his heart-flipping Henry Mercer smile wasn't aimed at Parker anymore. His eyes fluttered to hers for a moment, then back to me.

"Charlotte, before I forget, I wanted to tell you that you did an incredible job here."

I smiled, feeling the warmth in my chest set off like the upcoming fireworks.

The park had been empty when Nellie and I arrived this morning. We had a few other volunteers come out to help, but it wasn't until people started arriving with their picnic supplies and blankets to watch the band that the work we focused on for so long had been appreciated.

It had turned out better than I thought. "It's been great. People love it. Even Kirby's wife told me she liked how things turned out. It was a begrudging compliment, but I'll take it."

Henry laughed and wrapped his arm around my shoulders before he spied every eye turn to us.

Everyone in the park had given me effusive feedback, but hearing it from Henry meant a lot. Even though we had just parted that morning, I'd missed him all day.

"You must be so pleased. Everyone is impressed. Well done," he fawned, just as a marching band started playing "America the Beautiful" in the background. The whole scene was very Hallmark, and I couldn't have been happier to have been in our little bubble.

The spaces between the blankets were getting smaller as more and more people filled in any available stitch of grass. Emma had the foresight to send a couple of her office interns to scope out the best spot for viewing the fireworks and had them sit with our blankets until Nellie and I were finished setting up.

Emma, of course, was never done. She kept popping up and taking off at the slightest sign of something going wrong.

"Does she always do that?" Parker asked, watching Emma spring up from the blanket and power walk through the crowd toward the face-painting area. The line had to be twenty kids deep and they were starting to shut down and whine.

"Think outside the box? Always. It's her superpower, I think. I wish I had the ability myself," I said, staring across the field at the hundreds of people either milling about or sitting and enjoying the slightly cooler temperature since the sun set.

"No—well, yes, but mainly I'm wondering how a small person like her can down four or five beers and still function like she's

stone-cold sober. That, my friend, is a gift. And don't let me hear you
questioning your abilities or I'll kick your ass. You're not giving yourself enough credit, C," Parker insisted, holding up a plate of cookies
in front of me. "You come here, fully expecting the worst possible
scenario, and look at what happened in a short amount of time."

I shrugged, feeling the warmth creeping up my face. Praise was
always something in short supply when my mother was still alive.
Hearing it now was still a hard pill to swallow.

"It's been unexpected. Amazing? Brilliant? Not without fault, of
course, but still, this place is the opposite of everything my mother
ever told me about it. It's crazy how it gets under your skin. The
places, the people."

Parker scoffed. "My God, I'm going to slap you! You're so happy
here I might drown you if you don't stay here forever! You don't have
to go back, you realize that, right? You can stay. Make this your
home. Fuck New York."

I sucked in a breath. "Parker! There's kids around."

"What's left in New York? Honestly?" she continued, ignoring
the looks from the parents nearby.

"Parker, I—" I began, but she kept rambling.

"Think about it. Tell me what would make you run back there
when you have all this and all that"—she pointed to Henry—"here?"

"You?" I replied weakly. "I'd miss you."

"And I can come visit. Hell, maybe I'll come with you," she said,
glancing over to the other blanket where Henry and Cooper were in
a deep conversation. They didn't seem like they were arguing, but it
didn't look like an entirely pleasant conversation, either. I could only
hear bits of it: "What if it backfired?" and "I appreciate the thought,
but," and "I know it's only two hours, Cooper."

"What's that about?" Parker asked, following my eyes and glancing over at the friends, who noticed us watching them and turned
to hide their arguing.

"No clue. It's been weird around here lately," I said honestly,
taking a sip of my drink.

Parker took my hand. "I'm being serious when I say to think about it. You can start over anywhere. Why not have it be here where you're clearly very happy?"

"I decided to stay," I said finally, and waited.

"You what?" she howled, so loud and shrill that everyone turned. "Why didn't you tell me before I went on and on like an ass?!"

"Because you were going on and on like an ass!" I said, laughing when she pulled me into a hug.

"I don't know that there was one thing specifically that sold me," I continued. "But a ton of little things. Seeing that I can make a difference somewhere has done a lot for my mental health. I struggled with that so much and this place, this job, these people just seem to elevate that happiness for me.

"Tonight was sort of the ringer of it all. I know you're not supposed to work for praise, but hearing from everyone about how great the park looks, or how much they love what I created for them, has made me question what giving this place up would mean for me.

"I don't know that staying in Hope Lake is the answer to everything that I've been missing, but it's definitely a step in the right direction. I think I still need to figure out what else I need but I think I'm off to a damn good start. I only wish I found it sooner."

When I looked at Parker, she was glassy-eyed. "I'm so proud of you, C. Truly, beyond happy for you. I will miss the shit out of you, but if I've learned anything, it's that life's too short."

She looked over to Henry and Cooper.

I smiled. "It's not all because of him," I insisted, repeating it when she rolled her eyes. "I'm serious."

Parker patted my hand. "C, I never said it was."

I wiped the sweat from my brow. "Okay, good. Because he's a major factor, but it's about me, too."

"Interesting that you brought it up not once but twice," she remarked, smiling into her beer.

"Oh, shut up!"

"I didn't say anything."

"Your eyes, they're judging me."

Emma returned, squatting down on the blanket. "I'm officially out of beer and I'm sad. What did I miss?"

"Oh, not much, Emma. Just that my girl here is going to be your girl full-time. She's on loan, though, in case I need her once in a while."

Emma shrieked, drawing attention from Cooper and Henry. "Holy shit!"

"No, no, don't do that," I said, trying to calm her down. Each of them had one of my hands, so I couldn't use them to wave off a very nervous-looking Henry.

Emma mimed zipping her lips, but she was shaking, clearly giddy over Parker's words. "I know nothing. I'll say nothing," she whispered.

"I've got to make some calls and figure things out logistically. There are so many decisions about if I can do this without Lucille bankrolling it. Now is not the time for them—" I stopped mid-sentence when Henry, Cooper, and Nick joined us.

"The fireworks are going to start," Cooper explained, extending a hand to Emma. "I believe this blanket is too crowded for all of us."

"That's code for *I want to be alone with my fiancée*," Nick said with diluted laughter. "No hanky-panky under the blankets!"

"It's ninety-five degrees, who is going to have a blanket on?" Parker chided, and Nick shrugged.

"It's an expression," he retorted, and turned his back to her.

"Henry, why don't you sit?" I suggested, scooting over on the blanket. With the way everything was positioned on the grass, we would only be able to fit two people on my blanket, which was convenient, as I only wanted Henry and me on it. *Sorry, Parker.*

The blanket behind us was where Emma and Cooper were lying, and I supposed Nick and Parker would have to go to the blanket in front of us. I might be refereeing WrestleMania in a bit if they got aggravated with each other.

With his legs stretched out, Henry leaned back on his arms,

mirroring my position. I looked behind us, where our friends had set up camp. Cooper looked pleased, as did Emma. Her eyes widened when Nick and Parker approached.

They sat on opposite ends of their blanket.

"What were you and Cooper talking about earlier?" I asked, not looking at him. Given our close proximity, I felt his body stiffen. "Or, you can just say it's none of my business," I added quickly, feeling the awkwardness building up.

In my periphery, I saw Henry turn toward me. "I found out that someone was doing something to— Well, I guess you could say they were trying to help me."

I turned, leaning on my side and resting my head on my hand. "Well, that's not a bad thing. It was a friend? That was trying to help, I mean?"

He nodded. "My friends, *our* friends, are the best, but sometimes— and I'm sure you know this—their brains and hearts don't communicate."

"Naturally," I replied.

Henry smiled, but it didn't quite reach his eyes. "They think they're doing something that will be helpful when in reality they're messing with things they shouldn't. People's lives and emotions aren't something to toy with."

"Henry, this sounds serious."

"It is."

"Do you want to talk about it?" I asked, reaching out with my free hand and placing it on his.

"Later."

He looked down at my hand on his and grinned. I watched the dimple deepen on his right cheek. Henry licked his bottom lip absently, pulling the plump flesh between his teeth for just a second.

Swallowing thickly, I wondered again what it would be like to kiss him. Here in public, surrounded by everyone and everything that I had grown to love. As if reading my mind, his head lowered, but a loud pop in the sky drew our gaze upward as the fireworks started.

His skin was warm when he took my hand in his. All around us, people were paying attention to the explosions above us, but I couldn't look away from Henry.

It was as if the crowd had melted away and it was just the two of us on a blanket in the middle of a park. Alone together on a warm summer's night.

Slowly, Henry leaned down. I licked my lips, drawing his eyes to them.

I wish I wore a better bra. Do I have perfume on? How bad is my hair?

With a single searing press of his lips, the crowd surrounding us oohed, aahed, and clapped excitedly.

For the fireworks.

THE FIREWORKS, I think at least, were fantastic. I couldn't tell you what the finale was, nor did I care. I didn't remember saying good night to a tipsy Emma and Cooper, who stumbled away singing patriotic songs. Or remember Parker finding a crew of people to go have a beer with at Casey's.

Henry excused himself earlier to run to the restroom and still hadn't come back. I was still sitting on the blanket wondering why Nick, the only person left from our party, looked like he was about to throw up.

"Henry wasn't sending the letters," he blurted out, wringing his hands nervously.

"I know," I said absently, wondering where Henry went to and why Nick was doing this now. "I thought it was Max."

"They weren't from Max, either," he said, looking more nervous by the second.

"Nick, what are you saying?" I asked, a sinking feeling burning in my stomach.

"I sent them," he admitted, and held up his hands quickly. "Before you get mad. They weren't from me. I like you, but not like that," he rambled, keeping his hands up like I was going to strike him. "I promise I only did it for Henry."

For Henry?

"Wait, what? He asked you to send them?" I was so confused. "He said they weren't from him. Repeatedly."

He shook his head. "They weren't."

"I haven't even been drinking that much, and yet, I have no idea what the hell is going on. In the plainest of words, explain."

Nick began pacing. "I mean, he didn't know about it. I sent them on my own, *from* him to help nudge him along with you.

"I knew he was writing to you as a kid, and when you came back and had no memories, I thought maybe this would help. I figured if I made the letters *sound* like Henry, you'd think they were from him. So I found his books from the summer classes and took sections from them. Things he had bookmarked and highlighted. I figured it might help and you guys could put all the bullshit aside and just work it out but—"

"You didn't know that I didn't get the letters all those years ago," I said, my head falling into my hands. I rubbed my temples, trying to will away the headache that was forming.

"Correct. Once he told me about that after you guys, you know"—he blushed—"I stopped. I mean I wrote a bunch up, but I told him I wouldn't send any more since it would be super inappropriate. I felt like such an asshole. I didn't know it would bring up so many hard feelings for him. I just thought it would help. I'm sorry, Charlotte. I really am. I didn't really think it through or that anyone would get hurt."

"Nick, I don't know what to say," I replied honestly, looking for a description of what I was feeling. "I'm not mad. I don't know what I am, but I know it's not mad."

He looked relieved. "Thank God. I didn't want you to get pissed and hit me in the nuts like you did Henry."

It earned a much-needed laugh. "That was an accident!"

"I know, I just wanted you to smile. To help you remember why you and Henry were so special together. Don't be mad at him. He's super pissed at me because of it, and I feel bad that I muddied the waters with you guys. I didn't mean to make it complicated, and I didn't think that you'd assume it was Max. That was an unfortunate error on my part. I just knew—"

I held up my hand to stop him. "Promise me you won't pull a crazy stunt like this again, okay?" I said, thinking back to all the letters and how it never made sense with the timing that it was Henry or Max. This explained it.

"Deal. So, still friends?" he asked with his signature grin.

How could I stay mad at him when he had good intentions? I smiled back. "Still friends."

"I'm going to go meet some people at HLBC. Want to come?"

I shook my head. "I'm going to wait here for Henry to come back. We have to talk, too."

Nick gave me a quick hug before jogging away.

When Henry didn't return, I wondered if he'd left for the night, but I knew in my heart he didn't. We had to talk, and he knew it. He probably got sidetracked. I got up and threw my blanket over my arm. I collected the rest of my things and headed toward the park's parking area. It was mostly empty, a few cars lingering with people packing their cars with all their bags and coolers.

This. This is where I'd kill for an Uber.

Pulling the bag up higher onto my shoulder, I began to walk. It wasn't as if there weren't a dozen people I could call.

Turning onto Main Street, I slowed my pace. The night was perfect. Stars dotted the black sky. Locals and visitors milled about even though the shops were all closed. I sat on the bench in front of Late Bloomers. I still couldn't bring myself to call it my shop. I wanted to, but the words felt foreign on my tongue.

Looking into the darkened shop window, I thought about my mom sitting on this bench. Waiting for my dad. A small Charlotte was running around with other children. I willed the memories to come and they did. Nothing looked quite the same, but the memories were still there. All of them were helping to anchor me here where I belonged.

When I stood, debating whether to throw the bag into the shop to grab it tomorrow, I felt the energy around me shift.

"I didn't even need to turn to know that it was you."

"Charlotte."

"I was hoping you'd find me."

"You didn't wait," he said. "I got tied up, I'm sorry. People are chatty when they're drunk." He laughed.

"It's okay. I had a long talk with Nick."

"You talked to Nick?" he asked. He stood a good distance from me.

Nodding, I turned. "He explained the error of his ways. I'm not mad. I'm confused and have to process it, but I'm not mad. I can see why he did what he did. It's sweet if you only focus on the good parts."

He, too, looked relieved. "As soon as I found out what he was doing, I made him promise to stop. He was going through my books from the course and finding passages to send. Admittedly, I was impressed with what he chose from those couple that I read."

"He may not be the most experienced Cyrano, but I can appreciate that he wanted what was best for you," I said, putting my arm around his waist.

"If I asked you to come with me somewhere, would you come?"

Without a doubt. "Yes," I said, as he led me toward his Jeep that he had parked right outside the center of the square.

We drove, just shy of the outskirts of town—a spot that looked familiar, but I knew that I hadn't been there since I had been home.

"It's a bit of a walk," he explained, helping me out of the Jeep.

"I don't mind."

It wasn't long before we hit railroad tracks. "Is this part of that rail-biking thing? I haven't done that yet."

"No, these are still operational," he explained, helping me across.

"You're not going to ask where I'm taking you?" he said, and instead of an answer, I squeezed his hand and followed.

A few moments later, I did finally answer, sort of. "You're going to think I'm crazy," I said, looking around at what amounted to a ton of trees, wildflowers, and empty tracks.

"Try me," he said, leaning against a pole.

I paced slow and steady steps around the scattered boulders that lined the tracks. "This is tugging at a memory, but I can't quite put my finger on it. Which is insane, because why would I remember anything out here?"

He smiled, looking down briefly at his shoes. The moon was high above us, and when he looked up, the stars lit up Henry's face, making him look younger than he was. His big blue eyes didn't have the slight wrinkles at the sides. His hair was longer, curlier than it was now, and I realized that I was seeing a Henry from years ago.

"Best friends," I breathed, watching his face transform into wonder.

"What did you say?" he asked, taking a step toward me.

I pointed, just above his head. "The sign."

Walking past him, I climbed up onto the rock and reached out, touching the faded, chipped sticker with my finger. "You can't read it anymore, but it said 'Best Friends.' Right?"

He nodded, coming to meet me at the boulder. "Our initials were written, too, but they faded a long time ago."

"We were going to run away. That was the plan. We knew I was leaving, and you were going to come with me. But why?"

Henry didn't say anything. After a moment, he took my hand, holding it gently between his. "Even though we were young, I knew that I would have followed you anywhere. Even if that meant running away at ten. Or following you back to New York twenty-plus years later."

"What are you saying, Henry?" I breathed, slipping my hand free to cup his face.

He turned his head, kissing my palm lightly. "After you left the first time, I was heartbroken. I didn't know it then, but facing the notion that you were leaving here, and me, again, I recognized that the pain I felt then was a broken heart. Charlotte, I can teach from anywhere. Who knows, maybe a high school in New York would want a small-town English teacher? It's worth a shot. Or I stay here and visit a couple of times a week. I can stay there in the summer. We can do whatever it takes to make it work. I can't imagine my life without you again. I can't."

"Henry, I—" I began, pausing when he started kissing from my palm, to the inside of my wrist, to kissing each of my fingertips.

"You were saying?" he said, smiling when he saw my mouth open and close with nothing more than a squeak coming out.

"That I'm staying," I said, just before launching myself at him.

"You are?" he said, pulling me into a hug. "I can't believe it."

"I can't, either. I didn't think it would work. I don't know that it will, but I'm willing to give it a shot. I have a thousand things to work through. Where to live. How to keep working with the shop being owned by Lucille. Eventually I'd like to buy it, but that's a lot of money."

I rambled until he cut me off with his lips firm against mine. "We'll work it out. Not just you and I but everyone. Together."

"Together."

EPILOGUE

THREE MONTHS LATER

The temperature was cooling off, and I felt guilty not grabbing his coat from the house before I stopped at the school during dismissal. Three o'clock at a high school was like watching a stampede. The kids couldn't wait to escape. I knew the feeling as I was eager for the clock to strike three all day myself.

I was slowly learning that fall in Hope Lake was decidedly different from fall in New York. Not just the temperature but the feeling of the season all around. Deep in the valley, Hope Lake had the benefit of watching the colors transform from varied shades of green to splashes of oranges, golds, crimsons, and a color I could only describe as pure fire. It lit up the woods surrounding the house in the most magical way. When the wind blew, it looked like a wave of fire dancing through the trees.

What wasn't great about fall was that Henry was back in school mode. It was an interesting turn of events, though, seeing him dressed in sweaters and khakis instead of jeans and shorts. He looked damn good in a buttoned-down shirt, ready to mold the minds of Hope Lake.

It also meant trying to plan surprises for him was extra difficult because his schedule was the pits. October brought additional conflicts with his football coaching gig, and stealing him for an afternoon away was a challenge. I needed to enlist Nick's help.

"What's in the box?" Henry whined for the third time in five minutes. "Just give me a hint," he begged, shaking the box in his hands. I had picked him up from school, blindfolded him immediately, and handed him the box that I had been driving around with for two days.

"Stop, stop. You're like a toddler. You're going to break it. There's your hint. It's fragile!" I shouted, holding my hands over his on the box.

It wasn't actually breakable. It was wrapped in Bubble Wrap, but he didn't need to know that. The box was also totally unnecessary, but I wanted to throw him off.

He saw the box on the foyer table before we left for work and he nagged me via text message. All. Day. Long.

"Stop fidgeting with the blindfold. I swear I'm going to have to tie your hands up, too."

Henry stopped dead in his tracks, the crunching leaves kicking up around his worn brown boots. "Why'd you stop?"

It was hard enough navigating the damn trail on a good day. Leading my blindfolded boyfriend made it that much harder.

"Nothing, I just had an idea for later with this blindfold." He smiled in that cute yet sexy way that still drove me crazy. "That is, if you don't get us killed out here in the wilderness."

"Oh, for pity's sake. You can tell where I drove us to. We're practically in someone's backyard. That's hardly the wilderness."

I just needed to get us to our spot. And while it wasn't exactly the same as that fateful day that we were going to run away together when we were ten, it was still just *ours*.

At least for a little while longer.

"Okay, are you ready?" I asked, reaching up to tug at the blindfold.

He nodded, and I pushed the thin fabric up and over his head.

"I had a feeling you were bringing us here," he said, leaning down to kiss me. "Why the secrecy, though? We've been here a dozen times since you moved back."

I pointed to the sheet that was draped over a sign. It sat beside the rock we used to sit on. Just below the old rail sign that still had the faded BEST FRIENDS sticker on it.

"So I had this thought months ago, and I wasn't sure if I could pull it off."

"I wish you told me, I would have said you can pull anything off," he said sweetly. He transferred the box to one hand and rested it on his hip; the other was reaching out for me.

"You're honestly the sweetest."

"The surprise is under the sheet?" he said giddily, and a memory of Henry riding a pony at my sixth birthday sent a burst of love through me.

"Do the honors, sir."

I stepped aside and tried not to laugh at the way he lumbered across the deep crush of leaves toward the sign.

He didn't rip it off right away as I thought he would. It was more of a slow-motion reveal as he slid it off and rolled the sheet into a ball. He stepped back a few paces and stared at the COMING SOON sign.

It was designed to look as close to the original development sign as I could remember. When they had first announced that the Love Lane Community would be built and that our spot might go away, we had been devastated. We were ten, though, and really didn't grasp the scope of the project, or how we would have been affected.

"This was a team effort. Truly, I could not have done this without our friends and with the help of the city council."

He tipped his head to the side. "City council? Charlotte, what did you do?" he asked; this time the nervousness melted away and was replaced with excitement.

"With a nearly unanimous vote, Hope Lake received three cityscape grants from Pennsylvania to build a couple of very specific things. One of which will be right here.

"Lovegood's Park will be built here, in our spot, so that the kids of Hope Lake and the Love Lane development have somewhere fun and safe to play. They're fencing out the wooded area, as far as animals go, but it'll still be open, airy, and, above all, fun."

He didn't say anything until I walked up behind him and slid my arms around his waist.

"Charlotte, this is incredible. You did this—I can't believe how amazing this is. You're unbelievable," he praised, dropping the box into the leaves absently.

"Oh, I forgot. You can open that now," I said, leaning up to kiss him. "Good surprise?"

"The best, honestly."

He tore through the box, then the second box inside, and then finally he pulled out the thin manila envelope that contained *his* surprise in all of this. Sure, the park was part of it, but it was more the sentimentality of it. The functionality of it was the real key to all of this.

"What is this?" he asked, smiling down at the colorful drawing.

"That's Henry's Little Free Library," I explained, pointing to the birdhouse-style book house. "It'll be placed somewhere in each of the playgrounds around town and filled with books for the kids to borrow and return. They can fill them with their own offerings that they've read and loved and visit the little libraries all around town. So far, we have enough money to build three, but my hope is to get to six."

Henry pulled me into his arms, kissing the top of my head. "I'll never be able to explain to you just how happy I am that you came back, Charlotte."

In that moment, I did my best to let go of all the hurt, the uncertainty, and the struggle I felt over trying to understand why my mother did what she did. It wouldn't all go away, but I could at least try to bury it so that I could truly move on in a healthy way. Maybe it was like Emma had said and providence meant I had to come back when I did and not before. If it was earlier, when I was younger and not ready to settle, it wouldn't have stuck.

I pulled away, reaching up on my tiptoes to kiss his cold lips. "You mean that I came home."

ACKNOWLEDGMENTS

Many people have asked if Hope Lake, Pennsylvania, is real. While it is fictional, it's 100 percent based on the small towns around me. I took everything I liked about the area I'm from and turned it into a town that I hope you enjoyed visiting. The pizza place, the romantic restaurant by the water, the rail biking, repurposing the old, abandoned mills, and the delightful brewing company that hosts awesome events—real.

Books take a village to create. Literally. This book was a labor of love, and without the guidance and wisdom of Kimberly Brower, who I am convinced is a superhero, it wouldn't have become what it is. Kimberly, I can't thank you enough.

Molly Gregory at Gallery, thank you for your patience, kindness, and all the positivity you bring! To the entire team at Simon & Schuster/Gallery Books, I am grateful for everything that you do for all the authors that you tirelessly champion; Rachel, Abby, Jen B., Lauren, and Diana, many thanks.

SR, thank you for reading and giving much-needed feedback. You, my friend, are a gem.

To all the booksellers, librarians, bloggers, and reviewers who promote the world of romance with graciousness, light, and endless enthusiasm, I am indebted.

DON'T MISS THE THIRD INSTALLMENT IN
THE HOPELESS ROMANTICS SERIES

THE INGREDIENTS
OF YOU AND ME

AVAILABLE FROM GALLERY BOOKS IN APRIL 2020
KEEP ON READING FOR A SWEET SNEAK PEEK . . .

"You've made these nine hundred times, and yet here you are forgetting ingredients, measurements, and— Shit, I never washed out the mixing bowl!"

It wasn't just that my KitchenAid mixer held a suspicious-looking substance, but the same goop was dripping from the bottom of my white cabinet. When I plugged the mixer in, I didn't realize I'd left it in the *on* position. Needless to say, everything went flying up and out of the bowl.

Now chocolate—or something formerly resembling chocolate— was oozing down the side of the cabinet, plopping onto the counter and right onto the sheet of paper on which I was desperately trying to write down the recipe I'd been creating.

It had been like this all morning; nothing was going right. First, I'd tried to open a bag of chocolate chips with one hand. They sky-rocketed out of the bag with such force that I was surprised any of them landed in the double-boiler. I'd be finding chocolate chips in all corners of the apartment for the next month.

I didn't have any pie weights for my crust (not that it looked much like a crust), so I tried using cans—and ended up boiling a can of corn.

My poor oven would never be the same.

"This pie is one of the easiest things I make, but here I am, destroying my kitchen and what was left of my self-esteem." Frustrated, I paced the small room. Maybe some movement would help my synapses to fire on all cylinders. Hell, I'd be happy with just one cylinder working at this point. I shook out my arms and rolled out my neck.

The joys of being unemployed.

For the past few months, I'd watched more than my fair share of the Food Network. Then I'd switch to Netflix for the *Chef's Table* series just to mix it up. Unfortunately, nothing was providing the motivation I needed. Was it the best use of my time? No, but since inspiration was at a premium, I was focused on doing what I wanted, not what I *should* do.

Logically, I knew I could do this. Rote memory wasn't supposed to fail.

It didn't seem to matter, though, because for months my skills had been floundering. Even before I sold my bakery, I noticed a distinct shift in prowess. Things that used to come naturally were lacking in finesse. Perhaps I should have stuck to something simple right out of the gate. Like truffles—those were easy as pie.

Which was ironic, as I was trying to make what was once known as my signature pie.

"Maybe if I take a nap, I'll dream of the answer," I reasoned, but I knew from the other three naps I took the past week that a nap wouldn't yield anything but a headache and a crick in my neck.

I still took the nap.

When I woke up an hour later, as predicted I didn't feel any better, so I decided to make a cappuccino to wake myself up. After I poured the ingredients into my fancy cappuccino machine—at least I could still make coffee—I watched the slow drip of the espresso plop into the mug, one that my old roommate Charlotte left when she moved out. The mug had a Temple University owl logo on it that at one point had two fancy gold gems for eyes. Those were long gone, just like Charlotte.

She had moved out officially months ago—and moved *on*, I liked to add. Headed to a little touristy town called Hope Lake, about two hours away from our apartment in Brooklyn in the middle of a currently snowy Pennsylvania valley.

She was born in Hope Lake, living there until third grade or so. She only moved to New York City around her tenth birthday. That's when we met, and as dorky as it sounds, we'd been best friends and inseparable ever since. Since her mom wasn't around much, and her father was still in Hope Lake, she was with me and my parents a lot growing up. She spent almost as much time with my family as I did.

Since she'd left, we set aside Tuesdays as our day to catch up— spending an hour on the phone gossiping about her small town, her adorkable boyfriend Henry, and the group of her childhood friends that I grew to love when I visited.

But two months had passed since I officially sold my bakery Delicious & Vicious, and while Charlotte and I exchanged texts here and there during that time, we hadn't spoken. I kept finding reasons why I couldn't talk—I needed to run an errand or check out a new baking supply store—to actively avoid bringing up my lack of plans or direction. The last two months had been the longest, and potentially the most boring, time of my entire life. Which is saying something, because I took an entire semester of linear algebra back in college.

It was also the loneliest. That was another reason why I was avoiding Charlotte. Talking to her should have made me feel better, but it just amplified the feeling of being alone. Prior to selling my business, my days were so busy I never had time to be lonely. I always had someone to talk to, whether it was a client or an employee. But now the only real conversations I had were with Seamless delivery guys or the kindly old woman from my dry cleaners.

As I slouched in the chair in my small office space off the living room, my eyes were trained on the ceiling until I heard my cell phone buzz and then saw it light up on the desk beside me. Siri announced Charlotte, and I debated for a moment whether or not to ignore a call from her *again*. I figured that since letting the voice-mail pick up had been the solution for the past few weeks, I might as well let it be the thing to do today. After the phone stopped buzzing, I pushed the voicemail notification to hear what Charlotte had to say.

Her normally cheery voice was nowhere to be found. Instead, she sounded disgruntled. Rightfully so. "Listen, you're screening. Don't deny it. You know that I know that you're screening. I get that you're in a funk and weird headspace right now, but it's been like a hundred thousand hours since we last talked, and this is bull. I need to know that you're okay or I'm going to drive into the city— and I still only have a permit, so I'm not sure that's legal. That's probably jail time or something if I get caught. Call me back or I'm going to keep calling—"

It ended abruptly. But there wasn't another call. Just a *ding ding* that meant I had a text message. Then a swoosh sound indicating an email. Charlotte was being persistently annoying, but I knew it came from a place of love.

"Okay, okay," I said to the empty apartment with a smile. I pushed Charlotte's name to call her back. It barely rang once before she picked up.

"This is Charlotte Bishop. How can I help you?" she said with a long, exhausted sigh.

"Hey."

"Hey, yourself," she said, followed by a solid minute of silence.

Charlotte *was* persistently annoying, and another thing about her that hadn't changed since we were kids was her ability to hold a grudge. She wasn't going to make it easy, but I knew that. For example, she was still bitter over a slight from middle school when our friend Hillary got the lead in the school play over her. Hence, the reason I'd been avoiding the conversation in the first place. When you had a friend who knew all of your faults, your secrets, and your fears, it was hard to admit that you were scared, worried, and lonely without them because underneath it all, I didn't want Charlotte to blame herself for what was going on with me.

"I'm sorry I've been a shitty friend and haven't called you back." She sighed again.

"It's been a really rough couple of weeks," I added.

"And you didn't think I would want to help you with that? What do best friends do, Parker?"

"I know, I know—honestly I do."

There was silence for a bit, and I knew that meant Charlotte was contemplating forgiving me and putting her best friend cape back on.

She sighed. "Talk to me. What's going on? It's been a while."

I thought about her question for a moment, and the problem was that I didn't really have an answer for her. "I thought all this free time would be amazing, and yet . . . I don't know. I've gotten into my own head so deep that crawling out seems impossible. Have you ever been there? So twisted up over what's next that you're literally incapable of *doing* what's next, and as a result ignoring people in your life? I'm sorry that I've been such a shitty friend lately."

Charlotte grunted. "Stop saying that. You're not a shitty friend. You're going through a life transition, and I get that. I just wish you'd let me help you sort it out. You don't have to do anything alone—you know that, right?"

What I wanted to say was "No, I'm not alone, *but you're also not here*," but that would be selfish. She was the happiest I'd seen her in ages thanks to her move back to Hope Lake that she was originally resistant toward. I wasn't about to fill her in and have her rush to New York because I couldn't get my shit together.

I shifted in my seat, scratching a doodle onto the scrap pad on my desk. The word I kept tracing read BORED.

"Hey, you still with me?" Charlotte asked, jolting me away from my doodling.

"I don't know how anyone can help. I'm just so stuck. Uninspired and worried that I won't ever get a burst of creativity again. And the problem is, I don't even know what I want to do next. How am I supposed to find a new path if I can't see the forest through the trees?"

"Parker Eulalia Adams, you listen to me. You'll never be too far into the hole to get out because you've got people to throw you the world's longest rope."

"While I appreciate the sentiment—" I began, but Charlotte was on a roll. It's what I knew would happen after avoiding her for weeks.

"Maybe you're a little lost because you're forcing yourself to be creative. You're not letting it happen organically. You think da Vinci beat himself up if he had a day or two where he wasn't feeling the *Mona Lisa*?"

I laughed. "Number one, I can't believe you used da Vinci as your example for me, and number two, 'feeling the *Mona Lisa*'?"

"Shut up, I'm tired. All I'm saying is that I get that you're not used to relaxing or having free time, but try and enjoy it! Buy a latte, sit in the park and read the paper. Or visit a museum, take a pottery class. You can literally do whatever you want!"

I threw the pencil across the small room. "I'm trying! I have been doing *stuff*."

She laughed. "Parker, water aerobics? Canasta night? Crotchet club? That isn't you. You need a creative outlet that's going to kick your butt into gear. Something that sparks that fire in you. Something that inspires you to say *Holy shit* and run back to the kitchen to make a masterpiece. Going back and doing what you love is the answer."

I snorted. "Baking is what I love, and I can't seem to do it anymore. It's like I'm you now. I'm broken in the kitchen."

"Do me a favor, answer this." Charlotte switched the call from audio to FaceTime, and I was greeted by her lovely, freckled, and frowning face. Her reddish hair was pulled into Princess Leia–style buns, and she had a daisy sticking out of the top of one of them.

"I resent that remark. Not everyone is as adept at being culinarily inept as I am." She laughed, and I remembered how much I missed having her around all the time. Seeing her smile was a bit of a light at the end of the tunnel.

"You'll never be as bad as me in the kitchen. My lack of skills is a once-in-a-lifetime gift, and I'm not sharing it."

My smile was weak, its lack of confidence clueing Charlotte into the fact that I wasn't actually joking about my lack of success.

"Oh my God, you're serious. I thought you were exaggerating!" she said, her hand covering her mouth in shock. "Look at you, you're covered in flour. And oh, Parker, is that egg on your face? I can tell that you're working," she said with a pinched expression.

She was trying not to judge my wayward appearance. Rolling my shoulders back, I wiped at the smudge of flour that I knew was across my cheek. "I'm digging the bandanna, by the way—very farmer friendly."

I gave her the finger and touched the red bandanna that was holding back my long blond hair. "I ran out of hair ties. This worked, and I promise I didn't look quite so shabby pre–baking disaster."

"Enough about how gorgeous you still look even with egg, literally, on your face. What have you baked that failed? I don't believe it. I once saw you create a trifle out of leftovers and people offered to buy it."

The comment gave me a smidge of a pick-me-up. A reminder that I was in fact talented. My ego needed that bit of a nudge. Actually, my ego needed a swift kick in the ass, but I wasn't complaining about any amount of boost.

Pushing off the chair, I walked into the kitchen, where I turned the phone toward the trash so Charlotte had a bird's-eye view. In the bag were a dozen supposed-to-be chocolate-coffee cupcakes, a dozen chocolate-chip cookies, and a couple cinnamon scones that could have doubled as bricks in a fireplace if I needed them.

"See those?" I asked, picking one up and tossing it into the sink.

Where it landed with a loud thud.

"Oh, boy. Did that crack anything?"

"Cute. That's how bad we're talking."

"Are you practicing for Henry's birthday cupcakes?" she asked, trying to lighten my dark mood. "You know we'll eat anything you bake for him, even if it requires a visit to the dentist afterward."

"Thanks for the vote of confidence, but he can't eat these. It's all so bad." I reached into the trash and took out the scone that was on top. Holding it like a softball, I rapped it on the edge of the counter.

"Still want to eat this? I'm not paying your bill from the oral surgeon afterward."

When I turned the phone back toward me, my stomach dipped. Charlotte looked worried. Her gray eyes were missing their usual light, and she wasn't smiling the way she almost always was.

"Parks, what's up? Really? This is so unlike you!"

I shrugged. "The last, I don't know, *dozen* things I've made have been awful. Like Charlotte-awful—no offense."

She shrugged. "None taken. You'll remember I once burned water, and I'm not sure any of your failures beat that. The FDNY hasn't been to the apartment yet, right?"

I laughed. "Nope."

"Good, then there's still hope. Is there something I can do to help? To kick the mojo back into you? What about your idea to start the baking classes? Did you decide against it?"

"No, not for good. I couldn't do anything in the middle of selling D&V, and I can't exactly teach someone how to bake when I seem to be incapable myself."

"Valid point. Then what's next?"

I shook my head, admiring the colorful tile design in the floor. "I mean I have no idea. I'm stuck."

"When I get overwhelmed—which is often, you know that—I simplify. You've been doing some wild and crazy recipes for years now. Maybe you need to Betty Crocker it up. Make basic things that even I could swing. Like, I don't know, pound cake. Is that still a thing?" We both laughed. Even the most pedestrian recipe was out of reach for Charlotte. Thank goodness Henry was a great cook, or she would survive on Pop-Tarts and crackers.

"I've tried almost everything, Char, and I still can't bake anything worth eating," I answered with honesty.

"Okay" was all she said. But by the expression on her face, I could tell she was trying not to look concerned. Crap, now I was bringing her down.

"Speaking of Henry's birthday," I said, attempting to change the subject. "Any plans? Anything romantic and exciting?"

Her face lit up. "Nothing crazy, just dinner. Maybe"—she started chewing on her pencil—"you can come? I mean, you don't have much going on."

I threw my head back, laughing. "Wow, harsh much?"

"Am I wrong?" she deadpanned.

"No, you're right, but subtlety has never been your strong suit."

Charlotte waved at the stack of yellow order slips beside her workstation and then at the calendar that hung on the wall.

"I guess the florist business is keeping you pretty busy, huh?" I asked, knowing that she wasn't busy only with the work of running her own business but also with the details of trying to buy said business from the owner. If the calendar was any indication of how swamped she was, she needed some help—and fast. It was color-coded and positively filled with scribbles.

"As you can see, I don't have much time for subtle these days."

"Girl, you need help!"

"I know, I know. I'm working on it. Trying to find someone who can handle all this crazy."

"Well, your crazy is part of why I love you." I looked around the office she was in. "Busy tonight?"

She wiped her forehead dramatically. "So busy, but it's good. I'm still gathering all the paperwork that I need to get the loan to buy this place outright, but the bank says that everything is looking good and I should be the proud owner of Late Bloomers by summer."

Seeing her face light up at the mention of owning her own floral shop lit *me* up inside. Charlotte was so lost for so long, and she had finally found true happiness. If I didn't love her so much, I'd be rolling in jealousy. We couldn't be in more opposite positions.

"C, that's amazing. I'm so proud of you. Here you are in the process of getting your own business—your dream business—and I just sold mine." Admittedly, there *was* a little bit of jealousy in my heart. Which was something I wasn't keen on considering, since this was my best friend in all the world.

Just as easily as her face lit up, all that happiness evaporated at my words. "Parks, I'm sorry, that was so insensitive of me. I—"

I cut her off with a wave of my hand. "Stop it. You have every right to be over the moon about buying Late Bloomers. And I know selling D&V was the right decision. I was beginning to feel morally bankrupt, with all the divorce and cheating cakes. I still have no idea how they're going to franchise it, but—"

"It isn't your problem now, sister!" she teased, and she was right. It wasn't my problem.

"Have you been good otherwise, though? Shop's good? Friends are good?" I asked, trying not to sound like I was fishing for information.

"The business has been a godsend in terms of dealing with this weather. I'm so busy that I don't mind the cold, and because I can't drive, I get to carpool into town with my honey. If I was home, I think I'd lose my mind. I've never seen so much snow, and there's nowhere to put it!"

"It's only January, honey. You've got at least two more months of it," I explained, laughing when Charlotte pretended to tug at her hair in frustration. "Where's your delightful professor? Out shoveling?"

Charlotte was dating her childhood BFF, Henry, after reconnecting when she returned to Hope Lake last year. It was incredible to see the change that being back in her hometown had brought about in her—especially because she'd fought the relocation tooth and nail.

She smiled, looking dreamily at a framed photo on the corner of her workstation. It was from the Fourth of July last year, when I'd surprised her for a quick visit. Well, sort of quick. The photo included, me, Charlotte, Henry, her friends Emma and Cooper, and their friend Nick. I bit back my grimace at the sight of Nick.

Something struck the work table near Charlotte's hand. A couple of chunks of florist foam had fallen out of the precarious design she'd started. "Damn it, I'm so clumsy, lately. Anyway, where was I? Oh, Henry is back at school after Christmas recess, which was lovely because we both got a small break over the holidays. I wish you could have seen this place for Christmas. It looked like a Hallmark movie."

"Too bad I missed it," I said, twirling a pencil between my fingers.

"You should come visit Hope Lake—and soon! Like tomorrow-soon. Henry's birthday is coming up, plus you miss me, and who knows, maybe a change of scenery will help kick you in the ass a bit."

"That's not a bad idea," I said, and to my surprise, I realized I felt excited about the prospect.

"You can actually veg out for a minute. I think you deserve some free time." Charlotte winked, knowing damn well I was free *all the time* now.

"Again, I say to you, subtlety is an art you have not mastered."

Charlotte, suddenly serious, faced the phone head-on. She ET'd the phone, pushing her index finger onto the screen. I responded by placing mine against hers, causing the image to wobble a moment. "I miss your stupid face. Come visit."

"Well, with an offer like that, how can a girl refuse?"

"I'm serious, Parker. I know you; you're floundering."

"What's the phrase? My new normal? I'm trying to figure out exactly what that is. I spent years building D&V and now it's gone. I mean, I'm glad it is, because I was a zombie all the time, but what do I do now? Who am I without it?"

She sighed, and I was pretty sure that if we were face-to-face, and not screen-to-screen, she would have pulled me into one of her crippling hugs. "Delicious & Vicious was a part of you, but it's not all you are. Selling it was the best decision you made. You saw me last year when I was having a hard time. You didn't let me give up, and I'm not going to let you either. Come visit. Recharge your batteries and enjoy this godforsaken snow."

"How's the sledding in Hope Lake?" I asked, jumping up from the chair and setting the phone on a nearby table. I stretched my arms up over my head, hoping to ease the stiffness out.

Why was I hesitating? Really, what else did I have to do? Or lose? Besides a little bit of this ennui. It was now or never. If I didn't get ready quickly, I knew I'd back out. I grabbed a suitcase and began tossing essentials inside. What I didn't bring I could buy there.

"The best." Charlotte glanced at her watch. "If you catch the three o'clock bus, you'll get here in time for dinner."

"I hope you're not cooking," I joked before hitting the red button.